KU-021-003

OLD FLAMES

John Lawton is the director of over forty television programmes, author of a dozen screenplays, several children's books and seven Inspector Troy novels. Lawton's work has earned him comparisons to John le Carré and Alan Furst. Lawton lives in a remote hilltop village in Derbyshire.

THE INSPECTOR TROY NOVELS

Black Out
Old Flames
A Little White Death
Riptide
Blue Rondo
Second Violin
A Lily of the Field

OLD FLAMES

FLAMES

John Lawton

Grove Press UK

First published in 1996 by Weidenfeld & Nicolson, London, England

This paperback edition published in 2012 by Grove Press UK, an imprint of Grove/Atlantic Inc.

Copyright ©John Lawton, 1996

The moral right of John Lawton to be identified as the author of this work has been asserted by him in accordance with the Copyright, Designs and Patents Act of 1988.

All rights reserved. No part of this publication may be reproduced, stored in a retrieval system, or transmitted in any form or by any means, electronic, mechanical, photocopying, recording, or otherwise, without the prior permission of both the copyright owner and the above publisher of the book.

The extract from his introduction to *Philby: The Spy Who Betrayed a Generation* is quoted by permission of John le Carré.

The extract from his interview with Kim Philby is quoted by permission of Murray Sayle.

The extract from Graham Greene's introduction to Kim Philby's *My Silent War* is quoted by permission of David Higham Associates Ltd.

Every effort has been made to trace or contact all copyright-holders. The publishers will be pleased to make good any omissions or rectify any mistakes brought to their attention at the earliest opportunity.

1 3 5 7 9 8 6 4 2

A CIP record for this book is available from the British Library.

ISBN 978 1 61185 590 6

Printed and bound by CPI Group (UK) Ltd, Croydon, CR0 4YY

Grove Press, UK
Ormond House
26–27 Boswell Street
London
WC1N 3JZ

www.groveatlantic.com

For
Susan Freathy

Agent provocatrice

Acknowledgements

To **Daniel Edelman** of Ridgefield, Connecticut, who put a roof over my head while I wrote chunks of this.

To **Arthur Cantor**, who did the same in Manhattan.

To **Sarah Teale**, who got between me and the phone and the fax for the best part of four months.

To **Art Tatum**, who in 1956, the last year of his life, recorded session after session of his finest work, and kept me intrigued and listening forty years on.

'. . . SIS would not merely defend the traditional decencies of our society: it would embody them. Within its own walls, its clubs and country houses, in whispered luncheons, with its secular contacts, it would enshrine the mystical entity of a vanishing England. Here at least, whatever went on in the big world outside, England's flower would be cherished. "The Empire may be crumbling; but within our secret elite, the clean-limbed tradition of English power would survive. We believe in nothing but ourselves".'

John le Carré

(from his introduction to *'Philby: The Spy Who Betrayed a Generation.'* Page, Leitch & Knightley 1968.)

'To betray, you must first belong.'

Kim Philby

(in an interview with Murray Sayle 1967)

April 1876

April 1956

Prologue

April pretended to be spring. The cruellest month, and a bad joke. Midday in Moscow teased you with a sunbeam, and midnight froze you down to the bone. The heating in the crumbling hotel-cum-jail came and went with a chilling irregularity, and when it went you needed every scrap of clothing, every inch of bedding. Grey days, black nights, and a sting in the nipples that cotton wool in the end of the brassière did little to alleviate.

The little guy wore layer upon layer of clothes. Three or four sweaters, she thought, a thick navy pea jacket, mittens over his gloves, a woollen hat under a cheap rabbit-fur flapcap. The little guy, Yuri, was OK. As thugs went. The affable apparatchik. It was the big one, Mischa, she had to watch.

Little Yuri was teaching himself English. He'd never been out of Russia in his life and, thought the Major, probably never would, but he was delighting in the oddities of the language, and he seemed to relish any opportunity to talk English with her.

'Many a mickle maks a muckle,' he said to her one day.

'What the hell is that supposed to mean?'

He didn't know, no more than she did herself, but he produced a tatty magazine from his coat pocket and handed it to her.

'*I Belong to Glasgow,*' she read. 'The magazine for Scotsmen abroad. Sydney 1955. Where d'you get this?'

He shrugged.

'Can you get stuff for me?'

'Sure,' he said. 'So long as ...'

The Major understood. So long as Big Mischa never knew.

She asked for a copy of *Huckleberry Finn*. A week later he brought her one. In Russian. Translated in 1909. Good God, Twain was still living when this book was printed. They'd spelt it with a cyrillic Г. Геккельберри Финн. She guessed it was the nearest they could get. Gekkelberry. She'd never thought before how it would read in her native tongue. The most American word in her American vocabulary—it went with Hoboken, Hoosier and Hominy Grits—rendered into the language of her father and forefathers. She laughed till she cried and couldn't get Yuri to see the joke in either language.

'Is problem?' he asked.

'No,' she said. 'No problem. I'll read it. It'll make a change.'

She was almost at the end, those weak scenes where Tom Sawyer steps in and screws up the plot, when Mischa showed up. She slipped the book quickly under the mattress and watched as he unbuttoned his flies. So, this was it. At last. It had been a long time coming, but she'd always known he'd try.

It took him less than a minute to rip every shred of clothing off her. She fought hard, and as he held her down managed to get her thumb and forefinger into the socket of one eye. Mischa froze. He could move, he knew, but he also knew the hold she had on him, knew that he'd leave the eye behind if he did.

She squeezed a little, dug her thumbnail into the eyeball.

'Have they told you to kill me, Mischa?'

The other eye stared motionless at her.

'Speak, dammit!'

'No,' he said.

'If you finish what you've started, you'll have to kill me. 'Cos if you don't, I'll kill you. And if they still want me alive, I wouldn't want to be in your shoes. Capiche?'

She squeezed again. He yelled. She let him go. He backhanded her across the face and stomped out. After that he beat up on her regularly, but he never tried to fuck her again.

She'd already lost track of the days and weeks, but not long afterwards, it seemed, Yuri appeared in the early morning with one of her suitcases and one of her coats, the ankle-length black number she'd bought in Paris on her last trip there. He set down the case quietly and threw the coat to her.

'Cast not a clout till May be out,' he said.

'We're leaving?'

He nodded.

Was this the end? A car ride out to the forest, a bullet in the back of the head, an unmarked grave and her KGB service record erased? One more anonymous Khrushchev casualty?

'I'm sorry, Major,' he said. 'It's only to another hotel. We'll be there in half an hour.'

Half an hour. Half an hour outside. Light. Air. Movement.

The car was a battered Moskvitch saloon, a drab shade of no-colour, crude and angular like a pre-war Citroën, the classic Gestapo car, redrawn by a clumsy child. At least it had a heater. The Russians were way ahead of the French, light years ahead of the English, in putting heaters in cars. It smelt like frying tripe but it was warm.

Yuri drove. Mischa sat in the back with the Major, looking bored and tired, legs spread, fat thighs taking up the lion's share of the seat. The Major stared out of the window. Once or twice when he caught sight of her in the mirror Yuri could have sworn she was smiling to herself as one thing or another flashed by her gaze.

Two blocks from Red Square the thin line of traffic stopped moving, a few cars came up behind them, blocked the street and honked a couple of times.

'Get out and look,' Big Mischa said through a stifled yawn.

'Boss, it's bollock-freezing out there!'

'Do it!'

Yuri did up the top buttons of his pea jacket and stepped into the street, his breath billowing out in front of him in white clouds. A few minutes later he was back. He bounced into his seat and slammed the door.

'Tanks,' he said. 'Tanks and troop transporters and ICBMs and thousands of poor fucking Ivans all rehearsing May Day. It'll be half an hour before they pass the end of the street.'

Mischa looked behind them at the growing line of stalled traffic.

'Shit,' he said. 'We'll just have to sit it out. Pass the time.'

The Major watched. He undid his oatmeal-coloured, double-breasted overcoat, then popped his fly buttons and got out his cock. It rose up, uncircumcised and ugly, rolling back its little bonnet in greedy anticipation.

'Sweet lips you have, Major.'

He wasn't kidding. He was pushing his luck. She could hardly believe hers.

She put out her hand and stroked it. He closed his eyes and she felt an involuntary judder pass through him. Then she snapped it back and heard it crack like willow as ten thousand engorged blood vessels ruptured. He opened his mouth to scream. She punched him in the throat with her other hand and all that escaped him was a strangled wheeze. She put the hand into his jacket and pulled out the automatic from the shoulder holster a full second before Yuri could pull his and turn in his seat.

'Don't make me, Yuri. You been good to me. Don't make me shoot you.'

He held his gun up by the barrel and passed it back to her. 'Go,' he said. 'Before the slob comes round.'

She reached for the door and the last thing she thought she heard was Yuri softly saying, 'Good luck. By God you're going to need it.'

She had always been careful where Dorry was concerned. Dorry was her secret. Dorry was her escape route. She'd never been seen with Dorry. She'd never visited her except when she was certain she was not followed. She considered herself an expert at shaking off tails. Wasn't so hard. You took one cab, paid him to cross the city, got out round the corner, ran like hell and picked up one going the other way.

Dorry cried when she saw her on the doorstep.

'I thought for sure you were dead,' she said through her tears. 'It's been weeks. They stripped your apartment down to the floorboards and then they took up the floorboards.'

There was nothing for them to find. All that mattered was here. The passports, the travel permits, two thousand US dollars and an array of dreadful wigs.

Dorry got out the suitcase. The Major pulled out the false bottom and sifted its contents for anything incriminating. She'd need the passports. If she made it out of Russia she'd be half a dozen different people before she found safety. There was the letter from Guy Burgess. Why on earth had she kept it? It could get them both killed. Better now to burn it. But she didn't. She folded it over one more time and dropped it in with the passports.

Dorry had the stove door open and was feeding in oddments as the Major passed them to her.

'That too,' she said, pointing to Huck Finn.

'Nah. Not Huck.'

'It's a dead giveaway. It's your trademark. Besides, a book that thick, we'll get twenty minutes of heat off it.'

She pulled on the mousey wig, wrapped herself into the peasant overcoat. It felt like it had been run up from a mixture of horse blanket and candle wax. Then she passed the chic black number to Dorry.

'Oh no,' said Dorry, running a finger down the lapel. 'It's beautiful. It's worth a year's wages.'

'And it's a "dead giveaway". It'd never fit you. You're five feet nine, and I just about make five nothin'—burn it!'

'Where will you go?'

'West. Where else can I go?'

'Will you write to me?'

'Sure. If I can. I mean. When it's safe.'

'Send me something.'

'Like what? Scent? Lingerie? That sort of thing?'

'No. Send me an Elvis Presley record.'

'Elvis Presley? Who the hell is Elvis Presley?'

§ I

A blurred face swam at the end of a tunnel. Croaked like a frog.

'Is that it?' said Troy.

'Is that what?' said his sister.

'It, dammit, it. I mean the danm thing cost seventy guineas—is that as good as it gets?'

The man in overalls, crouching behind the set, twiddling with a screwdriver, looked over the top.

'It's in its infancy, you know. You can't expect it to look like the Gaumont, now can yer?'

The face swam fishily, rippling like a mustachioed and unwelcome mirage. Troy recognised him. Gilbert Harding. A figure made by the new medium, a tele-pundit, a man with an opinion on everything, and quite probably the most famous ex-copper in the land.

'I thought we invented television years ago,' Troy went on irritably. 'I thought we led the world in this sort of thing. I thought it was like radar. The stuff of boffins. Barnes Wallis, Logie Baird and all those chaps.'

'It's your own fault,' said Masha. 'If you'd got one for the Coronation like everyone else, it'd be fine by now.'

'You're not saying it takes three years of fiddling and twiddling to get it right?'

'Well,' she said, 'Sort of.'

'Then I don't want it. Take it back.'

Gilbert Harding stopped wobbling. Troy could hear him clearly for the first time.

'Am I right in thinking you're in the pottery industry?'

Applause. A voice off-screen said an utterly unnecessary 'yes'.

'Am I right in thinking you're a saggar-maker's bottom knocker?'

More applause. A third voice broke in, and the camera cut to a big, curly-headed man with a tough, if pleasing, boxer-like face, smiling genially at an embarrassed nonentity who had at some point thought it would be fun to waste thirty minutes letting four people in evening dress guess his occupation. It struck Troy as being bizarre in the extreme.

The telephone rang and saved Troy from throwing out the chap in overalls or physically assaulting his sister. Life with the goggle-box, he concluded, was not going to be easy.

'The Branch want to see you,' Onions said.

'I don't work for the Branch.'

'For Christ's sake, Freddie, knock it off.'

'Stan, I don't have to work for those—'

'Two of their blokes were killed today,' Onions said bluntly.

Troy weighed this up momentarily. Carrot or stick? 'You mean murdered?'

'No. Car crash on the A3.'

'Then I don't see what it's got to do with us.'

'It leaves them short. They say they need you.'

'Why?'

'Not over the phone, Freddie.'

Troy sighed. He hated this pretence of hush-hush, as though anyone other than Special Branch would be tapping a phone line in England. All the same, if they'd asked for him by name he was intrigued.

'Just see them,' Onions said. 'You don't have to commit yourself to anything. Just hear them out.'

It was an hour's drive to Scotland Yard down the Great North Road. Troy was due three more days holiday, but the drive into London had the added draw that it would free him from the attentions of his sisters, who had talked him into buying the goggle-box and would doubtless waste a whole evening talking him through their favourite programmes. If this guessing game were anything to go by, the damn contraption could be stuck in the servants' hall the minute the sisters left and he need never be bothered with it again. By the time they next suffered a misdirected bout of maternal concern for him, some other fad would have taken its place.

§2

Troy's Bullnose Morris had expired in 1952 at the age of seventeen. He did not want another. He had liked the car. He had even appreciated the mockery it had elicited in its tattier latter years, but he did not want another. For the first time since the death of his father in 1943 he had blown a portion of his inheritance on an incontrovertible indulgence—a five-litre, six-cylinder Bentley Continental Saloon with Mulliner's sports bodywork. Long, stylish and fiercely raked at the blunt end, it was a car in a thousand and, as all who knew him had pointed out, utterly un-Troy. The pleasure it gave him to deny familiarity beggared description.

He had the door open and was flinging his old leather briefcase onto the passenger seat when the other sister appeared. Sasha was drifting aimlessly in the spring twilight, clutching a handful of bluebells, humming tunelessly to herself as she approached the drive from the pig pens Troy had built at the bottom of the kitchen garden. She seemed to be in a very different mood from her twin. They read each other as though by telepathy but there appeared to be no rule in twindom that said they should think or feel alike at any one moment. When they did, of course, it was hell for those around them—two bodies with but a single personality, thought and purpose. Sasha was in meditative whimsy, Troy thought.

'Off so soon?' she said.

'The Yard,' muttered Troy, hoping this would suffice to kill the conversation.

'That Old Spot's turned out to be beauty. Are you going to have her put to the tup this month?'

'I think you only call them tups if they're sheep.'

Sasha thought about this as though it were some great revelation, startling to contemplate and worth hours of harmless fun. Troy sat in the driver's seat and reached for the door, but she put her hand across the top of the frame and emerged from reverie.

'Oh well . . . are you going to get her fucked by a daddy pig then?'

'Goodnight, Sasha.'

She let go of the door.

'Goodnight, Freddie.'

Troy slipped the car into first and let it purr slowly down the drive, the crunch of gravel under-wheel louder than the engine. In his rearview mirror he could just make out Sasha sitting on the steps of the house gazing idly at the moon. He rounded the row of beech trees at the head of the drive and could see her no more. The way ahead was clear, he eased out of the gates and set the Bentley racing south towards the London road.

§3

Onions was waiting in Troy's office, perched on the edge of the desk, back to the door, staring out at the moonlit Thames. He was often to be found this way. As Superintendent in charge of the Murder Squad he had developed the habit of office-hopping. Never, in Troy's recollection, had Onions once summoned him to his own office. He would drop in, unexpected, uninvited and on occasion unwelcome, at any time of the day and expect to be briefed, or else Troy would arrive to find him hunched over the gas fire pulling on a Woodbine, or as now, watching the river flow. Almost idly, it seemed—but it never was. Onions learned every secret in his squad by rooting around with his nose to the ground. He was adept at reading documents upside down as he talked to you across the desk, and Troy had long ago learnt to leave nothing much lying around unless he felt happy with Onions reading it. Becoming Assistant Commissioner had not changed his habits. Meetings were always held in someone else's office, information was still gleaned in this haphazard fashion. Troy returned the compliment. On days when he knew Onions was out he would go through his desk, as surely as Onions did his. The result: they had no secrets, except for the secret that they had no secrets.

Onions was bristling. A glimmer of something unknown played about him.

'Good,' he said simply as Troy walked in. 'Good, good.'

Troy took the mood for excitement. Something as yet unspoken was giving him a great sense of anticipation, quite possibly great pleasure. He slipped off the desk. Troy heard the thick, black beetle-crusher boots clump on the floorboards. Onions slid his palms across the stubble that passed for a haircut, as though neatening that which did not exist to be neatened in the first place, and smiled. Troy slung his briefcase onto a chair and stuck his hands in his coat pockets, the merest hint of petulance and defiance in his posture.

'Are you going to tell me what this is about, Stan? Or do I have to guess?'

'Ted Wintrincham's waiting for us in his office right now. Why don't you give it half a mo' and let him tell you.'

Troy had no idea what to make of this.

'Why?'

'Cos I think it might amuse you.'

'Aha.'

'Oh yes, laddie. In fact, if it strikes you as being half as funny as it strikes me, you'll be a basket case in ten minutes.'

'Stan, Special Branch are about as funny as Jimmy Wheeler's rice pudding joke.'

'Tell me later. When you've heard Wintrincham.'

He smiled in a roguish way that was almost out of character. It seemed from the barely suppressed grin that Onions himself might corpse at any moment. He led off along the corridor. As they mounted the stairs to Wintrincham's office, Troy fished.

'Who died in the car crash?'

'Herbert Boyle, and his sergeant. Young chap name of Briggs. Did you know 'em?'

'I didn't know Briggs. I knew Boyle. It was hard not to.'

'Aye. You could never say he didn't speak his mind.'

'You could never say he wasn't the most unconscionable bastard ever to walk the earth,' said Troy.

'Jesus Christ, Freddie, the man's not been dead three hours.'

They arrived at Wintrincham's door. Onions thrust it open without knocking. Ted Wintrincham was a Deputy-Commander, and head of Special Branch. Much Troy's superior, but it would never occur to Asst. Commissioner Onions to treat him any differently than he treated any other junior officer. One china shop was much like another to the bull. Wintrincham was seated behind his desk. He rose to shake hands with Troy and make the introductions.

'Good of you to come so promptly, Chief Inspector Troy. You know Inspector Cobb, don't you?'

Troy looked at the big man lurching unsteadily to his feet to take his hand as he extended it. He knew Norman Cobb by sight. He was well over six foot, a good sixteen stone, and rather hard to miss. Troy had seen him around the corridors of Scotland Yard for years without ever exchanging a word. He was Troy's idea of a surly bastard. Well suited to the Branch.

'I don't think I've had the pleasure,' said Troy.

Cobb gave him a bone-crunching grip and a brief glimpse of gleaming front teeth in an attempt at a smile. Troy threw his overcoat on the back of a chair and sat down next to Onions, facing Wintrincham. Cobb, Troy rapidly concluded, was cold or just plain huffy, sitting there in his natty blue gabardine mackintosh, buttoned to the neck—like a child sent by his mother to a party he'd determined to hate from the start. Wintrincham was a different kettle. He was the only Special Branch officer Troy liked, the only one with whom he'd pass the time of day without the sensation that he'd just had his pocket picked. He often wondered how the man had risen to the top of his disreputable job. He was a pleasant, friendly countryman. The best part of half a century in London had done little to clip his Hampshire burr, and he still spoke like a rustic and suffered the nickname 'Farmer' throughout the Metropolitan Police Force.

'Ye'll have heard about Inspector Boyle and Sergeant Briggs, I take it?' Troy nodded.

'I hate losing men at the best of times, but this is a bad time. There's a state visit this week—I'm sure that's no secret.'

Troy was looking at Onions. Onions looked back. Troy could almost swear he winked. Good God, how could the man sit on information like this and not burst? Suddenly he could see exactly what was animating Onions, could see exactly why he'd played on the element of surprise, could see exactly what was coming.

'The papers are full of it, after all,' Wintrincham went on. 'First Secerterry Khrushchev and . . . 'ave I pronounced that right, d'ye reckon?'

He was looking to Troy for an answer. Troy was almost at a loss for words.

'Perfect, sir,' he muttered.

'Anyway. First Secerterry Krushchev and Marshal Bulganin will be docking at Portsmouth in the morning and disembarking tomorrow a.m. I've been asked to provide the bodyguard, and I gather it's a matter of principle that the bodyguard should consist entirely of serving police officers. There'll be the usual security arrangements—motorcycle escorts made up by the Met divisions—but the personal bodyguard will be Special Branch. Boyle and Briggs were on their way to Portsmouth when they were killed. It leaves me two men short. It would seem that you are the only available officer who meets the necessary requirements. You've good Russian, I'm told.'

'Perfect, sir,' Troy said again.

'I know it's unusual to ask to second an officer of your rank, and I appreciate you've a squad of your own to run, but under the circumstances I'd be very grateful if you'd agree to help us out in this matter.'

'A week's secondment, I take it?'

'More like ten days. Mr Onions is willing. If you'd like a little time to . . . er . . .'

'No, no,' said Troy. 'I'm sure Mr Onions has already said all he needs to on the matter.'

Troy shot Stan a sideways glance, but he refused the bait and stared at the end of his boot.

'But I'd like the opportunity to put a few questions to you if I may. Who, for instance, is in charge of the operation?'

Cobb's voice cut in from the corner. 'I am.' It was guttural, flat and Midlands, and he coughed into his hand as soon as he had spoken, as though reluctant to exercise his voice more than the minimum.

'I see,' said Troy. 'How many men do we have?'

'Five,' he grunted again. 'Six with you. Working in double shifts. Four with Khrushchev. Two on two off. Two with Bulganin. Same method. You'd be with the Marshal, and you could have the night shift. Less for you to do. Leave the important stuff to my lads. They're trained for it, after all.'

This irritated Troy. He knew damn well that Special Branch training amounted to no more than matriculation in steaming open envelopes and kicking down doors. Any fool could do that.

'It doesn't sound as though I'll be needing much Russian,' he said.

'A precaution,' said Wintrincham. 'Of course, they'll bring their own translators. But it's been decided in another place that perhaps it would be better if everyone in regular contact with them spoke the language. That way nothing slips by.'

Another place. If the man meant MI6, why didn't he say so? Good God, could no one call a spook a spook any more?

'Slips by?' Troy said softly.

'Anything . . . shall we say . . . anything of importance. Anything you hear that might be important would be reported back to Inspector Cobb. And I need hardly add that as far as the Russians are concerned we're all coppers, and they've no reason to think we speak their language.'

'Other than their natural suspicion,' Troy said.

'Can't bargain for that. All I'm saying is if you keep your mouth shut and your ears open, the job should be no trouble to anyone.'

Troy looked again at Onions to find him looking back. In for a penny, he thought.

'Let me see if I understand you, sir,' he began, using a well-tried opening of understated, deferential defiance. 'You want me to spy on Marshal Bulganin?'

'Not exactly . . .'

'Ted,' Onions cut in. 'What else would you call it?'

'I don't know whether you're aware of this, sir,' Troy went on, 'but less than ten years ago when I arrested an agent of the American Government on four counts of murder—four counts on which he was subsequently convicted—officers of this department sent me to Coventry. The sole exception was the late Inspector Boyle, who called me a traitor to my face. I wonder also, sir, if you're aware that when we, every man jack of us, were vetted during the war, my vetting was, as Chief Inspector Walsh put it, marginal. A condition of which this department has felt it necessary to remind me from time to time when it's suited its own purposes to portray me as less than wholly loyal to the interests of the force. Am I to take it that my credit with this department has risen? Am I now, after so much water under a dozen bridges, being asked to spy on a Marshal of the Soviet Union?'

Wintrincham was stunned to silence. It occurred to Troy that he could scarcely be accustomed to being addressed in this fashion—the daily routine of Onions and Troy—by his own men. He was almost sorry. Wintrincham was behaving decently and giving him a choice, but the game was too rich to resist.

'Because,' Troy concluded, 'I won't do it.'

Wintrincham was looking to Onions to bale him out, but it was Cobb who spoke.

'Excuse me, sir, we don't have to take this shit. We can do very well without Mr Troy.'

'Hear the man out, Inspector,' Onions said.

'I rather thought Mr Troy had said his piece and shot his bolt, sir.'

'Shut your gob, lad. He's not through. Are you, Freddie?'

Troy was silently in awe of the timing. It amounted almost to telepathy. And the use of his Christian name amounted to sanction for anything he might now say.

'No, sir. I did have one more point to make.'

Cobb rolled his eyes at the ceiling. Troy thought he heard a whispered 'Jesus'.

'I won't spy on Marshal Bulganin.'

'I told yer,' muttered Cobb.

'But I will spy on Khrushchev.'

Cobb and Wintrincham looked at each other blankly. Troy looked at Onions, sitting there with his arms folded and smirking. Troy had often thought that he had no more liking for the Branch than he did himself. That the Branch was now under his command was simply a result of running C Division of the Yard. Troy could not believe this aspect of the command gave him any pleasure.

Wintrincham spoke at last. 'Who,' he asked Cobb, 'have you assigned to Khrushchev?'

'It was Inspector Boyle. As things are, I was going to take him myself, sir. It's my operation.'

'I don't want the operation. I just want Khrushchev. Preferably while he's awake. You'd be wasting me on Bulganin,' said Troy.

'What makes you think that?' Cobb snapped back at him.

'Where did you learn your Russian, Mr Cobb?'

'In the army. 1946.'

'I've spoken Russian all my life. It's my first language. Besides, compared to Khrushchev, Bulganin is taciturn. If you have to think what Khrushchev says once he gets on a roll he'll leave you standing. He's quick and he's bad-tempered. And when he loses it, he talks nineteen to the dozen. Can you honestly tell me that you have anyone else as fluent as me?'

Cobb stared back at him silently.

'Are those your terms, Mr Troy?' Wintrincham asked.

'Not terms, sir. I wouldn't dream of setting conditions on my service. I'm simply trying to be practical.'

'I don't think I believe you, Mr Troy. But it remains nevertheless that what suits your vanity is probably what suits the operation best. I'll assign you to First Secerterry Khrushchev.'

Cobb opened his mouth to speak, but Wintrincham got in first.

'Whatever your objection is, Norman, I don't want to hear it. I've made my decision. It's still your command. You've enough decisions of your own without wasting time questioning mine. If you've any orders for Chief Inspector Troy, issue them now and I can bugger off home to bed. It's been a long day.'

Cobb coughed into his fist. He looked up at Troy with undisguised contempt.

'Report to the garage at 6 a.m. We drive to Portsmouth for a briefing in the dockyard and weapons issue at nine-thirty. I'll pair people off then and issue rosters. We wait for the Russian ship and meet the visitors at disembarkation. Back up to London by train. Formal meeting at Waterloo by HMG. And the evenings are mostly black tie—you do have evening dress don't you, Mr Troy?'

Well, thought Troy, he had to have his little dig one way or another, didn't he?

§4

Back on their own landing, out in the corridor, Troy could not resist the cat-that-got-the-cream grin. Onions responded. A cheery display of nicotined teeth. For a moment he thought they'd both corpse. Onions was right, it was rich; it was irresistible, it was funny.

'What was the gag?' Onions said.

'Eh?'

'Jimmy Wheeler and the rice pudding.'

'I only meant it's not funny. Everybody's heard it. Wheeler cracks it every time he appears. Like Jack Benny playing the violin.'

'Funny?' Onions mused. 'I don't think I've heard it.'

Troy thought that Onions must be the only man in Britain who hadn't, but then he probably did not go out much, never went to the cinema or the variety and had probably never seen television in his life. For all Onions knew, Charlie Chaplin still wore a bowler hat and baggy pants, and Martin and Lewis was a department store.

'Tramp calls at the door of the big house. Toff opens the door. Tramp says, "Evenin' guvnor. Could you spare a tanner or a bite to eat?" "Well," says the toff, "d'you like cold rice pudding?" "Great," says the tramp, and the toff says, "Well come back tamorrer, it's hot now."'

Onions thought about this for a moment or two, as though puzzled. 'You're right,' he said. 'It's not funny.'

§5

There was scarcely enough of the evening left to do anything but go home, pack and go to bed. It was a short walk from Scotland Yard to his town house in Goodwin's Court. Over the years Troy had worked out and walked every possible route home. Along the Embankment, under Hungerford Bridge, up Villiers Street, across the Strand and in the back way via Chandos Place and Bedfordbury—which was rivery and, on the whole, quiet. Or straight along Whitehall, across Trafalgar Square, miss Nelson, pass St Martin-in-the-Fields, up St Martin's Lane and in the front way—which was far from quiet and for when he was in the mood to play the tourist. Or, as tonight, in mood perverse, over Whitehall, down Downing Street, where the lights still burned in the Prime Minister's offices—last-minute alterations to the agenda allowing Mr K to visit a pickle-bottling factory in Middlesbrough or morris dancing in Middle Wallop?—where the duty copper gave him an unexpected salute, out into Horse Guards' Parade, up the steps at Carlton House, up the Haymarket, and left into Orange Street—there to pause, to gaze quickly up at the top floor of an old, narrow house, and walk on, out into Charing Cross Road, through Cecil Court and in the front way.

When he got in the telephone was ringing.

'Freddie? Come out and have a jar.'

Why Charlie? Why now?

'Bad timing, Charlie, I'm off somewhere at first light. I have to pack.'

'I'm only in the Salisbury. I saw you pass by. Come on. Just half an hour.'

'Charlie, it's half past—'

'Since when did we give a toss about the time?'

The Salisbury stood on the far side of St Martin's Lane, opposite the entrance to Goodwin's Court. In the heart of the West End, all but sandwiched between theatres, it was a popular watering hole of actors. And, of a kind, Charlie was an actor.

Troy found him in the tap room, swirling a brandy and soda, a thousand trivial questions on his lips, his glistening, tangled web stretched out for Troy to settle into. Troy had known Charlie for thirty years. He was a matter of days older than Troy. They had started at school the same day, in the same dormitory, and had lived side by side for nearly eight years through the vicissitudes of an education that Troy had hated. Charlie had more tolerance of it, more understanding, Troy had assumed, of what it all meant. He had steered Troy through the course of it, around social and formal obstacles that left Troy baffled and wondering vaguely if the English were not a race of lunatics. All the same, each summer Troy asked his father if he could leave now, and each summer the elder Troy replied that he would never come to terms with the new country any other way and so must stay. 'Do you want,' he said, 'to be an Englishman or not? I recommend it wholeheartedly. They can be so unforgiving to wogs of any kind. If the club has opened its doors, I suggest you join. You don't have to believe. That is, after all, un-English. Remember Conrad—*Under Western Eyes*. They made their compromise with history long ago, and so believe nothing. And you don't have to like them either.'

Charlie led. Whatever the situation, Charlie led and Troy was an NCO. The benefits to Troy were great. At first he had wondered why Charlie had picked him, since more often than not he needed protecting from the perils of a closed society that he scarcely understood. And the price to Charlie had been great. He had stood up to bullies, with whom he personally had had no quarrel but for whom Troy, foreign in his looks and short in stature, was a natural target. And on more than one occasion had taken a beating meant for Troy.

'I don't feel it as you would,' he had said when Troy asked why he had owned up to whatever it was Troy had done. Troy did not for a moment believe this, and said as much. Charlie replied, 'Well, let's put it another way. They hit me a damn sight less hard than they would have hit you. They know you're not one of them; they think I probably am. But they're wrong. *Contra mundum,* Fred. You and me against the world.'

Troy had not understood this. All the same, Charlie had gone on saying it.

In its way their education had shaped each of them into what they were now. Each found a home outside the norms of English high society. Charlie had gone up to Cambridge in 1933, from there straight into the Guards, in which he spent the war. In theory at least he was still in the Guards, but this was all part of the colossal bluff that Troy thought went back to the war and perhaps to before the war. Guards meant spook, reserve meant active spook, attachment to our embassy in Helsinki meant important spook, attachment to our embassy in Moscow meant very important spook. All this went without saying. Charlie and Troy did not discuss it, had never discussed it. There was little need. Few men alive had Charlie's gift for small talk.

'How are the girls?' he asked, beaming his faultless smile at Troy.

'Not bad at all. They're forty-five now, and when I can struggle free of them long enough to be faintly objective, I'll admit they're good-looking women.'

'And Sasha? How's Sasha? I always had a soft spot for her.'

This was a lie. Passable enough, plausible enough if uttered to anyone else, but to Troy it smacked of Charming Charlie. At school some wag whose facility with words was as good as his perception had dubbed him Princess Channing. It reflected Charlie's good manners, his good nature, his sexual proclivities, his ready flattery and the inevitable result—Charlie usually got his own way. Six feet tall in his stockinged feet, a mop of unruly blond hair that seemed to roll down his brow just short of the cuteness of curls, a pleasing heart-shaped face, pale blue eyes and good, un-English teeth set in a wide mouth, Charlie's looks had made him a social success from an early age. Troy had seen him grow from a pederast's delight to the perfect ladies' man. In many ways he and Troy were opposites but, as the years had proved, enduring friends. Charlie lived recklessly, was always broke, and seemed to lurch from crisis to crisis untouched by the clammy hand of chaos. Troy had a vivid memory of the last time he had lent him money three or four years ago, if only because it *was* the last time and because, for the first time, Charlie had paid him back. Three hundred quid in used flyers, and a crystalline lie about having backed the winner in the Grand National. Prior to that, Troy had paid off bad debts, settled tailor's bills and seen off menacing bookmakers with a disheartening regularity and, the charm working like magic, no real resentment that he could remember. Time was, Troy thought, Charlie could talk his way in or out of anything.

'No you didn't,' said Troy. 'Nobody could. I can tell them apart physically. I always could. But I defy anyone to drive so much as a playing card between their characters. They're both the same, and they're both as bloody minded as they come. The idea that you could have a preference for one over the other isn't on, and the idea that any man could seriously have a soft spot for either one of them is preposterous. Even their wretched husbands can't aspire to that.'

Charlie grinned. 'How is *dear* Hugh?'

Sasha had married the Hon. Hugh Darbishire in 1933. He was an English uppercrust bore, far from brainless but safely, absolutely contained by the mores and interests of his class. Troy's father had remarked on the announcement of their engagement that no one should ever doubt what to buy Hugh as a present—shirts for him to stuff. 'Wretched', Troy knew, was scarcely fair. Hugh was probably as happy as one of Troy's pigs, for much the same reasons. He was blind to his wife's eccentricities and took immense pride in telling people what a marvellous wife and mother she was. On a good day, Troy thought, Sasha could just about remember her children's names. Last year Hugh's father had died and Hugh had gone to the Lords as the Viscount Darbishire. He had broken with his family's Liberal tradition and sat for the Conservatives. Hugh and Troy's elder brother Rod had not spoken since the day he called the family together to announce this. Rod had called him a 'chinless wonder', to which Hugh had weakly protested with an 'I say', which Rod had capped with, 'And you're a fucking idiot, too.'

'Charlie, you didn't get me here to chew the fat about Hugh.'

Charlie beckoned the barman and ordered another brandy and soda.

'No,' he smiled. 'Of course I didn't. I just wanted to say that you don't have to do it.'

'Do what?'

'You don't have to go to Portsmouth.'

Troy was perplexed.

'I don't?'

Charlie shook his head vigorously, then swept an over-long lock of blond hair from his face.

'It's my shout. The whole damn shebang is down to me. I only found out the Branch had roped you in about quarter of an hour ago. Honestly, you don't have to do it. It wasn't on for those buggers to go twisting your arm like that. If they didn't nurse the illusion of their independence so jealously and had asked me first, I'd have told them not to bother.'

It was the first admission Charlie had ever made to being a member of the Secret Service. But Troy had already made up his mind. Of course the Branch were a pain in the arse. He hated Special Branch even more than he hated spooks, but nothing on earth would now dissuade him from the prospect of spending a week in the company of Nikita Sergeyevich Khrushchev.

'No,' he said. 'It's OK. Honestly. I've told Wintrincham I'll do it and I will.'

'We don't need you. Really we don't.'

'I rather think you do. Where else are you going to find a Russian speaker as good as me? Outside your own ranks, that is. And of course you've been told to stay out of it, haven't you?'

'Do you really think Khrushchev is going to be indiscreet in front of a British bobby?'

'I haven't a clue. But you must think it's worth the chance or you wouldn't have surrounded him with paid ears, would you? Where will you be?'

'Out of it. I'll be in London. And if Cobb doesn't keep me posted I'll have his bollocks for conkers. If any of the Comrade First Secretary's men spotted me there would be a bit of a rumpus. How did you know we'd been warned off, by the way?'

'It's buzzing around the Commons. My brother remarked on it only a couple of days ago. Said the word had come from the top.'

'He's right. I got the works. Meeting with the PM himself. Five and Six to go nowhere near the old boy, or else.'

Yet more admissions, thought Troy. Charlie would hardly be summoned to meet Eden if he himself were not somewhere near the top of the spook's greasy pole.

The barman appeared over Charlie's left shoulder. Placed a brandy and soda in front of him, but spoke directly to Troy.

''Scuse me, Mr Troy. Friend o' yours in the back room. Askin' for you.'

'Johnny?' Troy asked.

''Fraid so.'

'Drunk?'

'Arseholed, Mr Troy. If you wouldn't mind. He is askin'.'

Troy got up. Charlie followed. The back room at the Salisbury was beautiful; a plush red box, a sumptuous crimson hole, a velvet glove in which to drink and dream. The man called Johnny was face down on the table, moaning softly.

'How did he know I was here?' Troy said.

'If you ask me, it's second sight. Like how does he always know who's just been to the bank, and how does he know which night the guvnor'll be round askin' to clear 'is slate.'

The man pushed himself slowly upright, his hands against the edge of the table. His black cashmere coat and his matching red scarf—the nearest thing to a toff's mufti—were spattered with vomit. He reeked of whisky. Wafts of it floated across at them as he burbled.

'Freddie, Freddie me old cocksparrer. Pissed again, eh?'

Troy put a hand under his arm and jerked him to his feet. Charlie took the other arm, and the barman grabbed a brown trilby off the hatstand and rammed it down on Johnny's head.

'Home, Johnny,' Troy said simply, and the two of them lugged him through the front bar to the street door.

'Can't,' he was burbling. 'Just can't, can't seem to get over it. D'y'knowwhatahmean?'

Charlie looked questioningly at Troy, but Troy had no time for the unspoken question.

'Flag a cab,' he told him.

'Freddie, me old mate,' Johnny went on, 'there are times when all you want . . .' He paused to belch loudly. 'When all you want is just to be, just to be ... dammit just to be able to talk to her. You know, you must know. For Christ's sake you're the only one who does.'

Charlie had bagged a cab. The driver pulled over to the kerb, looking doubtfully at the way the drunken lord sprawled across Troy.

Troy tipped Johnny into the back seat, prised his hands away and got the door shut on him.

The cabbie was leaning out of his window, neck craning backwards, eyes full of suspicion.

'Where to, guv?' he asked.

'Lowndes Square,' said Troy.

Then the back window came down and Johnny's head lolled out.

'Soon, old chap, soon, whaddya say?'

Charlie pointed south towards Trafalgar Square with his thumb. A long wail of Troy's name trailed after the cab as it shot away down St Martin's Lane.

Troy and Charlie stood facing each other on the pavement, neither making a move to go back inside.

'Friend of yours?'

'Johnny, thirteenth Lord Enniskerry, tenth Viscount Lissadell, ninth Marquess of Fermanagh, and well-known piss artist,' Troy recited.

Charlie looked at his shoes, then back at Troy.

'I see,' he said. 'Diana Brack's brother.'

He paused. Glanced back down the street after the cab.

'I wouldn't have said he'd make a natural friend.'

'Killing his sister isn't part of the equation. If the truth be known, I'd say Johnny was devoted to Diana. But in killing her I destroyed his father. And if there really is something the ninth Marquess and I have in common, it's a hatred of the eighth Marquess. I'm sorry, Charlie, but this puts a damper on the evening. If you'll forgive me I'm just going to stagger home to bed. I have to be up with the birds anyway.'

'You'll be OK?'

'Of course. I've put Johnny to bed pissed out of his brain dozens of times. I've listened to his drivel about his sister and his father more times than I could ever count. Always leaves its mark, but nothing I can't handle.'

Charlie hugged Troy. A quick embrace, with enough backslap to pass for rugged and manly. It was the sort of thing Troy hated, but it was Charlie through and through and he had long since learnt not to flinch from Charlie's promiscuous, public emotions. Troy had, he rarely thought, loved only four people in his life: his father, long dead; Diana Brack, also long dead, shot by Troy himself in the last year of the war; one Larissa Tosca, long since vanished; and Charles Leigh-Hunt. It would be foolish in the extreme to lose what little he had left.

He crossed St Martin's Lane, cursed Johnny Fermanagh for his lack of timing, and went home. Within ten minutes he knew that Johnny had ruined a good night's sleep and with it the prospect of an early night. Troy would not sleep. Sleep brought only the prospect of the same repetitive nightmare; the same which played itself out in his head a thousand times, in a thousand variations, but with only one ending.

He had been recently in Portsmouth—three days spent on a murder investigation in February. A pimp strung up from a lamppost by his tie, and the killer had hung onto his feet till the poor sod had strangled. Troy had stayed at a pleasant enough hotel only walking distance from the naval dockyard—the King Henry, run by a retired dockyard policeman. It was only a quarter to ten. If he threw a few things into an overnight bag and got a cab to Waterloo, he could be there by midnight or perhaps twelve-thirty at the outside. It would distract him from the headful of nonsense that Johnny Fermanagh had given him, and with any luck he might be ready for sleep when he arrived. Better still, he'd be able to lie in till seven or thereabouts. He called ahead.

'You're in luck, Mr Troy,' said ex-Sergeant Quigley. 'We got just the one room left. I'll be up till one meself. Always stock the bar before I goes to bed. Just bang good and hard on the door.'

Out in the street Troy flagged a cab. As he sat back in the seat, and the cabbie waited a moment for traffic to pass, the door of the Salisbury swung open and Charlie came out. He yawned, stretched, buttoned his coat, swung his scarf around his neck and disappeared down Cecil Court. Troy watched him go, wondering at the distance that time had placed between them, wondering how well you could know any man whose entire life was bound up with lies, and thinking that Charlie knew Troy, now, infinitely better than Troy knew him or could know him. It pained him. As boys they had had no secrets, even to the details of Charlie's vigorous queer love life; as young men they had had few secrets, even to the details of Charlie's gargantuan consumption of women. Now he told Troy little. And for once it dawned on him how little he had ever told Charlie of his affair with Diana Brack. But then, he had never told anyone. Far easier was it to own up to killing than to loving. Young Fermanagh had rubbed this home in one drunken fit by quoting Oscar Wilde's piece of appalling doggerel on the subject: 'We each one kill the thing we love.' It was quite possibly the only piece of verse Johnny knew by heart, and he had failed utterly to work out whether it was the brave man who had the sword or the other chap, and undoubtedly well-meant; but right now Troy could do without such platitude. He closed his eyes and asked the driver to tell him when they reached Waterloo.

§6

Quigley had a perverse flair for melodrama. His rambling, twisted, late-Tudor dockside inn had seen countless additions and changes, amongst which was electricity in the bedrooms. Not, however, in the corridors and landings, along which Quigley led Troy by the sweeping, sputtering glare of a kerosene lamp, arm held high, shadows leaping from wall to wall, less like a retired copper and more like a ham auditioning for the part of Long John Silver.

'You made it just in time. Another two minutes and I'd've barred the door and called it a day.'

Pieces of eight, thought Troy. 'Good of you to stay up,' he said.

Quigley thrust open the door to a vast barn of a room and pointed across the wildly sloping floor to the comfort and welcome of a half-tester bed, already turned down, inviting Troy to a sleep he fervently hoped would be dreamless. He dropped his case and sloughed off his coat, hoping Quigley was not in the mood for chat.

'Early breakfast, you said?'

'Seven-thirty, if that's not too . . .'

'Fine, fine, Mr Troy. One o' my girls'll be serving. Mary, my youngest. You'll remember her. We're pretty full tonight. Lots o' them reporter chappies down from Fleet Street to snap those Russkis tomorrow. Not that any o' them'll be up with the lark. I've one other early call. Salesman chappie from up north somewhere. So it'll be no trouble.'

Quigley paused. The obvious had occurred to him.

'I don't suppose that's got anything to do with your own visit, Mr Troy? Russkis an' all?'

Troy smiled and said nothing. Whatever answer he gave would only be to invite Quigley to natter, and he desperately wanted his bed. Quigley took the hint. Troy heard the floorboards creak all the way back down the corridor. The wind rose suddenly and he felt the room shake and the old oak flex under the strain like a mast in a storm.

Pieces of eight, he thought, and fell gratefully into the half-tester.

In the morning he woke early and stared at the light slanting in through the curtains. It could not be later than six-thirty; he could hardly have slept more than five hours. He closed his eyes again and the dream flooded back in on him, the searing images of Diana Brack: stalking him across a wasteland, gun in hand; curled sleeping in the crook of his arm; stretching, yawning, naked at the foot of his bed. His eyes snapped open. He threw back the sheets, bumped onto the drunken floor, and cursed Johnny Fermanagh once more.

In the dining room a flustered Mary Quigley met him. A dozen tables stood piled with chairs and in the midst of them one had been set for breakfast. A small man in a blue blazer sat with his back to them, his right elbow working vigorously.

'You won't mind sharing, will you?' Mary asked. 'Only I'm way behind this morning and as there's just the two of you, it does save setting two tables and running between them like a scalded cat. I'll be doing enough of that when those randy buggers from Fleet Street stir their stumps. Bottom pinchers the damn lot of 'em.'

Put like that, Troy could hardly say no. Of course he didn't want to share. Breakfast was the most private meal of the day. Selfish beyond reproach. His father had always risen early to be sure of taking it alone. His mother had always breakfasted in her bedroom. And the children ate with the cook, under strict instruction that they could not talk to their father until after his third cup of coffee and his second newspaper. He couldn't remember when he last shared breakfast with anyone.

The man in the blazer paused in his porridge to offer a hand to Troy.

'Cockerell,' he said. 'Arnold Cockerell.'

Troy shook the hand, which instantly resumed its porridge-shovelling, and sat down.

'Troy,' he said. 'Frederick Troy.'

'Gentleman of the press?' Cockerell queried, through his last mouthful of oats.

Troy had no ready lie. He heard, felt, the clank of cup and saucer, felt the splash of two sugars and the rattle of the spoon as Cockerell stirred his tea in the silence of Troy's own making. The last thing he'd ever thought he'd need was an alibi. What was he doing in Portsmouth at seven o'clock of a Wednesday morning?

'No, no,' he muttered. 'Just a bit of a break really.'

Pathetic, especially for a man whose profession necessitated practised skill with lies, but Cockerell seemed satisfied with the answer.

'All right for some,' he said, and Troy knew he was off the hook, knew what was coming next. With any luck all he'd have to do would be to nod occasionally through the clichés.

'I'm in sales myself,' Cockerell began. 'Just another working day for me, another early start. Still, it's the early bird catches the worm.'

Mary appeared at the table, balancing a large wooden tray bearing porridge and a pot of coffee for Troy and, almost beyond belief, a plate of kedgeree for Cockerell. The man's digestion, Troy thought, must be Edwardian. Who in hell could stomach porridge *and* kedgeree? For all he knew the man had started with a plate of devilled kidneys and worked his way down the menu.

'Dad says to give you coffee not tea. On account of how you never drunk the tea last time you was 'ere,' said Mary. She plonked the pot in front of Troy and was gone. Troy poured himself a cup and, as the aroma of a good dark roast wafted up, said a silent thank-you that Quigley knew how to make decent coffee. Cockerell had started on his plate of kedgeree. Troy hoped it might shut him up.

'During the war,' Cockerell sallied forth with a beginning Troy had long ago come to dread as a preface to whatever rubbish might follow. 'During the war . . .'

The phrase rattled around in Troy's brain. It stood for a certain type of man, a particular, though hardly peculiar, breed of Englishman. 'During the war'—a phrase of constant anticipation, heralding hours of harmless fun, yard upon yard of interminable reminiscence about the way things were. 'During the war'—Troy looked across the top of his cup at the bearer of this piece of traditional English nonsense, wondering if he were true to type or if, by some God-given miracle, he might just be a variation that he hadn't encountered in the eleven long years of constant nostalgia since the war in question had ended.

Cockerell was off on some train of his own about the 'Yanks' and 'over here' and how they always drank coffee and not tea and how he'd never understood how anyone could start the day without a good cup of the leaf. Troy was not listening. He heard Cockerell's words through gauze and cotton wool, but he saw the man quite clearly for what he was. Ever since the war, the English had rehashed it endlessly. Many of those who survived the bombs and bullets had been destroyed by blue blazers with badges. They could be found across the length and breadth of the nation. Propping up bars in RAF clubs and the British Legion. Yarn spinners and bluffers whose greatest hour had been square-bashing in Inversquaddie or nipple-greasing at RAF Cummerbund, whose lives ever after would be in sozzled thrall to this one moment. Men who had foundered on the rock of a pointless nostalgia for the good old days, which, if viewed objectively, had to be counted amongst mankind's darkest hours. Troy found them to be hopeless bores.

Cockerell's badge had no inscription, but from the coils of rope twisted around what might be an anchor, Troy deduced that he had whiled away the apocalypse in the Royal Navy. Clerk in charge of stores, perhaps? Mess waiter? He looked at the weaselly face opposite him. A narrow skull, a pointy jaw and a pencil-thin moustache. A familiar enough face. A face to be seen in a thousand pubs anywhere in the British Isles. One to be avoided like the plague. Troy put him down as a former petty officer, shore-based, whisky drinker, Senior Service smoker, and probably wearer of suede shoes. He was almost tempted to risk a dropped table napkin to confirm the latter point when it dawned on him that Cockerell was looking at him in a manner that indicated he was waiting for Troy to speak. If he'd asked a question, Troy hadn't heard him.

'Tell me,' Troy fudged. 'What exactly is it that you sell?'

The man beamed. Troy had just pulled the cracker for him. He paused in his kedgeree, wiped a fleck of boiled egg yolk from his bottom lip, rested an elbow on the table, and shone with pride and self-esteem.

'Modern furniture,' he said, so softly as to be almost reverential. 'To-morrow's look. The settee of Mrs 1960 in your lounge today.'

Good grief Troy thought. What hath God wrought?

'We're a stuffy old country,' Cockerell was saying. 'We do so like to cling to the past. Do you know most families in England today have never bought a three-piece suite? Never! We all live with the junk our parents hand down. Most homes you go into are still using furniture bought in 1925 at a tanner a week on the knock. We're living in the past. Europe's leaving us standing. I mean, is this what we won the war for?'

Troy had no idea why we had won the war. At the time it had seemed to him a marvellous stroke of good fortune. All the same, he was damn certain it wasn't won simply to facilitate the purveying of second-rate tat in the dubious name of modernity. He knew what Cockerell meant by 'modern'—coffee tables on black tapered legs, sticking out at odd angles, and hideous carpets with patterns looking like Jackson Pollock's rejects. But then, he had never bought an item of furniture in his life. His mother had furnished his house, entirely with odds and sods from her own. He was, he supposed, part of what Cockerell was getting at. What he called antique, Cockerell called second-hand. It cut both ways. During his brother Rod's last campaign, the General Election of 1955, one old trout in Hertfordshire had buttonholed Troy and informed him of her intention of voting Liberal. She could not vote for Rod—such a nice man, but a Socialist—and she could no longer vote for the Con-servative. Why? Troy had asked. He invited us in for tea, the trout had replied, and do you know he had shop-bought furniture! In her book, one closed to such as Cockerell Troy suspected, the only way to acquire furniture was to inherit it.

'Do you know what England is?' Cockerell blathered on. 'The land of the forgotten parlour, the last bastion of the antimacassar.'

Silently, wishing him no encouragement, Troy concurred entirely with Cockerell's opinion. It summed England up very well.

'My old dad kept the key to the front parlour on his watch chain. He'd open it once a week for my mother to do the cleaning, and the rest of the week it was locked to keep us kids out. Fifty-one weeks a year this rigmarole went on. We used the blasted room on Boxing Day, and then we shut it up again, with its immaculate suite, scarcely dented by a human backside, its antimacassars and its sea-shell ashtrays, until next Christmas.

By the time I inherited, the furniture was hopelessly out of date. About as fashionable as spats, and looking as new as it did the day the horse and cart delivered it in 1908. I'd've given it to a museum if I thought they'd have taken it. As it was I took it outside and I put a match to it. Good riddance, say I. We have to keep up with the times, don't you agree?'

Troy did not agree. He was not at all sure what this much-used phrase meant. Cockerell gobbled more kedgeree—a surprising appetite for a man so thin—and did not seem to expect an answer.

'I've three shops,' he went on. 'In the North and Midlands. One in Derby, one in Alfreton and my HQ in Belper.'

The precision of 'North and Midlands' struck Troy as oddly mechanical, somehow devoid of humanity. A place in which no one could really live. The stilted language of a contestant in the regional finals of a ballroom dancing competition. Troy knew Derby. He had spent the best part of a week there hunting down a poisoner in 1951. The other two were merely names, although for some reason Belper sounded vaguely familiar to him.

'I import and export. The Contemporary look. Mainly Scandinavia, you know. That's where the best of the new comes from nowadays. But I buy anywhere and I sell everywhere. All over Europe.'

Cockerell finished the last of his kedgeree, pressing his fork down on the last few grains of boiled rice. As if by magic, Mary appeared with the toast. One small silver rack for Troy, and one small silver rack for Cockerell. The difference was that Troy's toast was a uniform golden brown, while Cockerell's was white on one side and black on the other. Troy would be damned before he'd trade so much as a slice with this living monument to British boredom. Cockerell scarcely seemed to notice. He scraped away sturdily with his knife at a rock hard slab of refrigerated butter and prattled on. Had Troy considered the attractions of wall-to-wall carpeting? The phrase meant nothing to Troy. Cockerell explained and even drew the swirls and curves of his own favourite design on the back of an envelope for him.

'There,' he said proudly. '*Skaters*. It's all the rage. At least it will be. I've thirty rolls in the Belper shop.'

'Tell me,' Troy asked, finishing his toast and knowing he could duck out of any consequences. 'What brings you to Portsmouth? Wall-to-wall ward room? Scandinavian-design barnacles?'

Cockerell was more than momentarily flummoxed. Troy had said so little, perhaps, that any question, however sarcastic, might stun him to silence. But it seemed more than that. He reddened a little, looked down at his toast and marmalade, and then, shrugging, looked back at Troy, a faint smile on his thin lips, a lost look in his pale blue eyes.

'Oh, you know, bit of this, bit of that . . .'

It was a lie. As limp as Troy's own. But if a voluble bore finally resorted to a lie that dribbled down into silence, Troy would at least be grateful for the silence. What matter if the man was away from home, having, as English euphemism so tartly put it, his bit on the side?

True to Troy's definition of type, he pulled the glass ashtray towards him, pushed away his plate and took a packet of Senior Service from his pocket. The man positively reeked Rotary Club. Troy wondered once more about the suede shoes.

§7

Troy was late. He had dawdled. He checked his watch. It was a quarter to ten. A clear, crisp spring morning. The kind of April Troy thought presaged a good summer. The guard at Her Majesty's Dockyard Portsmouth—a place known throughout what remained of the Empire as Pompey—looked at Troy's warrant card and scanned a list of names.

'You're not the last,' he said. 'Not quite. I've yet to see hide nor hair of Inspector Cobb.' He turned, arm outstretched. 'Second hut on your left.'

Troy followed where he pointed. He thrust open the door of a wooden hut, and found himself facing a loose squad of five bleary policemen. Four of them sat at a table, one of them slumped forwards on his arms quite obviously fast asleep. Troy thought he recognised some of them. A young man, no more than twenty-five, got to his feet.

'Chief Inspector. I'm Huw Beynon. Detective Sergeant with the Branch,' he said.

Troy knew the face. He'd seen him in the corridors at the Yard. Too young to be a sergeant, far too young to be with those bastards at the Branch. Beynon introduced him to Sergeants Beck and Molloy, also of the Branch, and one of them saw fit to nudge Detective Sergeant Milligan, drafted in for the occasion from J Division, into something resembling wakefulness in the presence of a Detective Chief Inspector. He looked up at Troy, muttered a greeting. A greyish fuzz coated his chin. He hadn't shaved. If Troy knew Cobb, the man was in for a good dressing down. It wasn't his responsibility, and Troy felt vaguely pleased to be free from it.

The fifth man hogged the stove. A short, fat, miserable-looking man, and a poor-looking specimen for a copper. Oblivious to all around him, he buried himself in the pages of a large, hardbacked book. Troy approached, tipped the book forward to see the title. *Lolita*—of which he had never heard—by one Vladimir Nabokov—of whom he'd never heard either. The man adjusted his glasses and his focus, and stared for a moment at Troy.

'Lance Bombardier Clark?' Troy said.

'It's Detective Constable Clark now, sir. And I don't suppose you're an Inspector any more, are you, sir?'

'Chief Inspector. Are you with the Branch?'

'Lord no, sir. Warwickshire Constabulary. I got roped in for me languages. I've Russian as well as German. Truth to tell, all the time I spent in Berlin I'd have to have been deaf not to come away fluent in Russian.'

Troy had not set eyes on Clark since Christmas Day of 1948 in a snow-bound Berlin, to which the late Josef Stalin had laid siege. Clark, Lance Bombardier, Artillery, had been assigned by the British Army as his translator. Which reminded him that he had last seen Tosca only minutes after the last time he saw Clark. Troy pulled up a chair close to Clark. The policemen had been up since four or five in the morning. They were all drowsy and bedraggled. A private conversation was unlikely to offend.

'How did they get you?' he asked simply.

'Quite straightforward, sir,' Clark replied. 'I'd done fifteen years by 1952. I'd made Warrant Officer Class II. I knew I wasn't what you'd call officer material. Personally, I don't think I was even Warrant Officer Class I material. It was time to ask for me civvy suit. About that time the force started recruiting in a big way. There'd been that big purge of bent coppers, you'll recall. They sent a couple of blokes to the base I was on to blow their own trumpet. They told me I was just what the force needed. Languages an' all. The new breed of educated copper. Brains instead of boots. Fine, I thought. I volunteered. I spent the next three years pounding a beat back in bloody Birmingham. The only foreign language I got to use was if we got villains in from Wolverhampton. About a year ago I got out of uniform. Things've looked up a bit since then. This came out of the blue. A right treat. Couldn't believe me luck.'

'Nor I.'

Troy dearly wanted to ask Clark about Larissa Tosca. But there was a risk. What had Clark thought she was? That last night in Berlin, he had watched her back into the mess at RAF Gatow, dusting the snowflakes from her WAC's uniform and almost collide with Clark, on his way out. Did he ever learn that the uniform was utter deception? A relic of the war that she was no more entitled to wear than Troy himself? Did he ever realise which side she was on?

'When did you leave Berlin?' he ventured.

'Oh, I was there till the end. I saw it all. Mind you, nothing was the same after 1949. Once the Soviets eased up on us it was dull as ditchwater. Life without a few little fiddles wasn't worth living. They all said it. The army, the spivs, the spies. It was yesterday's rice pudding.'

Much as Troy wanted news, the ambiguities of ignorance appealed. Supposing Clark knew everything? He had surely seen her sit down with Troy that night? Supposing she had been exposed or purged in one of those countless show trials rigged up by Beria under Stalin's regime? Did he want to know, and if he wanted to know, did he want to know the worst?

Clark was looking across Troy's shoulder. He turned. Beynon appeared above him.

'Excuse us, sir. We was wondering like. It's past ten and not a sign of Mr Cobb. He dropped us here more than an hour ago. You don't suppose there's anything we should be doing? We was wondering. You being the senior man an' all.'

Troy was about to point out his raw recruit's status on the operation when the door banged open and Cobb bustled in, red-faced and sweating. He slapped his case onto the trestle table, jerking Milligan once more to life. He looked around him, gasping and out of breath, taking in the room in a sweeping glance. As Troy had expected, that glance came to rest on Milligan.

'You,' he barked. 'Shave and haircut the minute you're off duty!'

He turned his gaze on Troy.

'Good of you to join us, Mr Troy!'

'You didn't get my message?' Troy said softly.

'Yes—I got your message. But if you don't mind, for the future, once a plan's been agreed I'd be obliged if you'd stick to it.'

Troy slowly turned his left wrist around. Looked at his watch and looked at Cobb, making his point silently. Cobb ignored the hint. Whatever it was that had made him late, it had severely taxed his physique. The man was streaming sweat, as though he had just won first prize in the sack race.

'Right,' he began. 'Rosters!'

Cobb tore off his blue mackintosh and scattered the schedule for the next ten days across the table. Troy glanced down it. It was chock-a-block. Not a day out of the next ten seemed to have as much as a tea-break built in to it. Bulganin and Khrushchev were about to be bounced the length and breadth of the British Isles by all known means of transport, and to be wined and dined by every dignitary London could unearth, in a punishing round of sociability that would strain a man half their age. For the evening of the twenty-third they were to be the guests of the Labour Party at the House of Commons. Suddenly Troy spotted trouble, but if the Branch and Her Majesty's Government couldn't see it, it was, he thought, scarcely his job to point it out to them.

'First off. For those of you who've already spent good money at Moss Bros, there'll be no evening dress. Our guests appear not to have brought theirs, so we're all, to avoid embarrassment, to wear plain dark suits for the evening dos.'

Cobb looked briefly but pointedly at Troy. The follow-up to yesterday's wisecrack.

'Now—there's a few rules and regulations. A few dos and don'ts. Cock up and you'll have me to answer to. We all know why we're here, and we all know what the front is. Each of you will log on and off shift with me. I want to know when you pick up the nobs and when you drop 'em, and when you drop 'em I want a full verbal report. I'll be the one to decide what needs to be in writing. You won't have time to take notes and even if you have, I don't want anyone caught by the Russians jotting things down. For the purposes of clear communications, Khrushchev is codenamed Red Pig, Bulganin is Black Bear. Nobody uses their real names over the phone. Got it?'

He looked at them all in turn. For no reason Troy could see, he let his gaze rest on Clark.

'Got it?' he said again.

Troy heard Clark gulp and manage a faint 'yessir'.

'Right. Next on the agenda. Guarding Red Pig and Black Bear.'

He paused. Troy assumed he was straining for the pause to look meaningful.

'Not your job. Repeat. Not your job. My boys will be everywhere and highly visible.'

'What? Trench coats and bowler hats?' said a voice from the back. Troy saw Cobb's eyes home in. He turned to see Milligan receiving the gorgon stare.

'Shuttit, laddie. Just shuttit.'

Cobb broke the stare. Looked at the roster in front of him.

'As it happens,' he said, reddening slightly, 'it *will* be trench coats and bowler hats.'

Troy knew he was grinning. Unless God spared him quickly, a grin would become a snigger and a snigger a laugh and he would have Cobb down on him like an irate schoolmaster, armed with a piece of chalk. The thought of all those flatfoots swarming all over Claridge's Hotel dressed up like pantomime policemen was too funny to resist.

Cobb's finger shot out, aiming towards Troy.

'You! Stop bloody grinning!'

Troy looked back and realised that Cobb was pointing at Clark. The fat little man was smirking with repressed laughter.

'They'll do the real work, and they'll be recognisable. To everyone. But in the event of a real hoo-ha, there's a routine to go through. First. The only time you do not accompany Red Pig and Black Bear is when other security is provided, e.g., royal palaces, Downing Street. In all other places you stick to them like glue. No matter where. Nobody is exempt. If you have to sit in on a cosy chat with the Archbishop of Canterbury, you do it. Second, you always go through doors ahead of them. Third, if any nutcase has a go at them, you get them out of the room and you let my boys handle the assailant. You do not tackle anyone unless you've no choice.'

Beynon's hand shot up like an eager schoolboy.

'Excuse me, sir. But have there been any actual threats?'

'Threats?' Cobb sneered. 'Threats? Every bunch of cranks in Britain from the Empire Loyalists to the Last-of-the-Mosleyites has threatened 'em. They're all nutters and it doesn't mean a damn. If we believed every crank who thought Khrushchev was the anti-Christ there'd not be a copper left on point duty from here to John O'Groats. All the same, we play safe. Understood? And remember, the Russians wanted the KGB guarding their own blokes. We had quite a row convincing them we weren't going to have armed Russian bully-boys swanning around London. So—bear this in mind. If we fuck up, we'll never hear the last of it.'

Again he swept the room with a practised penetrating stare. Practised, no doubt, in front of a bathroom mirror from an early age. Cobb was, Troy decided, a brute of a man, but not the ugly brute he had first supposed. The man's waffle gave him time to look and appraise. The stare was disturbing, more than Cobb ever meant it to be. He meant merely to command, and he did it rather well. But his eyes seemed asymmetrical. It was the cock-eyed, strabismic stare of a one-eyed man. But Cobb had two eyes. Then the penny dropped. It was the eyebrows. The left eyebrow drew all the attention to the left eye. It was white in the middle. A one-inch strip of premature white hair, as startling to observe as Diaghilev's two-tone coiffure or the hennaed halo of Quentin Crisp. Troy remembered Cobb's reputation at the Yard as a ladykiller. He was beginning to see why he had it. There was a slob side to him, that could appeal to the tidy instinct in a woman—a man for whom the right woman could roll pairs of socks into balls ever after—but there was also a raffish, brutal handsomeness to the man. To Troy it bespoke the surly Special Branch bastard. But, it was conceivable that to some young WPCs he was Mr Rochester of the Yard. Brown curls fell across his forehead, his mouth was wide, his jaw strong despite the extra chin—and he dressed surprisingly well. The mackintosh was a Burberry; the neat, double-breasted, figure-flattering blue suit must have cost a packet. Troy was all but indifferent to clothes. He had his suits made in Savile Row out of nothing more than habit. He dressed well only because money let him and tradition paved the way. Taste did not come into it. And a suit as sharp as Cobb's he did not own.

'And lastly—'

Lastly? Troy must have missed something.

'Lastly. These.'

Cobb opened his case and tipped out six police-issue Browning automatics in their shoulder holsters. It was an odd moment. Troy had not seen a gun in a while. It had been well over a year since he had last had to request issue of one. They sat uneasily with his notion of 'copper'.

'Sign here. You get two extra clips of nine mill. And you account for every shell spent.'

Troy watched as Beynon, Beck and Molloy slipped into their shoulder holsters like practised gunmen. He fumbled at his. Clark fumbled. Milligan fumbled. It slowly dawned on Troy that the shoulder holster could not be used left-handed. It went under the left armpit or nowhere. Clark managed to sling it around his neck, with the butt of the gun dangling across his sternum. Mulligan was all but making a cat's cradle of it.

Cobb looked at them, making no attempt to disguise his contempt.

'Jesus Christ. Amateurs. Rank bloody amateurs. Beynon, you show 'em!'

He stormed out. Beynon gave Troy a look that said 'sorry'.

'It goes like this you see, sir.'

He whipped off his own holster and slowly put it back on for the benefit of all three, exaggerating each gesture—the patient Scoutmaster teaching the dimwits a useful knot or two.

'Left arm first. Down, around the back. Right arm through the elastic side, straight out and pull in. See?'

They saw. Mulligan got the hang of it. Troy and Clark looked like the last of the clowns.

'S'cuse the thought, sir', said Milligan, 'but if I ever get Mr Cobb behind the bikesheds ...'

'After me in the queue,' said Troy. 'If I knew how this thing worked, I'd shoot him myself.'

He put the gun into the holster and put his jacket back on. It felt awkward and it felt silly. It stuck in his armpit like a cucumber. He'd have to live with it. God help Nikita Khrushchev if he ever had to draw it.

Guns boomed in the dockyard. Over and over again. Troy did not need to count. There would be thirteen blasts, as tradition demanded, followed by a Soviet reply of twenty-one. It meant the Russian ships were docking—or World War III had begun. Troy put his overcoat back on and joined the others in the yard.

'You're in luck,' Cobb yelled at them over the sound of the guns. 'You get a personal introduction. We stand in line and the Foreign Office bloke will introduce you in turn as personal bodyguards. Whatever they say to you, for pete's sake look as though you don't understand and don't answer until the FO have translated for you. As far as the Russians are concerned you're ordinary coppers—just how ordinary I shudder to think. Right, follow me.'

Cobb led off under the worn brick arch to the berth set aside for the Russian ships. The sun shone, but as they cleared the arch a salt wind came up off the sea to remind Troy that it was still only the middle of April and the weather could turn any minute. The quay was crowded: a horde of pressmen, the gentlemen of Fleet Street, standing around in groups smoking and joking; a horde of Foreign Office bigwigs and littlewigs, the gentlemen of Pall Mall, standing around not smoking and not joking. And, as Cobb had said, the unmistakable presence of Special Branch in its Sunday best, belted trench coats, bowler hats and big feet. There could scarcely be a phone tapped or a skull cracked the length of Britain this morning, there was no one to do it. They were all here looking like they were auditioning for the role of Chinese policeman in a seaside production of *Aladdin*. Troy did a quick head count of his own party, realised they were seven, and tried not to think of Snow White.

The Royal Navy provided a guard of honour, and the Marines a band to play the round of dreary national anthems. Under the vast grey shadow of the Soviet Navy's battlecruiser *Ordzhonikidze,* the dignitaries lined up in precedence to prepare to greet the Russians. Troy found himself between Cobb and Beynon. Peering round Cobb, he could see the Russian Ambassador, Jakob Malik, and the two faces of Britain: the civil in Lord Reading, Minister of State at the Foreign Office, and the military in Lord Cilcennin, First Lord of the Admiralty. Quite what the difference was in their roles he could not say. Although both of them were in the Government, he could not be certain whether Cilcennin was actually in the Navy or not, or whether it was even necessary that he should be in the Navy. Neither of them mattered much. Dogsbodies sent out to do duty on a windswept quayside. Nothing mattered much till they got to Victoria Station, the back door to Westminster, and came face to face with the Prime Minister Sir Anthony Eden, a veteran of the thirties— that dirty, double-dealing decade—the bright young Foreign Secretary who'd had the courage to resign from the Cabinet over Munich and Neville Chamberlain's appeasement of Hitler, and who had for so long been heir apparent to the ageing and ailing Winston Churchill. Heir no longer—he had been PM for almost a year now, carrying with him the hopes of a nation deeply loyal to the old man, but desperately in need of the new man. The problem, as Troy saw it, was that heir apparent was a role one could play too long.

The idea of meeting Khrushchev rolled Troy back into memories of youth. When he was nineteen or twenty a cousin of his father's had visited England as part of a Soviet trade mission. He was the only Troitsky Troy had ever met. One of the few to have stayed and tried to make the best of a dire inevitability. Troy's father had entertained cousin Leo royally, keen for any news of the old country, lost in time like the Sisters Prozorova, dreaming of Moscow once more, drunk on Moscow once more. Moscow. Moscow was the fiefdom of the party boss of the city, a cunning peasant named Nikita Sergeyevich Khrushchev. It was the first time anyone had heard the name. A hardy survivor of the Revolution, Khrushchev was in the process of building Moscow's showcase Metro—the triumph of public works over private demands. From the outside it began to look as though the new Soviet Union was raising its head above the parapet for the first time. Cousin Leo had an abundance of tales of the eccentric, domineering, charming, drunken apparatchik in charge of the first burst of colour the Soviet Union had seen in almost twenty years. From time to time Troy had followed the career of this intriguing little man. The late thirties had seen him put in charge of the entire Ukraine—where he took to dressing like a peasant and imitating the accent of the region. More peasant than the peasant, full of old aphorisms and Ukrainian lore. The pretence had cost him. Ever wise to the weaknesses of his subordinates, Stalin had hoisted Khrushchev on his own petard. 'Dance!' he had told Khrushchev, and the fifty-two-year-old fat little Khrushchev danced for his life, flailing and sweating at his pastiche of the Ukrainian *gopak* for the delight of a man who would have thought little of putting him on the next train to Siberia or seeing him hanged in public. The war had found Khrushchev in uniform as a front-line political commissar, a Lieutenant-General—one better than Bulganin, whose title of 'Marshal' was hardly more meaningful than that of a Southern Colonel in Mississippi or Tennessee. Khrushchev had, by 1949, reappeared in Moscow as a full-blown member of the Secretariat of the Central Committee, complete with overcoat, Homburg and his place on top of Lenin's tomb each May Day. Soon enough the old dictator was dead. To those who hardly paid attention to matters Soviet there might have been some immediate confusion as to who had really inherited power—Beria? Malenkov? The mock Marshal, Bulganin? Or the real Marshal, Voroshilov? Nominally, the head of state was Voroshilov, and for the purposes of this visit it fell to Bulganin. Neither Troy, nor HM Government it seemed, had any doubts as to where the real power lay. As far as Troy was concerned, Khrushchev was a rocket waiting for someone to light the blue touch paper and retire. The only thing that was predictable about the man was that he was unpredictable. In his public persona Khrushchev had often struck Troy as having the fundamental defining characteristic of a kitten—a boundless, reckless curiosity.

Sometime between the war and the fall of Beria, cousin Leo had vanished. Troy's brother Rod had been in the Cabinet in the dying days of the Labour Government and had used what influence he could. All Rod's enquiries had yielded was that the man had never existed in the first place. A non-person, even in death. In a nation where simply to have survived was an achievement, Khrushchev was the survivor *par excellence*.

For weeks now rumours had circulated in the Western press that he had denounced Stalin, denounced him as a tyrant responsible for the slaughter of countless numbers of his own people. No one knew for certain, and no one had been able to quote a word the man said as gospel. The Twentieth Congress of the Communist Party of the Soviet Union had been addressed by Khrushchev in a closed session. Yet the effects were noticeable. Reports came in from Poland and from Hungary of a change in the political climate, amounting to a faith in the veracity of the rumour—it was, as so many journalists had remarked, the first sign of a thaw in the cold war, the tinsel rustle of political spring.

The Band of the Royal Marines struck up. Troy looked up at the ship. An interminable row of Soviet dignitaries stood to attention for their national anthem. At their head, two stout little men in vast black coats. Bulganin was not a well-known figure, Khrushchev was, yet they both seemed to Troy to be variations on the same theme as they made their way down the red-carpeted gangplank to the quay. They were stout men, they were little men, but their stoutness was at odds with their boyishness. He could think of no other word to describe them. With their round, smiley faces, and bright, darting eyes they were like two little boys, two schoolboys blown up into men with a bicycle pump.

They approached the start of the British line and began pumping flesh, Khrushchev following and smiling fiercely, Bulganin leading, smiling, it

seemed, more naturally, his beautiful blue eyes shining and his hair coif-
fured like icing on a cake. As he shook Troy's hand he looked to Troy like
a living parody of Sir Thomas Beecham, right up to the goatee beard.
And Khrushchev, Khrushchev only a foot away now, shaking the giant
paw of Norman Cobb and looking like the Russian peasant he really
was, another rendition of the Ur-Russian face that Troy had seen staring
back at him from countless pictures and photographs all his life.

Khrushchev let go of Cobb's hand. Troy let go of Bulganin's, and in
the twinkling of an eye he found himself clasping the podgy hand of
Nikita Sergeyevich Khrushchev, looking into the nut-brown eyes of the
leader of the Other World, and counting the warts on the face of the
most fascinating man alive.

§8

Khrushchev was a bore. A bully and a bore. There were no two ways about
it, the man was terrible. He had all the character and gusto that Troy had
expected of him, but shot through with the corruption of power, an easy
manipulation of others that manifested itself in an utter lack of regard
for the feelings of those others.

In public he deferred to the nominal head of state, Bulganin, and took
an impish delight in back-seat driving. In private he bawled him out,
shouted at him, called him stupid and told him to the nth detail what to
say. He was scarcely better behaved towards his son Sergei, a twenty-two-
year-old, slim, quiet version of his father, hidden behind what appeared
to be National Health spectacles, who smiled pleasantly at everyone and
seemed as eager to please as a boy scout.

But what really put Troy off him were the jokes. Troy thought of himself
as a man with a sense of humour, but Khrushchev's jokes struck him as
tasteless and adolescent, as though he were striving too hard to outrage.

The first evening they did a mind-boggling, whistle-stop tour of the
sights of London, faster than an American senator running for reelection
in the boondocks, pressing the flesh while double-parked. The Royal

Festival Hall, that stirring example of the British Soviet School of Architecture; dark, brooding, ancient Westminster Abbey; sublime St Paul's, a surviving Wren masterpiece in the midst of a sea of wartime ruins; and the floodlit white walls of the Tower of London at dusk, with its red and black romance of beefeaters and ravens. All in less than two hours.

At the RFH Khrushchev appeared singularly unimpressed. He looked at the prices on the bar tariff and said he'd come back on pay day when he could afford it. Not bad, thought Troy, some sense of the wage packet if nothing else. At the Tower, informed that, according to legend, the empire would cease when the ravens left, Khrushchev quipped that he couldn't see any ravens in the first place. Nelson putting the telescope to his blind eye. A few smiles were forced but no one laughed. Hardly offensive, but Troy began to wonder if the man had any tact.

At St Paul's—a building known to still even the arid souls of atheists like Troy—the old Dean showed them the vast dome, in an eerie silence of muted voices and leather footsteps, and remarked with some pride that this was the spot on which a German incendiary had landed in 1940, how the cathedral had been saved, the damage repaired, and how London had lost seventeen of its precious Wren churches. Khrushchev blithely remarked that the Dean wouldn't have to worry about repairs when the Russians dropped 'the bomb'.

He did not need to qualify the term. 'The Bomb' was 'THE BOMB'. Not HE or incendiary, not 500lb or a ton, but *mega*tons—a word still virtually incomprehensible to most people, often paraphrased in multiples of Hiroshima: twenty Hiroshimas; fifty Hiroshimas. The same town atomised time after time in the power of metaphorical fission. In his mind's eye Troy saw tiny atolls in the South Pacific going whumpf and disappearing from sight beneath the icon of the times, a colossal mushroom cloud.

The Dean looked blankly at Khrushchev. The presence of an interpreter, the passage of words through a second language and a second voice, seemed somehow to deflect the sense of just who had spoken, to deflate the sense of menace and the contrivance at outrage. Bought the time for tact that Khrushchev himself could not muster. The Dean led off, taking them in search of John Donne's memorial. Just behind his right shoulder Troy heard a muttered 'Jesus Christ' from Mulligan.

Troy rapidly lost count of the number of trips they had made. He seemed to be in and out of Claridge's and Number 10 three or four times a day; and each evening he would dutifully report to Cobb, usually telling him that Khrushchev had said nothing of any significance within earshot. Or did MI5 and MI6 really want to know that he had thrown a tantrum when he couldn't find a diamond cufflink, or that he complained constantly about the tea? And that on one occasion Troy had found him crawling around the bedroom of his suite on all fours, and had been unable to tell whether this was another search for the missing cufflink or capitulation to the effects of his favoured drink, red pepper vodka?

On the evening of the second day, Downing Street had given a formal dinner for their guests. B & K met C & A, former Prime Ministers Churchill and Attlee, and the Leader of the Opposition, Prime Minister-Apparent Hugh Gaitskell. The Night of the Nobs, as Clark put it.

It was an easy shift 'doing' Downing Street. One simply escorted the Russians there, handed over to the highly visible uniformed coppers and shuffled into a side room to sit out the occasion in something resembling a bad version of a dentist's waiting room. Nothing to read and nothing to do.

'What's that?' said Troy as a uniformed copper pushed the door to.

'It came yesterday, sir.'

It looked like a ten-foot-long wooden spoon.

'It's a ten-foot-long wooden spoon, sir. It was left on the doorstep. The PM ordered it brought in at once before the press saw it. We're to get rid of it as soon as the Russians are safely out of the country.'

Troy looked at the label attached to the monstrosity.

'From the League of Empire Loyalists. We fear it may not be long enough for tomorrow's dinner.'

'What do you think it means?' asked the copper.

'Isn't it obvious?' said Troy. 'A long spoon to sup with the devil.'

There had been a curious reception for the two emissaries of Satan, from the minute the train slid into Victoria station; and a curious form of protest. And what they both had in common was that they were lukewarm. Neither welcome nor dissent seemed to have feeling or meaning to it. Neither could muster a crowd large enough to cut through the roar of the traffic. This particular protest lacked wit. Whilst the duty copper might be the dimmest of flatfoots, and possibly the only person in Britain who had not heard the cliché, it was a symbol so obvious as to be pointless. The cliché of clichés. The League of Empire Loyalists were hardly typical of the British, a nation of non-joiners; but at the same time they were—the nation of non-joiners was also the nation of endless committees and self-appointed bodies. This was simply the silliest of many, the association of old men who had failed to grasp the way of the world since 1945. As Rod put it, describing so many of the institutions of the country from the Carlton Club to the magistracy, just another League of Little Men.

Molloy, with the practised skill of a career copper, had perfected the knack of sleeping bolt upright. Clark, as ever, had a book. Troy was the one who was bored. He wondered if he could get away with stretching his legs. He opened the door quietly. There was a hum of voices, a solitary young copper standing in the hallway. Troy expected a reprimand, but the man simply nodded and said a quiet, 'Evenin', sir', as though Troy had every right to be wandering about. Emboldened by this he strolled as casually as he could up the staircase past endless portraits of previous incumbents from Walpole via Palmerston and Disraeli all the way to Churchill, to the first floor and the reception rooms. The hum of voices grew louder. English and Russian. He could hear someone almost shouting, and deduced that this was translation for the deaf. He was gazing out of a front window when a door behind him opened, the volume surged and he saw what he momentarily took to be an elderly waiter shuffling towards him. It was not an elderly waiter; it was an elderly Prime Minister, a portrait come to life.

'Harumgrrum werrumbrum,' said Churchill.

Troy understood not a syllable. What could the former leader of the western world, the undisputed Heavyweight Champion of the Second World War, possibly have to say to him?

§9

The following evening, just before dusk, they took a launch down the Thames from Westminster Pier to Greenwich, one of the pleasantest trips London could offer. It had its effect. A man who talked nineteen to the dozen had shut up by the time they slid under Tower Bridge. Khrushchev did what any man with the slightest poetry in his soul would do. He stared. London changed from the dwarfing magnificence of St Paul's, hogging the horizon with not a building to equal it for height or breadth, to the dark depths of the East End, a skyline slashed by the blades of cranes and derricks, shoreline fretted by a hundred wharves and harbours, flashing with the rumpled black-and-red sails of countless Thames barges motionless in the Pool of London. As they rounded the Isle of Dogs, the hill of Greenwich came into view, the complex, eye-baffling beauty of the Royal Naval College, the distant outline of the Observatory perched on the hilltop, dividing East from West along an utterly arbitrary line. What better symbol could there be for this entire visit?

Khrushchev preached the new gospel of peaceful coexistence to the Senior Service, spoke of the speed of the arms race, described the *Ordzhonikidze,* the ship that had brought him to Britain, as state of the art technology that would be out of date within a matter of months. It seemed to Troy to be a sound argument. Depending on how you read it, it was a warning to us all or a threat to the West. Khrushchev tipped the scales, and added that the Russians had no wish to 'push you off the planet'. But then that in turn implied that they had the power to do so.

Within minutes of him resuming his seat Troy heard Khrushchev offering to sell the *Ordzhonikidze* to the First Sea Lord.

'Buy two, and I'll throw in a submarine for free,' he said in best adman parlance.

The Englishman looked utterly baffled by this. He had no idea whether to take it as a joke or to name a price. Troy had no sympathy with such men, and on any other occasion it might have been a good wheeze, a good ruffling of the feathers of these imperial peacocks; but Troy found the menace that lurked just beneath the surface of this unruly schoolboy behaviour too hard to stomach. Three days of jokes and he was beginning to think there was no such thing as a joke that didn't have hidden depths just like an iceberg. Perhaps the joke was the defence of the underdog? Coming from the topdog it seemed brutal, bullying and boorish.

Only minutes later Khrushchev turned his sights on the Chief of the Imperial General Staff. 'One day,' he said, 'one day soon we will be able to put nuclear warheads onto guided missiles. Believe me, it will change the face of warfare.'

Troy knew from the look on the man's face, as the interpreter put it into English, what was coming. His expression was the blinking, startled blankness of shock.

'I find that,' the interpreter reported back to Khrushchev, 'a shocking suggestion.'

Khrushchev shrugged a little. 'It may well be,' he said. 'It is nonetheless the future.'

The baldness of truth or the nakedness of threat? And once more Troy's sympathies swung. Khrushchev's party was over forty strong. They had required an entire floor of Claridge's, they were trucked out for all the interminable public functions in varying combinations in a logistic nightmare requiring a convoy of limousines, and enough coppers to mount an invasion of Latvia or Lithuania. Khrushchev meant to show off Russia with an eighty-legged advertisement. Prominent in that advert were Messrs Tupolev and Kurchatov, known respectively for their work on supersonic flight and atomic physics. If not to rub home the possibilities in the conjunction of the two, why else had Khrushchev brought them? To be shocked was the utmost naiveté. The man was CIGS. To be shocked was crass stupidity. If we too were not going to put our nuclear weapons onto rockets and aim them at the cities of our enemies, why else had we gone to the trouble of hijacking the German rocket scientists? Why, even now, was Werner von Braun, inventor of the V2, holed up in some American laboratory if not to invent a rocket capable of carrying a nuclear warhead? Or did this man really think that we could fight another war as we had fought most of the others, by sending a gunboat out to one mutinous colony or another, or an expeditionary force to a troubled ally—was the word 'Imperial' in his title so brain-befuddling that he could not see the world as it had been reborn in fire at Hiroshima and Nagasaki?

Both sides bored him rigid. He got into the habit of never being without a book or newspaper. Prompted by the Greenwich trip, he dug out an old copy of *The Secret Agent* by Joseph Conrad, in which a child is blown to pieces unwittingly carrying a bomb to the Observatory. Every time he was shuffled into a side room at Number 10 or stuck in Khrushchev's suite at Claridge's he would read a few more pages of Conrad and scan the newspapers. Occasionally the two worlds would meet. The world in front of his eyes would be reflected in the remote world-out-there, the world-in-print: thirty thousand dissidents released in Poland; Soviet Admiral of the Fleet Kuznetsov sacked; Stalinist Politburo member Andrei Vishinsky denounced for his part in the show trials of the thirties; the head of MI6 to be replaced. This was oddly timed. Why now of all times? And of course the newspapers did not name the new man. Troy made a mental note to ask Rod the next time they met. Rod could not resist a bet, and Troy had a vague memory of him putting ten bob on some chap called White, or was it Black?

On the Saturday, out at Harwell, the Atomic Research Establishment, Khrushchev hit rock bottom in Troy's esteem. Establishment was an odd term; it concealed more than it revealed about the true nature of the place. But, in part, it was a factory, and being such had factory workers. As the visiting party sped around in their white coats, they would pause like passing royalty for meaningless banter with the working man.

The working man departed from the script. A large man, northern accent, gentle face, huge hands, which he, playing the part to the hilt, was found wiping on a rag as the party approached. Troy had no idea what job he did in this complex of concealment—it seemed to him that the only reason they were here was to shove the notion of 'atomic' down Khrushchev's throat. All the way there Troy had heard him ask, 'Is this a factory, now? I asked for more factories.'

Khrushchev shook the working man's hand.

'Pleased to meet yer,' the working man said.

Then he looked at his hand, palm up, checking the level of grease and dirt.

'Yer'll not have to mind the muck,' he said. 'Honest toil, after all.'

He smiled. Khrushchev smiled at the translation. For a moment they seemed to be on the same wavelength.

'I'm a Union man meself,' the working man went on. 'Man and boy. Joined when ah were sixteen.'

Khrushchev clearly found this less than fascinating, but continued to smile.

'Ah wanted to ask yer, like.'

His eyes strayed off to the accompanying faces, seeking authority. He looked at Troy, Troy pointed discreetly to the young chinless wonder from the Foreign Office who had trailed after them all day looking lost.

'I mean, it's OK ter ask 'im a question, in't it? 'E dun't mind answerin' questions.'

The FO wonder looked nonplussed. Khrushchev's interpreter whispered it rapidly in his ear. Khrushchev said, *'Da, da,'* syllables so simple as to be comprehensible across any barrier, and gestured with his hand. A flicking, upward motion that seemed to Troy indicative of his dwindling patience.

'When are you going to have free trade unions in the East?' the working man asked at last, without a trace of the hesitation that had dogged him up to now.

The FO man gasped audibly. He'd obviously been expecting something about the price of cabbage, or Khrushchev's recipe for a bloody Mary. The interpreter, a man who seemed to exercise no censorship on anything put to him, rendered it precisely for Khrushchev. It was, Troy thought, the first sensible question anyone had asked. Khrushchev didn't walk off in outrage. Nor did he attempt an answer. He behaved like a politician; did what any politician, in any country, would do. He ducked it.

'We'll get nowhere if we start criticising each other. Consider our point of view and we will consider yours.'

Which meant absolutely nothing.

'He's just another damn politician,' Troy told Charlie when Charlie phoned to ask 'how things were going'.

'What did you expect? The new Messiah?'

'No. I just . . . I just thought he'd be . . . well . . . different.'

'Oh, he's different all right,' said Charlie.

And Troy found himself wondering whether he could wait long enough to find out how different.

§ 10

By the Monday following, as they piled into black Daimlers once more for dinner with the Labour bigwigs at the Commons, he found an old Hollywood phrase lodged in his mind: 'Who do I have to fuck to get *off* this picture?'

But as they entered the Harcourt Room to be greeted by Hugh Gaitskell, suddenly Troy realised the turn the evening was about to take. The big picture was about to start. All they'd had till now was Pearl, Dean and Younger and a short from the Three Stooges. Tonight they were showing in Cinemascope.

Gaitskell held out his hand. The interpreter rattled off his few words of greeting. Then Gaitskell said, 'Allow me to introduce my Foreign Affairs spokesman, Rodyon Troy.' And before the interpreter could get his twopenn'orth in, Rod was shaking hands with Khrushchev and chatting to him in his flawless, old-fashioned, pre-revolutionary, upper-crust, Muscovite-accented Russian.

Khrushchev's eyes flickered between Rod and Troy. The subtle, perfect double-take of a comedian. Jack Benny eyeing Rochester could not have done it better. Rod was taller, stouter, older than Troy, but the family resemblance was inescapable: the thick mop of black hair, the ebony eyes, the full mouth.

Rod led Khrushchev off into the room. He shook hands with odds and sods from the Shadow Cabinet, scarcely seeming to listen to the routine Russian rattle of Rod's Who's Who in the Labour Party. As he gripped the hand of Shadow Chancellor Harold Wilson, Khrushchev's piggy eyes shot Troy a reproachful glance, and he knew that whatever happened, the return to Claridge's would not be pleasant. Perhaps there was a God after all? Perhaps his wish had been granted, his cover blown—and in the morning Cobb would kick him off the job?

A Commons waiter appeared suddenly at his side.

'Mr Troy, sir. We've put you at the top table. Next to Mr Brown. Your sergeants at opposite ends of the furthest table. Mr Cobb said you should be spread out across what he called the field of vision.'

God, Cobb was an idiot. Full of jargon and fury. Signifying bugger all.

'Good,' Troy said. 'When Manny Shinwell pulls out his sawn-off shotgun I want to be certain of catching him in a crossfire.'

The waiter didn't seem to get the joke.

'Mr Shinwell will not be attending, sir,' he said quite seriously.

Perhaps Troy was catching tastelessness from Khrushchev? He found a place with his name card on it. There was nothing else to do, so he sat down, feeling the nip as his Browning in its ludicrous holster jabbed him in the ribs. A few minutes later, the table began to fill. Next but one to him was Sergei, next to him one of the interpreters, next to him Wilson, next to him Rod, next to him another interpreter, next to him Bulganin, then the last interpreter, then Khrushchev and then Gaitskell. He looked at the place name of the vacant seat between himself and Sergei. It said 'Mr Brown'. But which Mr Brown?

Way over the other side, he could see Clem Attlee take his seat; down the room Clark and Beynon looked distinctly uncomfortable, disturbed by, rather than appreciative of, the democratic touch that had led them to be seated at the table and fed, rather than stuck along the walls and ignored for the duration of a five-course dinner. He didn't envy them—ordinary coppers having to make small talk with the people's representatives, whose grasp of the people they represented was based on researchers' briefings and what the newspapers told them to believe. He'd no idea what he'd say himself if any of these unworldly beings deigned to engage him in small talk. Down there with Clark and Beynon he caught a glimpse of Tom Driberg. A friend from the war years. Too far away for a chat. Then he heard the scrape of a chair being pulled back and turned to see a short, stout, owlish man sat next to him. Brown. Of course. George Brown. MP for Somewhere-up-North. Shadow Minister for Something-or-Other. He had met him once or twice. Neither a friend nor an enemy of Rod's. Somewhat to the right of the party, and known for his outspokenness.

Brown exchanged a few pleasantries with Troy. Nice enough bloke, thought Troy. The chap on his left was deep in conversation with his neighbour, and when Brown started an awkward, mediated chat with Sergei, Troy realised he had been let off very lightly, and was free to graze his way through the awful House of Commons food and . . . well . . . dammit . . . daydream. In the event of any of the old fogeys really having a shotgun, Beynon could be the one to plug him dead.

He dreamed his way through the delights of a weekend back in the country, something he looked forward to after a fortnight traipsing around London. Of spotted pigs and sprouting Aprilish vegetables. And when he had dreamed his rural idyll away he seemed to see in his mind's eye the score of a Thelonious Monk arrangement he had spent a small age trying to master. *April in Paris.* The score was an illusion. He had never seen it written down—nor, he felt, had Monk—it was a visible pattern of fingers moving across a keyboard. An audible antipattern of deliberative tangents, of musical geometry.

He had dreamed a dream too far. He could smell pipe tobacco, pulling him back to the solid world. The meal was over. They were into the speeches. He hadn't noticed the pudding even as he ate it. Khrushchev was on his feet, the translator racing to keep up with him. And the seat next to him was empty. At some point Brown had sloped off. Troy looked around. Brown had moved around to face Khrushchev across the table, the pipe smoke was his. Suddenly Driberg appeared in the vacant seat.

'Fancy seeing you here,' he said, and Troy knew he was up to something. Khrushchev was still droning on about the new era of peace. Driberg all but whispered in his ear. 'I don't suppose you could get me an interview with Khrushchev, could you?'

'You suppose right.'

Driberg leaned closer. Oblivious as ever. 'It could be very useful to me. I mean . . . none of the papers have got a look-in. No press conference, nothing. The *Reynolds News* or even the *Herald* couldn't possibly turn me down if I brought them an exclusive.'

'Tom, fuck off.'

'Oh, come on. You could do it.'

'With Bulganin and the embassy staff and the interpreters hanging about?'

'You could get him alone. You speak the lingo.'

Troy took his eyes off Khrushchev and looked at Driberg. 'Tom,' he said softly, 'has it ever occurred to you that Khrushchev doesn't know that, and might not be supposed to know that?'

'Bugger,' said Driberg and lapsed into a silence that Troy knew from experience could only be temporary.

In the gap he suddenly became aware that Khrushchev's tone had changed. He was on a different tack, there was a passion in his voice which no translator could hope to convey.

'Peace has been too long coming. We have extended the olive branch time after time only to see it snapped off in our hands. We were a young country in 1919, building ourselves anew in the wake of a war that had almost destroyed us, free for the first time in history from the yoke of tyranny. We asked for help. What did you send? Soldiers to Archangel and Murmansk. An attempt to force a restoration upon us. Then in the 1930s— we were fighting Hitler long before you in Britain knew who he was.'

A ripple of murmuring dissent went around the room. Brown grunted so audibly that Khrushchev looked straight at him, missed a single beat in the rising tempo of his improvisation on a theme, then took it up again. He was jazzing. It was what the man did best. In his mind's eye Troy saw Monk's fingers flash swiftly across the keys.

'Do I need to remind you that the primary purpose of Nazism was opposition to the inferior race, the Slav; opposition to the demonic ideology, the Bolshevik? We were ready for Hitler throughout your compromises, ready for Hitler when he invaded Czechoslovakia—'

'Then why did Joe Stalin sign a pact with Hitler?' said a voice from the back of the room. There was a brief pause in the heat as the interpreter spoke rapidly to Khrushchev *sotto voce,* his hands upturned, their heads bowed into a private huddle.

Khrushchev had not seen who had spoken. It didn't matter. It seemed to Troy that any one of them could and would have said it.

'Necessity,' Khrushchev began again. 'Something you in the West seem scarcely capable of understanding. We either fought Hitler standing alone or we found some other way. That is necessity! We had troops massed on the border ready to aid our brethren in Czechoslovakia. The Poles would not let us through, because they took the line laid down by the French, by the British, by Chamberlain!'

Again the rippling murmur of concern. But no voice of dissent. Troy doubted whether even the Tories would be able to raise a voice that would defend Chamberlain.

'We had troops at the ready. A pact guaranteeing our help. What did the British do? They sent us a mission, who could say nothing, who could hear nothing, who could only sit and drink tea! And all the time your Government was egging Hitler on, prodding him eastwards away from your shores. If you and the French had understood us more, had shown us as a new, struggling nation, more understanding, instead of perceiving us as simply godless regicides, if you had cooperated with us, talked to us, I tell you now that the last war could have been avoided.'

This stunned the Labour Party. It was almost the unthinkable. But Troy had long since, ever since Winston had got on his hind legs the best part of ten years ago in Missouri and dropped the Iron Curtain, felt this to be an age that specialised in thinking the unthinkable.

Out of the slightness of silence, the mereness of murmur, one voice spoke clearly. Brown.

'May God forgive you!'

The interpreter showed a shred of tact. Troy could hear him whisper and the very angle of his arms and shoulders spoke denial—he was trying to tell Khrushchev he had not heard what Brown said. Khrushchev asked Brown to repeat what he had said. A buzz went round the room, a sizzling concern. Brown should not say it again. Brown went through the motions of relighting his pipe.

Khrushchev said, 'What's the matter? Are you frightened to make yourself heard?'

The interpreter, his tact and defiance exhausted in a single burst, rendered it instantly into English.

Brown waved out his match, drew once on the pipe and took it from his lips.

'No,' he said clearly and calmly. 'I said, "May God forgive you."'

Khrushchev did not take his eyes off Brown. He drew a deep breath and exploded. Troy had the feeling that he was not the only person to notice that Khrushchev had not waited for the translation. The translator had not spoken.

'No, little man. Your God may forgive you! Do you really think anything has changed since Archangel? Do you really think that your creeping Socialism makes you superior to us? Why, you are more opposed to us than the Conservatives! And if I were British I would be a Conservative! Your support for us has been non-existent. All you do is harass us over Eastern Europe!'

This brought Nye Bevan to his feet, wagging his finger at Khrushchev, saying, 'Don't try and bully us!'

'And don't wag your damn finger at me,' said Khrushchev, and took off into a tirade that the interpreter could not keep up with. Among a dozen insults Troy caught 'Наглость'—'cheek!'

Rod got slowly to his feet. Waited for the steam to go out of the man. The very fact that he stood there and said nothing seemed to bring Khrushchev to a halt, like an old engine gliding slowly to the buffers.

Rod spoke in the quiet, demonstrative tones that chilled Troy to the bone with their reminder of his father's technique for public speaking. He seized an audience by timbre—Troy could think of no other word for it—rather than by volume or speed; let the tessitura of his voice hold his listeners. It shut Khrushchev up. It shut the Labour Party up—and they hadn't a clue what he was saying.

'It seems, Comrade Khrushchev'—no other that night had called him comrade—'that this is an apt moment at which to give you this. These are the names of political dissidents in Hungary, in Poland, in East Germany, in Czechoslovakia, who are missing. I would be most grateful to you if you could be of any assistance to me in tracing these people and in informing their families of their whereabouts.'

Rod said no more, simply held out a single sheet of paper folded over. Khrushchev would not take it. A stalemate that seemed to drag on for the best part of half a minute followed, until the interpreter risked life and job by plucking the list gently from Rod's hand. The spell broke. The mirror crack'd from side to side. Khrushchev headed for the door. All over the room, chairs were pushed back. Troy had to run to reach the door before Khrushchev got through it. They met almost shoulder to shoulder, almost collided. Troy could have sworn he heard Khrushchev say, 'Bugger the lot of them'—and then they were out.

§11

Out in the Commons yard, in the April drizzle, Khrushchev was raging.

'Они насрали на Россию! Они насрали на Россию! They shit on Russia! They shit on Russia!'

He bellowed at the embassy staff, bellowed at Bulganin, and when his translator moved to get into the Daimler, he snatched Rod's list from his hand and firmly pointed him to the escort car. Troy followed, assuming he meant to simmer alone, but Khrushchev stopped him with a hand on his sleeve.

'No,' he said, almost calm. 'Not you. You get in the back.'

The car moved off towards Victoria and Hyde Park Corner—Clark in the front with the driver, the dividing screen fully closed, and Troy in the back with quite possibly the most powerful man on earth, wondering what on earth was coming next. Khrushchev looked out of the window of the moving car, not speaking to Troy. As they passed Westminster Cathedral he turned his head and ducked to get a look at the looming red-brick tower, but still he said nothing. No tourist question. No tasteless black joke. At Hyde Park Corner he took Rod's list from his inside pocket and looked at it for a moment or two. As his hand slid the folded paper back into his pocket, his eyes still focused on the street outside, he asked, 'Who was he? The man with the names.'

'My brother,' Troy answered.

'And where did you boys learn your Russian?'

'At home. In the nursery. From our parents.'

'From your parents,' Khrushchev echoed flatly. It sounded to Troy more like realisation, a gentle mulling over, than a question.

'The family name is Troitsky.'

'Aha . . . Whites!'

Khrushchev at last looked at Troy. A glint of triumph in the nutty little eyes.

'No,' Troy replied. 'Nineteen-o-fivers.'

'Mensheviks?'

'More like Anarchists, I think. But that was a long time ago.'

'Indeed. And now?'

'My brother, as you will have gathered, has made his peace with history and joined the Labour Party. Whatever you might think, they are Social Democrats, no more, no less than that.'

'And you?'

'I'm a policeman. I have no politics.'

'If a Soviet policeman made such a statement to me I'd have him fired for thinking I was stupid. You don't think there's a sentient being on this planet who can honestly say he has no politics, do you?'

Of course Khrushchev was right. Troy knew that. Years ago, in Berlin, not long after the war, a Russian spy had told him that his father had been an agent of the Communist Party of the Soviet Union ever since leaving Russia in the chaos of 1905. Frequently Troy had thought about this. It was something he did not want to believe, and in the end was something he had chosen not to believe. It was certainly not a conversation he wished to have with the First Secretary of that party.

'Where are you from?' Khrushchev asked.

'Moscow mostly. Before that Yasnaya Polyana. It's near Tula.'

'I know where it is. I've been there several times. The place is virtually a Tolstoy museum now.'

'I envy you, Comrade Khrushchev. I've never seen it. I don't suppose I ever will.'

'Come to Russia.'

Troy looked at Khrushchev. He was smiling. Perhaps he even meant it.

'I don't think that's possible. My family history is a bit more complicated than I could tell you.'

'Come to Russia,' he said again. 'I'll show you a good time. Better than this dreary traipsing round the monuments of Britain.'

'You've met Eden. You've met the Queen and the Duke. It hasn't all been St Paul's and the Tower.'

'Eden's a monument. The Royals are monuments.'

Troy agreed wholeheartedly, but felt it was not for him to say so at this or any other juncture.

'Where are the people? Where are the workers?' The fat little hands, with their stubby little fingers spread outwards, emphatically open and empty. 'Where are the peasants?'

Khrushchev had a point. The crowds had been thin on the ground from the start. B & K had been somewhat less than mobbed. In anticipation Troy had assumed that the visit would be little different from visiting royalty or a personal appearance by Frank Sinatra or Johnnie Ray; in reality he had almost begun to wonder if the English had been told to stay home, or if, perhaps, *Gone With the Wind* was showing nightly on ITV.

'I doubt the English have any peasants. And you met a worker on Saturday. You just chose to shortchange him.'

'You mean at Harwell?' Khrushchev was almost shouting again. 'The man was an Eden apparatchik! A stooge!'

Quickly Troy weighed up the risk and concluded it was worth it. After all, his cover was blown, and with it probably the cover of the entire squad, and he would, no doubt, find himself resuming his holiday with a flea in his ear from the Branch, on the morrow.

'With all respect, Comrade Khrushchev, he wasn't. He was speaking his mind. Quite possibly the only person you've talked to this entire trip who has. And I do not mean by that that I question the integrity of George Brown or of my brother, but they, like you, are politicians.'

Troy paused. In for a penny, in for a thousand roubles, he thought. If Khrushchev was about to explode again, so be it. He would be the one to light the blue touch paper, and with any luck he would be the one to retire safely. It really was irresistible.

'If you were to ask me, I would tell you that the trip, for you and for the Marshal, has been a diplomatic contrivance on both sides. Your own side doesn't want you meeting the people. It's a waste of their time. They'd far rather you chewed the fat with a dimwit like Eden or exchanged brown bears and harmless pleasantries with Her Majesty. The British don't want you meeting the people. They'd far rather you were perceived as someone stripped of normal human feeling by the godlessness of Marxism. The last thing Eden wants is you pressing the flesh among the proles.'

Troy paused again. Cobb would surely fire him the minute he learnt that Khrushchev had seen through their pathetic charade. He had nothing to lose, not a damn thing.

'However if that's what you want, it's not yet nine-thirty and I'm sure something could be arranged.'

Khrushchev twinkled, mischief rippling out across those chubby cheeks, lighting up the impish eyes.

'An English pub?'

'If you like.'

'A pint of "wallop"?'

'That's what they're for.'

'The metro?'

'We call it the tube, but if that's what you want, I'd be happy to show it to you.'

Troy looked back at Khrushchev, resisting the grin that threatened to split at any second. The best, surely, was yet to come.

'Ditch the embassy people,' he said. 'And we'll go on somewhere.'

The phrase pleased Troy enormously. He was not at all sure he'd ever used it before, or that his Russian rendered it precisely. It was a man's phrase, Charlie's phrase, the turn of phrase men like Charlie used to pick up women or to armtwist old mates into drinking longer after tolerance of pub crawling had expired. Somehow it seemed wholly appropriate for the daring into which he now tempted Comrade Khrushchev.

§12

Back at Claridge's, Khrushchev stormed up to the mezzanine, trailing Special Branch and KGBniks from his apron strings. In the anteroom of his suite he announced his exhaustion and with it an early night. No one seemed surprised, but there was hesitation. Troy could not count, but putting the English and the Russians, the police and the spooks, the scientists, the dutiful son and the embassy officials together, there must have been fifteen or more people standing wondering what they were supposed to do next. Khrushchev left them in no doubt.

'Out!' he bawled.

In seconds, Troy found himself in a group of four. Himself, Clark, a tall, calm young KGB officer and Khrushchev.

Khrushchev led off into the sitting room. The KGB man followed. Clark's expression was crystal clear. 'What now?' said the look in his eyes, the slant of his mouth. Troy waved him into a chair, and followed Khrushchev.

The KGB man opened his case and set what appeared to be a large ornamental box—the sort of thing one brought back from a foreign holiday and kept stale fags in ever after—on the coffee table. He flipped open the lid. Troy had a fleeting glimpse of dials and lights, then the man nodded to Khrushchev and left. As the door closed Khrushchev flung himself down on the sofa.

'It's all right. You can speak now. No one will hear us.'

Really? Troy could hardly believe this.

'There are no hidden microphones. My men swept the entire suite before we arrived last Monday. They're not tapping the phone either, which confirmed our suspicions. Your people have found a way to use a telephone as a radio transmitter. And we in our turn have found a way to jam it. Be a good boy and pour us both a vodka.'

He reached for the telephone.

'I hope you don't smoke. There was no room for any fags in the box once we'd installed the jammer.'

Troy opened a fresh bottle of red pepper vodka and pinned back his ears. It was a simple conversation.

'Дейстбуй,' said Khrushchev. 'Do it.'

There was a pause.

'Дейстбуй,' he said again, and hung up.

If he was wrong, and MI5 were tapping the line, then they'd learn bugger all from that, thought Troy.

Khrushchev belted back the vodka. Troy sipped at his, thought it an acquired taste, and abandoned it. Khrushchev disappeared into the bathroom. Two minutes later he reappeared, scrubbed fresh like a schoolboy, and red of cheek. A minute more and they faced a disbelieving Clark in the anteroom.

It felt to Troy like an audience with the headmaster. He looked at them dressed in topcoats and ready for the street, put down his book and stood up, as though trying to make the most of investing his short stature with a little gravity. His expression both mournful and incredulous.

'Oh, bloody Nora. Oh, bloody Nora. Tell me I'm wrong. You're never taking him out?'

'Just check the corridor and the back stairs, Eddie.'

'Mr Cobb'll hang us out to dry if you're seen. You know that don't you, sir?'

'And when have any of us seen Cobb after nine o'clock at night? Go and look.'

Troy and Khrushchev waited in silence for Clark to return. Khrushchev hummed a little tune and jingled the coins in his pocket. Troy thought he recognised the tune as 'Love and Marriage'—a recent hit for Frank Sinatra—'they go together like a horse and carriage'. It seemed improbable, but who knew what acid drops of Western culture had seeped through the bullet-proof windows of the Daimler to settle corrosively in the man's unconscious?

'You're in luck,' Clark said when he came back. 'There's Beynon outside the Marshal's door, there's one of Mr Cobb's men sleeping upright on the mezzanine stairs, and there's another three in the linen room playing pontoon. The bloke on the garage has retreated into the glass booth the jobsworth has at the garage door. He's the only one likely to see anything.'

'Fine,' said Troy. 'Wish us luck and we'll be off.'

'Luck be damned. You'll get me shot.'

Troy opened the door, looked both ways and they dashed for the door to the service stairs, which led down to the underground car park. It was dark and low; the glass booth at the entrance shone like a beacon. Troy could see Cobb's constable, sitting with the Claridge's man, hat off, feet up, sipping tea and nattering. Such was the contrast in light, it would be nigh impossible for either of them to see out.

He opened the boot of the Bentley.

'I thought you promised me the metro,' Khrushchev said.

'We need a car to get out of here. And you can't ride the tube looking like Nikita Khrushchev. You can't go into an English pub looking like the Russian bear.'

Troy pulled out an old gabardine mackintosh and a cloth cap he used on odd occasions when he needed to follow people without looking like a copper and told Khrushchev to swap coats. The mac was tight on Khrushchev, and suitably tatty compared to his own, but the cap fitted, and beneath their shabbiness he looked surprisingly English. Troy took the scarf Khrushchev wore so elegantly beneath his jacket and threaded it like a muffler, with a huge knot under his chin. Giving him the once-over, the ensemble still lacked a certain *je ne sais quoi*.

'Put your glasses on,' said Troy.

Khrushchev fished out a pair of wire-rimmed spectacles, in which he usually, Troy had noticed, managed to avoid being photographed. He blinked at Troy through them. Troy weighed him up. Not only did he look English, he reminded Troy of those sturdy Londoners, packed with muscle after a lifetime in the docks, now running gently to seed on a diet of chips and beer. It solved a problem. Despite the promise, Troy had had no idea quite where to take him. The Salisbury carried the danger of running into Charlie, any pub in Soho, from the Salisbury all the way to the Fitzroy, via the Coach and Horses and the Colony Club, carried the risk of an encounter with Johnny Fermanagh. The man's face had been plastered all over the papers for the best part of a week. Only the marriage of Prince Rainier of Monaco to the unbelievably beautiful American film star Grace Kelly had eclipsed him—the best joke of the entire trip had been when a bunch of undergraduates greeted the Russian leaders with a poster reading 'Welcome Grace and Rainier', and it rammed home the point: Khrushchev was as famous as any film star. Where in London would Troy find a pub whose regulars paid more attention to Grace Kelly than they would to Nikita Khrushchev? Like it or lump it, Nikita Sergeyevich was about to make a trip into the heart of London's East End, where, if they'd read them at all, yesterday's papers would be wrapping tonight's chips. He liked the idea. He'd not been down the Brickie's Arms in a long time. There was a place where it was possible to earwig conversations in Yiddish or Polish; Russian would hardly seem remarkable or worth remarking. He'd seen too little lately of George Bonham, the gentle giant, retired station sergeant of his old nick in Stepney, and a Brickie regular. George's good nature would not lead him to question Troy if he passed Khrushchev off as a distant relative, and his grasp of current affairs was almost nil. Troy had spent much of the war explaining the war to him. After the war he had spent almost as much time explaining the new welfare state.

So far, so good, thought Troy, as they rode the escalator down to the Central line at Oxford Circus. He had told Khrushchev to lie low as they drove past the Special Branch flatfoot in the glass booth. He parked the car two streets away, and walked with him the last quarter mile across Mayfair. Khrushchev was gazing about him intently, his expression flickering between fascination and disgust at the plethora of advertising that lined the escalator shaft, learning the English obsession with health and quackery—of the reinvigorating powers of Horlicks and 'Yeast-Vite'; and their careless obliviousness to health and common sense—of the strength, mildness, coolness, flavour, *ad infinitum,* of Kensitas, Churchman's No.1 and a dozen other brands of fag. And the breasts, a diagonal gallery of breasts, a moving staircase of tit and titillation, advertising every conceivable form of 'foundation', that is ways to wrap and pack women into their own clothes. It was little short of a national obsession; the day was approaching when tits could be used to sell anything. Divide and conquer. Up, out and cleave.

At platform level Khrushchev took in everything, poring over the multicoloured map of the tube lines, even begging a sixpence off Troy to try the chocolate machine.

They boarded an eastbound destined for Hainault. It was well past rush hour, and the train was sparsely populated with mid-evening travellers, not one of whom paid the slightest bit of notice to Khrushchev. Khrushchev stared openly. Troy tried seeing the English through his eyes. It must, he thought, strike him as very familiar, if all the clichés of the popular press's version of the USSR were to be believed. The English were a drab bunch. A uniform bunch. Grey men in grey clothes. Bad haircuts, bitten fingernails, nicotined fingers, clacking false teeth, leaking shoes, stained trousers that hardly saw a dry cleaner's from one year to the next and, on a night like this, a rippling sea of wet gabardine—a sensory assault of damp and dirt. Miserable, downtrodden men in a miserable downtrodden nation. A nation, he hardly dared think, in need of some sort of revolution. Not marching in the streets, not the storming of the Winter Palace—that after all was Sandringham, too far away, and so unpalace-like—but a cultural revolution, something to shake the cobwebs off the country. Had Troy felt any close identification with his nation, he too, like Her Majesty's Government, would have thought twice about showing it off to any foreigner.

At each station Khrushchev got out, stood among the jostle of passengers elbowing their way home, and looked around him rather like a jaded train-spotter, the amateur expert—seen it, done it—to whom no sight can ever be fresh. Troy passed on Holborn, stayed put in the car. Holborn had cost him too much already. By the time they reached Bank, Khrushchev was ready to deliver his appraisal.

'It lacks grandeur,' he said simply.

Troy thought about it. Grandeur was not part of it. The London Underground was a piecemeal creation of lines dug separately, by different, private and public enterprises over a period of almost a hundred years. They each had their own idea of how to dress up a hole in the ground, but Troy doubted if grandeur had ever been part of anyone's scheme.

'My metro, in Moscow. My metro can hold its own with the finest palaces on earth. It is a cathedral under the ground.'

There were many who thought St Pancras railway station as fine as any cathedral. Troy thought of going out of their way to show it him—a quick change to the Northern line now would have them there in ten minutes—but decided instead to tell him the old chestnut about the American tourist mistaking it for St Pancras' church and respectfully removing his hat as he entered. Khrushchev shrugged. Knowing nothing of the sheer beauty of Sir George Gilbert Scott's unearthly masterpiece of turrets and gables and countless tiny, dormer windows, he probably took it as merely indicative of American naiveté. The anecdote neither amused nor interested him. He was thoroughly preoccupied with the recorded announcements urging him in the strangled tones of pre-war received pronunciation to 'Mind the gap!' One day, Troy thought, when presumptive classlessness had rendered all England gorblimey, RP would survive in dark corners of the London Passenger Transport Board, still warning people to 'stand clear of the doors' and 'mind the gap' in the superfluous diphthongs of a lost age.

A far better place to change, Troy concluded, was Liverpool Street, London's terminus for the old Great Eastern Railway, where a Piranesi-like nightmare of catwalks in the sky, usually shrouded in a miasma of soot and steam, was mirrored by an equally labyrinthine network of gloomy tunnels underground. Besides, it was the only place on the entire Underground system where you could prop up a bar, pint in hand, without even leaving the platform.

Troy bought halves. He didn't want to be here all night.

Khrushchev sipped at his beer and pronounced it good. It wasn't, but Troy had instigated an expedition in search of the common man—it was not for him to reject the common man's taste. Tom Driberg had often urged him to drink beer as the first and simplest way to break the ice with the lower classes, but Troy hated the stuff and did not, in any case, share Driberg's sexual fascination with the working man. Khrushchev stood on the down Metropolitan platform, elbow on the bar, shoulder to shoulder with a working man, who was nose-deep in the late final *Evening Standard* and oblivious to his presence.

The platforms were deserted, devoid of Londoners but strewn with their litter, a windswept mess of toffee papers—the British had binged on confectionery ever since it came off ration—cigarette ends and old newspapers. Troy watched Khrushchev watching an old *Standard* with Grace Kelly's face on the front being wafted across the platform and onto the track. It flipped over completely as it left the edge and Princess Grace's face gave way to Khrushchev's own. Troy wondered, as the picture disappeared under the wheels of an oncoming train, whether Khrushchev had just felt someone walk over his grave. Instead he took his glass in hand, walked out to the middle of the platform and looked up the line, the knowing train-spotter once more. Past the end of the platforms, the blackened walls of buildings rose like a canyon before the tunnel to Moorgate swallowed the tracks. Beer and bar apart, it was a depressing pit. It required an odd mentality to like it, a twist in the mind that could enjoy this cold, subterranean world, neither indoors nor out. Sometimes Troy had it, sometimes he hadn't. Sometimes he could spend whole evenings down here. Sometimes he loathed the place. A couple of years after the war, Johnny Fermanagh had taken him on a classic pub crawl around the bars of the Circle line. Starting out from Sloane Square's southside bar with a horde of Johnny's drinking cronies, pockets stuffed with miniatures, they had boozed and schmoozed their way to the Hole-in-the-Wall at King's Cross, to Liverpool Street, to come full circle at Sloane Square, shedding cronies all the way, until just he and Johnny remained to attempt the round one more time, only to fall short and end up at Liverpool Street again, pissed and penniless in this pit of soot and iron. Years, decades after the ending of steam-hauled trains, the underground still smelt of soot. Aldgate, one station down the line towards Victoria, was quite literally a pit, dating from the plague of 1666. The engineers of the Circle line had dug the station out through archaeological strata of human remains. Liverpool Street, he recalled, was the site of Bedlam, home to generations of lunatics.

Khrushchev sniffed the air.

Soot or madness or death? Troy wondered. Railways always put Troy in mind of Anna Karenina's death under the wheels of a train. Grace Kelly had never, as far as he knew, played Anna—the version he knew was Garbo's. That mournful, miserable beauty. The moist smell of the underground, that ancient mixture of soot and humanity, was as strong as the reek of cordite to him, inseparable from the thought of death, the thought of the woman in black laying her head upon the tracks.

Khrushchev's gaze swept around from the low, dark, dirty roof, across the clutter of signs and posters to the lantern glow of the bar once more. He walked back towards Troy, his short legs shooting out stiffly like a tin soldier's, and placed his empty glass on the bar.

'It lacks unity,' he said.

Unity was an impossibility. Only in the 1930s had it even approached unity and that was in terms of aspects of style. Troy would put it no more strongly than that—Beck's map, the Nuremberg lighting at Arnos Grove, the modernist lines of the newer stations out along the far reaches of the Piccadilly line. By now, in the mid-fifties, that short burst of style had been absorbed and the true nature of the system reasserted itself. There was only one word for it.

'It's ramshackle,' he told Khrushchev. 'But it works.'

'It works, but can you be proud of it?'

'I don't think Londoners think of it with pride. I doubt whether they think of it at all.'

'Why not?' he said. 'A little awe for the works of men would not be out of place. You have cathedrals and palaces galore. Where is the palace of the people? *What* is the palace of the people if not a railway station?'

Troy had no answer as yet, and fielded Khrushchev's question with one of his own that had been nagging at him for quarter of an hour.

'What is it you can smell? You've done that at every place we stopped.'

Khrushchev breathed in deeply.

'Soot,' he said. 'Soot and . . . and . . . despair.'

Troy looked out towards the tunnel, to the drizzling misery of a black night in London. For so long now it had struck him as some makeshift shanty, shabbytown, shorn of all pride, laid bare, without dignity. But despair? How had Khrushchev noticed that? Where had he seen it—where, since it seemed his operational mode, had he smelt it? Was this what the national odour of wet gabardine spelt out to the perceptive nose?

'Soot,' Khrushchev said again. 'And despair . . . and someone frying bacon.'

He wanted Khrushchev to see Stepney Green. After his outburst to the Labour Party on the matter of who had done what in the war, it was fitting that he should see some of what London had been through. They left the underground at Whitechapel. By the Blind Beggar, a pub gaining a reputation for trouble, and deemed by Troy to be highly unsuitable for the experiment they were essaying, they crossed over the Mile End Road. At the junction of Hannibal Road and Stepney Green they turned right, down the side of the Green, past the London Jewish Hospital and rows of abandoned houses—windowless, some floorless, with the zigzag shadows of collapsed staircases scorched onto the walls and blackened hearths stranded halfway up without rooms to wrap them—and out into the blitzed remains of Cardigan Street.

It had not occurred to Troy before that every other street in this neck of the woods was named after one aspect or another of the last war Britain had actually fought with Russia—unless you counted Murmansk, which Troy did not and Khrushchev surely would. The importance of Stepney Green to Troy was that it was as flat today as the day Hitler had levelled it in 1940. Hundreds of homes blown to dust. Thousands of lives lost, many, many more disrupted and displaced. This corner of the East End had never recovered from the Blitz, had never retrieved its people from the dispersal of the war, nor reclaimed its identity in the peace. It was grassed over now, but to Troy the lines of rubble were still visible beneath the wilderness of green. As Troy told him this Khrushchev nodded, said nothing. Just looked and sighed. At last he said, 'I saw Stalingrad. I saw Moscow. I was there when we took back Lvov.'

It was not a had-it-worse-than-thou comparison. The sadness in his tone told Troy it was identification. He'd known the solid world to dissolve about him, the permanence of life to crumble in the dust of war.

'You should rebuild,' he said. 'I noticed from the train last week. And around St Paul's. So much of London is like this. I find it hard to see why. The Germans level our cities; we rebuild them. We house our people.'

Troy felt almost in need of Brother Rod, who could give Khrushchev chapter and verse ad tedium on Britain's failure to rebuild and rehouse in the aftermath of war. They walked along Balaclava Street towards the end of Jamaica Street. A huge chimney stack lay on its side like a slaughtered Titan. It had fallen almost intact, back broken like a ship run aground, but not shattered. Troy had no idea when. It had been standing the last time he looked, but that had been years ago. He usually avoided this route, almost unconsciously. It must have been five or six years since he had walked this way. Twenty years ago, as a beat bobby, he walked it every day. He found it hard to admit, but the place held too many memories.

'Do the English keep their bombsites as monuments?' Khrushchev asked. Troy had never looked at it this way before, but silently agreed that that was exactly what they did. Their finest hour laid out in blasted brick and broken glass. And when they were fed up with them as monuments, they turned them into car parks.

It had turned chilly. The warmth as Troy pushed open the door into the Bricklayer's Arms was welcoming. The people's palace sounded to Troy like a good name for a defunct music hall. He thought the notion that it could be reapplied to a railway station, any railway station, an absurd piece of Soviet pseudo-realism. If anything the people's palaces were public houses. In their relentless, unvarying shades, dirty red, dirty brown, they were, he thought, some sort of refuge from the cloying English privacy, the world behind the rustling lace curtains, and an escape from the new invader, the one-eyed god of the living room. The public bar was half full at best. Monday was hardly the best night of the week for an evening in a pub, nor was Tuesday, most people being flat broke from the weekend, lacking the courage to run up a slate until pay day—Friday—was visible in the near future—but it would have to do.

'Before we go in,' Troy said to his companion, 'I should warn you. It's Monday. Don't expect cheerful cockneys doing the Lambeth Walk and the Hokey-Cokey.'

'Hokey-Cokey,' said Khrushchev. 'What is Hokey-Cokey?'

'Forget it,' Troy said. 'It's too difficult to explain.'

And so saying concealed the truth, that he'd no real idea what it was himself.

The pub had hardly changed since the end of the war, it was if anything simply ten years shabbier, ten years deeper into its nicotine hue. Most noticeably, the spot behind the bar where Churchill's photograph had hung for so long was now occupied by one of the footballer Tom Finney, star of Preston North End, a suitably neutral team on turf naturally split between Millwall and West Ham and, as it happened, the hometown of Eric the landlord, a man who had been known to crack heads over the matter of local loyalties.

Troy found Bonham at a corner table playing cribbage with two other men. He introduced Khrushchev as Uncle Nikki. Bonham looked down at Khrushchev from his six foot six plus and scrutinised him.

'No he's not,' he said. 'I know your Uncle Nikki. He's a little fat bloke with a beard.'

'Well, this is a little fat bloke without a beard,' Troy said. 'This is my Uncle Nikki on my mother's side. And he doesn't speak English.'

'Good Eefenning,' said Khrushchev. 'Good Eefenning to you oll.'

'Well, that's his limit,' Troy said.

'A pleasure to meet you,' Khrushchev went on.

'Mutual,' Bonham replied and moved up the bench to make room for him. He looked at Troy.

'Are you quite sure?' he said.

Troy sat down opposite Khrushchev. 'It's just phrases, that's all. He picks up the odd thing.'

'Mind the gap!' said Khrushchev, smiling at his own parrotry.

Bonham looked quizzically at Troy. 'Are you two having me on?'

'Honestly,' Troy protested. 'It's just phrases.'

'Sounds pretty damn kosher to me,' said Bonham. 'I think you'd better get them in, Freddie.'

Over a pint of best—Troy had no idea where Khrushchev had learnt 'wallop'—they taught him the rudiments of cribbage. Khrushchev paid enough attention to pass muster but was clearly far more interested in the players than the play. Next to Troy sat Alf and Stanley, a docker and a jobbing carpenter respectively. From Alf Khrushchev learnt of the power of the trades union and the way they had wrestled a decent standard of living from their employers before the war under the leadership of Ernest Bevin. Khrushchev's eyebrows rose a fraction at the mention of the name. From Stanley he learnt of the uncertainties of casual labour on the building sites east of the Lea Valley, of tax-cheating cash in hand, no insurance and no questions asked, and of the long lay-offs when no houses were built and no carpenters required. The reassuring proof, the quick quick slow of capitalism's inherent cycle of boom and slump.

The kitten's boundless curiosity humanised Khrushchev. The nutty brown eyes sparkled; the fat, fleshy lips parted in a revealing gap-tooth smile that needed only to chomp on a cigarette holder to look just like Roosevelt's famous letterbox grin. Khrushchev delved into everything, asked about their families, their wives, the education of their children, and of course, he asked them how they voted and what they thought of their leaders. They were both solidly Labour, but Gaitskell was a mystery to them, too, too new a leader to have made any definite impression. Eden, Stanley told him, was a joke, a living anachronism. Why not, Alf retorted, the whole country was one 'bleedin' great anachronism'—were they living in 1926 or 1956? Bonham said he felt quite certain that life was better. There had been, he declared, progress. Lots of it.

'What do you mean?' Alf asked. 'Washing machines? Fridges?' And spitting contempt, 'The telly?'

'National Health Service?' said Stanley. 'Ain't that progress? Heard the one about the National Health Service?'

Alf groaned. Who had not heard the National Health joke? Only Troy's newfound Uncle Nikki. Troy dutifully translated it for Khrushchev, rendering Stanley's poor version of Max Miller as precisely as he could.

'This bloke on the building site. Comes in every morning, picks up a full sack of cement, grunting fit to burst, then throws it down. Next day, does the same thing, and the next day and the day after that. Eventually one of his mates comes over and says, "Bert, why do you fling a full sack of cement around first thing each morning?" "Well," says Bert, "I pays me stamp to the Government every week, and I've had me free pair o' specs and I've had me free set of false teeth—I'll be buggered if I won't get me free truss as well."

Khrushchev laughed. It might well have been the funniest joke the man had ever heard. He threw back his head and roared, slapped the table with the flat of his hand and hooted with laughter.

It was almost ten-thirty. Troy felt exhausted. He dearly wished they could call it a night. He had never guessed that being an interpreter for the nosiest man alive would prove so taxing. Nor would he have anticipated that the dialogue Khrushchev had sought so keenly would have touched himself so little. He added next to nothing of his own to the litany of complaint—the great British whine—that Alf, dejected middle age and Stan, frustrated youth, poured out for Khrushchev's benefit. It was left to Bonham to offer the inadequacies of moderation, the unconvincing reassurance that we had emerged from the world war with 'fings better than wot they was' and that 'never again' would we suffer the tribulations of the thirties. Troy had no heart for such argument, and when Stan aired his view that he'd be 'better off in America', that it was 'years ahead of us, years', and that he'd 'be off like a shot' if he'd the price of the passage, he rendered it precisely and neutrally and watched the glint in Khrushchev's eyes.

'Is this your Britain?' he asked of Troy. 'The Forty-ninth state, a nation of second-rate, would-be Americans? Do you all want to be Americans?'

The Bricklayer's Arms, like many local pubs, closed when the last policeman in the bar chose to go home. On the dot of ten-thirty, far from calling last orders, Eric the landlord came round to collect empties and fresh orders.

'Where's the little feller tonight?' Eric asked.

'What little feller?' said Troy.

'That little feller,' Bonham said, pointing off over Troy's shoulder. Troy squirmed round in his seat. At the bar was a short, ugly man in a heavy black overcoat, glistening with raindrops, Homburg pushed back on his head, *News Chronicle* sticking out of his pocket. If there was one man in London Troy could have done without tonight, it was Ladislaw

Konradovitch Kolankiewicz. Polish exile, Senior Pathologist for the Home Office, one of the finest minds at the Yard's disposal, and the most foul-mouthed, bloody-minded, cantankerous creature ever to walk the earth.

'Oh God,' Troy said to Bonham. 'What's he doing here?'

'Mondays and Thursdays. Our regular crib nights. He's been coming for about five years now.'

'Why didn't you warn me!'

Too late. Kolankiewicz had picked up his pint and was walking towards them, quizzically scrutinising Khrushchev. He sat down next to Troy.

'Inch up, smartyarse.'

Then he paused to suck the foam off his pint, all the time staring at Khrushchev across the rim of the glass. He set it down.

'Who's the new boy?' he asked.

'It's Fred's Uncle Nikki,' Bonham volunteered.

'I know your Uncle Nikki, he's a little fat bloke with a beard.'

'A different Uncle Nikki. On my mother's side,' Troy said, and dropping his voice to a whisper he leaned in close to Kolankiewicz.

'Listen, you Polish pig. If you fuck this up, I don't care how many years you've got left till retirement, but I'll see to it you never get another good body from the Yard as long as you live. I'll have you scraping the mud off the soles of suspicious boots for the rest of your days. The nearest you'll ever get to a corpse is your own funeral. Do I make myself clear?'

Kolankiewicz hadn't even looked at Troy. He took another inch off his pint and spoke directly to Khrushchev in flawless Russian.

'Nice to meet you, Uncle Nikki. It's not often I get the chance of a chat with a relative of Troy's.'

On the final phrase he turned to Troy and grinned the grin of the Cheshire cat.

Bonham scraped in the cards and dished out dominoes. The rules were simple enough. Only the principle of knocking required anything by way of explanation from Troy. Bonham took the first game; Khrushchev the second. He smiled gently, but he had stopped asking questions in the presence of Kolankiewicz. One round into the third Kolankiewicz raised his fist as though about to knock on to Khrushchev, then he unfolded it and one by one set his remaining dominoes on end.

'East Germany,' he said, reverting to Russian, as he set up the first. 'Czechoslovakia.' Up went the second. 'Hungary, Poland, Lithuania.'

He ran out of dominoes, looked across at Khrushchev for the first time since the play had passed to him, clenched his fist again, and tapping it lightly with the forefinger of his left hand said in a hoarse whisper, 'Soviet Union!' The fist crashed down to the table, and the dominoes toppled down one by one. Lithuania took out Poland, Poland took out Hungary, Hungary took out Czechoslovakia and Czechoslovakia walloped East Germany. He looked into Khrushchev's eyes and said softly and, it seemed to Troy, almost sweetly, 'One man's buffer zone is another man's home.'

In his heart Troy had always known he was not the stuff that heroes are made of. Pleasing, flattering to his vanity though the idea was, it was always going to be someone else who lit Khrushchev's fuse. That the someone should be Kolankiewicz, the Polish beast, the most rough-hewn of heroes, was wholly appropriate. He should have known that no threat, however uttered, would deter him. He waited for the explosion, for Khrushchev to erupt in a furious spurt of Russian cursing. Bonham and his mates looked baffled, having no idea what Kolankiewicz had said by way of preface to the gesture.

Khrushchev smiled back at Kolankiewicz, laid a six and three against Troy's six and one and passed to Bonham. Bonham studied his hand for what seemed an age, and finally knocked gently. The game went full circle, punctuated only by the banal chatter of play. Troy won, and as Bonham scooped up the dominoes in his colossal paws, found Khrushchev looking straight at him.

'Tell me,' he said. 'Do you suppose they serve vodka in this place?'

'Almost certainly,' Troy answered. 'It's immigrant territory. I should think they have Genever and Schnapps too if they're to your taste.'

'Vodka will do. Poland and I clearly have things to discuss that can only be thrashed out over vodka. Perhaps you would have two glasses—large ones—sent over.'

With that he beckoned to Kolankiewicz and moved to an empty table by the Jug and Bottle. Kolankiewicz looked at Troy. Sheepishly, Troy thought. Troy had never known Kolankiewicz hesitant in his life—sheepish he was not—where angels feared to tread he was usually to be found in residence, having rushed in hours before with a camp bed, a shooting stick and a full thermos.

'Go on,' Troy said. 'It's what you wanted. It's certainly what you asked for.'

An hour or so later, heading back to the West End in a taxi, Troy said, 'What did you and Kolankiewicz talk about?'

Khrushchev was staring out of the window again into the night and drizzle. He did not turn around.

'Oh, this and that,' he said with the stifling of a yawn in his voice. 'We redrew the map of Europe. What else should happen when a Russian and a Pole get together?'

'I thought that line went "a Russian and a German"?'

'Germans,' Khrushchev replied, 'are like policemen. Never one around when you want one.'

§13

It was one in the morning before Troy turned in at Goodwin's Court. He hung up the leather holster and the Browning on the bedstead and threw his shirt into the laundry basket. The gun had left an oily stain on the shirt, the shape of a tiny heart, right over his heart. He declined to see a symbol in it and fell into bed. Before he could even switch off the lamp the phone was ringing. It had to be Cobb.

'You didn't report in, Mr Troy,' he said. 'Where've you been?'

'Pubs,' said Troy simply and honestly.

'The procedure, I should not have to remind you, is that everyone logs off with me. Not four hours later, but when they hand over Red Pig.'

Troy hated this addiction the man had for code-words. Why couldn't he say 'Khrushchev'? The pretence of secrecy was absurd.

'Sorry,' he said lamely. 'Forgot.'

'Well . . .' Cobb paused. 'Anything to report?'

Troy remembered Khrushchev's 'Do it'. It puzzled him greatly and was undoubtedly the kind of thing he'd been placed to overhear. But, and there were two buts, Khrushchev had uttered the cryptic two syllables in full knowledge of Troy's command of the language, and, but the second, to tell Cobb anything now would be to invite his curiosity about the entire evening, when it was best that he asked no more and learnt no more. Troy was confident that their jaunt had—Kolankiewicz apart—gone undetected. He'd been, as Clark had pointed out, very lucky. The last thing he wanted was Cobb nosing around.

'No,' he lied. 'Not a damn thing.'

'Really? I heard there was quite a to-do at the Commons.'

'There was, but as it all took place in public, indeed in the presence of a sizeable gathering of our lords and masters, I hardly saw it as a matter of any secrecy or importance. Or am I now spying on George Brown and Nye Bevan as well Khrushchev and Bulganin?'

The irritation in Troy's voice produced the desired effect.

'Play it by the book will you, Mr Troy!' Cobb snapped, and then he hung up.

Troy put out the light, still wondering what Khrushchev and Kolankiewicz had said to each other.

§14

The following day he accompanied Khrushchev to the Strangers' Gallery at the House of Commons. A Tory MP, a man whose hobby seemed to be the Russian language, sat in as interpreter, and for once Khrushchev seemed genuinely interested by the farce that was democracy. At the best of times Prime Minister's Question Time could be like a bear pit, the semblance of English manners tossed to the wind—surely something any Russian could identify with? Khrushchev warmed to the occasion, upstaged the clowns in the pit by taking a bow every time someone looked up and recognised him, as though the cry of 'author author!' had gone up from the stalls. It was an anodyne session until Troy saw Rod get to his feet from the Labour front bench.

'Will the Prime Minister inform the House of what arms Her Majesty's Government have supplied to Egypt and Israel?'

Eden rose to answer him. Khrushchev looked sideways at Troy, seated on the far side of Bulganin.

Eden invoked security and declared that he could not answer the question. Rod rose with his supplementaries.

Khrushchev stopped playing the showman, became attentive to the line of questioning—as well he might. It was a drama in which he made many of the noises off. Colonel Nasser was rapidly assuming the proportions of a cult figure among the Arabs. He had asserted the simple truth that the old imperial powers had no business in Egypt or any part of the Arab world, and offered his vision of a Pan-Arabia stretching from the Atlantic to the Indian Ocean, from Morocco to Aden. He was held to be hostile in the extreme towards Britain, a nation which fondly flattered itself that it had done rather a lot for 'Johnny Arab'—indeed there were those who thought we had done rather too much in giving him the financial aid he'd requested for his hydroelectric dam across the Nile. Troy knew—Rod left no stone unturned when he wanted you to know—that this was a cynical ploy to keep Nasser out of the Soviet camp, and were it not for the prospect of a fat Russian bankroll, the moths would have stayed zipped up in the British purse. But that was part of the national failing—the white man's failing.

The British could not accept that they had no role in Egypt, as though to give away the Raj were quite enough for one day, or in Cyprus, whose Greek population were fighting the British in the streets for union with Greece—hardly a day went by without news of some British tommy being bumped off in Nicosia or Larnaca—or in Africa, where British Imperial jails were stuffed to the gills with men who one day would surely lead their countries, and more likely than not face their former captors across the table with more than a hint of resentment. For their part, the French had withdrawn ignominiously from Viet Nam and were looking to restore national prestige by taking it out on the Algerians. Sore winners the French. Along the borders of Israel—a country less than ten years old—and almost every other Arab state, were frequent skirmishes, spelling out, to those who watched, the possibility of imminent war. Only last month young Hussein, the Sandhurst- and Harrow-educated King of Jordan, had sacked Glubb Pasha, the British General of the Arab Legion, saying that his values, like his policies, were Victorian. Nasser had a point. Rod, Troy knew, rather admired the man. But the life he led demanded, if not outright duplicity, then from time to time devil's advocacy. Troy looked at Khrushchev to see if he steamed, as Rod, smiling wickedly, asked Eden if he would restore the balance of power by giving Israel as much in the way of weaponry as the Soviet Union had given Egypt.

Again Eden would not be drawn. Troy wondered how little the man had got away with telling the Russians.

In the evening the Russian Embassy returned the astringent British hospitality with a formal reception. Troy knew what this meant. The embassy would never admit armed coppers, any more than MI5 would let armed KGB agents escort B & K, as the papers had dubbed them, around London. They'd spend a boring evening cooling their heels in an anteroom with a silent KGB guard for company. The bulge in Clark's pocket was undoubtedly a book with which to while away the time. Troy had finished *The Secret Agent,* and forgotten to pick up a newspaper. Clark was never caught out by boredom.

They handed B & K over to the embassy staff and waited for instructions. Troy watched his charges vanish into the throng of Russians awaiting their first guests, and saw a tall, thin young man heading towards him.

'Gentleman,' he began. 'Tereshkov. Anton Tereshkov. Comrade Khrushchev has informed me that you are all to be our guests. If you would be so kind as to surrender your weapons to me, you may join the reception.'

Clark and Milligan looked at Troy, waiting for their cue.

'Go ahead,' he said. 'I doubt there's anything about a service issue Browning they haven't known for years.'

They handed over their weapons like schoolboys parting with illicit catapults. Troy fished his own gun out of the absurd contraption that stuck it sharply up his armpit and gave it to Tereshkov.

'A word, if I may, Chief Inspector.'

Troy gestured Clark and Milligan away, and they moved slowly and suspiciously into the crowd, glancing back at Troy and looking like two coppers reluctantly pursuing a suspect into a ladies' lavatory.

Tereshkov took Troy by the arm, gently swung him around into the kind of huddle presumed to exclude other ears.

'Chief Inspector. Comrade Khrushchev has invited you to visit the Soviet Union.'

Good grief, thought Troy, the old fool had actually meant it.

'There are complications,' Troy said, trying for tact. 'I'm grateful, but I really think it won't be possible.'

'The British would object? It would destroy the career of a Special Branch officer?'

'No, the British would not object. And I'm not in the Branch, I. run the Murder Squad at Scotland Yard. It's more personal. Do you see?'

'I see, Chief Inspector Troy, only as much as you wish me to see. However, the invitation stands. Comrade Khrushchev seems alarmed at the idea that you have never seen your homeland and extends his personal, his *personal* invitation to you. All you have to do is let him know through the embassy that you wish to come, and the necessary papers will be arranged by the office of the First Secretary in Moscow.'

'Do you really think the KGB will forward a letter from an English copper to the ruler of the Soviet Union?' Troy asked, more than a little incredulous.

Tereshkov took a notebook from his pocket and jotted down a word in Russian—Пирожки. Pirozhki. Literally, it meant fried dumplings. He tore off the page and gave it to Troy. Troy could not help feeling that the man whose job it was to think these things up was secretly taking the mickey.

'I am Comrade Khrushchev's man here. Any letter dropped into the embassy letterbox bearing this code will be sent straight to me, and by me straight to the First Secretary. No one else will know its content. Whatever dark secret you and your people are hiding—from us or the British—will be quite safe.'

But, of course, Troy had no idea what he was hiding. Whatever it was it had been hidden by his father long ago. To entertain Khrushchev's invitation as anything more than whimsy on the part of a mercurial old man was to risk ripping the lid off a can of worms. Since his father's death in 1943 not a week had passed when Troy had not wished him alive for five minutes to answer one question or another, and with every year that passed the list grew longer.

Far from being blown by the night at the Commons, Troy's cover, and hence the cover of the team as a whole, seemed intact. Khrushchev made no further use of his knowledge that they were all spies. This confirmed Troy's belief that the mission was hopeless from the start. He had thought all along that Khrushchev would never be indiscreet in the presence of the English. He now blustered and joked and raged in Russian, well aware that they all understood him, and dutifully paused for his interpreter as though the charade were real. The tasteless jokes resumed, the boundless curiosity pretended it was sated by more meetings with living monuments, more official statements, more damned statistics.

He did not speak directly to Troy again. They lurched through a manic schedule that seemed designed to put Khrushchev in an early grave. He was, Troy thought, becoming tired, bored and irritated. This resulted in petulance, boyish behaviour teetering on the brink of a boyish tantrum. An evening of Margot Fonteyn at Covent Garden did nothing to lift his spirits, and the next day that which Troy had expected for some time happened. Khrushchev stamped his foot and told the Foreign Office to 'Stuff your trip to Calder Hall up your collective arse!' The interpreter, for once, showed tact and told the chinless wonder from the FO that perhaps a visit to the Atomic Research Establishment was not possible after all. The FO expressed their regrets and took it on the chin. Anyone, thought Troy, among those awful types at the FO and MI5 who might have suffered from the paranoid delusion that Khrushchev might be anxious to glean every last secret about Britain's much-vaunted nuclear programme and would have to be watched every second of his trip, might just be dragged back to the reality: the man was bored by Britain and the British. Perhaps the obvious was surfacing? We had no secrets the Russians did not know about. Or were the spooks–and–powers–that–be incapable of reading the contempt that ran through Khrushchev's refusal?

§15

On the dockside Troy waited with an assembly of nobs in the chill wind of April. The sky was ominously grey, just like the ship, and the papers were still moaning about a drought this summer. The *Ordzhonikidze* moved off at a snail's pace, towering above them like a block of flats on castors, the Russian band on the deck blew its tuneless military pomp and the wind sucked the notes out of the air. Bulganin and Khrushchev stood and waved like the Soviet version of *The Last of England*. Cheerless and frumpish as May Day on Lenin's tomb. Today was the day of the fawn mackintosh, the dark trilby, and contempt for matching accessories. Troy could not but believe that they were glad to be off these islands.

Suddenly Khrushchev approached the rail, whipped off his hat, leaned out, looked straight at Troy and yelled with all his might. 'Bugger England!' he cried. 'Come to Russia. Distance doesn't matter. Come where we still have some spirit!' Then he threw in an idiomatic, 'Держи хвост пистолетом!'—the sort of thing one said to cheer up a miserable child, slouching home after a pasting from the school bully—'Hold your tail like a pistol'—which had an approximate English equivalent in 'Keep your pecker up.'

Troy glanced around. In the long minutes of waiting for the ship to cast off, the nobs had chatted and drifted. He was, he realised, closer to the *Ordzhonikidze* than anyone but the Foreign Secretary, Selwyn Lloyd, who was standing right next to him. The Russian ambassador, in protocol Lloyd's escort and vice versa, somehow had ended up about twenty feet behind them.

'Что, Что?' Troy heard him say. 'I couldn't understand a word of that.' Lloyd was looking baffled.

'It's for you, Foreign Secretary,' he lied. 'Comrade Khrushchev is telling you to come and see him in Russia.' He thought on his toes, cutting and pasting what Khrushchev had said into some semblance of diplomacy. 'Physical distance is nothing, spiritual distances are what matter. He tells you to—' Troy searched for something better than 'keep your pecker up', something utterly without ambiguity or innuendo—'To keep your heart healthy.'

'Healthy?'

'Pure. He means pure. It's an old Russian aphorism.'

He glanced at the ambassador once more. The man was cocking a hand to his ear and still muttering 'Что?' 'What?'

'Oh dear,' said Lloyd. 'These aphorisms. Why can't we have a few of our own. Er ... er ... Tell Mr Khrushchev ... er ... to put his hat on. It's rather cold. I'd hate to think of him catching cold.'

Pathetic, thought Troy. Lloyd smiled. Pleased with his own powers of invention. Troy yelled his translation back to Khrushchev. Khrushchev roared with laughter. Troy just made out a cry of 'Bugger England!' before the ship swung its bows seaward and he vanished from sight.

§16

Troy was back at the Yard in good time. The day had cleared wonderfully. By four-thirty of a beautiful spring afternoon he had had quite enough of paperwork and was gazing idly at the sunlight glinting on the Thames beneath his window. It was, he thought, almost identical to the view his brother Rod had from his office in the Palace of Westminster, a couple of hundred yards upriver. Out of office since 1951, Rod was a dutiful constituency MP. Often of a Friday evening he would call Troy in the hope of scrounging a lift down to the Hertfordshire mansion that his father had bought on his arrival in England in 1910. Troy wandered over to the Commons, down the tunnel that connected the Underground to Westminster, past a tired, Fridayish constable, saluting him in the most perfunctory fashion, and up the staircase to the office Rod, as Shadow Foreign Secretary, occupied on the south side.

The door was open. Rod was in shirt-sleeves, obligatory red tie at half-mast, also looking very Fridayish, and rummaging about among a vast acreage of papers on his desktop. Troy leaned in the doorway, looking at the clutter in which Rod seemed to like to work. The dark panelling and the huge gothic Thameside window were a Tennysonian, a Burne-Jonesy mock-mediæval, softened, humanised, almost modernised by the paraphernalia Rod accumulated around him. The window-seat cover his mother-in-law had sewn for him, the knitted tea cosy stuck in the in-tray, the sentimental relics of his kids' childhood—school photos, discarded mittens, outgrown caps, a one-armed teddy bear—all fighting with green-and-white Government papers for space atop the bookshelves. The personal and the political intermixed, crowned by a full outfit for a three-year-old, topcoat, bonnet, bootees and red Labour rosette included, hanging from the picture rail like the skin of some exotic insect long since turned into a more exotic butterfly. The butterfly was Alexander, Rod's eldest, now all of nineteen and far from butterfly-like. A big, robust man like his father. Not unlike Troy in looks but built on a grander scale. Rod was the best part of six foot, going grey, going gently to seed at forty-eight and looking, as Troy had thought just the other night, distinctly portly.

Rod heard the thought and looked up at him.

'I suppose,' he said, returning his gaze to the papers and the desk, 'that you've come to tell me I buggered up your week?'

'No. I haven't and you didn't. As a matter of fact it all worked out rather well. And I came, incidentally, to offer you a lift home.'

'Who's driving?'

'I am.'

Rod found what he was looking for and tossed the corkscrew at Troy.

'Good. Open a bottle. Your week may have been fine. I've just sat through a stinker.'

Troy opened the cupboard next to the fireplace and pulled out a bottle of what Rod called his 'stash'—the legacy of the late Alexei Troy—enough château-bottled wine to last a man a lifetime or two. Troy picked the nearest. A Gevrey-Chambertin 1938.

'It probably escaped your notice while you were out playing the spy, but it was budget week. I've just spent several days cooling my arse on the front bench, watching Harold Macmillan wipe the floor with us.'

Troy poured and handed the first glass to his brother. Rod sat on the window-seat watching the last of the sun and took up his litany of complaint once more.

'He's such a flash bastard. The only thing he didn't do was juggle the despatch box and the mace.'

Troy sipped at his glass. He'd no idea, nor had Rod, how long such wine kept. It tasted fine. He joined Rod in the window, wondering why he was so ratty. Rod's disposition was ordinarily so even; he was, Troy accepted, most of the time a remarkably well-balanced man.

'It's so bloody frustrating. Watching him, and not being able to get up and have a go.'

'You don't want the Chancellor's job, do you?'

'Want it? Of course I don't bloody want it. Who in their right mind would give up the Foreign brief now? Just when your new friend has made it quite possibly the most interesting job on the front bench?'

'You mean Khrushchev?'

'Of course I mean Khrushchev! If he goes on kicking over the traces in this way we'll be running to keep up with him. Stalin never sets foot outside Russia except to pow-wow with Churchill. Khrushchev tours like Liberace. That's the beauty of the Foreign job—wondering what the bugger's going to do next.'

Rod looked at Troy, as though expecting Troy to answer the implicit question.

'Well,' Troy said, silently wondering what Khrushchev had told Kolankiewicz, 'he didn't tell me.'

Rod drained his glass and held it out for the refill.

'But you did talk to him, didn't you?'

The glint reappeared in his eyes, the irritation of the day deserting him in a wine-red flush of nosiness.

'Perhaps,' Troy said coyly.

'Perhaps my backside. Out with it!'

'Well . . . I did get the chance of a bit of a chat.'

'I suppose you gave him your usual jaundiced view of the country? Did he realise you were spying on him?'

'Of course. He's not stupid.'

Troy paused, wondering how much he dare tell Rod. The trip to the East End, and the jaundiced views of the British working man, had better stay a secret. But there was no harm in recounting the old boy's views. He had aired them so freely as they rode the cab back to Claridge's.

'He as good as told me he thought Eden was mad.'

'As good as?'

Troy raised his left hand to his temple.

'He tapped the side of his head. Very much the gesture our grandfather used to use when he thought someone was a bit crazy. Then he said Eden was a few grains short of a bushel—which I took to be some sort of peasant aphorism or something he'd made up to sound like a peasant aphorism.'

Rod glugged his wine, and stared at the river for a moment.

'Good Lord,' he said softly. 'I would not have credited a man of such obvious bluster with such acute perception. He's quite right, of course, Eden is barking. I've thought so for a while now. Absolutely barking bloody mad. There's talk he won't last the term. I've bet Nye Bevan a tenner Macmillan will lead the Tories into the next election. He's backing Rab Butler.'

'And,' Troy went on, 'I know for a fact Eden buttonholed the Russians over Egypt. Tried a bit of armtwisting to get them to stay out of whatever rumpus is brewing out there. I heard Bulganin and Khrushchev rehashing it.'

Rod leaned his head back against the panelling and sighed gently.

'Ye gods and little fishes. Then he really is barking. It's the last subject I would have raised with them. Why give them the impression we're going to invade? The send-a-gunboat days are over. If he doesn't know that then our Prime Minister is the last man in England who hasn't heard.'

Troy made and cared nothing of this.

'And,' he pressed on, 'Khrushchev invited me to Russia.'

'Bloody hell! You must go. He invited Gaitskell. If he'd asked me I'd have been off like a shot.'

'Don't be silly, Rod. I can't go to Russia. Nor can you.'

'Why the hell not? There's nowhere on earth I'd rather go. And with Mr K's personal invitation you could escape the usual InTourist rubbish.'

'We can't go—either of us,' Troy said firmly. 'It simply isn't on.'

'Freddie, I spent my entire childhood listening to tales of the old country. Do you think I'd throw up a chance to finally see it for myself? I had to give Khrushchev that list of political prisoners. It was duty. But I knew damn well I was queering the pitch for myself as a visitor. If he's asked you, you have to go.'

'It's because I spent childhood listening to the old man and his old man blather on about the old country that I can't go. It's not a real place any more. It's a myth now. I'd rather keep it that way. It could never measure up. There's things back there I'd rather not know.'

'Such as?' Rod shot back, and Troy realised for the first time that he had embarked upon a conversation that could have no other result than Rod cornering him. He should have seen where it was leading.

He drew a deep breath and told Rod what he had put off telling him on a dozen other occasions.

'You remember when I was in Berlin in '48?'

'Could I ever forget?'

Troy ignored this.

'While I was there I met a KGB agent. A Pole I'd been investigating in London. He knew more about me than I did about him. He told me that the old man had been a Soviet agent all along.'

Rod slowly got up and crossed to the desk and the phone. He dialled and waited a few seconds for his wife to answer.

'Cid, I'm going to be late,' he said. 'Absolutely unavoidable. I'll come home with Freddie just as soon as I can. He's driving us down.'

He paused while his wife said something Troy could not make out. Then he hung up and resumed his seat in the window.

'Right, you bugger. Let's hear it.'

'You just did,' said Troy.

'That's it? That's the lot?'

'I thought it was quite enough, myself.'

'Some KGB spook collars you in Berlin and tells you your father was a spy. And you believe him?'

'I didn't say that. I thought about it. In fact, I still think about it. Most of the time I don't know what to believe. Sometimes I find it easy to believe it isn't true. I've never yet come to the point of believing it lock, stock and barrel.'

Rod leaned forward to Troy, demanding his attention, playing the big brother and confirming all the reasons Troy had ever had for not telling him what he had just told him.

'Freddie, it's preposterous. It makes no sense. No sense at all. The old man opposed Stalinism all through the thirties—even when it was fashionable to be a fellow-traveller he eschewed it. I often worked with him on the editorials for the *Herald,* and one or two for the *Sunday Post.* He would have to have been a conman extraordinaire not to have meant what he wrote.'

'Rod, there's plenty of people think the old man was a conman, and you have to admit he was certainly extraordinary.'

They had almost reached the bottom of the bottle. Rod pulled another from the cupboard without so much as a glance at the label, and proceeded to oil the wheels once more.

'You amaze me sometimes, little brother, you really do. How can you have knowledge like this and sit on it, not use it? For Christ's sake, if it had been me the bugger told I'd've come screaming round to your house like my arse was on fire!'

'I know,' Troy said simply.

'How could you not tell me?!?'

'Because I knew you'd react as you are doing.'

'Freddie—it's too important . . .'

'No it's not. You don't believe a word of it, so it can hardly be that important.'

'Yes it bloody well is . . . It's . . . it's undermining.'

'What?'

'It's undermining! I don't want to be forced to consider that my father's life might have been a sham. It doesn't shatter one's faith in the old man. It chips away at it in a shoddy, petty, corrosive way. He built a life here for himself. And he built one for you and me and the girls. I don't want to be made to doubt that, and if I doubt him I doubt the life. It's important to think he was committed to it.'

'To England?'

'Yes.'

'You know what I think of that.'

Rod rose up in rage. Glass in one hand, bottle in the other. He stormed a few paces around the room in his stockinged feet, leaving Troy wondering why Cid never managed to get him to wear matching socks, and returned to his seat, seething with anger and not a drop of wine spilt.

'You stupid, stupid sod. Let's not go through that again. We're English. That's what he made us. For you to go on raging against the English because you hated their damn schools and you can't grasp the first rule of their damn silly national game is just plain childish. For God's sake, Freddie, grow up!'

Of course Rod was right. Troy could not tell silly mid-off from deep leg. It ought to mean nothing, but at times was simply and neatly symbolic of his regard for the English as being other—'them' as he was wont to think of them. But on another level he too knew why Rod raged so madly against the idea. England—or rather that part of the English to whom it mattered at all—was still reeling from the defection of Burgess and Maclean the best part of five years ago. The scandal rippled through English society with a resonance and a force out of all proportion to the incident. Only last year some chap named Philby—Kim Philby, Troy recalled, son of the old Arabian explorer St John Philby—had been the subject of a Commons answer by Macmillan to the effect that he was not the third man in the case of Burgess and Maclean; and Philby had followed that with the unprecedented step of calling a press conference, so necessary was it to reinforce the general sense of his innocence in an atmosphere where the notion of a third man had reached the level of an Establishment paranoia. Establishment, there was a word at the heart of the mystery, buried so deep in the unwritten English code it was impossible to define and much of the time impossible to discern. But then the whole affair touched on unwritten codes—unspoken but understood meanings—the grasp of which, the consciousness of which, in Troy's eyes, was what separated the likes of the Troys from the English proper. Not to be shocked by Burgess and Maclean was to miss a fundamental meaning in post-war English life. As Rod had so succinctly put it, it was like not knowing the rules of cricket. The two errant diplomats had broken the rules, which stated, in the unwritten code of the English, that spies were much more likely to be one of the cloth cap and brown boot brigade—who had, after all, something to gain from the triumph of Communism—than to be 'one of us'. That the cloth cap and brown boot brigade had nothing and no one to spy on was neither here nor there. That Burgess and Maclean had each been 'one of us'—although Burgess had managed the neat trick of being flagrantly one of *them* at the same time as being 'one of us'—was at the heart of the offence. Contempt. It was what offended Rod now, the thought that their father had made him, and tried to make Troy, 'one of us', only to be in utter, secret contempt of the very notion. That was what hurt. That Alexei Troy might just have nurtured the same secret contempt, making fools of them all.

Troy had known Guy Burgess. They had a common friend in Charlie, a common friend in Tom Driberg. Troy had propped up bars in Soho with Guy a dozen times. He was a charming, sometimes outrageous drunk, who blathered about politics and Communism half the time but around whom there lingered not a whiff of ideology. But, then, that was what had so obviously lent conviction to the façade that he was 'one of us'. The English ideology could be summed up in some wag's definition of the C of E—'the creed of the English is that there is no God but that it is wise to pray to him occasionally'. Troy knew that he, Chief Inspector Troy, was not 'one of us'; he knew that it suited Rod to believe that he, Rodyon Troy Bt. MP, was, but felt that in his heart of hearts Rod knew he too was on the outside.

Troy taunted him, unnecessarily.

'Why is it causing you such offence?'

'Offence? Bugger offence. It's pain. Pain, pain, pain! I am hurt by the idea that the old man could be called a spy. It's insulting. More insulting than I can find words to express!'

'Aha?' said Troy. 'I don't suppose you've noticed, but you've called me a spy at least twice since I walked through the door less than an hour ago.'

'I have?'

'Yes.'

Rod was momentarily contemplative. Instantly calmer. They both knew what the next logical remark must be.

'It's true in its way, though. Isn't it?'

'Yes. I suppose it is. But that's not why I was there. Whatever they expected of me, I was there for the crack. I knew we'd learn nothing we didn't know already. If Eden hadn't told Five and Six to lay off, I'm sure they'd never have clutched at such a straw. As it happens, I was a spy who didn't spy a thing. My hands are clean!'

'They didn't,' Rod almost whispered.

'Didn't what?'

'Didn't lay off. They went right ahead and spied on the Russians. They sent a frogman out to inspect the hull of that battleship Khrushchev came in on. The Russian captain made a formal complaint to the FO before he sailed. It was a lot bigger and dirtier than they told you.'

Suddenly Troy was angry. His turn.

'Eden's denied it, of course. But you know in your bones it's true.'

Troy was angrier.

'Wouldn't surprise me if you and all the plods in Special Branch were just the decoys.'

Angrier still. He bit on the bullet, and refused to give in to the rage he felt.

'When?' he asked. 'When did this happen?'

'The word is that the complaint came in on Tuesday morning. The denial was immediate, but my sources say Eden's been in a paddy ever since because the spooks have admitted it.'

That Rod had 'sources' was hardly a surprise. It made perfect sense for Her Majesty's Civil Service to see to it that Her Majesty's Loyal Opposition knew what the Civil Servants wanted them to know. It was one way of ensuring their loyalty and it was easy enough. The Commons was a vast club, an elective Garrick, the voting man's Athenaeum. And the mandarins were nothing if not natural clubmen, nodding and winking at their blind horses. After all, Opposition might well be Government in a year or two.

Again Troy could hear Khrushchev saying 'Do it!' on the Monday evening. The remark made marginally more sense now than it had at the time. But he had created a situation in which it was now impossible to tell Rod that he had indeed heard something of worth in his spying on the Russian leader—impossible, without branding himself a liar as well as a spy in Rod's eyes. He realised once more why he so hated spooks and spookery: it clung to fingers, it left a bad taste in the mouth, a nasty smell in the air. All in all he had only himself to blame. He should have known better.

They all but rolled out of Troy's Bendey in Hampstead. Lucinda Troy took one look at her husband and brother-in-law and demanded the keys to the car. One day, she told them, as she eased herself into the driving seat, there'd be laws against middle-aged men driving pissed to the gills.

§17

Rod had been a toddler of three, the girls babes-in-arms, only weeks old, and Troy himself unthought of, when their father had paid a pittance for the vast Georgian pile that was Mimram House. He had saved the bedrooms from falling into the ground floor and the house itself from crumbling into the eponymous river Mimram. He had turned it into a hybrid of a Russian dacha and an English family home. It had remained that after his death, home to his mother, home from home to the sisters and Rod's constituency base, until their mother's death in 1952. Troy had been, as he himself saw it, at best a visitor. To everyone's surprise, not least Troy's, Maria Mikhailovna had left the house to Troy, stating simply in her will that it was only right as he was her last unmarried child with no family home of his own. This to Troy confirmed what she thought of his terraced house in Goodwin's Court, which she had always con- temptuously referred to as his 'bachelor residence', as though it would serve only until he too married. There was little prospect of that, and even his sisters, those indefatigable romantics, had long given up the game of matchmaking. He had hesitated, had almost passed the house back to Rod. He had come to think of himself as a Londoner. He had been there since the thirties. He had witnessed the privations of the war there, and the worse privations of the peace. But in the end he had accepted that there was a certain appeal to claiming the family seat. It would never be wholly his—Rod needed it most weekends, and nothing short of a moat could keep out a determined sister—and hence the responsibility need not be the millstone about his neck that at first glance it might seem. He could indulge a dream. He had long wanted to keep a pig and grow vegetables. And to his own surprise he had done things his younger self would never have dreamt of. He took weekends and holidays as weekends and holidays. Before cases out of London, he would let Onions bribe him with the promise of days off. After cases out of London, he would let Onions reward him with days off. He spent summer evenings in the country, motoring down just for the night, and rising at first light to be back at the Yard. He had come to look upon Mimram House as a pleasurable retreat, although retreat from what he could not say.

§18

He awoke on the Saturday morning to the promise of breakfast in bed, followed by a stroll down to the pig pens. He was sitting up in bed with a cup of coffee and the morning paper when Rod opened his bedroom door. Troy could tell from his expression that he had just a tinge of guilt, the nagging self-doubt that perhaps he had overdone it and made an ass of himself. Unlike Troy, Rod could never hold a grudge. He had nothing to feel guilty about, but guilt he could hold aplenty. He looked immaculate, freshly scrubbed and shaved, three-piece suit and a shine to his shoes, ready to meet his electorate and suffer their complaints.

'You haven't told the girls what you told me yesterday, have you?' he asked.

'No,' said Troy. 'Why should I? Can't wear it, can't fuck it. They wouldn't know what to do with it.'

'A deeply cynical attitude, if I may say so.'

Rod left. Nothing on earth would have induced Troy to tell his sisters. Their dismissive indifference would have been far harder to bear than Rod's absurd guilt. He went back to his newspaper, to the news of the departure of B & K, and a near-verbatim account of Khrushchev's last words to the Foreign Secretary. Some Fleet Street hack must have been closer than he thought. Except that they weren't Khrushchev's last words, they were Troy's, the lies of convenience by which he had stripped Khrushchev of his hostility and vulgarity. He was, he realised, a part of history. His lies were now lies of record. Oh, the accursed vice of lying. Troy threw back the covers and yawned his way to the bathroom.

Under the oaks at the bottom of the kitchen garden he found a large, fat man seated on the makeshift bench of planks and oil drums, sipping tea from a thermos flask. When Troy had first met him he had seemed merely big. He was bald too, but his baldness had not altered—there was nowhere for it to go—but his growing girth had forced Troy to reappraise him from big to fat. He still wore, as so many of the British did, the shabby remains of his wartime uniform. All over Britain on Saturday and Sunday mornings shades of blue and khaki could be seen on the backs of digging men on allotments or peeping out from the bonnets of old bangers in back yards. It had become, by dint of durability, the mufti of the working man. There seemed to be not a dustman in England without his khaki blouse. The Fat Man had put leather cuffs and elbows onto the dark blue serge of his old LCC Heavy Rescue battledress, though Troy doubted very much whether he could still fasten it, but these details apart he looked scarcely different from the night when Troy had first encountered him in the gloom of the black out, tending his large white sow in the heart of Chelsea. These days you could search Chelsea from river to square, the length of the King's Road from the Royal Court to World's End, and find not a trace of a pig.

'Mornin' cock,' he said as Troy wandered over.

Troy had never known him to use names, his own or anyone else's, a habit which had made him, on occasion, hard to keep track of. He had always told Troy, with a tap of the finger to the side of the nose, that he worked for an amateur detective, 'a gentleman, like'. Troy took this with a pinch of salt. The Fat Man would disappear from time to time and occasionally Troy would wonder what became of him, but he always showed up at the punctuation points in the calendar of a pig's life, and Troy had long since given up asking him questions. He would, after all, only resort to 'ask no questions, you'll be told no lies', or some such phrase, which irritated Troy intensely, so reminiscent were they of childhood.

Troy leaned over the side of the sty. The large Gloucester Old Spot sow was scarcely visible in the shade of the tree, well camouflaged by the natural black and white of her markings and the odd splash of mud. She grunted a greeting. Troy could just make her out, sitting on her haunches, rolling her head at the sky in anticipation of the coming sunshine.

'I's'll 'ave 'er put to the boar next month,' the Fat Man said. 'We should get a good litter this year. She's in the pink of condition.'

Troy sat next to him on the planks and declined the offer of sickly sweet, milky tea.

Troy had sought him out to get his advice on building the pens and breeding pigs. One hot summer day in 1953 he had roared up the drive on his motorcycle combination, still in his blue jacket, wearing goggles and a leather helmet. In the sidecar sat a patient, self-possessed pig, a large specimen of the Middle White. It, too, wore a leather flying helmet.

Troy had stood in the porch with Sasha watching the bike approach. It ground to a halt in a spurt of gravel. The Fat Man pushed up the goggles and beamed at Troy.

'Wotcher, cock,' he said as though they had last met only yesterday.

Sasha drifted over to the bike, walked slowly round it, delicately, bare-foot on the gravel, feigning appraisal. At last she said, 'Who's your friend?'

'Randolph,' the Fat Man said.

'Randolph?'

'Randolph. On account of his father was called Winston.'

Sasha corpsed. A fit of girlish giggles. The Fat Man did not, clearly, see the naming of pigs as a source of mirth. He looked stonily at her doubled up with laughter. The pig, for its part, continued to roll a pebble round in its mouth, it eyes narrowed to slits, staring straight ahead, oblivious to her hysterics, listening to the sound the pebble made on its teeth. For all Troy knew, what sounded like utter monotony to him might well have been music to the pig.

'Ere,' the Fat Man said to Troy, 'is she taking the mick?'

'Most of the time she does little else,' said Troy.

'Right, Randolph. Time to show 'er your stuff!'

He plucked the leather flying helmet from the pig's head, and the porker leapt from the sidecar and put his nose to the ground. He sniffed a second or two and was off.

'What's happening?' Sasha cried.

The pig had the acceleration of an MG. He had almost reached a gallop and was approaching the corner of the house with the Fat Man in hot pursuit.

'Come on,' he yelled over his shoulder to Troy. 'Shake a leg! Or we'll lose the bugger!'

Troy looked from the Fat Man to Sasha. She was clutching the hem of her skirt and hopping madly from one foot to the other.

'I've nothing on my feet!' she squealed, desperate at the thought that she would be left out of anything.

'My wellies are behind the door,' Troy said.

He took off after the pig and the Fat Man, already vanishing around the corner. The pig had a head start on them, but Troy soon drew level with the Fat Man.

'What are we doing?' he gasped.

The Fat Man wheezed and creaked and spoke in rapid snorts.

'We're finding the pig spot.'

'What's a pig spot?'

'The best place to build a pig pen, old cock.'

'How do we know it when we find it?'

'Simple. The pig stops. We stop. When yer pig finds his spot he'll stop. Either he finds something worth eating or he knackers himself. Either way he stops. And that's where we builds 'is little piggy 'ouse.'

Randolph was out of sight, darting between the greenhouses and the cold frames. From behind them came a shrill 'View halloo'. Troy turned his head to his sister galloping after them in outsize wellington boots, skirts tucked into her knickers to keep them free of the mud.

'Mind you,' said the Fat Man, 'a good pig in his prime can run you ragged. I've known Randolph give you a right round the 'ouses when 'e's a mind to. I 'ope that mad woman as appears to live with you 'as got the energy to keep up. He'll do for me in a couple of rounds. If he starts circling the 'ouse I's'll sit it out and nab 'im on another lap.'

Sasha's cries were getting closer. Windows were going up in the house. He saw Rod lean out, heard him yell, 'What the bloody hell is going on?'

'A pig! A pig!' cried Sasha, as though this alone would suffice as explanation.

The pig doubled back on Troy, caught him in the narrow corridor between two greenhouses, pigdozed him aside and headed back to the house. One circuit of the house and the Fat Man, true to his word, decided to sit it out, pulled forth a large white handkerchief and sat on the edge of the verandah, mopping his brow. Two, and Troy joined him, leaving only Sasha to keep up the chase. She and the pig orbited the house, she squawking and hooting, the pig threatening at any moment to lap her and pursue the pursuer.

'Has she been barmy long, then?' the Fat Man asked.

'Don't ask,' Troy replied. 'By the way, I have very bad news for you. There's two of them.'

'Eh?'

'Twins,' said Troy.

Troy pushed the Fat Man to one side as Randolph came hurtling across the verandah and shot between them.

'Right,' said the Fat Man, lumbering to his feet. 'This looks like it.'

The pig disappeared southwards.

Down by the oaks, a couple of hundred yards from the house, Troy found Randolph snuffling among layers of dead oak leaves and digging vigorously with his front feet. Was this the pig spot?

Sasha came bounding up, well ahead of the Fat Man, speechless with giggles, capable only of hooting, 'A pig! A pig!' She drew a deep breath and at her third attempt managed a short, full sentence.

'Has the pig come to stay?'

'No. He's a breeding boar. To be honest, I don't know why he's come.'

A wheezing Fat Man came slowly down the slope. 'I might've known,' he said. 'Haycorns.'

'Wrong time of year,' said Troy.

'Nah, 'e's diggin' for last year's, buried under all that leafmould.'

He gazed up at the spreading branches of the great oak tree.

'So this is it, eh? This is where you wants yer piggy 'ouse, is it?'

The pig snuffled and dug and ignored him.

'Is an oak tree the best spot?' Troy asked.

'It'll do. Shady, doesn't have to walk far, food just drops off the tree to him. On the other hand, if you doesn't want a pig livin' right under yer tree, you just picks a bit o' waste land, like them brambles over there, and you tosses in an 'andful of haycorns, and yer average porker'll turn it over for you better than two horses and a plough.'

So saying he took a few acorns from his jacket pocket and tossed them among the mass of nettle and blackberry. The pig gave up his dig and tore into the brambles with his trotters, slashing away with a demonic ferocity.

'And when 'e's through, all you 'as ter do is put up a sty and bob's yer uncle.'

'That's it?' said Troy. 'That's how you find a pig spot? It all seems a bit arbitrary to me. You could just start off by throwing the acorns into the brambles and not bother chasing the damn pig all around the garden.'

The Fat Man looked hurt, suddenly deadly serious. A sharp intake of breath, a shake of the head, as though Troy were defying ancient pig lore that might be almost sacred to him. He stared at the ground a while and then looked up at Troy.

'But then you'd miss all the fun,' he said.

That had been three years ago. The Fat Man still regarded Sasha with great suspicion, and never referred to her by any other name but 'the mad woman'. Masha—when he was certain it was her—he was scrupulously polite to. But then she hardly ever went near the pig pens anyway. He acknowledged the fact of twins with a degree of doubt, much of it due to Troy's too-often repeated assertion that they were one dreadful woman with two bodies. Today he and Troy sat on the plank bench and followed the pig's example in looking at the sun.

'Are you goin' to say anythin'? Or shall I drink up me tea and go home?'

'Sorry,' Troy said. 'Things on my mind.'

'What you should have on yer mind is muckin' out. A mornin' shovellin' pigs' doins should take yer mind off whatever it is.'

He was right. And in the afternoon, following lunch outdoors, they walked down through the village, cut a five-mile circle through the leafing woods and came back to the house from the north in a bobbing sea of bluebells and an unearthly tangle of uncurling spleenwort. They chatted about nothing much; the Fat Man was a committed cockney and Troy doubted that he could tell Love-in-a-Mist from Hole-in-the-Head, but he added to Troy's knowledge of pig lore, and Troy thought the old man made most of it up and minded not one bit—and he told Troy what he thought of Arsenal's performance this season, a subject of which Troy knew no more than he did of cricket. And at the end of it Troy returned home feeling pleasantly sane, delightfully buffeted by the inanities of a normal conversation. It was an art so difficult in his own household, so far were the Troys from normal. Their father's legacy; his character, split up so oddly among them, and none of them easy, normal people. Rod, inheritor of the old man's political earnestness, his journalistic nose. The Sisters, heirs to the mercurial, whimsical, self-indulgent side of his nature—a man who could crack jokes in five languages, who could be reduced to hysterics often by the slightest thing—oddly crossed with their mother's stern humourlessness, evident on the days when nothing would make them see the joke. And Troy—what had he inherited? Troy knew full well. The tendency to secrecy. The habit of playing his cards close to his chest. Put together with the nosiness of a journalist, it was what made him a copper, but it was also the source of the very problem from which pig and pigman had so pleasurably distracted him.

Rod, too, seemed to have recovered his form. He entertained them all over dinner with his account of events in Westminster—a wicked caricature of Macmillan announcing a thing he called a Premium Bond, a lottery by any other name. The very way Rod said 'orf' reduced the twins to giggling heaps. They cackled like demented hags when he screwed up his face and imparted to his eyes the sad slant of an old bloodhound.

Troy looked at the one in-law present—Lucinda, Lady Troy. Laughing quietly, a delightful, shy smile, the bright blue eyes in the pale face. Neither Hugh nor Lawrence, Masha's husband, had come for the weekend. So often these days Lucinda was the only outsider present. If nothing else it ensured that they spoke English. Russian evenings bored Troy with the sense of their exclusivity, the retreat into a private language. Rod had married Lucinda in 1936, the year of the three kings. She was about the same age as the girls. Troy thought he had a good relationship with her—she had none of the girls' tendency to bully, and none of that preordained idea that he was inevitably 'younger' and hence disqualified from judgement for the rest of his life. He had often envied Rod the choice, the step towards normality he had made. The choice of an indisputably English woman.

Suddenly, as they were finishing the last course, Sasha was on her feet announcing she must dash, trying to be home before the pumpkin got her. And the meal, and with it the evening, dissolved around her. Rod had papers he must read before bedtime, Masha's favourite programme was on the goggle-box in the yellow room. There was half a bottle of Pouilly-Fumé '52 left in the ice bucket.

'Shall we finish it?' he said to Lucinda.

'I'd love to, Freddie,' said the indisputably English woman, 'but I'm worn out. I didn't know Sasha was going to cut and run, but now that she has I'd rather like an early night.' She yawned. 'I seem to have spent so many nights sitting up listening to Rod get his speech right, or waiting up for him to come in after a division. Sorry.'

Troy took the bottle out of the bucket, grabbed his coat from the hall stand and walked through his father's old study to the south verandah. It was still not yet May. The day had lost its warmth. He slipped on the coat, sat on a creaking wicker chair and finished the bottle in natural silence—the mechanical clatter of a pheasant, the distant bark of a dog-fox, the wind, gently, in the willows. The willows divided the garden from the river and were overhanging badly. He had put off pollarding them last year, and as they vanished from sight into the encroaching night, he knew he could not put it off again. He loved the sweeping shape of wild willow—a pollarded willow was always a squat thing, with too regular an array of branches, but if left they would split down the middle and die.

In the deepening gloom a pair of bats began to criss-cross the lawn at first-floor height, cutting the night into invisible squares, in search of prey Troy could not even see. As one cut in from the north, the second would come in from the west, missing each other with unerring accuracy, with scarcely a flutter of the skinny wing, weaving the warp and weft of their nightly pattern.

He sat until the darkness was complete and his hands turned numb with cold. Looking back, he would come to think of it as the last peace he would ever know. In the morning the warp and weft of one life began to tear themselves apart and thread themselves into the matted conspiracy of another.

§19

He was taking coffee alone in his father's study, scanning the Sunday papers for any admissions by Her Majesty's Government that bore out what Rod had told him. He sat in his father's chair, facing the window. For a while after the old man had died he had sat on the other side of the partner's desk, facing into the room—his father's pen and blotter exactly as he had left them—giving in to some fearful sense that it was a form of sacrilege to occupy his place. Then, one day, he had thought, sod it, the view's better, moved around to the other side, and gave the matter no more thought. Today, for no reason that was immediately apparent, Masha appeared, perched on the edge of the desk, put her feet on his father's chair, helped herself from the cafetière and smiled her sweethag's smile.

Troy said nothing. They sipped coffee in silence. He waited to see if the visit had any purpose.

The telephone rang. He picked it up and heard his brother-in-law Hugh asking if he could speak to his wife.

'Sasha?' Troy said, puzzled, and before he could say a word more the phone was snatched from his hand.

'Hughdey,' Masha crooned. Only Sasha ever called Hugh Hughdey. 'Darling. [Pause.] Yes, darling. [Pause.] I'll be back after lunch I should think.'

There was a longer pause. Troy could hear the Bakelite crackle, the baritone rasp of Hugh's voice, without being able to make out a word of what he was saying.

'Oh,' Masha resumed. 'Nothing special. Lucinda came down too, so it was dinner *en famille*.'

She paused again.

'Yes. After lunch.'

She blew him a smacking kiss and hung up.

Troy stared in near-disbelief.

'Does Sasha provide the same service for you?' he said.

'Don't ask.'

'Do you think he'll fall for that?'

'Well—he always has in the past.'

'Hugh isn't a complete fool, you know.'

'Wanna bet?' said Masha.

§20

Onions rang forty minutes later.

'Pack a suitcase. You're booked on the night sleeper to Aberdeen.'

'A juicy one?' Troy asked.

'Arsenic. Four bodies. Same MO, and the locals are stumped.'

This appealed. He had not had a good body in a while. He had not investigated a poisoning for about five years, and now the prospect of four at once.

'What about the squad?'

He heard Onions sigh deeply. The squad was under strength. When Troy had told Khrushchev's apparatchik that he ran the Murder Squad, he had clipped the truth. He was its acting head in the absence of Superintendent Tom Henrey. But Tom had been absent since Christmas.

'I doubt Tom'll be back,' Onions said at last. 'It's cancer of the pancreas. But until he tells me one way or the other, to relieve him of the job permanently seems like piling it on—like I was hurrying him into the grave.'

'Of course,' Troy said. 'I'm not asking to be promoted, but I think we have to get someone else in lower down the ladder, as soon as we can.'

'I'd be hard pressed to give you another inspector.'

'A sergeant will do.'

'Anyone in mind?'

'Yes,' said Troy. 'Clark, Edwin Clark. Warwickshire Constabulary, currently with Birmingham CID.'

Onions thought for a second.

'OK. You're on. I'll get Sergeant Clark transferred.'

'Constable Clark.'

'Eh?'

'He's a constable now. He'll be a sergeant once he's on the squad.'

'God, you ask a lot. Is he up to it?'

'Of course he's up to it. In fact, he may be just what we need. A solid anchor man, someone who's good with paperwork.'

'It'd be nice to set foot in your office and be able to see young Wildeve. Lately the pile of paper's been bigger than him.'

Troy knew he would have no difficulty justifying Clark's presence. A fortnight with him left alone to pervade the office with his unrufflable calm and his methodical, military efficiency and Onions would soon appreciate him—and the contrast in temperament between such a cool customer and two men as volatile as Troy and Wildeve.

§21

Aberdeen took longer than he or Onions had guessed. When Troy stepped from the overnight sleeper into the dusty morning light under the arches of King's Cross railway station in early June, he had been gone the best part of six weeks. London had roared into summer.

He was feeling that curious mixture of the contentment of success and the niggling doubt of a loose end. The murders had indeed been arsenic, but the mistake that had thrown the Aberdonians was in presuming a common *modus operandi*. Troy had seen at once that this was not the case. The four doses of the poison had been administered in wildly differing quantities, and the emergence of a fifth body two days after Troy had arrived only added to the spread of evidence. They were not looking for a murderer, he had told them, but for several murderers. His task had been to redirect the team, to rake over the evidence accumulated in the best part of a year, to interview all over again those potential suspects who had not fitted the previous assumptions about the case.

It had been a long haul, days without break, often starting at break of day. Occasionally he would pick up a newspaper and scan it quickly. Egypt still simmered, Cyprus still bled and the Government made no admissions about the Portsmouth spy. The press made endless speculation, particularly those papers owned by the Troys, and Troy knew that some of that speculation was being fed to them by Rod. The mysterious spy had gone missing, or he was not really working for the Secret Service at all but had been hired by the rightwing Empire mob / the left-wing anti-Soviet Trots / the White Russian exiles / the Zionists, or he had been kidnapped and was now in Russia, or he had died on the job and was now at the bottom of the Solent—perm any two of three, delete as appropriate. He had no time to follow the story in depth, but then, he thought, the only depth the story had was that in which this mysterious frogman spy might be buried.

He had gained a confession to two of the murders from the victims' own family doctor; the local inspector had managed the same with the brother of the second victim; the team as a whole had built a case against a third man for the fourth murder that Troy was certain would convict him in court—but the fifth case he could not solve, and he returned to London trailing behind him the thread of his first failure in several years, much inclined to write it down to imitation, the copycat syndrome as he believed the Americans were now calling it. There was a lesson to be learnt in keeping some things out of the papers. It was, he concluded, a loose thread that was unlikely to be tugged in the near future. At the earliest he would be yanked back to Scotland at the end of the summer to give evidence in court.

It was seven o'clock in the morning. A fine summer morning. The sun coursed down the Pentonville Road, over the rooftops of Islington and Clerkenwell to pick out the magnificence of St Pancras' Midland Hotel in all its grime and glory. London was waking up. Two million kettles sang on hobs. He threw his case in the back of a cab. After coffee and a bath he was quite looking forward to walking to the Yard.

The old Ascot Patent Gas Water Heater perched on its iron bracket above the bath worked well enough if you knew the knack. Begin in the bathroom. A small trickle will emerge from the nozzle. Turn knob fully counterclockwise. Run downstairs, wallop pipe next to sink with heel of shoe, held firmly in left hand. Run upstairs, turn knob half-clockwise, press button to ignite. Go to airing cupboard on landing, wallop pipe at back of cupboard with shoe, held firmly in left hand. Return to bathroom, trickle will now be a lukewarm, modest flow. Disrobe. Lukewarm, modest flow has now become hot, generous flow. Get in bath. Flow cuts out at four inches of hot water in obedience to World War II guidelines.

Troy had no idea why his Ascot had never got over the war. So much of England had not, after all, and it might well be a simple matter of the machine's sympathies, but after this rigmarole nothing would induce him to answer the telephone. It rang as he settled into the bath, and it rang again five minutes later. He stood his mug of coffee and his slice of toast and marmalade on the soap rack and lay back in the suds. A gentle kick with his foot on the up pipe and the Ascot would yield a second harvest to create something resembling a decent bathful. It just required a little patience. Whoever it was on the phone could go to hell.

He sipped at his first good cup of coffee in weeks, and was strongly reminded of Larissa Tosca, of her utter immodesty which led her to hold court in the bath, of him perched awkwardly on the loo while she sank into foam like a Hollywood starlet in a musical comedy. Bath nights had never been the same since.

The walk to the Yard was pleasant beyond all his anticipation. There were days when he loved London; there were days when it sparkled through the grime, and one could be seduced by the lie that fog and winter were not its natural condition.

He scarcely recognised his office. It was neat and clean and orderly. Someone had emptied the waste paper bin. Someone had cleared that pile of files off the floor and filed them. Someone had unjammed the window to let the breeze in off the river along with the odd toot of the traffic. Someone had taken down years' old notices from the board. Someone had wound the clock. Someone had replaced the broken chair with one of those swivel things that glamorous secretaries sit on while they hoik up their skirts and take dictation. And the desks. Jack's desk was almost bare. His own was stacked with papers, but a small, far from glamorous, stout little body was sitting in his chair calmly working his way through them, sorting the urgent from the routine, occasionally annotating, he presumed for his, Troy's, future benefit. It made no sense. Had they fired him *in absentia* and replaced him with a real policeman? Was he one of the three bears? Was this the fat version of Goldilocks?

'Good morning, sir,' said the stout little body.

Clark. It was Clark. He'd quite forgotten about Clark.

'I bet you could use a cup of coffee, couldn't you, sir?'

Before Troy could say that he'd just had a cup and that nothing short of desperation would induce him to drink Scotland Yard coffee, his eye was caught by a contraption on the corner cupboard, next to the gas fire. It seemed to consist of a Bunsen burner, several glass flasks, a yard or two of glass and rubber tubing and a large, round condenser from which a deep brown liquid appeared to be dripping into a beaker.

'Do you like it, sir? I designed it myself.'

'Like it? I don't even know what it is.'

'It's a coffee machine, sir.'

Troy looked at the bubbling glass maze. Piranesi could not have bettered the design. He inhaled deeply. It was coffee, and it smelt rather good. Better than the stuff he made himself.

'Where did you get the apparatus?' he asked as Clark poured him a cup.

'From Forensics, sir.'

'You mean Kolankiewicz parted with half a ton of his clobber to let you make coffee?'

'Not exactly, sir. I requisitioned it with a chitty.'

'A chitty?'

'Yes, sir. I find that if you catch Mr Wildeve when he's trying to leave, particularly if you already know from his diary that he's got a date for the evening, he'll sign almost anything without reading it.'

This was bad news. This was pretty much how Troy got Onions to sign chitties. It was all a matter of knowing when Stan had arranged to play bowls or dig his allotment. It did not bode well. How many scoundrels could fit into a single office?

'You're not back to your old fiddles, are you, Eddie?'

'Well, sir. I paid for the coffee. Besides, if you lived in the Police House you'd make your office as comfortable as you could. A home from home, if you like.'

'Is that where they put you?'

'Just till I can find a place of my own, sir. I'll be a few quid a week better off when I get my first sergeant's pay packet. I might be able to afford a small flat somewhere, you never know.'

Troy was not sure whether this was a tip of the hat from Clark acknowledging his promotion or another episode in the great British whinge. Promotion meant about thirty shillings a week to Clark, Troy estimated, still leaving him short of five hundred pounds per annum. It might be enough to set him up in a place of his own. It might not. It wasn't a great sum. Troy himself earned the maximum allowed to a Metropolitan Chief Inspector, less than a travelling salesman, and well short of the social yardstick of one thousand pounds per annum—the enviable 'thousand a year man'—but then he had never lived off his salary and had never had to. Clark had a point. A single man would not be anyone's priority in London's struggle to house its people in the battered buildings the Blitz had left standing.

'Is there anything I should know about?' he said, pointing at the pile of paperwork.

'Half a dozen things you should read. Nothing that can't wait. Though this might amuse you.'

He handed Troy a copy of the *Police Gazette,* folded open at the promotions and transfers page.

'J Division has a new DDI, sir.'

Troy read the short piece announcing 'the appointment of Detective Sergeant Patrick Milligan as Divisional Detective Inspector, J Division, based at Leman St., London E1, following the death of DDI Horace Jago'. Leman Street had been Troy's first station twenty years ago.

'That's quite a promotion,' he said. 'Who would ever have thought he had it in him?'

'I don't think Mr Cobb brought out the best in Paddy, sir.'

'My recollection is that he was asleep half the time, and the other half he was scheming ways to get even with Cobb.'

'Weren't we all, sir? Oh, by the way, your brother's been trying to reach you all morning.'

'Urgent?'

'I wouldn't know, sir.'

Troy called his brother. Next to the phone was a copy of *The Times,* folded open at its daily crossword. It was nine-thirty in the morning and Clark had already finished it.

'What's up?'

'I've a treat for you,' Rod said. 'Can you meet me in forty minutes?'

'I've got a fortnight's leave due to me. I'll be at Mimram tomorrow morning. Couldn't it wait till then?'

'No. It's special.'

'Rod—'

'Just meet me. Won't take long.'

'At your office?'

'No. At the *Post.* Lawrence is making an announcement.'

In 1945 Rod had called the family together. He could not, he said, take responsibility for the family businesses and be an MP. Whatever the rules said, he could not and would not do it. Did they, he mooted, wish to get out of the business of Fleet Street and sell the lot? No, was the chorus answer. It would be selling everything the old man had put together. To Troy's surprise his brother-in-law Lawrence, still in uniform himself, stepped into the breach and offered to run the *Sunday Post*. He had no experience of such work; he had been a barrister when he married Masha, had spent a frustrating war wearing the red flashes of a staff officer, had never in fact seen combat or set foot on foreign soil. He was, he said privately to Troy, itching for a challenge. And he had risen to it. The *Post* was now the most contentious Sunday paper in the country, and Lawrence the most litigious, cantankerous, campaigning editor. All in all a man pretty much like their father. Rod might be right, it might be worth hearing. It might be another of those occasions like the time when Lawrence accused Attlee of selling out his principles after he had imposed charges on the National Health Service to pay for Britain's part in the Korean War. Or the time when he had personally signed an editorial calling for Churchill's resignation on grounds of senility. Subscriptions all over Britain had been cancelled. Ex-colonial colonels and mad majors had written in in droves and patriots bunged half-bricks though his windows. Lawrence had his moments.

§22

The lobby of the *Sunday Post* was full of grumbling hacks complaining yet again of the absurd vanity of Lawrence calling a press conference. The other newspapers might have sent their trainees and their hasbeens, but they would not ignore Lawrence, and the chance of another row. There was at least an inch or two of column space in reporting the antics of the competition. They cliqued unto themselves, talking shop, but then so did the other faction present.

London was a city of exiles. Here and there, statistical probability implied, there might just be the odd refugee from the fall of the Second Empire. Some nonagenarian brought across the Channel in childhood. The Empress Eugénie herself had lived on in Chislehurst on the southern edge of London into the 1920s. But Russians fleeing their revolution, London had had aplenty in its time and, it seemed, every living London Russian exile Troy had ever met or even heard of, including several he had thought long dead, was there. They were not a pleasant bunch. The last scions of displaced and dying lines, the final bearers of ancient and occasionally bogus titles, the last believers unwilling to recognise the course history had taken, not-so-old men who still thought the storming of the Winter Palace might be undone, that Ekaterinburg might not have happened after all. As a rule, he avoided them.

The USSR was the fine line of the century. Its most heated topic, from the old guard of diehard monarchists to the fellow-travellers of the thirties. Though both were thin on the ground these days, there was still a peculiar species of egghead who could bore for Britain on the subject of the Soviet Union at the drop of a hat. It was the most attacked, the most defended, and the most mythic country on earth, that about which we knew least and talked most. People turned out for Russia.

'If this lot are meant to be indicative of the tone or content of this hullaballoo,' Troy said, 'I'm leaving now. It's beginning to look like a freak show. I take it Lawrence has dug up some new scandal on the USSR? And the gathering of the clans is meant to celebrate the cocking up of another Five Year Plan or something equally silly?'

'Bear with me,' said his brother. 'There's more to it than a handful of old fools and clapped-out hacks.'

At the back of the room Troy caught sight of one of the few people he would still listen to on the matter of the Soviet Union. Seated on a foldaway chair, Homburg far back on his head, eyes closed as though snatching a nap mid-morning, was his Uncle Nikolai, Troy's father's younger brother. The last of the Troitsky brothers, and the only one to accompany Troy's father to England. He looked old to Troy, though he could not say with any certainty how old he was.

The old man's consistent opposition to all Russian regimes, from Nicholas II to Lenin and Stalin, to Khrushchev and Bulganin, had enabled him to keep intact his wartime role as British Intelligence's man on ships and planes and bombs and rockets, right into the peace, and right past his retirement, despite his obvious Anarchist leanings. He received a 'clearance' that was in all probability denied to Troy, a serving copper, and to Rod, a former Government minister and, if the Tories blew the election in 1960, most certainly the next Foreign Secretary. Nikolai had given up his chair in Applied Physics at Imperial College, but hung onto his office and a fellowship, hung onto his advisory role. Nobody knew more about ships and planes and bombs and rockets; his mind was an attic cluttered with the dust of these horrors. A mind that was much like his father's—Troy's grandfather's—tending to dust off the attic at unexpected moments and wheel out something arcane, to interrupt a conversation with a diversionary tack—the wooden horse of physics, the abandoned rag doll of pre-Soviet history. His grandfather would suddenly burst with nostalgia and reminiscence, bringing meals and conversations to a juddering halt. Even Troy's father, Alexei Rodyonovich, that garrulous piss artist, could be silenced by unanswerable interjections from the elder generation, a Slavic rumble from deep in the enveloping beard and tunic. Nikolai was more focused, arcane it might be, or amusing, or important, or deadly accurate. He had the unsparing knack of putting lives to rights in a sentence or two without even recourse to 'you know what your trouble is?' Troy added it silently to many things the old man threw at them, and he was pretty sure Rod did the same.

Troy felt Rod nudge him. Lawrence had appeared in front of the lectern and was waving for silence with a piece of paper, Chamberlain-style.

'For many weeks now, we have all of us been hearing rumours, emanating from the Soviet Union, concerning a secret speech made at the Twentieth Party Congress by Nikita Khrushchev. Details of this speech have been speculated upon since February, and I think I speak for Fleet Street when I say that it is now widely believed that Khrushchev used this secret session to denounce Stalin. I can tell you now that this is true.'

Somewhere in the ranks of the cognoscenti a raspberry was blown, and a second voice said simply 'Big deal'. This was hardly news.

'I can tell you,' Lawrence went on, 'because I have obtained a copy of the speech.'

No one sneered. The press ranks exploded with cries of 'How?', 'Where from?'

Lawrence carried on regardless. He had their attention now. They'd all been upstaged and they knew it.

'From, shall I say, sources overseas.'

Lawrence had a simple code. Russia itself would be 'unnamed sources', a contrived British leak would be 'friendly sources', and the US was always 'sources overseas'. So, Lawrence had a nark in the State Department? This should not surprise the hacks. What was surprising was that this should be Khrushchev's way of leaking the truth. Who did *he* have in the State Department? It was a neat trick—it had in-built deniability. Khrushchev could leak it and deny it at the same time. Lawrence's sense of theatrical timing gave the hacks a minute or two of hubbub before he closed in for the kill.

'The full text will be published in the *Post* this Sunday. All 26,000 words of it. In the meantime I can tell you something of the atrocities denounced by Khrushchev. There are some truly shocking revelations. I think we have known for some long time now that history is unlikely to offer a larger rollcall of the dead. Khrushchev does not deal in figures. Indeed I doubt that we or he will ever know the full carnage of the Yezhovshchina, but he deals in methods and principles—the methods of Stalin's madness and the principles of his paranoia.'

Lawrence rattled on. Troy looked at Rod. His face said, 'I told you so,' and his lips formed the words seconds after Troy had read them in his eyes.

'Told me what?'

'It's a hoot. It's a coup.'

'No it's not.'

'How so? It means Khrushchev was serious about peaceful coexistence. Or are you going to insult me in your habitual fashion and tell me that "he's just another politician"?'

'Worse, Rod. He's an actor.'

'Eh?'

'I saw a wee bit more of the man than you did, and take it from me, he's Grimaldi and Alec Guinness rolled into one.'

Lawrence was almost through with his press-tease, saying nothing and something at the same time, and he ended by quoting Khrushchev's own words.

"Comrades, we must abolish the cult of the individual decisively, once and for all." And if you want any more, you'll have to buy the *Post*. Thank you, gentlemen.'

Lawrence stepped down to half-hearted applause, beaming with pleasure. He had pulled off a coup, stuck one to the rest of Fleet Street *en masse* and he knew it. Every editor on the street would have killed for that speech. Most of them would run it in full just as Lawrence was doing, revelling in the showmanship, knowing full well that not one reader in fifty would get halfway through it. Troy made a mental note to buy the *News of the World* instead. Comrade K could not compete with tits and bums and wayward vicars, the rightful, the traditional subjects of the English Sunday papers, as British as the fish and chips they would be wrapping by next Tuesday.

From behind them Troy heard a sigh that seemed to bear the weight of history on its breath, an infinite weariness, the like of which Troy had not heard since the days of his grandfather. It could only be Nikolai. They both turned at the same time. Rod and Troy looked at their uncle, his head resting on the wall, the brow of his Homburg pointing skyward, his eyes looking up to the heaven in which he surely did not believe.

'Nikolai,' Rod said, softly, with caution. 'Are you all right?'

'I am fine, my boy,' he said without looking at either of them. 'It is you and yours I fear for, not myself. Stalin is dead—long live Stalin.'

'Eh?' said Rod for the both of them. It struck Troy as the most logical response he could make.

'Do you know why Khrushchev will not enumerate the Soviet Book of the Dead? Do you know why he will not add up the millions upon millions? Do you know what this man did in the first years after the war?'

The question did not seem to either of them to require an answer.

'Stalin regarded anyone who had allowed themselves to be captured by the Germans as a traitor. He ordered returning prisoners of war to be interrogated, and an arbitrary number of them to hanged. Guilty or innocent, he did not care; but enough should be hanged to let the people know the power of their leader. This man, Nikita Sergeyevich Khrushchev, hanged his fellow countrymen in countless numbers. His denunciation of the monster Stalin comes ten years too late to be believed.'

In the midst of the hubbub, the room-filling buzz of ardent hacks whose hands had quickly tired of clapping, there opened up a silence which seemed to engulf the three of them.

'There's no such thing,' Rod said gently. 'It can never be too late. Khrushchev has done now what was right. Regardless of what he might have done in the past.'

Again the heaven-bound, world-weary, earth-sent sigh.

'Regardless?' he queried. 'I find it impossible to disregard such things. What he did then is surely indicative of what he will do next. My country

—our country, though I know you boys haff never seen it—has become a country of programmed change. Each change is a rewriting of the history of what has gone before. Each change has meant a new set of victims, a new herd of scapegoats to be staked out in the sun. Do you really think this will be different? Do you really think this is anything we haff not seen before? There may not be show trials—that, after all, would seem to run against the grain of what the man is saying—but for all that do you not think that heads will roll? That purges will surely follow, that there will once more be disposable people, that the little people will suffer? In sloughing off the guilt of a generation onto one man, Khrushchev has accepted the cult of personality even as he would seem to reject it. But the one man is dead so the burden will fall on those who served him. Little people.'

'Apparatchiks,' said Troy.

'People,' said Nikolai.

'Apparatchiks,' said Troy.

'People like you and me. Little people, caught in the tide of a history they could neither make nor unmake.'

'Don't ask me to care about apparatchiks,' Troy said, ignoring the slow pressure of Rod's foot on his. 'There's nothing on earth could make me care.'

If nothing else, Troy had seized the old man's attention. He had lowered his eyes from heaven and was looking at Troy with a deep sadness in his eyes.

'Perhaps,' Nikolai said slowly, 'perhaps, they are not people like you and me. Perhaps I am wrong. What distinguishes us from them but the matter of choice? And if there was one thing your father's genius did for us all, to say nothing of his money, it was that he gave us choice. Me as much as the two of you. These are people who know no choice. If I were Khrushchev's head of KGB, I would not bank on collecting my pension, but if I'd been one of his apparatchiks, as you insist they are, under Josef Stalin, I would now fear for my life. Believe me, heads will roll. This denunciation is but prelude to another purge. The dead will pile up in heaps uncountable yet again. This is not freedom. Your man is wrong about that. This is the false dawn before the new nightmare. We are a long way from freedom.'

Rod seemed flabbergasted, speechless, but had stopped treading on Troy's foot in the vain hope of shutting him up.

'You know,' said Troy, picking his words brutally. 'You might as well ask me to care about the fate of the guards at Auschwitz.'

Nikolai got to his feet, shrugged off Troy's unanswerable remark. He made his way slowly, painfully, towards the door. He stopped. The very posture, the angle of his head and body, betrayed the action of memory at work. Then he turned and spoke, looking at them with a sad air of mourning about him, his voice scarcely audible.

'I considered all the oppressions that are done under the sun: and behold the tears of the oppressed, and they had no comforter; and on the side of their oppressors there was power; but they had no comforter.'

The old man's voice rose, the softness of tone vanishing in a burst of anger, hammering out the verse with a hard emphasis.

'Wherefore I praised the *dead* which are already *dead* more than the living which are yet alive. Better is he than both they, which haff not yet been, who haff not seen the evil work that is done under the sun.'

Nikolai walked slowly out, leaning heavily on his walking stick, and did not look back.

'Good God,' said Rod. 'What was that? Lear on the blasted heath?'

'It was the Old Testament,' Troy replied. 'Don't ask me which book. Even old atheists can't escape their upbringing.'

'Do you think we've upset him?'

'Yes—but for once I don't care. He can't ask us to shed a tear for the jobsworths of Russia. I couldn't give a damn about his apparatchiks any more than I could about all the spooks from Torquay to Timbuctoo and back again. And I cannot conceive of the force that could make me. He's wrong, and that's all there is to it.'

§23

He lunched with Inspector Wildeve, who yawned his way through canteen meat and two veg and seemed to hear very little of what Troy had to say. Troy did his best to sort out what mattered from what did not. Jack could complain till he was blue in the face about a workload that kept him from his bed until four in the morning, there was little Troy could do about that. With a fortnight's leave due to him—the first since Christmas—he did not intend to let Jack's whingeing deflect him from it. What mattered was that he had clicked with Clark, that Clark had significantly eased the workload of which he complained so bitterly. Indeed, towards the end of a bowl of canteen rice pud, and a cup of murky tea, Jack was willing to admit that his Yard duties had kept him at it until only midnight, after which he felt like some fun and had squandered sleep and salary in a West End nightclub. Jack had been slow growing up. He was thirty-six, a bachelor, and burning the candle at both ends, much as he had done when he and Troy first met nearly fifteen years ago. Troy was not sympathetic. He did not frequent the clubs of Soho, and only occasionally ventured into its pubs.

In the evening, on his way home, after a desk-clearing operation designed to leave him unmolested for the next fortnight by anything more demanding than a pig or a parsnip, he just fancied a pub, and a drink, just the one in each case. What he did not fancy was walking so much as twenty yards out of his way to find one. And so, eight-thirty found him pushing open the side door of the Salisbury.

The usual patrons of the Salisbury were out-of-work actors. Loud voices and sweeping gestures were the house style. On a bad night you had to fight your way in through a few dozen monologuing, name-dropping hams, and the occasional stage door Johnny waiting for the stage door to open in a couple of hours' time. The man at the bar in the creased white shirt was singular in his stillness and silence. It was the doyen of stage door Johnnies—Johnny Fermanagh. Troy almost turned on his heel and walked out, but the poise of the man, the concentration in his stillness, stirred his curiosity. He walked over to the bar. Johnny stood with his palms on the bar, arms braced straight, head down, staring intently at an empty pint glass and a full shot glass of whisky. So, he was on beer and a shot. A textbook example of how to get roaring pissed in the shortest possible time.

Johnny did not move. Did not seem even to have noticed Troy.

'What's up?' Troy said to the barman.

'Don't ask me. It's been going on for more than an hour.'

'What has?'

Before the barman could answer Johnny let out a strangled cry, his head shook and his right hand crept slowly out towards the glass of whisky, then with the speed of a hungry snake he knocked it back in one, slammed the glass back on the bar and groaned like a beast in pain.

'Aaaaaghhhhhhh! Nya, nya, nya. Yeworrayeworrayeworra. Same again, Spike.'

The barman topped up both glasses. At last Johnny seemed to have noticed Troy.

'Freddie, old horse. Stick around, I'll be with you in a jiffy.'

He hitched up his shirt-sleeves by their silver armbands, pulled his tie down an extra inch or two to dangle at the third button and reassumed the pose. The face twitched a little as he sought composure, then the right hand aimed at the pint, sank it in a single, ten-second gulp, and once again he proceeded to stare at the shot glass.

Spike spoke confidentially to Troy. 'Thing is, Mr Troy. He'll eyeball it a while, then he'll scream, then he'll knock it back, and then he'll look like it chokes him and order another. This is round four. Seconds out.'

'Do you think there's a point to it?'

'Search me.'

Minutes passed. Troy could hear a ham in the back of the room doing what sounded like a bad impression of Robert Newton, punctuated by the constant clink of glasses and the ever-present cry of 'Darling'. Johnny pulled back, still staring at the glass of whisky. Slowly he drew himself up into some sort of drunk's dignity, and waved the glass away with his hand.

'Done, done. Get thee behind me, single malt! Take it away. Take it away!'

'Did I hear you right?' said the barman.

Johnny reached up to the pegs and was slipping on his jacket.

'Yes, yes. I'm through with the demon drink. Give it to one of these poor thesps. Drink it yourself. I don't care.'

He turned his sights on Troy once more.

'Tea, tea,' he said. 'Let's go to your house and drink tea.'

'On the slate, Johnny?' the barman asked.

'No,' said Johnny. 'No more slate. No more tick. No more *mañana*. Tell me the sum outstanding and I shall write you a cheque at once.'

He reached into his jacket pocket and pulled out a Mullins Kelleher chequebook, its cheques the size of a pocket handkerchief, its script a florid pre-war copperplate.

'Twelve pounds, three shillings and ninepence, Johnny.'

Inwardly Troy winced. Who in their right mind would run up a bill that size just for booze? But Johnny wrote out a cheque, tore it off the stub as though he relished the sound, and presented it to Spike with a flourish.

'Free,' he said. 'Free, free, free.'

He turned, aimed for the door and walked his drunkard's crooked walk to the street. Troy followed, wondering what this could be about. Rather than giving booze away, it was Johnny's habit to scrounge it off anyone with the price of a round. Troy did not think he'd ever seen him walk away from a full glass before.

'There's the rub,' said Johnny. 'The very point. The glass was full. I am not.'

They crossed St Martin's Lane, into Goodwin's Court and up to Troy's front door.

'Not full, perhaps, but pissed just the same,' said Troy with his hand on the key.

'Pissed, pissed—but hardly the same.'

'Do I get a prize if I spot the difference?'

He let Johnny flop into an armchair while he put on the kettle. He could have his cup of char and then Troy would throw him out.

'What are you up to?' he asked as he poured.

Johnny pulled himself back from reverie, smiled, gazed into his cup and looked up at Troy, dark eyes lost in a messy forelock of black hair. He swept the hair from his eyes, a gesture Troy had seen his sister perform so many times.

'Any fool can give up the booze when he's sober.'

Not a bad point, thought Troy.

'The trick is to give it up with a glass in front of you. If I can walk away and leave a glass on the bar, then I know I can go the whole damn hog. D'ye see?'

'I see that it gets you tight of a Friday night, just like any other Friday night.'

'It's the only way, the only way. You order beer and a shot. You drink the beer. Only when you can leave the shot glass full and walk away with the beer inside you do you know that you've got willpower, and without willpower you've got bugger all.'

'But you had to drink four pints to get there.'

'Four pints and three shots of malt!'

113

'Which is why you're pissed.'

'Absofuckinlutely. Pissed? Of course I'm pissed. But never again. That's it. *Finito!*'

'Drink your tea,' Troy said.

Johnny sipped at his cup of Best Orange Pekoe and pulled a face.

'I'm going to have to get used to this, aren't I?'

'You've made your bed,' Troy said. 'What puzzles me is why?'

'Hmm,' said Johnny.

'Do you know I pulled your record from CRO a while back? Just to see how many times you've been done for Drunk and Disorderly.'

'Go on. Amaze me.'

'Fifty-seven times.'

'I should copyright it. Sue the blokes who can the beans.'

Johnny thought his joke hilarious and disappeared into a drunken cackle.

'Do you remember your first?' Troy asked.

'Could I forget it? November 1934. My first term at Oxford. Courtyard of Wadham. Climbed in late. Bit of a tussle with a porter. The beak fines me five bob for D & D, the college stings me for a guinea and reminds me I'm pissing all over traditions going back as far as my great-great-grandfather and blahdey blahdey blah.'

'Instead,' Troy went on, 'you've set up a twenty-two-year tradition of reckless pissery.'

'And now it's over.'

Johnny pushed himself up from his seat. Propped himself up on the mantelpiece, breathing deeply and making an effort at sobriety. He stared into the wall only inches from his eyes.

'If you'd had my old man, Freddie, you'd have been a piss artist too.'

'What is it that makes you finally want to bury the old bugger now? He's been dead eleven years.'

Johnny drew a deep breath. Turned to look at Troy.

'The love of a good woman,' he said.

The trouble with clichés is that they all begin as truth. Only excess of use ever leads one to think that they are other than true. Every so often, against the odds, someone will use one with a straight face, or a straight pen, and with a bit of luck and the wind behind them they will disinter the original truth long since buried. Troy knew he should not laugh—not so much as a snigger. Johnny, transparently, believed every word of his cliché. But what woman in her right mind, good or downright malevolent, would take on Johnny? Some title-grubbing, gold-digging hag who'd put up with a raving husband in exchange for being addressed as Marchioness? Some sorry-for-drunk self-martyring silly cow?

'Might I ask who?'

'Can't tell you, o' man. Wish I could, but I can't.'

'I see.'

'Do you, Freddie? Do you?'

'A married woman, I take it?'

'Oh. You do see. How d'ye know?'

'Just guessing.'

'Give me a little while to get things sorted. I just need a while. Or truth to tell she needs a while, not me. Just to get sorted. Then I'll tell you. I'd love to tell you now. But I can't. It's all over between her and her husband. They've been out of love for years. But she has to tell him, you see. She has to tell him. I can't say anything until she does.'

A friend could say only one thing. And Troy was a friend, wasn't he? This was how he had come to regard Johnny by a process of attrition. Frequency and familiarity wearing away hostility. The friend as furniture? A dozen variations, but only one essential thing for a friend to say. Two of them sprang readily to mind.

'Well done, Johnny. Congratulations.'

Johnny smiled and blushed. He really seemed to be happy, far from his common condition.

'I'm very happy, Freddie. She makes me happy. I haven't felt like this since I was a boy.'

Troy envied this. He was never at all sure that he was happy. Certainly no other *person* made him happy.

'And I wanted to ask you . . .' Johnny let the sentence trail off. 'I wanted to ask you . . . about Diana.'

Mentally Troy began to ease him out. As quickly as he could he would physically ease him towards the door, out into the courtyard, out into the street. Out.

'About you . . . and Diana.'

'Johnny. You and I have known each other for ten years.'

'Have we?'

'You came up to me in the Muleskinners' Arms in the autumn of 1946. "I know you," you said. "You're the bloke that killed my sister."'

'Did I? I must have been out my skull. I'm most awfully sorry.'

'Think nothing of it. It is, after all, true. I did kill your sister. I cannot change that. But ever since you have assumed, it has been implicit in your conversations with me, that Diana and I were lovers. I have never said any such thing. None the less you have assumed it. It is a fixture in your mind, much as, until tonight, you were a fixture in half the bars in Soho. Why now, Johnny? Why do you choose to ask me now?'

'I have to know. Really, I have to know.'

Troy said nothing.

'I have to know that . . . somebody else can feel as I do. I don't want to think that this is a delusion peculiar to me. I've lived my life apart. Never been in the mill of things. A drunken lord, a music hall joke. There's hardly ever been a dash of normality about me. I don't know what's real. I don't know what I should feel. Only what I do. I'm left, after years of a bent existence, craving normality, about which I know bugger all, wishing to God I could grow up, straighten up, and fly right. And I don't know if I'm the only man ever to feel this.'

This, Troy thought, was why we read novels and poetry. To know that what we thought and felt were not total solipsisms of the mind and heart.

'Ask one of the marrieds, Johnny. We have plenty of friends who are married.'

'Name one.'

Troy could not.

'You can't do it because we haven't got 'em. Most people we know are like you and me. The marrieds paired off donkey's years ago. Who sees them any more? Who among us keeps the company of married men? I have to know. I have to know that you can feel as I feel. Otherwise I'm stuck inside of it like a starfish in a glass paperweight. A world of my own. That's the achievement of twenty-two years of reckless pissery. Help me, Freddie.'

Troy said nothing.

§24

Diana Brack tumbled through his dreams, dragged out of her hiding place in some cupboard in Troy's mind by her brother, yet again. He awoke to find himself with the beginnings of a foul mood, and to the Sunday papers on the mat.

It was a rash promise. Only to himself, but one he could not keep. Well before noon Troy had begun to wish he had nabbed the paper boy and bought a *News of the World* off him. The *Sunday Post* lay upon the wicker table on the verandah, a fat unreadable wadge. He read the first paragraph of Comrade K's message to mankind and yawned into his morning coffee. Guilt and salvation when what he needed was tit and titillation. Perhaps he would get out his bicycle and ride into the village for a copy of the *News*. On the other hand perhaps he'd just sit and yawn.

He was still yawning on his second cup of coffee when his sister Masha appeared out of nowhere. He had not heard a car on the drive. Rod had scratched his weekend, driven up for morning surgery on the Saturday and gone straight back to a meeting in London. Troy had been looking forward to being alone, except for the Fat Man. It was his motorbike he had been listening out for. How had he missed a car, and what was the damn woman doing here today?

'You bastard!'

Troy blinked at her, not much interested in what it was he might now be supposed to have done. She threw her hat at him.

'What have you been saying to Nikolai?'

'Me?'

'The pair of you! You unconscionable bastards! I had him on the phone Friday and yesterday in one of his tizzes. What have you and Rod been saying to him?'

Troy gathered his dressing gown around him. This was no way to spend his first Sunday morning off in six weeks. He picked up the *Sunday Post,* threw it towards her. She caught it with a little gasp, but didn't look at it.

'Here,' he said. 'You read it. I can't be bothered. And when you have, you go and talk to him about the fate of the little people. Of necessity and choice, of shoes and ships and sealing wax, of apparatchiks and kings, and why the sea is boiling hot and whether pigs have wings. See if you can't irritate him far more than I can.'

He left her clutching the paper and went back to the kitchen to make more coffee. On the kitchen table was a note from the Fat Man. Thick pencil on lined paper.

'Pig in Pudding Club. Your ole pal, . . .' Then a long scrawl which Troy took to be his signature. All he could make of it was that it was indeed very long.

Damn. He'd missed him. He must have come and gone before Troy was even up. 'Pig in Pudding Club.' Troy tried to work out the date. The gestation period of a pig is 117 days. That made it . . . September the . . . well, near enough the end of September. He'd have to remember that. It would be a shame to be in Aberdeen or Aberanywhere at that moment.

On his way back out he heard the telephone ring in his father's study. Then he heard Masha's voice answer. She was cooing unctuously. She could only be talking to her husband. Then the penny dropped. A husband. Not hers.

'Of course, darling. Of course. Well, I think Masha wants to take a walk through the woods this afternoon. I thought perhaps we'd make up some sandwiches and . . . what? No, he won't come. He'll stay at home with his blasted pig. I'll call you about five, shall I? Bye, Hughdey darling.'

Troy waited till she had finished and then crossed the room to the verandah. He did not care that she must know he had heard; he did not care what lies she told.

Masha reappeared next to him as he sat down and reclaimed her hat.

'Don't ask,' she said.

'I wasn't.'

'And don't judge.'

Which he certainly wasn't.

He heard Masha banging around in the house for another ten minutes or so, then he heard the scrunch of gravel as her car disappeared down the drive. He was just starting to wonder about the problem she had left him with if Hugh phoned back asking for Sasha, when the phone rang. If it were Hugh, he'd no idea what to tell the poor cuckolded sod.

It was Rod.

'Well, did you see it?'

'I could hardly miss it. It weighs as much as a side of bacon. Whatever happened to paper rationing?'

'No, not Khrushchev. Bugger Khrushchev. Page seven, bottom left. Got 'em! All I want now is the name!'

Troy rang off and turned to page seven. Any subject but Khrushchev would do, but all the same he had no idea what Rod was on about. Then he saw it. A small piece buried between a bit of Khrushchev and an advert for Horlicks.

'Sources close to Downing Street have revealed that Her Majesty's Government will make a Commons statement early next week on the matter of the Frogman Spy, following several questions tabled over recent weeks by Sir Rod Troy (Lab.—Herts. South), the Shadow Foreign Secretary. It is believed that the Prime Minister will admit the error, and offer an unreserved and full apology to the Soviet leader and to the captain of the *Ordzhonikidze*. It is understood that while the purpose of sending out a naval frogman was to test new experimental underwater equipment, the exercise was open to the wrong interpretation and is to be regretted.'

Fine, thought Troy and turned to Uncle Todger's gardening strip at the back of the paper.

'Aye up,' said a bubble coming from the lips of a caricature northern bloke on his allotment behind the mill, waistcoat, muffler, cloth cap on head, string around the knees of his tatty trousers. 'Did you know that now is the right time to make a second sowing of Cos lettuce so you can have lettuce right through the autumn? I thought not.'

This was more like it. In the absence of tit and titillation, Uncle Todger was infinitely preferable to Khrushchev or the Frogman Spy. Rod could keep the spooks and spookery. This was the real world of rhizomes and tubers, of scab and blackleg, of pricking out and earthing up, and putting horsemuck on rosebushes. Not that Troy was entirely sure what a rhizome was. All the same, he took Uncle Todger at his word, and as soon as he had bathed and dressed went down to the kitchen garden, took up the rake and hoe and made a fresh sowing of lettuce.

It was late afternoon before the telephone rang again. He was mentally striving for the last frame of Uncle Todger's strip—of every strip, on every Sunday—the scene of pastoral reconciliation in which he sits upon a barrel and puffs gently on his pipe, while Nature blooms abundant all around him, fed and watered by his own hand . . . all that's made to a green thought in a green shade. It was almost five, a sunny, moderately warm June afternoon, the height of the English summer, peaceful Sunday, blessed Sunday . . . bloody Sunday. He was not succeeding; the tooth and claw crouched waiting beneath the green and pleasant, and he was beginning to think that perhaps he and Uncle Todger were not cut from the same cloth. Where was Uncle Todger in the fury and the breaking thunder when it came to rage against the heavens? What price this Nuncle on the blasted heath? And—he was half expecting Masha to show up any minute and reinforce her sister's alibi. He picked up the phone, wanting it not to be Hugh in his cuckold's horns, and heard Jack's voice.

'I'm in the office.'

'On a Sunday?'

'Just clearing up a bit. Look, there's an airmail letter turned up for you. It's done the rounds a bit. It's dated last Tuesday. It was addressed to "Sergeant Troy", except that the "y"'s been smudged. It's ended up in your tray. Probably late yesterday. Shall I open it?'

'Yes.'

'It says "Hotel de l'Europe, Amsterdam. Till Thursday next week. Lois Teale." You don't know anyone called Lois Teale, do you?'

'No,' Troy lied. 'I don't.'

§25

Amsterdam is a city of concentric circles, of concentric canals. Prinsengracht, Keizersgracht, Herengracht and, as near to the middle as dammit, the Singel.

Troy had last been in Amsterdam as a child late in the 1920s. One of his mother's musical grand tours. A little night music in Vienna, on to Hannover to hear Walter Gieseking—in the days before his dubious, disgraceful association with the Nazis—play the entire Debussy *Preludes*, with *Estampes* thrown in for an encore, and ending in the Concertgebouw in Amsterdam and the full blast of Mahler's Second. He had no recollection of the Mahler, it had merged with a dozen other performances over the years, but to this day he had only to close his eyes and imagine the sound of the third *Etampe*, 'Jardins sous la pluie', to see Gieseking's huge frame and bald head bent over the keyboard, his giant's hands somehow producing the most delicate music he had heard in his young life. And when he saw Gieseking he saw not Hannover, but Amsterdam.

The war and occupation seemed to have left Amsterdam physically unscathed. A seventeenth-century mercantile city left intact by the blitzkrieg that destroyed Antwerp and Rotterdam, Coventry and Plymouth. It had none of the ambitious design of Hausmann's Paris, a city reshaped to the military column—he could not imagine the Dutch marching in columns. Nor was it the mess with occasional concession to scheme that London was—a city in which no grand scheme had ever run more than a few streets without merging once more into the chaos that was natural to it.

Tall, narrow houses, no two alike it would seem, squeezed each other for room on the canal banks—odd shapes, uneven heights, gables sharp as steeples, some tilting at precarious angles—the city seemed to Troy to loom over him, to wrap itself around him, to contain him and thrust him at its heart. Accordingly, he found himself on the innermost circle, the bull's-eye, as it were, at a sharp curve in the Singel at about five in the afternoon, on the day following the cryptic airmail letter. He presumed a degree of secrecy and so did not telephone ahead. He presumed also that Lois Teale would be expecting him. He looked up at the outside of the Hotel de L'Europe, seven storeys of red brick, edged in white and topped by a Hollywood-scale sign, rising to a host of dormer points, St Pancras in miniature, hesitant, wondering what he might find. June light danced on the water of the Singel. It had been a blazing, blistering summer's day, one of those days when the canals turned to glass and lit the city from below, creating a mixture of spotlight and shadow, a dappled city, revealing as much as it hid.

He could leave now. He could turn right around, get on one of those creaking old trams and go back to the Central Station, the way he had come. He could pretend that he had never received the airmail letter. He could learn the lesson of youth, admit he had grown up a bit, and not get involved again.

A flower-seller was pitching his wares from a wooden cart, only a few feet away. An eye-catching display of summer's reds and yellows and blues, against the flaking Balmoral green of the old wagon. There had been one much like it on almost every corner. The flower-seller eyed Troy expectantly.

'Why not buy her some flowers?' the flower-seller asked in English. Two assumptions in a single expression, so put as to make Troy instantly self-conscious. Was he really so transparent? Did the look on his face say 'woman'? Worse, did it say it in English? He had no idea what to buy. To buy tulips seemed nothing less than corny.

'Yes,' he said. 'Roses. A dozen white roses.'

As English a choice as he could make, a dozen York roses. Since, he was, it seemed, so recognisably English.

He crossed the iron bridge to the other bank, a few feet nearer the heart, walked into the lobby of the hotel and asked for Miss Teale. Did he mean Mrs Teale? There was a Mrs Teale in 601. Yes, he was sure he did. An American lady? They would have to ring up. No visitor could be admitted unannounced. Mrs Teale had been quite insistent on the point.

He tapped lightly on the door of 601. It opened at once, an inch or two of light showing, a face in shadow thrust to the crack, a brown eye peeking at him.

'That you, baby?'

'Yes.'

'I—er—I need a minute. And we're right out of the hard stuff. Could you go round the block to a liquor store and get me a quart of Jack Daniels?'

The door shut on him before he could argue a syllable.

Back across the iron bridge, he asked directions of the flower-seller and two side streets away found a liquor store which had very expensive, imported bottles of Wild Turkey. It would have to do.

He gave her a full quarter of an hour and tapped on her door again. Her voice answered faintly from inside.

'It's open. You can come in.'

She stood between two double beds, facing him, back to the window, curtains half drawn to whittle down the daylight to a single shaft aimed at him, framed in the doorway, lit as by a natural spotlight. The room resolved into vision for him, and he saw that daylight was not the only thing aimed at him. The thing in her hand was a small automatic, a .25 Beretta or some such, the classic woman's gun, tailor-made for the handbag.

She was dressed in a neat Chanel deep-blue two-piece, oh-so-high heels, a nervous, flickering grin on her face, that failed to make the evolution to a smile, her blonde hair bobbed, her fathomless, fleckless brown eyes staring at him.

'Long time no see,' she said, lowering the gun.

'Yes. It's been a while.'

'You can close the door now.'

He kicked it to with his foot. She put the safety on and dropped the gun on the bed behind her.

'Had to be sure. You see that, don't you?'

Troy was not at all sure what he saw. He felt encumbered, bourbon in one hand, flowers in the other, and neither seeming much to matter any more. He put them gently down on a chair and moved slowly round her in an arc towards the heavy brocade curtain. She turned as he moved. He grabbed the curtain with one hand, her arm with the other and pulled. The shaft of light became a flood and he drew her to him, cupped her face with one hand and rubbed his thumb across her cheek. He knew now why she had stalled him, why the curtains had been drawn. The cheek was thick with make-up. She squirmed and yelled but before she had pulled free he had seen the bruises, purple ringed in yellow. He caught the hand that came at him spread to slap. Two of the fingernails had been half torn off, the pulpy flesh beneath bright pink and swollen.

'What the hell is going on?'

She lurched across the room and picked up the first thing to hand. A dozen white roses hurtled at him, followed by the bourbon. He caught the flowers in his right hand and the bourbon neatly in his left.

She flung herself at him, hands flailing. She caught him a couple of stingers round the ear. A clenched fist to the diaphragm almost winded him. He found himself encumbered once more, the flowers and the bourbon had simply changed hands. He drew her to him, smothered her anger in a clumsy half-embrace, like hugging someone in too many overcoats and outsize mittens.

She kicked his shins, but he simply tightened his grip until she stopped moving altogether. It seemed to him that minutes passed, before she moved again. He had no idea how long. He could hear the sounds of traffic in the street, the occasional hoot of a barge on the canal, and when they were silent all he could hear was the thumping of her heart.

'Troy, Troy, Troy, Troy, Troy,' she said into his chest.

'Tosca,' he said, looking down at the top of her head. 'Or do I call you Mrs Teale?'

She wriggled, tilted her head up at him. One clear brown eye peeping out, a teardrop poised in the corner. Her voice rough and throaty, as New York as lox and cream cheese.

'Tosca, schmoshca. What's in a name?'

§26

It had been a wet night in the winter of 1944. The last bombs of the 'Little Blitz'. His second meeting with M/Sgt Larissa Tosca WAC. The first counted for little. He remembered feeling sodden and miserable, on the verge of giving up, when he had caught sight of her, making her way from Ike's Overlord HQ in St James's Square to her billet in Orange Street. Not that he knew it was Orange Street, or he would not have tried to follow her, would not have wasted time, would not have had her turn on him, first accusing then challenging him.

The challenge was sex—she assumed, she had told him, that he was following her because he fancied his chances. He had no way now of knowing whether this was true or not, and perhaps it didn't matter. He had tumbled willingly if clumsily into her bed less than half an hour later, and so embarked on a perilous course that had damn near cost him his life, and if the Yard had ever found out about his liaison with a witness, his job too.

He had been seduced, in every conceivable sense of that word, by this pocket Venus, this pizza-toting, bourbon-guzzling, much-hyphenated Italian-American, a Manhattan moll born and brought up on Spring Street, wise-cracking, foul-mouthed, Bowery-brash and brassy—and utterly, completely, totally false.

At the height of summer, almost exactly this time twelve years ago—8 or 9 June, he thought—she had vanished, leaving her Orange Street billet swamped in her own blood, and he had reported her dead. Jack had been with him, but when push came to shove, Jack was the most reliable person he knew, the best of lieutenants, and he knew to ask no questions.

Then in the winter of 1948 M/Sgt Larissa Tosca WAC, Italian-American, had surfaced once again in a Berlin locked in Stalin's iron fist—just when he needed a guardian angel—mysteriously transformed into the Russian-American Major Larissa Dimitrovna Toskevich KGB, NKVD? P&O? . . . or whatever initials the Cheka had had at that time. He could not keep track, and if there was one thing that characterised secret police all over the world it was that they were alphabetically mobile, changing initials at whim, it seemed.

Tosca had helped him trap Jimmy Wayne, alias John Baumgarner, the most elusive criminal Troy had ever set his sights on. Christmas Day 1948, and from that day to yesterday, the Sunday Jack had read Lois Teale's air-mail letter out loud to him, he had heard not a whisper of her—Tosca, Toskevich, Teale—what, indeed, was in a name?

§27

Troy woke late in the morning, nearer eleven than ten. The heap in the bed opposite did not move. Larissa/Lois Tosca-Toskevich-Teale was sleeping soundly. Late the previous night she had pointed him to his own bed and said she was exhausted.

'You don't mind, do you?'

'Mind,' he had said. 'What's to mind?'

'Separate beds. Separate beds is to mind. But—'

'It's all right, I understand.'

'Do you Troy? Do you?'

He had tried to persuade her out for the evening and failed. She had not wanted to leave the room, had not left it in a week.

'How do you manage?' he had asked.

'Room service. I live off the delivery menu. I been all the way through the damn thing once already. I'm back to cold roast chicken again. I've eaten more pickled herring than Moby Dick. I could kill for pepperoni and mozzarella pizza or spaghetti vongole or even just a warm bagel.'

So they sat on the floor, backs against the matching beds, tore apart a whole roast chicken, which he downed with Perrier and she with slugs of bourbon. There were a thousand questions he wanted to ask, but he doubted he'd get answers to a single one, so instead he let her ask a thousand questions and did his best to answer them all. Until they came full circle, once more through another menu.

'You were famous for a while, d'y'know that?'

'Even in the Soviet Union?'

'The Man Who Shot Jimmy Wayne. Quite a reputation.'

'It sounds like a good title for a cowboy film. But I didn't.'

'You didn't shoot him?'

'No. Why would I shoot him?'

'I heard you went up against him at Heathrow armed with a handgun. And he pulled a gun on you, and you winged him.'

'Not the way it happened. High Noon At Heathrow isn't exactly the English way, is it?'

'Glad to hear it. And that's an *awful* title for a movie.'

'I did have a gun. A necessary precaution. But I also had six armed constables surrounding the plane he was on. And I didn't have to shoot him for the simple reason he wasn't armed.'

'How d'he die? I know he never made it to the gallows.'

'Suicide.'

'Well, KGB gossip got that right. Hang himself with his suspenders?'

'Cyanide capsule in one of his teeth. A legacy of his time in Berlin I should think. As soon as the Old Bailey handed down the sentence, he was put in a paddy wagon to be taken back to Brixton prison. He was handcuffed, but there should still have been someone in the van with him. Lazy sods rode up front so they could smoke and natter. He was dead when they opened the door at Brixton. If the trial hadn't been in camera there would have been one hell of a row, but—hang on a minute, it was in camera, how did you know he was dead?'

'We leaked it. Did you think I helped you catch him for old times' sake? The British tried him in camera, fairly predictable after all. To try a CIA killer in public would put the last nail in the coffin of the special relationship. But we had our sources and we leaked it. Every newspaper in the western world knew Wayne was on trial and for what. Some of the French papers ran it for a day or two till the fist came down. Too late by then. We'd sown the seed of doubt. Probably more valuable as rumour than if Fleet Street had printed it in full. You were lucky not get the Order of Lenin.'

He got out of bed and tugged at the curtains. Another cloudless June morning. The bourbon bottle lay on its side, half-empty. The roses lay on the dressing table, sad and wilting where she had left them, petals fallen like giant snowflakes onto the lavender-coloured carpet. He didn't think he'd bother buying her flowers again. And if she could drink like that he didn't think he'd buy her bourbon again either. He pulled the sheet gently off her. Still she did not wake. He looked at her. She was thin, almost wasted by comparison with her old self. A stone or so underweight. It looked to him as though she'd been eating badly and too little and as though she had not seen the sun in a long time. He had vivid, tactile memories of the curve of her backside—it was one of the great backsides—which now seemed flattened, and the muscles of her calves seemed slack, and her back was a mass of bruises as bad as the ones she buried under pancake on her face. He'd seen such marks a hundred times in the course of the job—a good kicking to the kidneys.

He washed, shaved and dressed and came back to find that she had not moved. Only now her eyes were open.

'Get up.'

'Nuuuhh?'

'Get up. We're going out.'

'Out?'

'You can't stay in this room for ever.'

'Wanna bet?'

Tosca dragged herself to the bathroom naked, and emerged fully clothed, with another thick layer of make-up to her face, pulling a glove over the torn fingers of her right hand. She did not seem to bother with the left.

'What d'ya have in mind?'

'Lunch. We'll go to lunch. And we'll talk.'

All Troy wanted was a clean, well-lighted place. A view of the canal would be nice. Any canal, it didn't matter which. But all the way out, on every corner Tosca was looking over her shoulder, checking in the reflections of shop windows in an atrocious parody of fugitive caution.

'Stop it,' Troy said.

'Stop what?'

'All this cloak and dagger nonsense. If the person you think is following us is any good you won't spot him, and if he isn't, I'd've spotted him pretty quick myself.'

They had stopped by some law of serendipity outside a small café on the Prinsengracht. Troy decide to look no further and all but dragged her inside. To appease her they took a window table. Troy could see to the next bend in the canal one way, Tosca the other. She waved away the menu and ordered 'coffee, black, lots of it'.

'Who do you think is following you?' he asked.

Tosca said nothing, did not return his gaze and made tramlines on the tablecloth with her fork.

Troy wondered how to break the silence. Her right hand let go of the fork and disappeared below the table. Glove or no glove he assumed she was acting upon an instinct to hide it, but the hand came up again clutching her handbag.

'I got a letter for you.'

'A letter? For me?'

'Well, a note really.'

'From whom?'

He had a momentary, illusory vision of long-lost cousins he'd never met and never heard of somehow encountering Tosca in the lost domain of family history that was the Union of Soviet Socialist Republics. She fished into her handbag and brought out a tiny piece of paper folded over many times.

'Burgess.'

'*Guy* Burgess?'

'Yeah. I got to know him pretty well, he gets bored easy, never really learnt Russian. He used to take me out drinking just to have a conversation in English.'

'And you and Guy Burgess talked about *me*?'

'Well, no, not exactly. I guess your name came up at some point. I mean most of the time he wanted to talk about England, he loved the fact that I'd lived there. That I'd not been there for a good five years before he split didn't seem to matter, just to know the same bars and restaurants was enough. We ran through the names of everyone we knew there till he found a name we had in common. I never thought it would be you. He said if I was ever in England I should give you this.'

'When did he say this?'

'Christmas before last.'

Troy held out his hand for the note, but she unfolded it and began to read.

'Hold on. I can't ... it says something like please send one dozen jars ... jeezus it looks like ... pappum papperum. Jeez, I dunno. Anyway that's the stuff he wants you to send him. I guess it's the English equivalent of a Hershey bar. You miss 'em like hell, then the first one you get you damn near barf and wonder what you ever saw in them.'

Troy snatched the scrap of paper from her. It read 'Patum Pepperium', in Burgess's upright, loopless hand, his letters stiff and straight like lead soldiers in their box—the opposite of the man himself. Patum Pepperium, an anchovy paste which called itself 'the Gentleman's Relish', much as Heinz boasted of its fifty-seven varieties. Burgess gave an address at the Moskva Hotel and sent his best wishes. Troy screwed up the note and dropped it in the ashtray.

'No,' he said, 'Guy can go fuck himself for his Patum Pepperium.'

'If Burgess could fuck himself, he'd be the happiest man alive. As things are, he's one of the unhappiest.'

'Bad as that, eh?'

'If you ever defect, defect to Paris or Monte Carlo—not Moscow, anywhere but Moscow.'

'I hadn't planned on it. Reminds me of a scrawl I once saw at Liverpool Street station. Where the sign says, "Harwich for the Continent", some wag had written, "And Paris for the Rest of Us" underneath.'

She smiled. Without nervousness, without forcing it. A natural reflex action. The first in the many hours they had been together.

'He's right, whoever he is. Burgess is holed up in his hotel, pissed half the time, watched all the time. It's no life.'

She paused to turn the tramlines she had scored on the white table-cloth into a chequerboard.

'Tell me,' she said, looking up. 'Do you remember when you were interrogating Diana Brack?'

He could scarcely believe she had raised the name, but the look in her eyes showed no anger, no sensibility that he too might feel anger, or remorse, or pain. He nodded.

'She said talking to the old British Socialists was like spending an evening with the guys who planned the bus routes or mapped out the sewers or something like that. Well, I've seen the Soviet Union from the top since then, and believe me, the damn woman was right. You could take a job lot of council clerks and town planners and dump them down in Moscow or Omsk or Tomsk—and they'd feel at home in ten minutes and Russia would feel at home with them. It's *the* bourgeois country, Troy. They've enshrined the practices of Middle England, even as they reject the values. They have a form for that, a Ministry of Circumlocution, a Department of Bumf. Jeezus, it's a miracle they achieve anything! Russia has become the natural home of the little guy with the rubber stamp. For every heroic, bleeding Stakhanovite you hear about, there's a dozen Mr Efficiencies running a world the borough surveyor from Fogtown and Bogshire would find recognisable. Praise the lord and pass the Turkey.'

'How did you stick it?'

'You sneering? Troy, you wouldn't be sneering, now would you?'

'It's an honest question. I've never been there—but it is the most fantasised, the most imagined country since Lilliput.'

She shrugged her shoulders, stirred the tablecloth chequers into messy, concentric circles with her fork. And suddenly he realised that he had unleashed the flood. He had no idea what he'd said to achieve this, perhaps it was not of his doing at all, perhaps he had Burgess to thank for breaking her silence? But she was talking.

'I guess I wasn't there a lot. The whole point in having someone like me who can pass for an American is to send 'em abroad. Mostly I played Western Europe. I spent a lot of time in Berlin, but I got pulled from there not long after you snatched Wayne. It was too public a place. Every other guy was a spy. There was a risk of me getting too well known. And when I was home I was well treated. Until '53, that is.'

''53? What happened in '53?'

'Stalin died. I thought you might have heard.'

'I don't quite see what you mean.'

'When the top man goes there's little guys all down the line who get reshuffled. It's like a house of cards or a row of dominoes. One tumbles, they all go. Although the death that mattered was Beria's. Once he was gone there was a purge of his people.'

'You mean you were one of Beria's people?'

'Not directly. Not in any real sense. I mean I never even met the guy. But reason is not the way these things operate. Somewhere up the line a guy I had worked for was held to be too much the Beria man, so he was out. So then they look down the line, I was his as he'd been Beria's. So while I wasn't out, I was downgraded, reassigned to safer stuff and my promotion was stopped. I'm still a Major. I been a Major for seven years. Since 1953 all I've been is a low-level courier in cities that are considered relatively safe like Paris or Brussels or Zurich, places that have never been carved up into zones, places where the concierge leans in a window smoking cheap cigarettes for the hell of it instead of noting everyone who passes for one goddam secret service or the other. I did that for three years, just shuffling packages around, live drops and *duboks*. Then this March they pulled me off it. I began to wonder if some defunct apparatchik in some prison somewhere hadn't fingered me to cut a deal for themselves. Or maybe Khrushchev's denunciation finally did for me. Old Joe is knocked off his pedestal and the domino ripple finally reached me, the last apparatchik in the stack. God knows, I don't. I wasn't just off the job, I was under arrest.'

'In the Lubyanka?'

'God, no. I don't think I was important enough for that, I wasn't even in Dzerzhinsky Square. I was in one of those cheap hotels the KGB have. If they have one they have twenty. Lock you in a room, beat the shit out of you, and no one will hear because the place is empty or else everyone else in every other room is getting the shit beaten out of them at the same time.

'You know what? They didn't even ask me questions. That's how unimportant I was. There was nothing they wanted to know. They just did it for the hell of it. They did it because it was their job, and they didn't feel they were doing it properly any other way.'

She held up the gloved hand and turned it slowly. Made a fist and dropped it back to the tabletop.

'As torturers go they weren't very inventive. At the end of April they decided to move me. God knows why. One hotel to another, but it meant crossing Moscow two days before May Day. Most of the time you could play baseball in the street in Moscow; there's almost no such thing as traffic or traffic jams. But Mischa and Little Yuri have been guarding me for a month. Yuri's OK but Mischa is a slob. Beats up on me because he likes it. The only reason he didn't fuck me too was because I told him he'd better kill me afterwards, 'cos if he didn't I'd never stop till I got him. So he hit me some more, pawed every part he could reach, but he didn't try and fuck me. Who knows, I could beat the rap and be back at work in a few weeks. It's been known to happen . . . I mean, pigs fly, Al Smith was a Republican. He wasn't going to take that risk. But crossing Moscow we meet a military convoy getting into position for May Day, and the traffic stops. Yuri's driving, I'm in the back with Mischa. Cocky bastard didn't even bother to cuff me—after all, where can I run to? And he decides a good way to pass the time in a traffic jam would be for me to suck him off. Get's his roscoe out and hard and says, "How about it?" Dumb cluck. I snapped his dick back with my right hand, snatched his gun with my left, then hit him in the throat as hard as I could. Yuri reaches into his jacket and tries to turn in the seat. I put the gun on him and said, "Yuri, do you really want to die just because this schmuck wanted his dick sucked?" He tosses his gun over the seat and says, "On your way." Mischa is unconscious or he fainted, I don't know, so Yuri throws in a "Good luck." I get out of the car and I walk away. Took me six weeks to get here. It was a month before I dared to leave Russia. I figured they'd look for me at every port or crossing for a week or two and then assume I'd got through and switch their resources. I wasn't that important any more. Then I came across Finland and down through Norway and Denmark. Nice and slow. But now comes the problem. I ask myself what I'd do if I had to track me. I wouldn't waste manpower and time on the land crossings, there's too damn many of them. I'd watch the one place I have to end up. I'd watch England, I'd watch the ports. If I really wanted Larissa Tosca back I'd have guys watching every ferry that docked at Dover or Folkestone or wherever. This is where I come unstuck. I've no plan to get myself across the water. I live by my wits, I live by plans and deceptions and I can't get around this one. The fuckers're gonna nab me the minute I set foot in England. And if I stay on the Continent, it's only a matter of time. The disguise that suited the KGB so well is the same one that makes me stick out like Paul Robeson at a Klan meeting. They're gonna get me. I know it.'

'Don't worry,' Troy said. 'I'll think of something.'

She simpered, smiled, almost contrived to blush, dipped her face and gazed up at him through fluttering eyelids.

'Gee, big boy—I was hoping you'd say that.'

He would have, he realised, to get used to being sent up.

§28

Back at the hotel, Tosca kicked off her shoes, took apart her vanity case, ripped up the false bottom and tipped out a dozen assorted passports into a heap on the carpet. They sat as they had most of the previous night, inches apart on the floor, like children playing.

'Now. Who am I? Take your pick. Lois Teale has had her day. Time to be somebody else.'

Troy picked one up off the pile.

'Greta Olaffssonn. Born 3 August 1912, Duluth, Minnesota.'

'Nah. I been Greta too many times.'

'Are they all fake? How did you get them?'

'Fake? Of course they're not fake. Most are got through the old trick. You find out the name of some poor kid who died very young, never applied for a passport, and you get one in her name with your face on it. Works every time. Greta never made it to her second birthday.'

Tosca picked up another and looked at the name.

'Clarissa Calhoun Breckenridge. Well, I never been her, but with a name like that is she from the Deep South or is she from the Deep South? I'd never manage the accent. And I don't know how to cook chitt'lins.'

She tossed it back on the pile. Troy picked it up.

'Born Hoboken, New Jersey, 22 August 1913,' he said.

'Well. Whaddya know? I could do Hoboken. It's Sinatra's hometown. It's only a spit and a ferry ride away from Manhattan. I'll have to remember that. Ole Clarissa could come in handy.'

Troy picked up another.

'Nora Schwartz. Born Chicago, 10 June 1911.'

'Nah. Don't like the name. If I'd been born Nora Schwartz I'd've changed it. Betty Boop, Minnie Mouse, anything but Nora Schwartz.'

'Larissa Dimitrovna Tosca. Born New York, 5 April 1911. This is yours. And it's still valid. This must be a fake. It's only four years old.'

'No. It's real. And Tosca's my real name too. It was all immigration could make of my old man's name. My last passport ran out in '52. I just took it to the American Embassy in Lisbon and got a new one.'

'But the Americans think you're dead. You died in a bloodbath in Orange Street in 1944.'

'Yeah. But apart from the guys I worked with at the time, why should anyone know that? Just 'cos you filled in a few forms at Scotland Yard and posted 'em off to Grosvenor Square? Troy, the world is not that efficient. Who matches births to deaths? It's the same as getting a ringer. You show up with the right face and the right papers, who gives a damn?'

Then, the penny dropped. He should have seen at once. Such a simple solution. The right face, the right papers, who gives a damn?

'Look. I think I've found the solution.'

'Aha?'

'You have to become British. We get you a British passport.'

'How do we do that?'

'You have to marry me.'

'Not the cutest proposal I ever received, I can tell you.'

'You have to marry me, because marriage confers citizenship. And once you're a citizen you can apply for your own passport. You enter Britain as Mrs Frederick Troy, British subject. Tosca no more, Greta no more. We'll marry in Vienna. We'll have to wait a few days, quite possibly more than a week, while the embassy issues a passport to you. Then we go into England through the back door.'

'Back door?'

'Ireland.'

'Why Ireland?'

'Because there's no immigration control between the republic and the mainland. And we fog the trail by stopping over at the Isle of Man. Ships from there are not counted as international. We dock at Liverpool at a domestic berth. No customs, no passports, and hence no reason for any of your spooks to be watching.'

'It'll work?'

'If we can get into Vienna without being spotted, yes.'

'And then what, a plane to where? Dublin?'

'Yes.'

Tosca stared at the carpet, then she looked him in the eye.

'Mrs Frederick Troy.' She enunciated the words very slowly.

They lapsed into silence. He filled it.

'It's just a convenience.'

She stared at him.

'It doesn't mean anything.'

'Liar,' she said.

She scooped up the passports and clutched them to her chest.

'It's OK. I'm game. But I don't see how we can work this scam from this side of the Channel.'

'I have a friend,' he said.

'Aha?'

'At our embassy in Vienna. Are you known in Vienna?'

'Nah. I never played Vienna. Too many goddam spooks.'

She fanned the passports out like a hand of cards and spread them on the carpet.

'Who am I?' she said.

'You'd better be yourself. That's a risk we have to take. The entry stamps on your passport would be useful, and the marriage and hence the citizenship will only be valid if you're Larissa Tosca. I can't marry you as Minnie Mouse or Betty Boop. There'd be no point. You have to enter Austria and marry as yourself.'

'I understand. But what I meant was, "Who Am I?" Capital W, capital A, capital I.'

'I don't understand.'

'Nor me. That's why I'm asking, Troy. Who Am I?'

§29

Gus Fforde was a rogue. A rogue, a wag and an old friend. He and Troy and Charlie had been schoolboys together. Charlie was the leader, Troy and Dickie Mullins very much the NCOs, and Gus the inspired, reckless subaltern. Fforde it was who had taught Troy how to disable a car by shoving a potato up the exhaust, how to blow out the down-pipe on a lavatory cistern with gun-cotton so that the next poor sod to flush the bog got a free shower, and how to catapult stink bombs in chapel. Of these, Troy had only found the first to be of any lasting value.

Fforde was also First Secretary at Her Britannic Majesty's Embassy in Vienna, capital of the newly reconstituted Austria—its democratic government only weeks old, the Russian and American troops that had been there since 1945 having departed a matter of months ago.

'A passport, you say?'

'Yes, Gus. For my wife.'

'She's not English then?'

'Of course not.'

'Okey doh. And when did you get married?'

'Tomorrow. You can be a witness if you like.'

'Freddie, there wouldn't be anything . . . how shall I say? . . . untoward about this, would there?'

'Untoward, no. Downright dodgy, yes. In need of discreet assistance from an old friend, yes.'

'Quite,' said Fforde. 'What are old friends for?'

Fforde did his bit. Witnessed a civil wedding, pronounced Tosca, even with her haggard look and pancake make-up, to be 'a stunner', discreetly intervened when the clerk raised the vexatious matter of 'residency', popped the champagne and served the Sachertorte in the lobby of the Sacher Hotel, and rushed through a British passport, asking no questions and stepping lightly over embassy staff who remarked that it was all a little irregular.

'Speaking of the irregular,' he said. 'Seen anything of Charlie lately?'

Troy thought about it.

'No,' he said. 'Wish I had. But I don't think I've set eyes on him since April.'

'I have,' Fforde went on. 'He was through here only a week or two back. All nods and winks, nothing definite. Wouldn't tell me a damn thing. Do you think he's still at it? After all these years, I mean.'

What are old friends for? Fforde had been immeasurably good to Troy. God knows, this whole thing could rebound on him, and a lesser friend would have told Troy to go home and sort it out there. But Troy's debt to Gus could not include such truths. It seemed odd that in his position he did not know, but if he didn't Troy could not be the one to tell him. Of course Charlie was still at 'it'. And 'it' was something Troy would not go into. He shrugged it off and mourned the days when they had all told each other everything. What were old friends for?

§30

It was a smooth crossing. Over the Irish Sea. Aboard the *Maid of Erin,* out of Dublin, bound for Liverpool via Douglas I.O.M. Within sight of the Isle of Man, not far off the uninhabited southern island, the Calf of Man, they stood at the rail watching the gulls circle, and the herring boats bobbing in the distance.

'Give me the gun,' Troy said.

'What? I mean why?'

'Just give it to me.'

Tosca looked around, checked no one could see, took the gun out of her handbag and slipped it to him palm to palm. It was so small he could conceal it almost completely in his hand. He looked around, exactly as she had done, and dropped the gun over the side into the grey surf.

'We don't need guns,' he said.

'We don't?—No—I guess not.'

'Now,' he said. 'Let's agree on a story.'

§31

He stopped the Bentley in the curve of beech trees, resplendent in their bottle green, the late June sun glinting off their leaves as from a thousand tiny mirrors. The house was just visible beyond the curve, a quarter of a mile or so in the distance.

Tosca said, 'Last night I dreamt I went to Manderley.'

He looked at her, surprised and pleased that she knew an English novel, that she knew anything that wasn't Huck Finn—she was always reading Huck Finn—but she wasn't smiling.

'Is this poetry or premonition?' Troy asked.

She flapped a dismissive hand at him.

'Oh, don't mind me. It's just—well—it's just that that's what it looks like to me. Y'know, Hollywood England, green shires on a back lot.'

So, she had not read the book after all, she was merely remembering the Hitchcock film—Olivier, darkly romantic, and George Sanders playing yet another supercad.

'I wouldn't mind,' he said. 'But Joan Fontaine so mangled those opening lines.'

'She tried, baby. We all do. Now, do I get to meet Mrs Danvers?'

'If you're going to take the mick—'

She leant her head on his shoulder and elbowed him until he put an arm around her. He slipped his foot slowly off the clutch and let the car crawl gently up the drive in first, steering as little as it needed with the fingertips of one hand upon the wheel. For a moment or two it was plausible, the seductive lie that this was the opening page of a lasting romance. Every bone in his body wanted it to be true, and every cell in his brain told him it wasn't.

'Of course you can meet Mrs Danvers,' he said. 'But you mustn't let her play with the matches.'

Mimram to him was a series of shapes and spaces, colours and sequences arranged in transparent time—a glass onion. The house of childhood, still visible through adulthood, nestled at its core, laid out in the order in which he had discovered it.

Tosca pulled a face at the stuffed black bear standing in the hallway.

'Jeez, but he looks moth-eaten. I mean, does he have to stand there, like the first thing you see when you come in the door?'

True, he was ugly as sin, had lost one eye, one ear and seemed daily to lose more and more of his stuffing, but to Troy he was Boris the Bear. He had stood on the same spot since 1919, and Troy saw no reason why he might not be found on the same spot in 1969. One of Troy's earliest memories was of Boris wearing a tin hat and waving a Union Jack on the first Armistice Day. He had worn a red poppy every November ever since; someone, not always Troy, remembered to pin one on him. He was part of the structured maintenance of childhood, as, indeed, was so much of the paraphernalia of the living house. In the main drawing room, the blue room, a battered Congolese carving of a Pygmy mounted upon an ebony elephant, the human figure far, far larger than the animal, had stood in the fireplace longer than he could remember. Sasha had nicknamed it Minnie, as a child. Once Troy had moved Minnie from the left-hand side of the fire to the right, only to see Sasha, on her next visit, move the figure back, without comment, or, Troy thought, consciousness. He would have difficulty explaining things like this to Tosca. The sheer solidity that the old man had placed around them, the spun, set spidersilk of airy nothings—his genius, as Nikolai had put it, for wrenching choice out of necessity. Tosca had lived her life out of a suitcase—three countries, a dozen passports and countless cities. Her cry of 'Who am I?' was not one he had ever asked of himself. He had doubts by the score; he knew Rod did too, and if they ever rose to any level resembling self-knowledge it was possible the sisters would too. He knew who he was; he was a Troy. And the best protection he could give her was to make her one too. If she would but accept.

'Pick a room,' he said to her, as he dumped their bags on the first-floor landing.

'Whaddya mean, "Pick a room"?'

'You did say you would like your own room.'

'I know—you gotta give me some time. I mean I—'

'No, no I wasn't arguing with you. I'm saying pick any room that isn't occupied. Make it your own.'

'Any room?'

'Any that isn't occupied.'

'Well, how many are there?'

'I've never counted, but I should think between fifteen and twenty.'

'How do I know which are occupied?'

'Slippers at the foot of the bed, dressing gowns on the back of the door, and the ones that aren't will probably smell a bit mothbally.'

She wandered from room to room, every step and word echoing around the empty house. She took a liking to Masha and Lawrence's room, bathed in the rosy western light of late afternoon, tinting the off-white walls Masha favoured with a wash of pink, and for a moment he wondered whether he might not have to persuade his sister to swap, but on the south side of the house she plumped firmly for a small dark room with faded wallpaper and a view of the river and the willows.

'It's kinda my size. You know what I mean? Well, you ever lived in a Moscow apartment, you would.'

'Yes. I know. It was my room when I was a boy.'

'You grew up in this? This was where you read *Winnie the Pooh,* sat up nights with Kennedy's *Shorter Latin Primer,* and jerked off to dreams of Carole Lombard?'

'Sort of. But I had a preference for Barbara Stanwyck.'

'And now?'

'I took my father's room at the end of the war. It's next door. Look, why don't you bathe and change. It's been a hellish journey. I'll rustle up some tea, and then we can look over the rest of the place.'

He had not contrived the situation, but once it had arisen he could not deny the familiarity. Tosca up to her tits in a bathful of bubbles, teacup in hand, blathering away at him; him sitting on the bog seat, partly listening partly daydreaming, his mind drifting between present and past. This was how things had been. This simple juxtaposition with a naked, garrulous woman had set like gelatine in the mind as one of his 'fondest' memories. And he dearly wished he had a better word than 'fond' for it. It had ended in blood, hers and his, and half his left kidney blown away.

Tosca stretched out a leg to soap and he saw the unmistakable marks of cigarette burns—the scars would be permanent—and the arm that held the soap still bore bruises that had faded to medicinal yellow. Again he wondered, how hard had they hit her for the marks to last the best part of two months? He could not ask again until she was ready to tell. God only knew whether he had the tact to discern such a moment.

Dressed, powdered, perfumed and, he thought, quite possibly pleased, he led her from room to room, each one still in the soft, powdery, floral colours in which his parents had found it in the summer of 1910, five years before his own birth. Each colour had been maintained, restored. The blue room, the largest drawing room on the south-west corner of the house—Tosca paused over the scratches on the window, where Sasha had carved her and Hugh's initials in the glass with the diamond of her engagement ring—Alexandra Troy and Hugh Darbishire—AT & HD, entwined above a heart and the date '30th Jany 1933'.

'Time and chance do that to you,' said Tosca, tracing out the letters with her fingertips. 'Make you look like a romantic fool, before you can so much as blink.'

'Eh?'

'"January 30th 1933"—the day Hitler became Chancellor of Germany.'

He waited to see if she would elaborate. She didn't. But he thought he knew what she meant—the lives of little people measured against the mark of history. What mattered at the time seen with the devastating benefit of hindsight. Sasha had meant to etch the date of her engagement into glass for ever, and inadvertently achieved a different commemoration, of an event that would eclipse any other that day.

Troy threw open the doors to the smaller red room, with its bay window where a Christmas tree stood every year. And the rest of the year, his mother had often sat in the bay sewing or lace-making or working at any one of a dozen quick-fingered hobbies that ruined her eyes by the time she was seventy. To the pink room—not so much pink as washed-out sainfoin magenta; to the yellow room—primrose and cowslip, 'Patent Yellow' to the discerning eye; through the deep Prussian of the dining room, through the layers of the onion to his father's study, its colour a dark, obscure nothing, a faded something.

At some point his father had lined the room with bookshelves, and when they had been filled, he had stuffed books into cupboards and when they too had filled, he had left books in piles on the floor, where they stood to this day. And in front of the books he had piled anything that caught his fancy. Three long-case clocks of differing height—remarkably, Troy now thought, like the Amsterdam skyline—which no one had ever managed to synchronise. A complete orrery—complete but for the undiscovered ninth planet—in brass, which no one had wound and set in motion in years. A harmonium whose leather lungs had long since perished. A player piano on which the hands of Gustav Mahler, Igor Stravinsky and George Gershwin could be brought to life from a punch-paper roll. A large, hand-painted, flaking, plaster of Paris globe on an iron pedestal, depicting the world in pastel colours as it had appeared in the days of empire and eagles. Extinct countries like Austria-Hungary, Imperial Russia, and no hint of neogeographic entities such as Yugoslavia. The existence of Poland was a mystery to the boy Troy, a country which came and went like the little man in the weather house, now you see it now you don't, and which, since his father's death, in its most recent incarnation, had leapt bodily some five hundred miles to the west. The old man had used the globe and his stamp album to teach Troy geography and history. His stamp album ran from a plethora of penny reds and the young head of Queen Victoria to the inflated millions on the denominations of the Weimar Republic, to the tasteful browns of Hitler's portrait, via vanished confederations of British East Africa, and the oddly colourful stamps of South Sea islands, where the head of George V could be found offset by palm trees and giant tortoises. Troy wondered, did the king have a tortoise at home with him, grazing the lawns at Buckingham Palace? And the naming of places puzzled him. Who was Gilbert? And were he and Ellice married? And did they have children after whom other islands might be named? The spelling of Yugoslavia, with its interchangeable J or Y, had taken him an age to learn.

'I'm almost sorry to waste your time,' his father had told him. 'I doubt it will be there long. You cannot invent a country. If you can invent yourself you're doing quite well enough.'

Tosca's gaze came to rest on the wall between the windows, just above the desk.

'I ain't seen one of those in years.'

He could not make out what she was looking at, but then she reached up and took his father's gun off the two wooden pegs that supported it on the wall. It was a large, heavy, semi-automatic pistol.

'It was my father's,' he said.

'Yeah—my old man had one just like it. You know what it is?'

Troy shook his head. He had an aversion to guns at the best of times.

'It's German. It's a Mauser 1896 Conehammer. A semi, a machine pistol—kinda like a hand-held machine gun.'

This meant nothing to Troy. It might as well have been a Howitzer.

'My Dad had one in the Civil War. Shot his way across Siberia with the damn thing—least that's the way he told it.'

'Maybe that's its purpose in life. It lends itself to legend. My father claimed to have shot his way onto the last train out of Russia in 1905.'

'Don't you believe him?'

Troy shrugged. He had never known how much to believe of anything his father told him. If his life turned out to be one colossal work of fiction, Troy would not be surprised. And, unlike his brother, he would not be offended.

'A train, perhaps. The last train, I doubt. Shot his way through, I doubt that too. Talked his way would be more in character. He may well have waved the gun around a bit while he talked. Just for show.'

Tosca flipped out the magazine, checked it was empty and pushed it back into place in front of the trigger-guard.

'It's a cavalry pistol,' she said with all the enthusiasm of a trainspotter. 'It's got a side-mounted hammer. You're supposed to have it in a saddle holster. Then when you have to draw it, you roll it over your thigh, which cocks the hammer, so the gun comes up ready, like this.'

So saying, Tosca stood on one leg, raised her right thigh and cocked and levelled the gun at him in a single action. He found himself looking down the barrel of a gun yet again.

Then there was silence, then there was stillness. Neither of them knowing what to do next, both of them rendered uneasy by the presence of a weapon, Tosca perched on one leg like a dwarf flamingo. A burst of pheasant's rattle from the garden broke the silence. She lowered the gun and her leg, blushing a little and clearly feeling as silly on her end of the gun as he did on his. He took the gun from her awkwardly and put it back on its wooden pegs, in the mind's eye seeing some burly Russian soldier teaching a little girl how to fire a lethal weapon, and wondering at the nature of paternal wisdom.

'Best place for it,' said Troy.

'Sure,' she said softly.

In the green room—sage panels lined in deeper green—stood the Bechstein his parents had shipped from Vienna in 1911. He had spent hundreds of hours at this learning from his mother.

Tosca ran a finger over the lid and came up with a crown of fluff.

'You don't play any more?'

'Of course I play. I just haven't played this particular piano for a while.'

He opened it and played a quick scale.

'Still in tune,' he said. 'Any requests?'

'One of the old guys. Cole Porter or Gershwin? I always loved Gershwin.'

'Yip Harburg?'

'You mean like "Over the Rainbow"?'

'No, I mean like . . .'

He played the opening five chords that spelt out 'April in Paris'. She smiled and he began again. He gave it his best shot, and when he saw that she was still smiling, propped against the piano, her chin upon her hands, her eyes closing, he risked all and let his hands tinkle forth Monk's interpretation, every angular note adding, as he thought of it, to the romantic pull of the song, giving all and taking nothing. She let him get all the way through before she opened her eyes. He had half dreaded the protest of a purist.

'Gee—but that's beautiful. Even the bum notes work.'

'I think you might have stumbled on a definition of Jazz. Bum notes that work.'

'What's new?'

'What's new?'

'I mean new new. Really new. Like hot off the press. You get so starved for new in Russia. Old we got plenty of. It's new we don't get. The hottest thing when I left Moscow was Judy Garland singing to Clark Gable's picture. "You made me love you, didn't wanna do it, didn't wanna do it." Now how old is that?'

'I don't know. Donkey's years, I should think.'

'That figures. We got plenty of donkeys too.'

Every so often Rod would make a trip to America, fulfilling his duty to party and country, taking, as he saw it, his life in his hands, and flying in one of the huge new airliners: Comet, Constellation, Caravelle, that sort of thing, they all seemed to begin with C to Troy. The hero of the Battle of Britain firmly maintained that the aeroplane was not meant to be bigger than a six-seater and that the bigger they were the more likely they were to crash. All the same he did it, and never forgot the souvenirs for his family, button-fly blue jeans for the teenagers, records for Troy. Among the last batch Troy had found on top of the gramophone in the study was a record for which new seemed almost inadequate as an adjective.

'OK,' he said, and began to play.

A little more than two minutes later he had finished, delighted that he had kept to the tempo—it was a fast and difficult tune—and breathless from singing, which was not his forte, but without which the song seemed less than complete.

She stood before him, mouth open, eyes wide. Horror or fascination, he could not tell.

'Is that it?'

'Well, yes.'

'I don't get it.'

'What don't you get?'

'Well—who is this Daisy woman?'

'Dunno.'

'Why does she drive him nuts?'

'Not nuts, crazy.'

'And who is Sue and what does she know how to do?'

'I'd be guessing.'

'And the words. I couldn't understand half of them. Awobbly dobblynobbly—what the heck is that?'

'Know what you mean. Took me a while. Look, why don't we take it a phrase at a time?'

'Sure,' she shrugged. 'Why not?'

'Awop,' he said tentatively.

'Awop,' she echoed, and there was the beginning of a look in her eye that made him suspicious.

'Awopbop.'

'Awopbop.'

'Awopbopalubop.'

'Awopbopa—what?'

'Lubop. It's lubop.'

'How do you spell that?'

'God knows, but it's pronounced Awopbopalubop.'

'OK—Awopbopalubop.'

'Awopbopalubopalopbamboom.'

'Awopbopalubopalopbamboom.'

She slammed the flat of her hand onto the piano.

'Awopbopalubopalopbamboom! Goddam it Troy, you know what that is? It's straight out of some goddam Mississippi juke joint. Goddammit Troy, it's nigger music!'

'Quite,' he said. 'I believe they call it Rock'n'Roll.'

A polite cough was heard behind her. Troy looked up, Tosca turned on one ankle, her elbows on the piano, one leg slightly raised, her toes tucked in behind the knee, looking as though she'd just finished a smoky rendition of 'Cry Me A River'. Rod stood in the doorway, and behind him Nikolai, and just behind him Sasha and Masha, and behind them Hugh and Lawrence, and behind them . . .

Tosca eased herself off the piano.

'Well,' she said, and in her heavy Muscovy accent, 'Это что ли пистолет у тебя в карнмане, или ты просто рад меня видеть?'

§32

They pleaded the wear and tear of a long journey, left Rod and the sisters at the table to see in midnight, drinking and squawking round the debris of the meal. Lawrence and Masha seemed on good terms. Hugh and Sasha, Troy concluded, were in the midst of another row and had diplomatically reached a truce for the evening. Nice of them—he had known occasions when they would not, but their rows never lasted long, and pretty soon Hugh would revert to his self-deluding, obliviating view of his wife's virtues. Rod would get drunk, have a hangover and regret it. Sasha and Masha would get drunk and appear magically unscathed in the morning, immune to the ravages of booze, or the criticism of husbands. Nikolai had excused himself before the coffee. Cid climbed the stairs with them, pecked them each on the cheek, smiled and said nothing. More than most, Troy thought, she would appreciate the dilemma of joining a tribe.

When she had gone their awkwardness remained.

'Well,' he said. 'What do you make of it all?'

'Tutti frutti,' said Tosca.

And they went to their separate rooms.

Hours later, it seemed, he was awoken by the door of his room opening. Someone climbed into the bed, next to him, inches away, not touching.

'Y'awake?'

'Stupidest question in the world. Supposing I said "no"?'

'But you are.'

He half turned to face her, and her hand pushed him back.

'No, don't move. Just stay still. We'll go to sleep now.'

'Before you do I have a question.'

'Okey dokey.'

'You rehearsed that bit of Mae West, didn't you?'

'Sure. Be yourself, you keep telling me. Takes practice. I been somebody else for years, I been several somebodies else—being me takes a lot of practice. Besides, it did no harm. He didn't have a gun in his pocket and he was pleased to see me.'

When he finally decided that she was asleep, he squirmed around as carefully as he could and stretched out a hand. Before he could reach anything a sleepy, hoarse, bedroom whisper said, 'Don't touch.'

§33

In the morning she was still there. It was familiar and unfamiliar. He had not woken up next to Tosca in years. Not that he would or could forget it. Christmas Day 1948. But the unfamiliar troubled him. For the moment he could not quite put his finger on it.

It was early still. He lay and mused for a while, watched the sun dance behind the curtain, flapping gently in the open window, and listened to the birdsong. Then it dawned on him. He had last woken up in this bed next to someone in April. Or was it March? The week the sisters had forced him into getting a television. He had not seen his mistress in . . . weeks . . . months? He'd get hell for this. He could hardly put it off much longer.

The telephone rang. He reached over and picked it up before it rang twice, but Tosca had not stirred.

'Hello, Troy?' said Anna's voice.

'Hello,' he said. 'I was just thinking about you.'

§34

Troy and Anna always met at the Café Royal, in the Quadrant of Regent Street. It was pretty well midway between his office at Scotland Yard and her surgery in Harley Street, and her husband, who scavenged half the watering holes in London, had never, to their knowledge, been sighted in the Café Royal.

'I've pushed my afternoon appointments on a bit,' said Anna. 'We'll be OK till about half past two.'

Anna had begun as a pathologist, assisting Kolankiewicz. With the commencement of the National Health Service she had moved into general practice—struck a bargain with the striped trousers and fancy waistcoats of Harley Street and helped a bunch of incomprehending old men into the post-war world and a practice that combined treating those who could pay with treating those who no longer had to. Troy missed her skill at making sense and peace out of Kolankiewicz, but admired the idealism.

'I thought we should meet,' she said.

'It's been a while,' he agreed.

'I've been meaning to talk to you.'

'Me too. I've been meaning to talk to you. A bit of news, I suppose.'

'Rightie ho—shall I go first?'

'If you like,' he said, sensing an imminent bollocking.

'Angus is back.'

Angus was her husband. A preposterous drunk, a daring drunk, as decorated as Rod for the same reasons. A do-or-die RAF flyer who had done and had not died. But then he had not put the war behind him with the scarless aplomb that Rod had achieved. His benders were notorious.

It had occurred to Troy that the real reason he was not seen at the Café Royal was that they wouldn't let him in.

'I didn't know he'd been anywhere.'

'It was a metaphor, Troy. I mean that he's back with me. I mean that I've taken him back.'

Angus had never actually left the marital home. He had simply moved all that mattered about him to the planet Angus—and not for the first time.

'You mean he's sober?'

'I think I do.'

'What's he saying?'

'He says he wants to make a go of it.'

'And that if he does he'll stay sober?'

'Sort of.'

'Sort of?'

'You know Angus.'

'I know that you can't believe a word he says where booze is concerned.'

'I know.'

She paused in a sadness that Troy could not fathom. Anger was so often more her *modus operandi*.

'The thing is, you see, I want to believe him.'

'Yeees . . .'

'The thing is, I want to make a go of it.'

'I see.'

'I'm thirty-eight. We could still start a family. It's not too late.'

'Quite.'

'It's not as if we were passionate about one another.'

The 'we', he realised, referred to himself.

'You and I never worked up much in the way of passion, did we?'

'I suppose not,' he agreed.

'I mean—we came together sort of in the spaces in between.'

Indeed they had. It was a tune played only on the black notes of the keyboard. They had known one another since the second year of the war. It had been late 1949 before they had tumbled into bed, and perhaps for both their sakes they should have done it sooner, but the possibility had been inherent from the start—only her loneliness and his fecklessness had ever led them across the line he knew existed. He rather thought she knew it too.

'If you like,' he said.

'I want to make this work, Troy, really I do. And for God's sake stop saying "if you like".'

She was crying quietly. Her handkerchief came out to dab at her eyes.

'If you'd seen him when I married him . . .'

They hit silence. This was not a line he would pick up, not a sentence he ever wanted to hear the end of. Troy waited while she found composure. It was unlike her to show quite so much feeling. What they had in common, he had long thought, was the tearless cynicism of people who made their living in death.

'It's all right,' he said at last. 'I understand.'

'Could you try to be a bit less understanding?'

'Eh?'

'Never mind. Why don't you tell me your news?'

'My news?'

'Yes. You said there was something you wanted to tell me.'

'Well,' he said. 'I'm not sure how to tell you this.'

'Just spit it out. It can hardly be as deadly as what I've just told you, now can it?'

She smiled through the glaze of tears.

'I got married the other week,' he said simply.

The smile vanished. Slate clean.

'Troy—you shit. You complete and utter fucking shit!'

§35

One Friday morning at Goodwin's Court, late in July, Troy was cooking breakfast for the two of them. He had heard Tosca get out of the bath, her feet slap on the floorboards above, and begun to fry the bacon and heat a saucepan for the scrambled eggs. She had been an age in the bath. The scent of bath salts had drifted down the stairs, the sound of her rhythmical, rather flat and raspy singing had come with it, floating into the kitchen: 'Gonna wash that man right outta my hair.' He hoped it meant nothing. 'And send him on his way.' He was sure it meant nothing. He flicked on the wireless in time for the news. A best Home Service voice crackled forth.

'It was announced in Alexandria last night that Egypt is to nationalise the Suez Canal. Colonel Nasser has declared his intention to reject the terms of the 1888 agreement whereby Britain and France retain control of the canal until 1968. This is believed to be a response to last week's withdrawal by Her Majesty's Government of financial aid for the Aswan Dam project . . .'

The telephone was ringing. It had to be Rod. It was a Rod moment.

'Mr Troy? Bill Bonser. Detective Inspector, Portsmouth CID.'

Troy moved the bacon off the hob.

'How can I help you, Inspector?'

'I was wondering if you could find a few hours to come down to Portsmouth. We've found the body.'

'*The* body?'

'Well . . . I say the body. I'm not one hundred per cent sure it's him.'

'Who?'

'Him, sir. The Portsmouth spy.'

'I hope I'm not being dense, Inspector, but what exactly has this got to do with me? It doesn't sound like a typical case for the Murder Squad.'

'No—it's not. But it would seem you were the last person to see him alive.'

'To see who?'

'The spy, sir.'

The merest hint of exasperation was beginning to creep into his tolerance of rank.

'I still don't get it. When am I supposed to have seen him?'

'Oh . . . How shall I put this without seeming rude. Have you by any chance been out of the country for a while? Away from the papers?'

'As it happens I have. Most of June.'

'Ah . . . then you won't have heard. HMG named the spy about four weeks ago. Cockerell. Lieutenant Commander Arnold Cockerell, RN, retired.'

The name meant nothing to Troy. Then a mnemonic flash. Suede shoes. Suede shoes. The weaselly bloke, with the Ronald Colman moustache, the navy blazer and the suede shoes.

'As I said, sir, we've a body. Fished out of the sea, over Chichester way on the far side of Selsey Bill yesterday morning. But we're having a little difficulty getting a positive ID.'

'Sorry, Inspector. I was being slow, but I'm with you now, and I can tell you that I wasn't the last person to see him alive. Ex-Sergeant Quigley saw him after me, and he's right on your doorstep.'

'I know, sir. He can't say for certain. And his daughter won't look. The squeamish type, I'm afraid.'

'Next of kin?'

'There's a wife sir, but . . . well . . . she's upset right now. She may give us an ID in the future, but she can't or won't confirm at the moment. If you could come down, sir, it might result in a quick clear up of the case. As it is, things are a bit awkward. Mrs Cockerell's still here and I might be able to persuade her to take another look, but it is . . . well . . . it's awkward, d'you see?'

'OK,' said Troy. 'I'll be there after lunch.'

He put the bacon back onto the flame, tipped the eggs into the gleam of butter in the bottom of the saucepan, listened to Tosca banging about as she finished dressing, listened to her start a new song—'I'm just a gal who cain't say no!'—and wondered why Rod hadn't bothered to tell him about Cockerell. Only weeks ago it seemed he had been obsessed with screwing an admission out of Eden. But the answer was almost obvious. He had come home with a wife, and at that a Russian wife. Rod, the happily married man, who could conceive of no man being happy out of marriage and no man unhappy within it, had had his cup filled to the brim, and as it ran over he had forgotten that anything else mattered. Troy had thought Rod would never stop laughing at Tosca's Mae West line. She could not have cracked the ice more perfectly. He had clasped her to his chest, or as far up it as she came at five foot two inches in high heels, and laughed till he cried. It was typical of Rod's passions that they eclipsed each other like the moon going round the sun. Sooner or later he would have told him.

§36

Awkward was not the word Troy would have chosen. Most of Cockerell's face had gone. And with it the whole of his right hand, his left down to the knuckles, all of the right foot and two toes off the left. The top of his head had been sliced off and the back of it crushed like a peppercorn. He'd been in the water more than three months. His rubber suit had protected his torso but the fish had lunched on anything that was exposed. The one eye hanging loose and half eaten from the remains of its socket was enough to make the strongest stomach heave.

He looked at the naked mess that might once have been the pathetic little bore from the carpet saleroom, stretched out on a green rubber sheet. The exposed flesh was streaked and stained; the flesh uncovered by the peeling away of the wetsuit was as pale as flour, bloated like a white slug on a cabbage leaf.

He turned to the sergeant Bonser had sent in with him.

'You've got to be joking,' he said. 'His own mother couldn't identify him.'

The man was indifferent or callous or just young. He shrugged his shoulders.

'There's always the teeth, I suppose. And prints off the three toes.'

For some reason this irritated Troy.

'Look at his jaws. Do you see any teeth? Isn't it obvious the man wore false teeth?'

The sergeant crouched and peeped into the black, lipless hole.

'Oh, I see what you mean. Where are they now?'

'I don't know. Perhaps you should dredge the Solent?'

The sarcasm of this went over the man's head. He probably *would* dredge the Solent for a set of false teeth.

'And whilst you can get prints off toes, when does anyone bother to record toeprints?'

The man shrugged again. He was easy with death. Death didn't bother him. It bothered Troy. He couldn't wait to get out of the room.

The door to Bonser's office was open. He was resting his backside on the front edge of his desk, leaning low over the hunched, juddering figure of a woman.

'Surely you can?' he was saying. Then, 'After sixteen years of marriage?'

His tone of voice was somewhere between the incredulous and the hectoring. It did not, to Troy's ears, sound pleasant, particularly in the light of his assumption that the sobbing woman must be Cockerell's wife.

Troy tapped gently on the glass.

Bonser prised himself off the desk and came over to the door.

'Any luck?' he said.

Troy had no wish to speak in front of Mrs Cockerell. He shook his head.

'What, nothing? Surely you—'

It was the same 'surely' he had used a moment before on the grieving widow. Troy refused to respond to it, cut him off before the verb by walking past him and placing a hand on Mrs Cockerell's shoulder.

'Mrs Cockerell?'

She unwrapped a little, looked up at him, her face contorted into a mask of ugliness by tears. A frump of a woman well into middle age. Overdressed for the weather in a heavy tweed coat; overdressed for the occasion in one of those stupid hats that women wear to be formal. But, then, what was more formal than a dead husband?

'Frederick Troy. I'm a chief inspector at Scotland Yard. I met your husband briefly last April. I can't tell you how sorry I am.'

Her eyes flashed with panic. She swivelled in the chair, looking sharply at Bonser, then at Troy again.

'It's not him, you know. You haven't told them it's him, have you?'

Troy looked at Bonser. More than a bit of a slob, a big bloke, with a boxer's nose, standing in the open doorway in his striped braces, his tie at half-mast, his hands thrust into his trousers, Biro sticking out of the breast pocket of his bri-nylon shirt, as though he'd seen far too many episodes of *Dragnet*. She was alarmed, almost demented by the thought. How long had Bonser had her in here putting on the screws?

'No. I haven't. I couldn't in all honesty say that I recognised the body as your husband.'

'It's not. You do see that, don't you? It's not him. It can't be.'

Bonser took his hands out of his pockets.

'Oh come on now—'

Troy cut him off, raised his voice just a fraction louder than was necessary and stared him down. It was known as pulling rank.

'Have you had lunch yet, Mrs Cockerell?'

She shook her head. A lock of grey hair fell free from the ridiculous hat.

'It's nearly three. You must be famished.'

Troy held out a hand to her. She took it and stood up. A little taller than Troy, slim and fiftyish. He could see her clearly for the first time. Her face powder creased by rivulets of tears. Her bright red lipstick smudged. She did not, thank God, seem to wear mascara or she'd look like a coal chute, thought Troy.

He sat her in the front of the Bentley. Ducked back into the station. Bonser was unhappy but short of protest.

'I'll talk to her,' said Troy. 'You'll get nowhere if you lean on her.'

Bonser shruggged, began to gather up the scattering of paperwork on his desk, his mind already moving on.

'Maybe you're right. But it'll drag on now, won't it?'

'What will you do?'

'What can I do? Follow the book. Put him on ice.'

He tossed a file into the open cabinet and slammed it shut.

'Coroner opens an inquest and adjourns it indefinitely. You know the routine. In the meantime I've got an unidentified body and an open case. Makes a mess of the figures.'

This was universal copper-speak, an appeal through rank to Troy's sympathies.

'There are worse things,' said Troy. Then he added, 'The post mortem. You'll send a copy of the report up to the Yard?'

'If you like,' Bonser said, as though it were a matter on which he was wholly indifferent.

Troy swung the car into the yard of the King Henry. It was out of hours, and he was relying on the goodwill of Quigley. The door was propped open, Quigley was behind the bar drying glasses, a towel demonstratively laid across the pumps.

'Mr Quigley?' Troy began. 'I don't suppose there's any chance of a late lunch?'

'I'm sure I can manage something,' Quigley said.

'And a drop of brandy?'

Quigley looked at the dial-faced clock over the bar. He knew exactly what time it was. The clock simply provided reassurance, and passing drama. There was a barely audible, hammy intake of breath.

'It's not for me,' Troy said. 'I've Mrs Cockerell with me.'

'Say no more. On the house. That way the law can't touch us, now can it?'

They sat alone at a table in the centre of the room. Quigley took one look at Mrs Cockerell and set a very large brandy in front of her. Troy coaxed. Persuaded her to take off her coat, to sip at the brandy. Her tears had stopped. The grief had lapsed into silence. She did not speak to Troy until Quigley returned with two plates of roast beef and boiled spuds in pools of gravy. She unpinned the silly hat, set it down on the spare chair, shook her hair out of her face, straightened her posture and assumed the forced look of bearing up in adversity.

'It's not him, you know,' she said bluntly.

Tact not truth, thought Troy.

'I'm sure you know best.'

'That Inspector wanted me to say it was.'

'No—I think he was just doing his job. Just asking you to be sure.'

She took a mouse's bite at a potato, chewed half-heartedly, decided she liked it and began to take bigger forkfuls.

'No,' she said. 'It was more than that. He wouldn't take no for an answer.'

She spoke calmly. It did not seem to him to be the reaction of hysteria. Besides, Troy had to admit to himself that this squared with what he had seen. It seemed wrong, however, to agree with her and let her go away with the idea that Bonser had been heavy with her. Peace, if attainable, lay in denial. The truth came a poor second.

'Tell me,' he said, 'were there no distinguishing marks which might have been unique to your husband?'

'He had a scar on the back of his right hand. And a mole on the side of his neck. But there was no right hand, was there? There wasn't much of a neck. I told that Inspector all that. He still seemed to think I should know.'

Troy decided to let it drop. She ate slowly but steadily, seemed quite capable of getting through it all. Mary Quigley brought over two bowls of plum duff and synthetically yellow custard. Troy preferred his Technicolor on the screen rather than the plate. He declined and took the chance to seek out Quigley.

'Mr Quigley, when you were on the force, did you know Bill Bonser?'

Quigley uncorked the brandy bottle and poured two shorts for himself and Troy, far, far smaller than the one he had given to Mrs Cockerell. He pushed Troy's across the bar to him. Cleared a space to take the elbow upon which the process of confidentiality demanded he now lean.

'Came from Liverpool the year I retired. He was a sergeant in them days. If you ask me he shoulda stayed a sergeant.'

'Why do you say that?'

'Well, what qualities would you pride yourself on, Mr Troy? Intuition, imagination—flair, would you call it?'

'If you like,' said Troy.

'Billy Bonser ain't that sort. He's what I'd call a born sergeant.'

Quigley paused to knock back his brandy. Troy still couldn't see what he was driving at.

'But you're not saying he's bent?'

'Bent? Billy Bonser? He's so straight you could use 'im for a truncheon. Straight, bent—that's not the matter. Matter is—what separates the goat from the sheep? Nouse, Mr Troy. Bonser don't have nouse. Bonser has—well—loyalty, obedience. The stuff you'd want in a good sergeant. 'E don't 'ave the imagination to be bent. You give Billy Bonser an order and 'e'li follow it over a cliff. 'E was in 'ere the day I reported Cockerell missing. That was two days after you was last 'ere. Comes in. Asks to check the register.'

Quigley reached under the bar and pulled out the register. He flipped it open and ran his finger down the torn seam between pages.

'Looks at the page with Cockerell's name on it, yours too as it 'appens, and blow me he rips it right out and tells me 'e was never 'ere. Then yesterday he comes in and asks me to identify the body. Typical Bonser. Orders to lose Cockerell, one day, orders to see to it 'e's identified the next, and he follows both to the letter. Bent—not on your life. Straight as a die. Born sergeant.'

Troy considered that as Quigley had spent twenty years as a sergeant there was an odd mixture of generosity, objectivity and sheer perversity in the view, but it did prompt a question.

'Whose orders would he be following? Why would anyone down here want Cockerell lost?'

'Nah. Not down 'ere, Mr Troy. It'd be one of his mates in Special Branch. Before he got this posting Bonser was a sergeant in the Branch up in Liverpool. Mind you, it was too late. I'd already had a reporter in 'ere. And he'd seen it first.'

'Reporter? Did you ask which paper?'

'He said he was from the *Sunday Post*. Local stringer. If you ask me, 'e'd heard it from a nark down at the nick. So 'appens he moved quicker than Bonser.'

'Did you tell Bonser this?'

'No. Why upset him?'

This put a piece of the puzzle into place, the *Sunday Post* being owned by the Troy family, edited by his brother-in-law, Lawrence. Anything of use to Rod, Lawrence would undoubtedly pass on—which was how Rod had been able to harangue the Government long before it was common knowledge that there was a spy. It also spelt out to Troy that Rod had known all along that the Portsmouth spy was Commander Cockerell. He had never named him. He could imagine the delight Rod had taken in forcing Eden to name him, the off-the-record hints by which Rod would have let Eden know that he knew. Except that now—now it seemed that the Portsmouth spy might not be Commander Cockerell?

Troy offered Mrs Cockerell a lift to London. She declined, saying her train changed at Reading and she'd be fine if he would just drop her at the railway station.

'It's not him,' she said again, with her hand on the car door, paused to get out into the station forecourt. 'Really, it isn't.'

It was a habit. A bad one, and more often than not meant as a brush-off. Troy gave her his card. His rank, the Whitehall 1212 number, the most famous telephone number in Britain.

'If there's anything I can do—' he said meaninglessly, knowing he would never hear from her again.

And for a month he did not.

§37

He had retreated to his father's study—his study, as he habitually failed to think of it. The summer rain pelted the windows, setting the glass rattling in its frame. He stuck Art Tatum on the gramophone, picked Graham

Greene's *The Quiet American* off the shelf and decided to while away a wet Saturday afternoon and quite possibly a wet weekend in solitary pleasures. Somewhere in the distance he could hear the sisters' prattle. Rod was up in his office with a deskful of papers, as he was every Saturday; Nikolai was sleeping off lunch in the conservatory; Cid was in the kitchen discussing the evening's menu with the cook. He had no idea where Tosca was and for two chapters of Graham Greene he did not wonder.

To enter his thoughts seemed like word magic—as though he could summon her up simply by thinking of her, she opened the door softly and came in. The creature he summoned was dressed bizarrely. All the clothes were his, rescued from the box he put aside for gardening and pigging. His old grey cotton trousers, rolled up many times at the ankle, and a Tattersall shirt, shot at the collar and cuffs. She was bored. He was getting used to that. She was so easily bored. She was in all probability drawn by the music, the rippling, sentimental piano of Tatum, the oh-so-mellow saxophone of Ben Webster, the Chekhovian thud of the string bass. He had no sense of intrusion. Indeed, he wished she would show more initiative and pick up a book and put on a record without waiting for him to make the decision. He had weaned her off Huck Finn, convinced her that there were other writers besides Mark Twain. But he was rapidly coming to conclude that he could not please her—in any sense of the word.

'Y' OK, baby?'

She sat on the edge of the chair opposite, not relaxing into it. More like his daughter than his wife. Irritable, irritating and curious.

'I'm fine.'

'Y' don't mind me just . . . sittin' here?'

'Not at all. You're my wife.'

'Buys a lot of favours, huh?'

He did not answer.

'Sorry. That was bitchy. I been hangin' out with your sisters too much.'

The rain shook the french windows to fill up the silence. It let him put off what he knew he must say and would rather not, such display being alien to his nature.

'That's OK. I didn't mean I owned you. I meant what's mine is yours. As corny as that.'

She smiled and unsmiled, all in a split second.

There was no way out. He'd better say it. Knew he had to say it. He put down the book. His own inadequacies rushing in to meet him black as storm clouds.

'I meant, I loved you.'

'That so?'

A whisper, not half-hearted, not uncertain, no sense of doubt. But it seemed to him that it did not register with her; so much did not, after all, and this was her only response, and it seemed the words she used did not mean what they said.

The telephone rang. It was far nearer her than him. She was looking intently at him, smiling shyly, stuck for words. She let it ring, until Troy said: 'Pick it up. It's probably for Rod. Usually is.'

'Hello,' she said quietly, and he saw the blood drain from her face, saw her eyes lock onto his with an expression little short of terror.

'Yeah, yeah [pause]. Yeah, he's here. Sure.'

Then she put her hand across the mouthpiece and screamed her whisper at Troy.

'Aaaaaagh!'

'What's the matter?'

'Aaaaaaaaaaggggghhhhhhh!!! It's Ike!'

'Ike who?'

'Eisenhower, dummy!!! The goddam President! Jesus Christ. Take the damn thing off me!'

Troy ran around the desk.

'What does he want?'

'He just called to ask if I'm happy. Jesus Christ, Troy! What do you think he wants? He wants Rod!'

Troy snatched the phone from her. She hopped around the room screaming quietly, dancing from one foot to the other as though walking on hot coals.

He ran upstairs. Rod took it all very calmly. Yawned, picked up the phone and said, 'Ike,' as though he had seen him only yesterday.

Afterwards, he sat in the study and watched Tosca rant and rave, still tearing around the room on fire.

'Jesus, baby. Suppose he recognised my voice?'

'It was twelve years ago.'

'Dammit, Troy. I saw the old guy every day for weeks, months even! I mean, he used to flirt with me!'

'He didn't have a clue. You're dead, remember?'

She returned to her place, perched on the edge of the chair, toes drumming nervously on the floor.

'You're right. I'm dead. I find it hard to remember sometimes. I mean, here am I trying to work out who the hell I am, eyeless in Gaza, clueless in Hertfordshire, lost in the desert of the English home counties, marooned between the Co-op and Dorothy Perkins, caught between the devil and the woman in the deep-blue dress who just popped in from the Women's Institute, adrift on a sea of good manners and guilt about masturbation, wondering whether property is really theft or does my fawn handbag really not go with my twin-set, driven crazy by not knowing which'll destroy us first, the H-bomb or the wrong fork at the dinner table, forgetting all the time that I'm dead. Well—fucky wucky woo!!!'

For several minutes all he could hear was rain and the gathering rumble of thunder.

He leaned back, the chair on two legs, and flipped the switch to start the record again. Tatum glided into 'Gone With the Wind'—the prewar song from which Margaret Mitchell had taken her book title, which in turn had become a film, which in turn had became another, utterly unrelated tune—and competed with the rain on the window pane. There was scarcely a mood to recapture, but he loved and hated the fragility of silence under rain. Almost erotic. The temptation to shatter it was too strong. He'd tried once and failed dismally.

He reached for his book. Then she leapt from her chair, knocked the book from his hand, threw her arms around his neck and wept onto his chest.

The record spun on its final groove. One of Mr Sod's favourite laws was that the autochanger never cut out when you wanted it to. She prised her head off his chest, sniffed noisily, looked at him nose to nose.

'Y' remember what Twain said?'

He shook his head.

'Rumours of my demise are greatly something or other.'

'Exaggerated?'

'That's the word.'

161

Then she kissed him, drew up her legs, wedged her stockinged feet between his thighs and buried herself in his neck. She smelt of perfume, nothing he could name, of soap flakes, and of Tosca.

§38

Rod took the bellows to the last of the fire. A man of no real practical skills, he was devoted to the two or three things he did well. He was excellent at pancakes, though rarely called on to prove it since his children hit adolescence, mixed a mean Martini, and would always undertake the lighting of fires with repeated cries of, 'Don't touch it, don't touch it!' And on cold summer evenings such as this could be found bent over the embers, arse uppards, blowing a spark into flame. The fire once lit, he would be reluctant to waste so much as a therm of heat and light, and was often to be found crouched over a fire with parliamentary papers, or the novels he rationed to himself, past midnight, past sociability, yawning and nodding off. In the days when he had been a minister, Troy had saved him from a scorching when a Government white paper slipped from his lap into the grate and set fire to his trousers.

Dinner had dissolved, the family dispersed to their rooms. Troy walked the length of the table snuffing out the candles with his fingers. He had first taken the precaution of closing the door. He sat by the fire, hoping for a fireside chat—a phrase not much heard since the death of Franklin Delano Roosevelt. Rod achieved ignition, sighed and sat back in the chair opposite.

'Staying up, are you?' he said.

Which was by way of a hint. It meant 'sod off' in Rodspeak, but Troy was not to be sodded.

'Aren't you going to tell me what's going on?'

'Meaning?'

'The President of the United States is usually to be found on the golf course on a Saturday morning, not making clandestine calls to minor British politicians on their home numbers.'

'Minor! Clandestine!'

'I didn't even know you knew him.'

'I was in and out of Overlord HQ dozens of times in the run-up to D-Day. I can't say I was on first-name terms with a five-star general, but I knew him. I saw him again a couple of times in '54, and I led the Labour group to Washington this June while you were off gallivanting with your newfound wife.'

'And you just happened to give him this number?'

Rod put aside the sheaf of papers he had sat clutching. It indicated that Troy had at last won his attention.

'Off the record. Right?'

'I'm not a Fleet Street hack, Rod.'

'It's part of the job, his and mine, to meet the Opposition leaders, you'll agree. Nothing odd about that, so don't pretend. The fact that we knew one another in the war helps. After all, he didn't know Gaitskell. He told me in June that he was worried about Egypt—the Baghdad pact and all that—said it would be useful from time to time to know what Her Majesty's Opposition felt without the formalities and frills. And no, I didn't give him this number. He had it already. Asked if I minded him calling me here, but said he knew for a fact that the line wasn't bugged. Which is more than can be said for my office. He said we could talk without anyone else knowing—not his people, and not mine. What prompted him to ring today was that television address to the nation Eden gave the other night. Ike, it seems, had the London embassy stick the phone next to the set so it could be relayed direct to him in the White House. The upshot is that he thinks Eden is not getting the message. He says Dulles is being as clear as can be that the Americans will not back us over Egypt—"we will not shoot our way through the canal" and all that guff—bit subtle for Eden, really—and we cannot expect them to. But he thinks Eden is just blind and deaf on the matter.'

'So what's new? Ike must have known Eden during the war. I doubt his character has improved.'

'Quite. That is part of the problem. I doubt whether Ike has ever had a deal of confidence in him. However, there is something new.'

Rod paused, seemed almost to sigh with regret.

'We're going to invade.'

Troy thought silence the better part of discretion. Just keep him talking.

'The Tories have signed a secret pact with France and Israel. Israel strikes at Egypt across Sinai, towards the canal. Then the British and the French steam in as peacemakers, and on the way nab the canal for themselves. It was all in writing, it seems, but Eden has burnt his copy of the agreement, and sent a Foreign Office chap to France to get the French copy. But he couldn't get the Israeli copy. Eden's lied to the House and if we drag him back for a special session he means to go on lying.'

'How does Ike know this?'

'The CIA got a look at Israel's copy.'

'Why is he telling you this?'

'He just wants me to know.'

'I don't believe that. Nor do you. I don't see how you can use this. When did anyone last stand up in the house of clowns and call the Prime Minister of the day a liar? If you do, every journalist in Britain will ask you for your source. What are you going to tell them? That Ike calls you at home? Because no one will believe you. That you have a hotline to the CIA? That'll do you more harm than good. You'll have your own left wing shooting at you with everything they've got.'

Rod leant forward. No one could possibly hear them, but still he lowered his voice.

'He says that he'll pull the rug from under the pound if Eden goes through with it. It'll drop like stone against the dollar. In the autumn we're due to pay interest on the post-war loans the Americans gave us. We'll probably have to default. The Exchequer will be passing the hat round and we'll be borrowing from anyone with a five-bob postal order to lend. From imperial power to international beggars in less than ten years. At which point Ike has us by the balls—and one of Ike's maxims is that when you have a man by the balls his heart and mind soon follow.'

'Jesus Christ,' said Troy. 'That's Machiavellian. But I still don't see why he's gone to the trouble of telling you.'

'Special relationship?'

'Come off it.'

'He wants us to be ready.'

'Ready for what?'

'Government.'

'Government? There's no bloody election due till 1960!'

'Eden will go. Ike has decided. When he goes there's a good chance he'll bring the Tories down around his head like Samson. We'll be back in government by January.'

'So Ike is acting like a bookie's runner. Giving you a hot tip?'

'All in the interests of continuity.'

'Rubbish.'

'It's called diplomacy.'

'Sez you,' said Troy. 'I could think of half a dozen other words for it.'

It was Troy's turn to lean in close over the sputtering fire, to usher in the tones of a spurious confidentiality. Secrets where there could be none. Home truths where there could only be alien lies.

'Tell me, don't you find it in the least bit disturbing to be on the receiving end of CIA operations? Aren't you just a wee bit apprehensive about an American president deciding to swap governments in Britain? Because if they can do it to the Conservatives, they can do it to you.'

'Strange times, Freddie, make strange bedfellows.'

'If I went to bed with the CIA I'd count my bollocks in the morning.'

§39

The Quiet American was not where he had left it. With only a couple of chapters to go, he was quite looking forward to finishing it in bed.

He tapped on Tosca's door and went in. The windows were wide open to let in the night air and the last reluctant drops of rain with it. Her trousers, knickers and socks trailed across the floor from the door, exactly as she had stepped out of them. The room was turning into a marginally neater version of the pit she had had in Orange Street all those years ago. She was sitting up in bed. The Tattersall shirt had become a nightdress. She was reading his book. He decided to say nothing. He'd start another.

'I'm sorry about this afternoon.'

'That's all right. You must have been scared.'

'Shitless would be the word.'

She paused, put her thumb between the pages and clutched the book to her bosom. Drew her knees up to support her chin.

'It makes me wonder. Y'know. Could be anybody. Anytime. I mean—we'll never know. We can never be certain, can we?'

She was looking at him. A look he could not fathom. She had wrapped herself around him, slept off the fear of the day in the sleep of a frightened child. She had never done that before. She had clammed up over dinner, let Rod and the sisters make all the running, occasionally reached under the table cloth and held him by the hand or grabbed him by the balls. She had done that dozens of times. He did not know what she wanted of him now.

'No,' he said. 'We can't.'

§40

It had been a sodden summer. Wind and rain, with the odd day of outstanding sunshine to pepper the calendar and remind the English that they didn't have summers like they used to—before the war. One glimmer of 'sunshine' remained—earlier in the season England had thrashed the Australian touring cricket team in the test and reminded them that Len Hutton had retired, but that perhaps his spirit played on.

The desk copper at the Yard had the reliability of a good barometer. He would talk about the weather or he would talk about cricket. In either case, he had the same solution.

'It's the bomb,' he told Troy one morning at the end of August. 'Stands to reason.'

Troy loved 'stands to reason'—it was, when used by a certain kind of idiot, specially bred by the English, the signal, the preface, to the preposterous, to a statement that would, beyond a shadow of a doubt, be quite devoid of reason.

'Definitely the bomb,' the copper said, as Troy walked in from Whitehall.

Troy waited. Cricket or the weather?

'We never had weather like this before you had all them atoms in the air! It's the atoms. We got too many of 'em just whizzing around in the atmosphere.'

Play or pass? Play, he thought. Absurdist's gambit.

'It rains in Japan all the time.'

'Yeah, but there's always the trade winds. We're on the same trade winds as Japan, you see. The wind blows all their atoms from Hiroshima and Nagawotsit over to England.'

This required little thought. Troy could see mate in a couple of moves.

'Of course,' he said, Knight to Queen's Bishop 4, 'Japan never was any good at cricket.'

'Stands to reason,' said the copper, and went into a manoeuvre known to Troy as the cracker-barrel loop, the homespun philosopher's ploy of repeat, sigh and wonder at the majesty of God and Nature. Troy quit. They bred a particularly hardy species of idiot—the English.

Up in his office the phone was ringing. And not a sign of Clark or Wildeve.

He did not recognise the woman asking for Chief Inspector Troy.

'It's Janet Cockerell,' she said.

'Yes,' he said neutrally.

'You said to call you if—'

She could not complete the sentence, but it didn't matter. The 'if' had been universal. Bread cast upon the waters. Anything and nothing with a preference that it should be nothing. But she had called.

'I've heard from that Inspector Bonser again.'

So had Troy. A post-mortem report lay unread in his in-tray. If he'd had a reason for asking Bonser to send it, he'd quite forgotten what it was.

'He wants me to go back to Portsmouth. And I was wondering. Well. Do I have to go?'

'No, Mrs Cockerell, you don't.'

'He can't make me?'

'No, he can't.'

Troy was not surprised to learn that Bonser had asked. How else was he ever going to get the body identified? If anything, it was odd he'd left the matter as long as he had.

'But,' Troy went on, 'I'm sure you'll appreciate how little Mr Bonser has to go on.'

'You're not saying I should do it?'

'No. I'm not.'

'It's not him. I can't say it is if it isn't.'

Troy had heard all this.

'It's the way he asks. I feel I'm being bullied.'

He was not wholly sure why he was prolonging this conversation, or where it was leading.

'Mrs Cockerell. Why are you so certain your husband is not the body we saw?'

'He's still alive. I know it.'

'I've been investigating suspicious deaths for twenty years, Mrs Cockerell. Most people who begin as missing persons show up as corpses. There's not a man in ten thousand can effectively engineer his own disappearance. The old ploy of leaving your clothes on the beach doesn't work. If he's still missing after nearly five months the chances are—'

'My husband didn't leave his clothes on a beach! He left them at the King Henry Hotel,' she protested.

'Quite. Doesn't that tell you anything?'

'No.'

'Well. It tells me that your husband has not staged a disappearing trick. Clothes are one thing. Your husband left his wallet, his case and his car, his toothbrush, his razor. If he's roving England, he's roving it without so much as a farthing to his name.'

'Doesn't that tell *you* anything?' she threw his question back at him.

'Such as?'

'That perhaps it all comes down to money. That maybe he's got a nest egg stashed away somewhere?'

'You may be right. But—'

'It's money, Mr Troy. It all comes down to money. If you could just come and look.'

'What?'

'If you could come up here. To Derbyshire. And look.'

'I'm on the Murder Squad. I can't look into missing persons or missing money.'

'But you don't think he's missing. You think he's dead!'

She had rounded on him in a quick twist of logic. Afterwards he often had cause to wonder why he had agreed to make the trip to Derbyshire, to involve himself in this bloody, cloying mess. Even as he jotted down her address, the name of the town—Belper—seemed oddly familiar, as though he'd heard it recently in some other context. She was right: he did believe, if only from a combination of experience and instinct, that Cockerell was dead. She was right too, in that, for all that he could not offer Bonser the legal certainty he needed, he too thought the corpse was Cockerell. The weakness in it all was that if the corpse was Cockerell, it was not his problem—let the spooks handle that one—but if it wasn't, what logical consequence followed from his assertion that the man was dead? Dead where? Dead when? And by whose hand? No—it was not her logic that gripped him; it was his own. That and the dead cat curiosity of wanting to stick his nose into the Cockerell affair, simply because he was intrigued that his own brother should have concerned himself so much with the political capital to be made out of it. Rod was playing an odd game. Of late Troy had been surprised at the lengths to which he would go and the methods he would use, the people with whom he was prepared to deal. Strange bedfellows, as he had called them. He remembered the long spoon at Downing Street. And he remembered Rod's stinging suggestion that perhaps Troy and 'all the piods in Special Branch' had been only decoys in the episode of Commander Cockerell. He doubted the use Rod was making of all that he knew and he doubted the source of all that he knew—but worse, far worse, he hated the thought that he himself might have been used, hated the idea that he'd been in a sideshow when all the time he thought he'd been present at the main attraction.

He looked at the neat, small stack of paperwork on his desk, so controlled and so ordered since the arrival of Clark. The opposite of his life.

'I'll be there sometime tomorrow,' he said to her.

He rang off and pulled the post-mortem report from his in-tray. All good cases begin with a good body. And whoever he was down there on the slab in Portsmouth, he was the ripest corpse in a long time. Foul, fish-eaten, putrid and stinking. The pathologist's report made a disgustingly enjoyable read—up, that is, to the heading 'Contents of Digestive Tract, Stomach, Duodenum, Colon & Examination of Rectum'. At which juncture disgust overwhelmed even the most perverse of policely pleasures, and Troy dropped the report in his out-tray. He did not have a pending-tray. Perhaps Clark was working on that? Perhaps one day soon he would walk in and find his life casually dumped in that centre tray?

§41

When it came down to it he could not face the drive. The thought of the hours spent crawling up the A5 and then up the A6, across Northamptonshire and Leicestershire and halfway up Derbyshire, filled him with boredom. You could spend hours stuck in traffic before even leaving Greater London, and the road north could move at a snail's pace. Britain, it had to be said, was choking on its traffic. What Britain needed was Autobahns. They were the one positive thing the late Adolf Hitler was remembered for. Visitors would return from the newly reconstituted Germany and whinge about the backwardness of Britain when it came to roads. Every so often you could meet a buffoon in a bar for whom the mark of a civilised country was that it let him cruise at 105 mph along a concrete superhighway. But, then, that was the post-war syndrome. Troy was getting used to the fashionable rediscovery of the Continent—or Europe as people were tending to call it these days—the costly summer holiday abroad from which the well-to-do British would return boasting that they'd found somewhere in France that served English beer or a nice cup of tea—or, increasingly, on the opposite tack, that they'd discovered things that 'simply hadn't caught on in Britain yet', and never would while we remained 'insular'. Troy remembered his first sight of a garlic press, a bottle of Chianti and red Tuscan pottery. And that little blue book of *Mediterranean Food* by Elizabeth David, stuffed full of 'calamári'—whatever that was—and 'courgette', better known in its bloated form on the allotments of England as a 'prize marrer'—that had a lot to answer for. Either way, either response, was part of the great British talent for self-flagellation.

He reached into his desk drawer for a copy of the railway timetable and began to search for a suitable train. The old Midland line out of St Pancras. He liked trains, and Britain had an extensive network of lines that seemed to connect pretty well everything with pretty well everything else. Unlike Mussolini's trains, they rarely ran on time, but they did get you into the nooks and crannies of the country, whether the nook was Midsomer Norton in deepest Somerset or the cranny Monsal Dale in the heights of Derbyshire. The railways were like the underground, as he had described it to Khrushchev—ramshackle but they worked.

Belper? Why did he know that name? Belper. He found it on the network map. It was about ten miles north of Derby, a one-horse town, wedged between a tributary of the Trent and the tail end of the Pennines. And it did indeed have a railway station.

§42

The engine was a shabby specimen, still bearing the insignia of the old London, Midland & Scottish Railway, long since nationalised as part of British Railways. Troy had been a train-spotter as a boy—so many lines passed through Hertfordshire on their way north—but had outgrown the delights of childhood by the time this type had appeared. All the same, he knew it for what it was under the grime and neglect of the new order. It was, he recalled, a Jubilee class 4–6–0, named for the year of the old King's Silver Jubilee in 1935. Not as grand as the Coronation and Princess Pacifics, not as powerful, but sleek, neat, and usually red like the story-book engine—not dirty black as it was now.

The rhythm of steam, the mechanical inhalation and exhalation of the iron beast, was always soporific. He fell asleep, appropriately enough, somewhere in Bedfordshire. When he awoke it was dark and the train was chugging through the flatlands of the Trent Valley. He could not remember passing Leicester or Loughborough. He peered out of the window into a clear sky lit by a near-perfect half-moon. A station passed swiftly by—Long Something or other. He leant against the worn cushioning of an LMS Third Class railway compartment and fell back into sleep again.

Someone was nudging him. He opened his eyes. It was dim in the carriage, dark outside and the train had stopped. The someone was a railway guard.

'Belper you said, guvner? Look sharpish or you'll find yourself in Manchester.'

Troy leapt from the train, still half in the land of nod, and found himself in the land of he-knew-not-what. Far Twittering or Oyster Perch? The train pulled out, deep rhythmic sighs, and disappeared slowly into the stone cutting to the north. As the chug-hiss and the smell of smoke and steam faded, other sounds and scents took their place, opening up like flowers in trick photography. A delicate waft of night-scented stock, the fainter scent of late-flowering cabbage roses, the strong aromatics of nicotiana. He found himself facing a well-ordered flowerbed. In large white stones in the centre of the display, offset by an outline of scarlet geraniums, the letters B-E-L-P-E-R were picked out as though freshly whitewashed. High on a stone wall, a gas lamp perched upon its iron stem and hissed gently into the scented air. From its two arms hung baskets of trailing nasturtium and lobelia. The sound of the engine finally died in the distance, and from beneath it emerged a throaty musical burble, a multitude of deep cooing voices, dipping in and out of the silence. The silence. That was what was so startling. Somewhere in the distance an open window let out the indecipherable but unmistakable sound of a wireless tuned to the Home Service, but apart from that and the odd burbling noises, Troy could hear nothing, not a car, not a voice, nothing. A scented silence.

He looked around. He was standing next to a peeling red railway building, somewhat in the style of a Swiss chalet. The door to his right bore an enamel plaque saying 'Ladies Only'. Off to his left a man in porter's uniform was loading wicker crates full of racing pigeons onto a cart. The pigeons cooed at him, and there was a swift flutter of feathers as he lifted each basket in turn. He bore a remarkable resemblance to Oliver Hardy. The same rotund face, the same layered jowls jammed between chin and collar, the same clipped, old-fashioned moustache—the same colossal girth.

'Excuse me,' said Troy, 'I don't suppose there's a station hotel?'

Troy half-expected him to straighten up, fiddle with his tie or cuddle his hat to his chest and fluster a little in best Georgian modesty, rocking his head from side to side and pursing his lips. He said nothing, simply carried on loading his burbling baggage onto the cart. Troy regretted the implied negative in his question. Sod the English and their ungrammatical manners. All he meant was, 'Where's the nearest hotel?'

Without looking at Troy, Hardy pointed up the narrow track towards the town.

'Up there?' Troy asked. He was aware such men existed. People who scarcely dealt in language.

'Top o' the slope. Across the square. Kedleston,' said Hardy, in a surprisingly high, soft voice, barely raised above a whisper, still not looking at Troy. He plonked the last basket high on the load, walked to the front of the cart, and pressed a button. An electric motor kicked in with a whirr about as loud as a sewing machine, and the loaded cart wobbled off up the slope with Hardy perched at its head. Troy followed the railway caravan in search of the caravanserai, bemused by his silence, dreamily letting the sound of pigeons and the scent of stock wash over him in the warm night air. A Pennine Arabian Night.

It could not last. The Kedleston was a hole. A hole that had last seen a paintbrush or a new roll of paper sometime in the reign of Edward VII. His room was tiny and the bed the width of a coffin. Its springs, long since exhausted, protested to him most of the night and when they did not the man in the room next door, from which Troy seemed to be divided by two sheets of wallpaper glued back to back, broke wind frequently as though in sympathy with the tortured bedsprings.

He awoke, aching and tired, to find himself facing the only item of twentieth-century furniture in the room. Designed and built to be makeshift, the rational extension of the wartime motto 'make-do-and-mend', Utility furniture had proved surprisingly durable, and God knows, there might even have been people who found the plain plywood tallboy, an identical item to which could be found in homes the length and breadth of the land, attractive. It was alchemy in wood, necessity transmuted into virtue.

He washed and dressed to the sound of thumping water pipes and the deafening roar of emptying lavatory pans. The hot ran cold, and as he waited for the trickle of water to gain temperature, the sound of feet descending the stairs banged past his door and rattled the ornamental vase of plastic flowers on top of the tallboy.

He was the last down. The small dining room was full. Men with moustaches. Men in brown suits, who all seemed to know each other, and to be deeply submerged in greasy eggs, greasy bacon, greasy, milky tea and knowing shop talk. A smell of stale tobacco and hair oil glided gently across the worst that breakfast could exhale. One or two of the brown suits said, 'Mornin',' to Troy, and the one nearest to him asked him what he sold. Listening to their proud, jargon-ridden banter, Troy soon realised he was sharing a table with pioneers at the cutting edge of the brush and bathroom-fittings trades.

He emerged into the street. An Indian Summer's day. The bright light of belated sunshine, racing to make up for the cold of August. He looked around him. A bustling main street, banks and drapers and building societies and butchers, drenched in a sudden rush of smoke and steam as a northbound express roared through the cutting in the heart of the town. He looked up past the painted shop fronts to the stone upper storeys and the town shot back a century or more to the plainer solidity of the original Victorian; and above them all rose green hills, wrapping the town on three sides. It was not the landscape he had seen from the train, just before he had last nodded off. This was not the flood plain of the Midlands, this was a stone-built, sturdy northern town, climbing the sides of a Pennine valley. The landscape, if his matriculation all those years ago in School Certificate Geography served him well, of cotton and coal.

The waitress who had served him a disgusting breakfast of congealed something with cold something, which had to recommend it only that fact that there was lots of it, had drawn him a rough plan of the town. He turned it this way and that, trying to find north, and set off up the main street towards the eastern hill, looking for the Heage Road, for the address Mrs Cockerell had given him. He had not seen quite so much stone since he last killed a dull afternoon in Westminster Abbey. The town seemed to be carved from it. The odd outburst of brick seemed like an afterthought, a failed gesture in the direction of modernity. The town, like so much of Britain, did not strike him as well-to-do. The age of austerity had gone, but its defining attribute lingered on like a persistent cobweb. An air of the poor, stopping short of poverty.

So many of the houses were shabby, the paintwork peeling and the woodwork rotting, the people Orwellian, seeming to Troy like characters from *The Road to Wigan Pier*. Ascending the steep hill out of the town centre he passed what was obviously a doss house. A gaunt man stood outside wearing the remains of an army greatcoat, the flashes of a regiment still visible, the buttons dull and unpolished ten years or more, the hands clutching the lapels, one above the other as though cold in the warm light of morning, and the lips moving softly. As he passed him, Troy heard the syllables clearly 'che, che, che . . .'—a stammer leading nowhere. He would never get past the first syllable of whatever it was, and the worn, post-war, post-what figures emerging, shuffling and farting, from the blistered maroon door of the doss house did not wait for him to finish. They shuffled on, up or down the hill. Sad and silent. Post-war, post-what? Troy often wondered what private tragedy brought men to this. Britain after the war, any war, the First had been no different, seemed to litter itself with its unhealing casualties. But it was hard to believe that the public tragedy could account for all this. Beneath, beyond, the tangible fact of war were the multitudes of intangible facts of God-knows-what. As a child Troy had thought that there must be some special place from which such men came, almost like the factory of a mad scientist where rags were arranged into the form of man, the island of Dr Moreau where the half-men were half made. So often would he meet them in the dusty lanes of Hertfordshire, so often would a talking bundle of rags ring the bell at the kitchen door of his parents' house to be given leftovers. The reason Jimmy Wheeler's rice pudding joke was not funny was not that it had been told too often. It was not funny because it was true.

From the crest of the hill he could look back on the town. Over to his right, looking north, was a vast, blackened, brick chimney. So, it was a mill town after all. And, doubtless, if he'd been up and about earlier he would have passed streams of women pouring out of stone cottages in stone streets, walking in for an eight o'clock shift. Instead, at nine-thirty going on ten he was checking the names on the gates of large houses in a street of a different kind. Heage Road was, clearly, the posh end of town, the houses bigger, better maintained, further apart, lacking uniformity, suffering the gables and crestellations of passing architecture. He found Jasmine Dene, a large, between-wars Tudorish bungalow in black and white, set well back from the road, behind double gates, each gate post topped by a large square, wooden basket of hanging flowers. He opened one of the gates, parting Jasmine from its Dene. The garden was immaculate. Perfect to the artificial—rollered turf in stripes like the grain in wood, a razored edge, with borders of precisely aligned bedding plants, verging on the regimented, verging on the unattractive in the precision of their symmetry. The author of this British line and square was bending over the blades of an upturned lawnmower. A man of seventy or so, in black trousers, black waistcoat and a collarless, patterned cotton shirt. He looked up at Troy through enormous grey eyebrows. It was Uncle Todger come to life.

'Art lookin' fert missis?' he said.

Troy had no idea what he'd said. 'Yes' seemed like a good answer to try, then if the man whipped out a subscription to the *Reader's Digest* or a pledge to Jehovah's Witnesses he could try sign language.

'Yes,' Troy said.

'Tha'd best ring t'bell then, anntya?'

It didn't seem like a question, but Troy heard the upward inflection that implied it might be. He resorted to a 'jolly good', always handy in time of doubt. The man bent over his jammed lawnmower once more and Troy stepped between two half-barrels, in the ubiquitous black and white, chockful of primulas, and yanked on an iron bell-pull.

Grief is a deceiver. This was not the woman he had seen in Portsmouth. This woman was a well-preserved fifty. Tall, slender and elegant, and whilst he could not honestly say she was good-looking, she kept herself; carried herself and dressed herself in a way that made it seem inconceivable that she was the same person.

'Mr Troy, you're bright and early. Do come in.'

She smiled and threw the door wide, and when she smiled her eyes lit up. She was wearing a boiler suit of many zips in mid-blue, the same colour as her eyes, doubtless dyed from its wartime dirty grey, belted tightly around her narrow waist, and the blue was smudged and smeared with a hundred different hues. And in her left hand she clutched two paintbrushes, one with a dab of Chinese White and the other with a shade Troy recalled from childhood as Burnt Umber, fixed in his memory with an unanswered question as to why a box of watercolours had no paint called Raw Umber. She pulled a Liberty scarf from her head, shook her hair, part brown and part grey and well-cut, free from its bond.

'You've stayed in the town somewhere? God, I bet you could kill for a decent cup of coffee. Let me rinse the brushes and I'll get a pot going.'

A long corridor led to the back of the house. Mrs Cockerell strode off down it, leaving Troy to follow at his own pace. She had disappeared like the white rabbit, through a doorway to the right. Troy paused by the first door, knowing she was somewhere at the back of the house. Double doors opened into a front-facing sitting room. Nosiness drew him to the threshold; discretion kept him hovering on it. There, in the piercing eastern light, breaking incongruously through the leaded windows of the original mock-Tudor, were the artefacts and icons of the new, the substance of the gospel according to Cockerell. Ashtrays on stilts. A portrait of a stern Chinese woman, whose skin was green. The skater-pattern carpet, the coffee table with its laminated, clear plastic top and its inlay of plastic sea-shells—the factory version of Mother Nature's bug-in-amber—the non-matching wallpapers, whereby two walls faced each other in pale stripes and two in dark swirls and spirals. And the curtains—curtains in Mediterranean, sun-bleached tints, depicting an assortment of ubiquitous Chianti bottles, the symbol of all we were not—a sun-loving, easy-going, *mañana* people. It was not a room in which he could have felt comfortable. The studio-style, studded PVC leatherette furniture, so delicate on its black tapered legs and brass-shoed feet, seemed fragile compared to the robust representatives of the new technology—the double-doored television set, the huge, multi-functional radiogram, with an array of creamy, off-white push-buttons rictus-grinning like false teeth in a tumbler. You could not be comfortable. The furniture might break beneath your weight, then the machines might eat you.

'Arnold gave you his lecture, then?'

She had appeared quietly at his side. He was about to apologise, but suddenly it seemed unnecessary. She leant on the door jamb and peered in.

'You know. The Contemporary Look. All this tat.'

Troy smiled.

'Yes. He did.'

'Bet he bored you silly with it, didn't he? He'd have done the whole house out this way if I'd let him. Come and look. I kept one room, just for me. Arnie's allowed in on condition he changes nothing.'

Right at the back of the house was a large room opening out to the garden through french windows. It was an afternoon room, facing south and west, but even in the morning light it was obvious what she meant. Not a scrap of Contemporary had made it past the door. Walls papered in a pattern of English wildflowers, muted yellows and washed-out blues; a polished parquet floor; a few old, worn Persian rugs, a deep, sturdy Edwardian three-piece suite, reupholstered in pale colours; large Colefax and Fowler flowers on a cornfield chintz. A solid wall of tatty, broken-spined, well-read books. And twenty to thirty watercolours scattered across the other walls. It was traditional, it was comfortable, and it had more of an individual mark on it than the other room would have if lived in for fifty years.

She had gone again, away to the whistling of a kettle. Troy was drawn to the paintings. Mostly, he assumed, they were her own. The peaks and valleys of Derbyshire, the watercolours of the Early British style. Unfashionable now, but she worked through that, pushing, it seemed to him after he had looked at half a dozen, through the representation of landscape to an unsentimental abstraction. He had gazed a minute or more at one such abstract until the signature told him otherwise: 'Janet Cockerell. Combe Martin, Devon. 1948.' What he had taken as abstract was a seascape dazzling in the silver light of North Devon, the beaten-metal sea, the red-rippled, iron rocks of the coastline. He blinked and looked again. It was abstract once more.

He was staring, envious of her taste, at the few paintings that were not her own work—a portrait by Gwen John, a pseudo-religious scene, quite possibly a gospel story, in the unmistakable, irresistible heavy hand of Stanley Spencer—when she returned.

'Shall we have coffee in the garden? After all that rain I think we might be in for an Indian Summer.'

He followed her out through the french windows. The same division of property seemed to apply to the garden. This was not the immaculate military layout of the front; this was a wilder place altogether. Herbs and flowers competed with vegetables in the same bed—a straggling thyme bush, the crisp, blackened flowers of marjoram, dozens of onions, their tops folded over to ripen in maturity, a ragged, unpruned late-flowering red rose, petals bright as blood, a rambling, fruit-laden quince, a thousand wallflowers turning woody, and being left to seed themselves.

An easel stood facing the south-west, across the smoking chimneys of the town, down across slate roofs, over the Orwellian maze of stone streets. The merest outline of an image appeared. She had clearly been at work a matter of half an hour or so before Troy's visit distracted her. She set down her tray on a wicker table—a cheap and cheerful Suzy Cooper pattern of crockery, and a large pot of steaming hot coffee. Troy took the chair furthest from the house, and found himself perched almost on the edge of a cliff, looking down into the overgrown remains of a quarry. Instinctively he pulled his chair a foot nearer the house.

She said nothing until he had a cup of aromatic, strong, black coffee in his hands.

'I know I'm playing with your sense of paradox, Chief Inspector, but my husband is not dead.'

'Not dead.'

'Not dead. Running.'

'Running?'

'Hiding.'

'From what?'

She set down her cup. They had in a few, short strokes arrived at the heart of the matter it seemed.

'I think my husband was living beyond his means. I think we've lived high on the hog for far too long, and I think whatever he'd been doing to finance our style of living was about to break, his chickens were coming home to roost. And he ran.'

'The things he left behind him in Portsmouth?'

'All planned. Designed to make us think he was dead.'

'The body?'

'Coincidence. A remarkable coincidence.'

'And the conviction the Government have that your husband was working for them?'

She shrugged, much as he would have done himself.

'I don't think the right hand knows what the left hand's doing.'

Troy could agree with that. In fact, it was the best summing up he'd heard of the governmental mess that had seeped out around the clumsy attempts to conceal whatever had been going on—worthy of a leader writer.

'Why would Her Majesty's Government use a man like my husband? He wasn't the best frogman in SOE, even in his prime. And that was more than ten years ago. He was a stringy, seedy, out of condition fifty-two-year-old, far too fond of cork tips and whisky. He was thirty-five when the war began. If he hadn't been in the Navy anyway he would never have been called up, not at his age. The idea that they'd get him out of retirement to do another job is preposterous.'

'What do you think he was doing in Portsmouth?'

'Preparing his own disappearance. Scattering a few red herrings. It just so happened it was the spies, his old pals, who picked them up and not the ordinary bobbies whom I'd yet to inform of his disappearance. I didn't report him missing until ten days after you met him. Right now he's abroad somewhere, puzzled to read that he was a spy, cockahoop that it lets him off the hook and scuppers his creditors.'

'Have they approached you?'

'No.'

'Doesn't that blow a hole in your case that it was a problem with money?'

'No. I've the evidence of my eyes. It may be they don't know they've been had. It could take a long time to surface. What I know is that we lived very high on the hog these last few years. And I know we can't afford it.'

'How long do you think this has been going on?'

'Five or six years. Since the Festival of Britain.'

She laughed at her own exactitude, looked down into her coffee cup, smiling wryly.

'He came back from that telling me, "I've seen the future and it works—works in any size and colour you want." He always told me business was booming. Once Labour was out he used to bang on about economic growth. We had a businessman's government, he said. He'd hold forth on that on the golf course, in the Conservative Club and when he was slumming in the British Legion. It took over from, "What I did in the war." I was pleased not to have to listen to his war any more, but I thought it was twaddle. And five years later we have three shops—I used to scream if he used the word "emporium"—a warehouse stuffed with all the tat he seems to think people want—and he's a better authority on that than I am—a Rover and a Jag in the garage, and he could afford to abandon an MG in Portsmouth. Our current account is absurdly healthy and our deposit is stuffed. None of it adds up. He couldn't have come by it legally.'

Troy thought it odd that debt or fraud should force him to disappear, when his bank accounts were lined. Equally he thought it odd that she should be telling him all this.

'Supposing you're right and he is alive. Supposing I find him. You would, in effect, have shopped him.'

'He ditched me. I don't care.'

'And the business?'

'I haven't touched it. I'm a director. All I've done is sign cheques for the managers and leave them to it. If I'm right and Arnold's alive and you find him, then I'll sell the business over his head, pay off the people he's swindled and to hell with him. If you're right and he's dead, then I'll get probate. Either way I don't care. I don't need the money. My father left me a trust. God knows Arnold didn't need to fiddle anything. We had quite enough as it was. But he had his honour. He held it as a principle that we shouldn't spend my money. A man's not a man who's supported by his wife. That sort of thing. Men and their wretched honour. Just another of their lies. Something they thought up for their own convenience. I never had a lot of time for Arnold's honour.'

Troy remembered a line Conrad put into the mouth of his old sailor Marlow: 'He made so much of the dishonour, when it was the guilt alone that mattered.' Of course, she was right. But Troy doubted the worth of mentioning a book quite so male as *Lord Jim*.

'Tell me,' he tacked. 'Who came to you?'

'I don't quite follow you, Mr Troy.'

'You reported your husband missing . . . in the conventional way.'

'Yes. The local inspector came up. Harold Warriss. I suppose you could say he's a friend of the family. I've—we've known him for years. He was blandly reassuring. Told me Arnold would turn up soon enough.'

'And when he didn't? When the papers became chock-a-block with spy stories?'

'Nothing. Nothing at all. I didn't associate those stories with my husband.'

'And nor, it seems, did Warriss?'

'Well, if he did, it didn't prompt him to pay me a second visit.'

'And when the PM named your husband?'

'Oh, the Prime Minister has old-fashioned manners,' her voice rippled with the sarcasm. 'When he finally decided to make a statement naming my husband, which he must have been planning for weeks, he sent a chap to see me.

'I heard nothing at all until about a week before Arnold was named. It had, honestly, never crossed my mind that he might be the anonymous Portsmouth spy. Then one day, without warning, a chap from the Foreign Office turned up. Daniel Keeffe, about your age I suppose. Good-looking young chap. Very shy, very nervous, stammering an apology on behalf of Her Majesty's Government. Arnold would be named in a Commons statement the next week, and it had all been a dreadful mistake.'

'He actually said that?'

'No. His exact words as I recall were, "It's all been the most dreadful misunderstanding. I'm so dreadfully sorry. I'd no idea that he meant to do it."'

'"I" not "we"?'

'Yes. He seemed to take it very personally. He was very upset. I'm sure I should have asked him more questions, but I didn't. I didn't believe Arnold had been the Portsmouth spy. I still don't. As far as I was concerned he was still missing. It's very convenient for the Government to say it's Arnold. Ties up a loose end, doesn't it? But it isn't Arnold.'

'And the press?'

'Oh, they hung around at the gates for a few days. The old pals' act finally worked for Arnold. Warriss put a man in uniform outside the house until they cleared off. Then nothing. Other fish to fry, I suppose. What's a dead frogman compared to Nasser?'

'You know,' said Troy, after a while, 'most men don't disappear over money. It's usually women.'

She laughed, a short, bitter snort.

'Give over, Mr Troy. You saw my husband. Do you think he has the makings of anyone's fancy man?'

It called for, and Troy deployed, a standard line from Teach Yourself Detection.

'It takes all sorts,' he said, squirming at the phrase.

'Believe me, Mr Troy, my husband wasn't interested in women, or sex. At least not in—'

She stopped herself. Passed over the moment by pouring another cup of coffee for him. But it was impossible to let the remark go.

'At least,' he said, 'not in ordinary sex?'

There was a pause so long he thought she would not answer, but then she drew breath and picked up his gaze.

'No. Not in ordinary sex. He was over-fond of his frogman's suit. He wanted us to do it while he wore the damn thing. I never would.'

'And you don't think he might have found someone who would?'

'No. It's the kind of thing he could get from whores in all the cities he visited from Manchester to Stockholm. God knows he spent enough time travelling to know half the whores in Europe. That would not surprise me. But the idea of another woman actually offering him such nonsense as part of a sexual relationship—no. I can't find that believable.

My husband could not sustain such a relationship. It wasn't in him to do it. When I told him I wouldn't let him into the bed in his rubber suit, he took to undressing in the bathroom. I haven't seen him naked in ten years. I don't think he could show his body to a woman. I saw more of the man on the slab in Portsmouth than I ever did of my husband . . .'

She paused for breath. Troy hoped she would pick up; he did not want to prompt her in any direction with any word of his own.

'That, that Inspector Bonser. Do you know, he actually asked me if I could identify . . . I mean . . . he actually thought I could recognise my husband by his . . . thing.'

She paused again. He said nothing.

'Of course, I couldn't. But he would ask. It was what he was going on about when you walked in. He really would not believe that a woman could not know that.'

She slammed down the cup onto its saucer. Anger, worked up in an instant, to save her from her tears. She leant back, her face tilted to the sky while the moment passed and the prospect of tears with it. When she turned her eyes back to Troy, she was almost calm, and she was harder and sterner. Suddenly he existed for her. She was aware of her listener as well as her own narrative.

'You know, I'm not at all sure I should be telling you all this.'

'I'm a detective, Mrs Cockerell. I need clues.'

'Yes—the detective detects. But what I detect is the inward sneer of the man. You are sneering at all of this, aren't you, Mr Troy?'

Damn the woman. He had not thought she would be so acute. Sneering? Of course he was sneering.

'Don't reproach yourself too much, Mr Troy. There's probably a lot to sneer at. I imagine a house called Jasmine Dene is enough to make your home counties sensibility heave. My husband wanted to merge our names and rename the house, but that yielded "Jarno" or "Arnoja". I suggested "Dunswimmin" might be appropriate for an ex-frogman, at which point he gave up and we left it with the name it had when we bought it. Not a great sense of humour, my husband.'

Troy felt he had tacked into the wind. It had been short of explosive, but it had still been an outburst. He picked up the line and gently pulled her in.

'Was he a frogman when you met him?'

'Yes. I met him in the spring of 1940. The last weeks of the Phoney War. We married that summer. Everybody did, after all. Summer of the Battle of Britain and the quickie marriage. He spent most of the war teaching men fifteen years younger than himself how to be frogmen. That hurt. He came home irritable as hell. "Boys doing a man's job," as he put it. Then as the war hotted up he went into active service. I think Special Operations must have got short of qualified swimmers, possibly desperate to have taken Arnold off the back burner—perhaps all those boys he trained were dead by then?—and from the summer of 1943 he was tapping the side of his nose, using phrases like "hush-hush" and banging on about work of "national importance", about which he couldn't possibly tell me anything. He never realised I didn't want to know. I think he would have loved it if I'd wormed a secret out of him.'

'But afterwards—surely he told you then what he'd done?'

'Yes. Of course. I suppose he was right. It was "hush-hush". He was surveying French beaches looking for the D-Day site. He did some genuinely dangerous work, I'll give him that. He once swam into Brest to set magnetic mines on German ships, that sort of thing. But he wasn't anything special, he was just inordinately proud of it. I don't know what the magic ingredient was, but those five years of hell and want seem to have imbued us all with a preposterous national pride.'

She paused. Looked at Troy quizzically. Weighing up his reaction.

'I'm sorry, Mr Troy. I'm not unpatriotic. It's . . . well . . . it's just "men", isn't it? I suppose you're of an age. You did your bit in the war, I wasn't trying to offend—'

Troy cut her short.

'I wasn't in the services, Mrs Cockerell.'

She raised an eyebrow at this. There could be few men of Troy's age without a war record of some sort. It was his generation's war.

'I was a WREN,' she added bluntly.

He said nothing.

'At Bletchley Park. Cryptography. That sort of thing.'

Troy was quietly amazed. Her casual 'that sort of thing' had been the best-kept secret of the war. Odd things had come to light in the years since, but it was still true to say that it was also one of the best-kept secrets of the peace.

'My father died in '43. Left us this house. Arnold got an early demob. We were installed here before the results of the '45 election were out. He went onto the reserve list, but I think if they'd given him a choice he would have stayed. He wasn't a conscript after all, he was a regular, even though his time would have been up in '44 anyway if there hadn't been a war. But he got his orders soon after VE Day. All they'd looked at was his age. He was forty-one. I suppose it was generous in its way. Discharge the married men first, the middle-aged, those with dependent families. Of course, we didn't have children. We'd spent most of the war apart. And by then it was too late.

'We stood in King Street at the end of July and cheered when Labour got in. Everybody did. The next morning I found Arnold cleaning his frogman's kit. He put it in the garage, in a steel trunk. Once or twice a year, he'd take it out. Clean it. And put it back. The only swimming he did after that was on our holidays. We used to go to Woolacombe. My choice—the North Devon light is quite incredible, I've been painting it for years—but the sea was warm and blue if you wanted to swim. We went every year in the forties, but I never saw him do anything more than swim a few yards like any holiday maker, then he'd laze around on the beach, and then he'd prop up the bars, boring people with his war.

'The last few years I've been on my own. Arnold's been on his foreign jaunts—buying, selling, roister-doistering. God knows.'

In the midst of all this had been a telling statement. Troy wondered if he could make her pick it up again.

'You say he kept his frogman's kit in the garage?'

'Yes—in a trunk. If I'd let him he'd probably have hung it on the wall like a trophy.'

'Is it there now?'

He had clearly uttered the unexpected. She stared at him for a moment unblinkingly.

'You know—I haven't looked.'

She led the way back across the lawn, through the side gate to a double garage—about the most colossal status symbol a suburban house could display; to own one car was posh enough, two, or three as they appeared to have, was a rare display of the ostentation of wealth.

Mrs Cockerell prised open a warped wooden door to reveal a shiny black Rover 90—the poor man's Rolls-Royce as it was so often called.

At the far end of the garage was a thick steel chest. She lifted the lid. It was empty.

'Doesn't mean anything, you know.'

Troy said nothing.

'If he's planned it all as carefully as I think, then this is just one more red herring.'

'Didn't the police ask to look at it? Or the chap from the FO?'

'I didn't think to mention it.'

She strode quickly out of the dimness of the garage and back into sunlight. Troy found himself facing the upturned backside of the gardener, bent over the lawnmower once more.

She folded her arms, thumbs pressing deeply into her flesh, and composed her face against the anger she so clearly felt.

'I know what you're thinking. But believe me, Arnold was clever. He planned ahead. This is just another twist he thought up. And besides, it doesn't square up. None of it does. Do you know what the papers said? They said he'd been testing experimental equipment for the Navy. In a pig's eye, he had. And if he was, why would he need his own kit? And that line doesn't match what young Keeffe told me. If it was all a "misunderstanding", where did he get hold of this so-called experimental kit? In an Army and Navy surplus store? Mr Troy, you can surely see what a cock-up this is? They can't even get their stories straight. Arnold just provided them with a convenient scapegoat. I shouldn't think he gives a damn. Wherever he is, he'll be flattered to think he was of use to the Navy one last time. Ironic, isn't it?'

The man with the lawnmower moved off slowly across the lawn, creating the even stripes, the green herringbone, filling the air with the smell of freshly cut grass. It seemed to Troy that the pattern in the grass was the only one Mrs Cockerell was willing to see for herself.

'For a second, Mrs Cockerell, indulge me and pretend that your husband might be dead. Then ask yourself why you so much want him to be alive in the teeth of the evidence.'

'I may take it this question does not allow of matters of the heart or even the mereness of sentiment, Mr Troy?'

'You may.'

'Then I think that perhaps we understand one another after all. I want him alive, I want him alive, and I believe him to be alive, because if he's dead, then he's got away with everything.'

It was a showstopper. A number to ring down the curtain and bring the audience to its feet. He followed her back into the bungalow. She went to the back room, her room, flipped down the lid of a writing desk and picked up a set of keys.

'Take these. The main shop is closed for the moment. The manager wanted his summer holiday. So I let him take it. Look at anything you like. I have no secrets; they're all Arnold's. Somewhere in there is the key to how he did it. A colossal fiddle, I'm sure. Who knows, if you find out how he did it we may discover a trail of money, a paperchase. And at the end of it, there he will be.'

'I'm not wonderfully experienced at fraud cases, Mrs Cockerell.'

'But you'll do your best.'

It grew slowly, a heaving, dragging curse, uttered from deep in the bowels of the planet, spreading its damnation until at the pitch of madness a sound like a tortured banshee wailed in through the open french windows and chilled him to the marrow. He moved to the edge, looked out across the garden, soaked in its incongruous southern sun, and heard the unmistakable, but almost forgotten tones of an air-raid siren.

She had followed him, peering around him, shoulder to shoulder in the door frame.

'What's the matter?'

He was speechless.

'Oh, the siren! I wouldn't let that bother you. They use it at the mill to announce the change of shift.'

She turned her wrist and looked at her watch, showing him the face.

'See, it's noon. On the dot. You'll hear it again at four. It's mounted on top of Woolworth's. I suppose it ensures that everybody knows when the Moloch wants them.'

The arrogance of it. He could scarcely believe it. The modern equivalent of the knocker-up, and to achieve it they perpetuated the most frightening, the most evocative sound in England. Dragged the past into the present, and momentarily dragged him back to 1944. To dark cold nights, the frozen wastes of East London. Darkness, death, the wail of the siren. Darkness, death, the ripe smell of cordite. He could almost taste it.

'Mr Troy. Are you all right? You've turned very pale.'

He was not all right. He felt breathless and sick to the pit of his stomach.

'I haven't heard that sound . . . in a long time.'

'We're used to it.'

'Yes,' he said. 'I'm sure.'

She held out the keys. He took them.

'You'll be in touch?' she said.

'Yes,' he said.

§43

Commander Cockerell's main emporium, his 'HQ', stood at the top of the market place. A large blue-and-white sign said simply COCKERELL in letters eighteen inches high, spanning the shop front, and that of the one next door. It said nothing else—from a distance he could be the butcher, the baker or the man who sold pea-green boats. At some point in the recent past the two shops had been knocked into one to create a barn-like room in which the angular Scandinavian sofas could be displayed in clusters of three, like broken squares, with a coffee table at each centre and sci-fi-looking, technology-defying lamps, no more than thin strips of steel or coiled springs bearing light bulbs, perched at the corners. It was termed, he had read somewhere, a 'conversation pit', a social device designed to bring one's kneecaps into close contact with other, perhaps lonelier, kneecaps; a dexterity-stimulating device, designed to teach you the rapid juggling of cups of instant, powdery coffee, glasses of warm white wine and little trays full of nuts and things; a sense-numbing device, as you watched warm blobs of oil rise and fall in the tapered cylinders of illuminated liquid table lamps. All in all, it brought out the snob in Troy.

Troy looked around for anything resembling an office. There was none on the ground floor. A steep, curving staircase led up to the first floor, and curved around again to climb to the second. In the space between the two was a wood and glass cubby hole, its walls formed by a simple partition from the main room, its ceiling by the angle of the ascending staircase. A single bulb, in a frosted glass shade, hung precariously from the ceiling on a twisted, cloth-covered cable, through which flecks of black and red baked rubber showed. Troy flicked the brass nipple on the wall switch, half expecting sparks and flames to spurt from the wires. Forty watts dimly illuminated the room. A cramped, poky little hole, whose height fell away to nothing as the stairs met the floor, but into it Cockerell had stacked everything he needed. The only remotely new item was a telephone. The filing cabinets, the desk, the rows of dusty pigeon holes, looked as though they had frozen in grime and time some fifty odd years ago. A small sliding panel, no more than six inches across, was set in the wooden wall at waist height, as though at some date long since receipts and tallies had been passed through by an army of shop assistants to the lonely clerk in his corner booth. The swivel chair burst with horsehair and the roller on the roll-top desk was jammed at three-quarters open and no force on earth would budge it. There was still a discernible pattern to the faded wallpaper that lined the sloping ceiling and one of the walls. Troy knew from childhood forays into the upper floors of Mimram that it was Victorian, the greens and the yellows were unmistakable, and it had probably adorned the walls of Cockerell's office for more than seventy years. He found it hard to believe that Cockerell did any real work here. Found it hard to believe that the John the Baptist of the New Look could live or work contentedly among such obvious relics of the hated past.

A pipe rack had been crudely nailed to the wall above the desk. Three pipes, blackened and stained but long unused, hung at odd angles. Just inside the door an umbrella stand held a collection of walking sticks, a dozen or more—one with a brass duck's head, one with knobs on, looking vaguely Celtic, and a shooting stick with a perished leather and canvas seat. He flipped through a couple of the pigeon holes—a catalogue of spare parts for paraffin stoves, dated September 1922, a dozen back issues of *Health and Efficiency* all dating from the 1940s, an old AA handbook (where to stay in the remotest shires and a few spidery road maps of Britain)—a couple of copies of *Fur and Feather Monthly* and he would have enough for a dentist's waiting room—and the first sign of recent occupation, *Parade,* February 1956—a risqué magazine, with none of the wholesome illusion of *H&E,* full of tits and backsides. All of which told him nothing. He turned his attention to the row of dusty books on top of the desk. *Whitaker's Almanac* 1951, the Lith–Zyx volume of Webster's *Universal English Dictionary* and dozens of well-read, broken-spined, paper-back books. Mostly the work of the late Peter Cheyney, a master of racial and social snobbery, creator of superior, ruthless, womanising Englishmen and wise-talking, slang-obsessed, rod-packing, punchy Americans. The villains were, inevitably, spawned by the lesser races—Jews, Negroes, anyone from Eastern Europe. Troy had read one or two Cheyneys in his early teens, and found them distasteful. Cockerell's recent reading was more interesting. The new bloke, already beginning to cause a bit of a fuss—Ian Fleming. Cockerell had *Casino Royale, Moonraker* and *Live and Let Die,* all featuring Fleming's hero James Bond, Commander James Bond RN. Troy caught the connection. Any fantasist might read, and some would enjoy, the pre-war world of Peter Cheyney in which the Englishman was still God, pushing through crowds of gibbering foreigners, waving Her Britannic Majesty's passport and shouting 'Imshe' but, perhaps, the man had a closer identification with Bond. The naval commander, the secret agent, socially superb, sexually confident, emotionally damaged—vulnerable enough to permit even a weasel like Cockerell the passing glimmer of identity. Besides, Fleming himself was supposed to be the real thing, an old Etonian, a close friend of the Prime Minister, part of our shady secret services during the war and quite possibly after, a silken charmer with women, nattily attached to one end of a long cigarette holder, but if Rod's parliamentary gossip was to be believed, a loser too since, as Rod would have it, while Fleming smoothed and smarmed his way around the heights of society, Hugh Gaitskell coolly, and in utter secrecy, was having an affair with his wife.

The left-hand pillar of the desk appeared to be one large cupboard. It was locked with two locks, one far newer and stouter than the other. Troy quickly went through the bundle of keys Mrs Cockerell had given him, and after a couple of tries found the pair that opened the cupboard. It was a model of neatness compared to the room which housed it. Neat stacks of thin cardboard folders: bank statements held together by bulldog clips, with each quarter dated; the stubs of his chequebooks; a paying-in book for the Hereford and Worcester Joint Commercial Bank, Great Malvern branch; a sheaf of annual statements from the Ancient Order of Derbyshire Foresters Savings Society, with whom Cockerell had a small mortgage, and a sheaf of quarterly statements from a bank in Stockholm, presumably where Cockerell acquired most of the 'Contemporary' furniture that filled up the floor below. Troy was, he knew, next to useless with this sort of thing. It was one of the reasons he had leapt at the chance to transfer Clark; neither he nor Jack had a scrap of patience where figures were concerned.

Seeking anything to put off the moment when he would have to examine the books of the business, Troy rummaged among the pigeon holes, not knowing what he was looking for or could expect to find. A covering letter from a travel agent, a pocket diary full of dates and assignations, a small black book marked 'Read This for Clues'? The best he found was a torn postcard. An English seaside resort, one of those long, pleasureless piers stretching out into the cold offshore waters of the Channel or the North Sea, Southend or Skegness or some such. The address side was intact—Mr A. Cockerell, and the shop address—but little remained of the greeting and the postmark was smudged. He puzzled a while over the remnants of the message—a woman's hand he was sure—but could do little with 'ing', 'ou' or 'eine'. 'Eine' at least was interesting. Few English words ended that way.

At last he could put it off no longer. He drew up the splitting horse-hair chair, blew five months' dust off the desk and turned to the less than riveting papers accounting for the proper running of a small business. Why, he wondered, long enough to gaze down the length of the main street and up at the looming Pennines, why had Napoleon dubbed the English 'a nation of shopkeepers'? He took a last look at his watch. He had wasted time, it was gone two. He must keep track of the time. If that damn siren was due to wail again at four he wanted to be ready for it. The last thing he wanted was for it to catch him unawares.

Cockerell was right to boast. His business was doing very nicely, far more nicely than one might suppose given that he was in unfashionable Middle England, far from the fashionable Heart of England. His wife was right to be suspicious. He was turning over a very tidy sum indeed. But beyond that Troy could not tell; the requisite skills were not his. He began to wish that Cockerell might be dead, that someone had killed him; it would at least bring him back within his own domain. You know where you are with a murder. It had taken him an hour or more to reach even this basic conclusion. He glanced at his watch. It was 3.58. Any minute now. He looked down the street once more. A steady bustle of afternoon shoppers, housewives with bulging shopping bags, the to and fro of delivery vans. He began to see why Cockerell had sited his office where he had. It was great spot for an idle mind to be idle in. Hours could be whiled away. The siren took up its wail. Troy sat it out. Stared at the hills above the town and waited.

It was a while before he perceived the sound beneath the siren. Loud and tedious now, rather than disturbing, but it masked almost completely the vigorous pounding at the shop door. By the time he had worked out that that was what it was, the man at the door had had time to pass through exasperation to anger.

'And who the 'eck might you be?' he said as Troy opened the shop door to him.

It was another of the weaselly men. He stood below the step, in a tatty tweed jacket and grey cavalry twill trousers bearing a multitude of unseemly stains, a cigarette stub burning between the longest fingers of his right hand. This specimen was more robust than Cockerell, taller and fleshier, but with the same scrawny look to him, the same fondness for the pencil-line moustache. But seediness had taken a different toll on this one; he was not simply scrawny, he was scrawny with a potbelly, scrawny with deeply nicotined teeth, scrawny with badly chewed fingernails. He was about five feet nine or ten. Troy estimated his age as fifty-five or so, and not wearing it well.

There was a visible frisson as Troy showed him his warrant card and returned the greeting word for word.

'I saw the light on,' he said. 'I thought it was Janet—Mrs Cockerell.'

'I'm sure you did, but you haven't answered my question.'

'Oh, I'm George Jessel. I've come about the books.'

'You're Cockerell's book-keeper?'

'Oh no. Arnold kept his own books.'

'His accountant?'

'No—he did that too. I'm the auditor.'

He fumbled inside his jacket and produced a dog-eared business card: 'George G. Jessel—Chartered Accountant, 23 Railway Cuttings, Belper.'

'I do the audit twice a year. It's overdue.'

The cigarette, burning down to his stained, coffee-coloured fingertips, was suddenly applied to the tip of a fresh one and discarded. A rapid bout of deep inhalation was followed by a rapid fit of coughing. He heaved and hoiked, and spat globules of phlegm onto the pavement, bent double with the effort of putting the torch to his own lungs.

He almost smiled as he straightened up.

'Long overdue as a matter of fact. Would it be all right if I picked up the last six months' figures now?'

Time for silence. Spin it out, thought Troy. Let him fill the vacuum. So he stared and said nothing.

'I did ask Janet—I mean Mrs Cockerell—but she said she couldn't be bothered. But it's got to be done, hasn't it?'

Troy said nothing. Jessel drew deeply on his cigarette.

'It's women,' he prattled. 'You know what they're like.'

'No, I don't. And the answer's no. You can't take anything now. If I decide you can have the books, I'll let you know. In the meantime they're part of my investigation. Now, can you be reached at this address?'

He held up the dog-eared card.

'Oh aye, nine till five-thirty, weekdays.'

'Then I'll be in touch.'

He stood some moments on the doorstep after Troy had closed the door on him. As he walked off down the street, he looked back several times and before he had gone fifty yards lit another cigarette from the stub of the old and coughed his lungs up again.

Troy watched him from the upstairs window. It was not long past four. If he zipped through the rest of the papers, Troy thought, he might just catch Mr Jessel in his office at closing time. He was not at all sure Mr Jessel would enjoy the meeting. The prospect of a live human subject to investigate rather than a set of figures galvanised Troy. Nothing quite so focuses the mind as knowing you might be able to hang some other bugger in the morning.

In an hour or so he had read all he wanted to. The rat, if such creature it be, that Janet Cockerell could smell, was smelt by him. It didn't add up—except, of course, that the metaphor was ill chosen, for add up was precisely what it did. The smell was beyond, beneath and all around the unlikely fact of such addition and precision.

Without doubt he was going to have to spend another night in this one-horse town, sampling the delights of the Kedleston. He looked at the row of books again, and, preferring what he knew to what he didn't, stuffed *Casino Royale*, the one Fleming he had read, into his coat pocket. It would pass a dull night in a small town.

Railway Cuttings was almost opposite the railway station, an alley of soot-blackened Victorian cottages running along the edge of the deep cutting that carried the tracks through the middle of the town. At best it was eight feet wide, and one side of it was made up of the thick granite restraining wall that topped off the cutting. The tracks were visible over the low wall, gleaming off to meet at infinity, polished like stainless steel with constant use.

Number 23 was some sort of lapsed warehouse. He could just make out the faded, cusped lettering of an old sign for a Seed Merchant and Nursery, high on the wall facing the tracks, but down at eye level were two small rectangular plates—new and painted, 'Belper Urban District Council Refuse Disposal'; old and brass, 'George G. Jessel, Chartered Accountant. 2nd Flr'.

The staircase had no carpet. Bits of old linoleum tacked onto the worn treads. Flakes of ancient off-white distemper floating down from the ceiling. The hand rail worn into deep curves by the passing of many hands. At the top were two doors. One half-open, marked 'G. Jessel'. The other, closed, marked 'Private'. Behind the first was a small, square office, packed with filing cabinets, with a small desk at the centre, overburdened with a huge manual typewriter sitting under its nightly plastic dust cover, its shift arm sticking out like a splint. He turned to the other door, heard the sound of papers rustling, and tapped gently. The door opened. Jessel's head appeared in the space. Dark brown cow eyes peering out at him.

'You found it, then?'

'Yes. I found it.'

Jessel backed away, ushered him into a room scarcely bigger than Cockerell's office. Tiny, triangular, but a complete contrast. It was a model of neatness. Everything shipshape and orderly. Not a speck of dust to be seen or a paperclip out of place. Although Jessel had a cigarette glued to his bottom lip, and had developed the knack of talking without dislodging it, the ashtray was wiped clean, as though he tipped it out and dusted it after every couple of fags. It startled Troy, but he could see the logic behind it. He had expected a reflection of the physical man, a man who, it seemed, kept a record of most recent meals on his shirtfront and lapels, stained from collar-stud to fly-buttons. Of course, the room reflected the mind of the man, the ordered categories of the accountant mind.

Jessel pulled an upright chair away from its place against the wall and set it in front of the desk for Troy. He sat on the other side, across the narrow strip of shiny oak and worn red leather—a small silver fob watch, a row of freshly sharpened pencils, a cut glass inkwell, and two marble-finish Waterman fountain pens laid out like toy soldiers in battle formation.

Jessel opened his mouth to speak and the roar of a train in the cutting made him think better of it. The room shook, the pens and pencils danced a jig across the desktop, a whiff of steam-laden smoke rolled in through the open window and Jessel picked up the fob watch and tapped the face.

'The five-fifteen out of Derby. St Pancras to Sheffield. Same time every day. Three minutes later on Saturdays, and never on a Sunday.'

'You've seen Mrs Cockerell, you say, and she—'

'No,' Jessel cut in. 'Not seen. On the phone. I've talked her on the phone.'

'And she won't let you see the books?'

Jessel detached the cigarette from his lower lip, the lip puckered and gave up its spittle adhesion reluctantly. How often, Troy thought, did the man skin himself doing that? Jessel picked a fleck of tobacco from his mouth—the hard stuff, no filter tips—drew on the fag, managed not to cough and flicked the ash into the otherwise pristine ashtray.

'Right. I don't blame her. She says Arnold will tackle it when he gets back and it should all just wait. I suppose it's important to her to believe he will come back. But the figures are piling up, even without all the foreign trade, and besides, it's not legal is it?'

'Quite,' said Troy. 'It's a matter of the law that brings me here.'

From the look in his eyes Troy knew that Jessel was instantly regretting having introduced the notion of law.

'Arnold's death.'

'Arnold's disappearance.'

'He's not dead then?'

'Mrs Cockerell is unwilling to confirm that the body is his.'

Another deep drag on the weed, a cloudy breathing out of noxious, high-strength tobacco smoke.

'If he's not dead, what's the problem?'

'Money,' said Troy simply.

'Money?'

'Lots of money.'

Jessel sucked his cigarette down to the knuckle, lit up another from the stub and bought himself as much time as he could.

'Nothing illegal about money,' he fluffed, and Troy knew he was on the defensive, knew down to his copper's toes that Janet Cockerell was right. And if she was, he would leave this man no stone under which to hide.

'How long have you been covering up for him?'

Jessel coughed, retched and looked to die. Troy sat impassively, watching the sweat beads form high up at the hairline and head slowly south across the reddening face to be mopped up by the frayed shirt collar. It was theatrical. Dragged out as long as he could muster phlegm, heaving till his ribs ached—and it wasn't going to work.

When he raised his head above the desktop, Troy was staring at him.

'Is . . . is . . . herrummmphhickerrwyerch . . . is that what she told you?'

'Is that what you're doing?'

'You don't want to believe everything Janet Cockerell tells you. They didn't exactly get on like a house on fire, you know. She's had it in for Arnold for years.'

'There's an awful lot of money passing through Cockerell Ltd. A small fortune for three small shops in the Pennines.'

'It's all legitimate. You're forgetting the foreign trade.'

'Goods that never enter England, but show up via his bank account in Stockholm?'

'Exactly. But you make it sound sinister. It's not. It's all above board. Declared and taxed. Perfectly legal. Men like Arnold Cockerell—the backbone of Britain. Expanding into Europe. Pioneers.'

He was beginning to sound like one of those dreadful Party Political Broadcasts that television had made into a form of boredom unique to the medium. It was a hangover from the war, when Churchill and Roosevelt felt obliged to chat to their people over the airwaves. In peacetime it was an' anachronistic bore. A prominent politician would address the nation, pompous and pretentious, and reading the stuff very badly from cards. Worse still the next night, the other side would talk you silly with their right of reply. Export—that was one of their favourite ways to bore for Britain.

Troy had too little to go on. Jessel could refute him step by step. But, where was the man's sense of outrage? Troy had called him a crook to his face, and now he sat there reasonably defending himself and Cockerell, when, Troy felt, an honest man would have shown him the door and told him to come back with a warrant.

'There don't appear to be copies of Cockerell's tax returns among the papers at the shop,' he said.

Jessel's cigarette had gone out. In the effort to be reasonable in the face of Troy's accusations he had forgotten to smoke. He rummaged in his pocket for matches.

Troy gambled.

'You have them, don't you?'

Jessel had just got a light to the nud end. His hand shook furiously. Cigarette and flame refused utterly to meet. The match burnt down to his fingers. He winced and struck another.

'I'd like to see them.'

This, above all, was the point at which outraged citizenry told him to come back when he'd got a warrant. Even if they did not know what it meant—and a chartered accountant surely did?—they'd all seen it at the pictures. Coppers sent packing by the right phrases in the right tones, as though they were unsolicited carpet sellers. Just short of a second singeing, Jessel managed to light up. Neither the gesture nor the tobacco brought him any relief. He was trembling and sweating worse than ever.

'I ... er ... can't put my hands on them right now. My ... er my secretary ... goes home at five.'

This was fine by Troy. He was happy to sweat Jessel overnight. He could hardly be so stupid as to destroy papers that were already a matter of record. And if he were, it was tantamount to a confession.

'Very well,' he smiled at Jessel. 'I'll see you first thing in the morning.'

From the look on Jessel's face Troy might just as well have suggested an appointment in Samara. But, he roused himself. Enough energy for the semblance of normality. He bustled past Troy, opened the door for him, put the chair back against the wall, where it came from, and, in a gesture Troy found curiously fastidious, whipped out his handkerchief and quickly dusted the seat, waving at it with an airy motion, the linen barely glancing off the oilcloth.

'Fine,' he said, the cigarette flapping from his lower lip once more. 'Tomorrow it is.'

§44

He made his way back up the hill in the cool of the evening, his briefcase bulging with the collected papers of Cockerell Ltd. Janet Cockerell was still in the garden, the painting pretty well finished, a few more dabs and shades added to the motley of her boiler suit. But the working day was done. She was sipping white wine and staring off into the redness of the evening sky. She fetched a second glass and the bottle. A well-chilled hock, flowery and not too sweet.

'Why didn't you mention George Jessel to me?'

'I can't think of everything.'

'No more than I can believe everything.'

She was far too smart not to know when she'd been called a liar.

'I suppose the real reason is that I don't want to have to think about him at all. I'd rather not give a man like Jessel head room. He's a toad. I don't like him and I don't much like Arnold when the two of them are together. He's the most unsavoury of Arnold's cronies.'

'Cronies? Why cronies? Why not just say friends?'

'I haven't looked it up in the dictionary, but I would hardly be surprised to find that the definition of "crony" was "disreputable friend".'

The next time Rod referred to Driberg or Fermanagh as being 'one of your cronies', he would have to remember to feel insulted.

'Or,' she went on, 'were you thinking of a more conspiratorial meaning?'

'I think perhaps I was.'

'Then I'm sorry to have kept him from you. But now you've met him I think you'll see my point. If Arnold was up to something, George Jessel is the sort of chap would lie through his teeth for him, and think it nothing more than matey loyalty, wouldn't he?'

'Yes, I rather think he would.'

'Are you planning to see him again?'

'Oh, yes. He can marinade overnight and I'll roast him tomorrow.'

Back in the joyless Kedleston, he spread Cockerell's records out across the bed and found he had no heart for such joyless reading. He skimmed the headlines in the *Manchester Guardian*. Read another lengthy piece on the burgeoning crisis in Suez, and fell asleep without even opening the Ian Fleming.

§45

He breakfasted among the brown suits. Something hot, something taste-less, washed down with something lukewarm. He gave Jessel the best part of half an hour to gather himself, a safe margin to let the anxiety build in him, stuffed all Cockerell's papers back into his briefcase, and on the dot of ten climbed the staircase to his office. In the first room, the typewriter stood unused under its plastic cover. He had expected to find some young woman filing papers or her nails.

The door to Jessel's office was ajar. He pushed gently at it without knocking. Jessel was sprawled in his chair, head back, eyes open, dead.

'Shit, shit, shit!' Troy said.

He put his fingertips to the side of Jessel's neck. Warm, but definitely dead. He stood by the corpse, slowly turning his head to take in as much as he could. He had just as much time as it took till the next person, whoever that might be, arrived.

He heard a rustle from the outer office, across the landing.

Shit, shit, shit.

A young woman was lifting the cover from the typewriter. As she raised her face to him, he could see the side of her cheek was badly swollen.

'Are you Mr Jessel's secretary?'

She mmmed at him and nodded vigorously.

'Call the police,' he said. 'The local station, not 999.'

She froze. Stared anxiously at him.

'You have the number?'

She nodded again, fumbled at the telephone pad and dialled. He could hear the ringing tone. She pointed to her cheek. The police station answered.

'Awo,' she said. 'Poweese?'

There was a pause. Troy could hear the plod on the other end saying, 'What?'

'Poweese. Ish Bwenda Bwock. Geosh Jeshll's Shecetwy.'

She held the phone out to Troy.

'They can't unnershtann me. Bin to dennish.'

He took it from her.

'This is Chief Inspector Troy of Scotland Yard. Get over to 23 Railway Cuttings at once. I've just found George Jessel dead.'

There was a whumphf as Brenda Brock fell into her chair. Troy slammed the phone down, took her head and pressed it down between her knees. At least, thank God, she wasn't screaming. In less than a minute she raised her head, pale and tearful, looked him in the eyes and said, 'No kiddin'?'

'No,' he said. 'No kidding.'

He left her. Went back into Jessel's office. The top drawer on Jessel's side of the desk was open a couple of inches. A sheaf of papers peeped out invitingly at him. He pulled them out. A couple of dozen pages stapled together in two lots—Cockerell's tax returns for the last five years. So, he meant to show them to him after all. He stuffed them into his inside pocket, and looked around. There was no sign of violence. Jessel was slumped, as though he had suddenly snapped at the shoulders and the knees like a puppet whose strings had been cut. There were five nud ends in the ashtray. Having seen the way the man chainsmoked, that was probably representative of the first half-hour of the working day. He was kicking himself hard. The arrogance of 'letting him marinade overnight' came home to him. He'd had his chance and he'd lost it. The cheap detective's ploy of waiting half an hour before showing up, just to string him out. He'd had a second chance and he'd lost it. All in all he'd made an utter balls-up of the business, and any minute now he'd have to face the local plod and pretend he was playing by the book. It would not be pleasant.

He heard footsteps on the stairs, took a last look around the room and darted back into the outer office.

Brenda Brock was staring down into the cutting, crying silently, her mascara dribbling across her swollen, hamster cheeks.

A burly man, overdressed for the weather in a mackintosh and trilby, appeared in the doorway.

'Warriss, Station Inspector,' he said bluntly, staring hard at Troy. 'Now—who the bloody hell are you?'

Troy recited name and rank and produced his warrant card.

'Don't be going anywhere,' Warriss said. 'I'll be wanting to talk to you, sir.'

The inflection on the 'sir' safely expressed a mixture of anger and contempt. A younger man, in his late twenties, appeared on the landing.

'Detective Sergeant Godbehere,' said Warriss. 'My scene-of-crime man. We've the big boys with us today, Raymond. Chief Inspector Troy of the Yard, would you believe?'

He turned to Troy, utterly unintimidated by rank.

'In there, is he?'

'Yes,' said Troy.

Warriss and Godbehere left him with Brenda. Five minutes later, Warriss came back alone.

'You've touched nothing?' he asked.

'Of course not,' Troy lied.

'And the lass?'

'She hasn't been in there.'

Another clumping on the stairs produced another large man in mackintosh and trilby. This one clutched a doctor's bag. Obviously the County Police Surgeon.

He nodded in Troy's direction, and greeted Warriss with a simple 'Harold.'

'In there, is he? Grim reaper finally got 'im? Silly bugger.'

He lumbered off across the landing.

Troy heard him say, 'Well now, Ray me lad, what have we got here? Oh dearie, dearie me.'

Troy's eyes were on the door, following the doctor, in his mind's eye following the routine he would now go through. Warriss's voice cut through, pulled him sharply back.

'A word with you, Mr Troy. Outside, if you wouldn't mind.'

He led off down the stairs. Troy looked at Brenda Brock. Beautiful green eyes looked pleadingly back at him, but whatever the plea, he could not meet it. He followed Warriss. At the turn in the stairs he passed an elderly woman in a flowered bri-nylon overall, dusting the landing windowsill.

Outside Warriss waited, an elbow propped on the embankment wall—a presumptive posture of might and right. Troy was about to be bollocked by a man ten years his elder, a rank his junior, and he hadn't a leg to stand on.

'Tell me,' Warriss began, 'does the word protocol mean anything to you, or are all you young buggers down in London ignorant clever dicks?'

'I'm sorry—'

'You'd bloody well better be. How long have you been on my patch?'

'Only since yesterday morning.'

'And what interest does the Yard have in George Jessel that it did not see fit to share with the local force?'

'Nothing. Jessel was not the object of my investigation.'

A light of sheer pleasure came into Warriss's bloodshot eyes. The glint of revelation.

'My God. My God! You're here for Arnold Cockerell, aren't you?'

'Yes.'

'You're with the Branch?'

'No. As a matter of fact I run the Murder Squad.'

Warriss was not impressed.

'Is that so? Who's been murdered, then?'

'Cockerell.'

'News to me. Last I heard the Russkis had got him. We do get the news up here, y'know. We're not all brown ale and whippets.'

'I was asked to look into the disappearance and possible death of Commander Cockerell.'

'I see,' Warriss mused. 'And you don't think your first port of call might have been the local nick?'

'I've said I'm sorry.'

The same glint appeared in Warriss's eyes—the same smug satisfaction in his own powers of deduction.

'It was her, wasn't it? The wife. She dragged you up here, didn't she. The bitch, she never trusted me. I'm handling Arnold Cockerell's disappearance, not the bloody Yard!'

He tapped his own chest with a stubby index finger. His voice rose. He was shouting, now. Not the faintest shred of pretence of respect for rank.

'It's my case, Mr Troy! The matter was reported to my nick, to me personally. I'm in charge of the investigation. Dammit, I've known Cockerell ten years or more. He was a friend! You want to carry on an investigation on my patch, you go through me!'

A convenient express roared through the cutting, southbound, and shrouded them in smoke and steam. As the air cleared Troy tried the only ploy left to him. He looked Warriss clearly in the eyes and put on his best no-nonsense voice.

'However. There is now a second case. Murder is my business. George Jessel's murder will be my business.'

Warriss laughed. Troy was expecting another tirade, and the man laughed.

'Murder? George Jessel? We'll see about that.'

He pointed off towards the door of the building behind Troy. The Police Surgeon was emerging, his bag half-open, the rubber tail of a stethoscope dangling from it. He held out his hand to Troy. Troy shook it. It was the first semblance of good manners he'd seen so far.

'Jewel,' the man said. 'Joe Jewel. County Police Surgeon.'

Before Troy could say a word Warriss cut in sharply.

'Whatever you're thinking, don't say it. There's not a joke about Jewel and Warriss we haven't heard. So just save your breath.'

One would think, thought Troy, that to have the same name as the most famous pair of music hall comedians in the land might be some incentive to behave less like a clown. However, he knew the thought would be wasted if uttered.

'Well,' Warriss said to Jewel. 'Am I right?'

'Oh aye. His heart. Finally gave out.'

'You'll sign then?'

'Oh aye. Open and shut.'

Warriss seemed almost to grin at Troy. A silent, smirky 'I told you so.'

'I don't want to interrupt the smooth working of an efficient team,' Troy said, 'but when a man is found dead in suspicious circumstances, it isn't open and shut.'

Warriss seemed not have switched on his patent sarcasm detector and let his other half answer.

'Oh, believe me, Mr Troy. It is. Y'see. Being a Police Surgeon in this neck o' the woods isn't full time. There isn't the call. We don't get the bodies. I'm a GP most of the time. So happens George was a patient of mine. He'd chainsmoked for forty-five years, he swigged scotch like it was Tizer, he'd got a heart about as strong as a bathroom sponge and arteries as hard as treacle toffee. Believe me, Mr Troy, this is natural causes. He died of a massive, and entirely expected, heart attack. And I've no qualms about signing his death certificate.'

Warriss found his twopenn'orth.

'The only thing suspicious is the fact that you're here. And you've already said you weren't investigating Jessel, so that's that.'

'I want a post mortem and I want the matter reported to the coroner,' said Troy, softly and emphatically. 'If you do not go through the motions now and of your own volition, I will call the Met Commissioner and your Chief Constable and I will report the pair of you for obstructing an investigation.'

Jewel looked at Warriss. Warriss looked at Jewel. A practised double-take.

'You London shites are all the same,' Warriss snarled. 'You think you can come up here and—'

'Just do it!'

Warriss eased his elbow off the wall. For a second Troy thought he was going to hit him. Then a uniformed constable came dashing down the alley.

'Langley Mill on the phone, boss. Urgent.'

Warriss worked his arm vigorously. He was not going to hit his superior officer. He had lounged so long in his posture of arrogance that the nerve in his elbow had gone to sleep. But his face was red and his voice was hoarse. If only the wit could be found he would surely have flung a *bon mot* or a clever insult at Troy.

'Cunt,' he said, trying his best. 'You'll get your PM, but if you're still on my patch tomorrow you report into the nick, and that goes for every day you stay. Sir!'

He stomped off down the alley. Jewel shrugged a little. Closed the clasp on his bag.

'It'll be in the post, laddie. But you're wrong. You'll see.'

He followed Warriss. The cleaning woman in the flowered overall appeared at the threshold of number 23, shaking her yellow duster. Troy approached her.

'Excuse me?'

'Why, what yer done?'

'I'd just like to ask you a few questions.'

'Ask away, me duck.'

It seemed to Troy that the gap between the local argot and received pronunciation was considerable, but he would endeavour.

'Do you clean the whole building—all the offices?'

'Ah do.'

'Mr Jessel's office?'

'Oh aye. Very partickler is Mr Jessel. Every morning, quart to nine.'

'I see,' said Troy. 'And you didn't see anyone come in between then and ten o'clock?'

'No. Only Mr Jessel. He came in about quarter past. Then ah took me tea-break, like. 'Ad a bit o' snap. Ah were back in afe an 'our. Ah saw thee come in. Then young Brenda not five minutes later.'

'And you cleaned Mr Jessel's office.'

'Ah just said ah did. Cleaned and polished every mornin', same time.'

Troy shot up the stairs, praying silently that Detective Sergeant Godbehere had more brains than his boss.

He found him, sitting on the chair he had sat on himself the day before, reading the *Daily Mirror*. He was tall, slim, and when he looked up at Troy's entrance seemed to have a mercifully intelligent look about him. He had had the decency to drape a sheet across the late George Jessel.

'I'm afraid you're going to have to help me,' said Troy.

Godbehere folded his newspaper.

'Why is it, sir, that at the sound of those words the hairs on the back of my neck stand up?'

'Copper's instinct.'

'I'm supposed to wait till the meat wagon gets here. And when Brenda's recovered I take her statement, and when you've got your bollocking from the boss, I take yours. And that's all I'm supposed to do. You do know that, don't you, sir?'

'Indeed. I've already been bollocked, and I think common courtesy will allow Brenda another half hour in which to grieve. In the meantime I want you to dust the place for prints.'

Godbehere stood up and reached for his bag of tricks.

'You'll get me shot.'

'I'll carry the can.'

'You'd better,' Godbehere said without inflection. 'Now, where do you want me to start?'

'Desktop. It was wiped clean at about nine this morning.'

'Handy,' said Godbehere, and he pushed the chair away to make room in the tiny space available to him.

'Just a minute,' Troy stopped him with a hand on his arm. 'Did you pull up the chair to sit down?'

'No. It was here, by the desk. I just parked me backside.'

Troy saw in the mind's eye that fastidious gesture. The precise aligning of the chair with the wall. The flapping handkerchief. It was a gesture born entirely of habit. Surely Jessel, a fussy man Troy concluded, did this with every visitor? Set the chair out and put the chair back. He looked at the patch of claret-coloured carpet by the wall. Four deep ruts had been impressed in the fabric by the habitual presence of the chair legs.

'I'll tell you now,' said Troy. 'Whatever Jessel died of, he did not die alone. Someone was here. Someone sat exactly where you were sitting when I walked in just now. Dust the lot, doorknob, chairback everything.'

'You'll get me shot,' Godbehere said again, unpacking his case, and seeming indifferent to the prospect even as he stated it.

Troy knelt down and looked across the leather top of the desk at eye level. Something obtruded, a speck or a blob, just off-centre to the right. He took out his pocket handkerchief. Put a corner of the Irish linen to the blob and watched as a tiny brown stain spread a thirty-second of an inch up the material. He stood and put the cloth to his nose. Oil. Definitely oil. And if those two weeks walking around with that ridiculous Browning stuck up his armpit had been at all useful, they had taught him the smell of gun oil.

He folded the handkerchief carefully and put it in his inside pocket where it nestled against the papers he had pinched from Jessel's desk. Godbehere dusted the edge of the desk with white powder and offered an instant opinion.

'There's something here. No doubt about it. D'ye reckon that cleaning lady was thorough?'

'You saw her. Looked to me as though she cleaned Pandaemonium for Lucifer on a regular basis. No brimstone left unturned.'

Troy looked down at the powdery smudges. This, like money, was not one of his strong points. He was about as capable of reading the signs as he was of deciphering the hidden meanings in wallpaper. Godbehere seemed to realise this only too well.

'I'll get on better on my own, sir. Why don't you do whatever it is you have to do and come down the nick to give me your statement a bit later. I'm there till six today and I'm on again at eight-thirty tomorrow. The nick's out on the Matlock Road. Ask anybody.'

Troy left to do whatever he had to do. It was just that he had no idea what the whatever he had to do should be.

He stood at the end of Railway Cuttings, pondering the dilemma. Either he placed a great deal of confidence in Godbehere, or he steamed in uninvited, set up his own investigation, knowing full well that the connection to Cockerell, and Cockerell's connection to what Stan would inevitably call 'spookery', was enough to make Onions hesitate in backing him. And if he did, Troy would then find himself stepping on the toes of every local plod for miles around and making himself the most unpopular copper in England.

Someone was honking a car horn at him. He looked at a pale Daimler or Jaguar parked a little way up the street. All he could see in the windscreen was a reflection of the street outside, crowded with shoppers. Then the driver's door opened and a stout, owlish figure beckoned to him.

'Get in,' he yelled.

It was George Brown. The penny dropped. The Somewhere-up-North for which Brown sat in the Commons was Belper. This was his constituency. Good God, he should have realised.

He pulled open the passenger door and got in. Brown eased the large car into traffic and headed slowly down the street.

'I don't have to ask you what you're doing here, do I?' he said.

'Is it that obvious?'

'Only two things have put Belper on the map since the industrial revolution. Me, and Arnold bloody Cockerell!'

'You knew him?'

'You couldn't miss him. Local nob. Rotary Club. Chamber of Commerce. Treasurer of the Tory Party for a couple of years. Always giving me gyp at public meetings. But I can't honestly say I knew him. Mind you, if it's local knowledge you want, I'm meeting two of my chaps for a drink at the Legion in five minutes. You might as well join us.'

Brown swung the car left at the next junction.

'Did anyone raise the matter of Cockerell's disappearance with you? As a constituency matter, I mean?'

'His wife did. But of course, by then it was what you'd call a Commons undercurrent. Your brother was masterminding it. I had a word. He said 'leave it to me', and I was glad to. I was supposed to have blotted my copybook where the Russians are concerned, as I'm sure you gathered from Brother Khrushchev. It was better all round for Rod to handle it. I told Cockerell's wife what I could. Wasn't a lot.'

Brown paused.

'I have to ask you this. Your brother didn't ask you to come up here, did he?'

'No. And I think I can say that he'd have told you first.'

'I've big feet,' Brown said. 'Easy to tread on.'

He swung the car left again and brought it to a halt in front of a sturdy, squat example of twenties architecture. The Royal British Legion. Watering hole of old, and not so old, soldiers.

Troy could not recall that he had ever been inside a British Legion. He had, after all, no entitlement. He had not only not done his bit, he would have lied, cheated and run away to Ireland to avoid doing his bit. It had never come to that—Onions had kept him out of the forces as an essential worker. He did not think that Brown had been in the forces either. It was an odd feeling; it set them apart from their generation. At most Brown was two or three years younger than Troy, one of the rising stars of the Party, if the fogies of fifty or so—Gaitskell, Rod—ever gave them space to spread their wings. The next election was four years away and closing with every crisis. Gaitskell looked set to win it hands down. It would be a very long time before the generation of George Brown and Harold Wilson found room at the top.

'You're not a member, are you?' Brown was saying as he locked the car door.

Troy shook his head.

'Then Walter had better sign us in. I'm not either, you see.'

Troy wondered if this admission had undertones. Did a British man, let alone a British politician, of their age automatically feel the divide of fought/not fought? Was it for ever going to be held up as the central action, the defining experience of their generation? Worse, when they got in there, to the Legion, what did people—men, it was always men—talk about? Could a bunch of forty-year-olds rehash 'what I did in the war' till the day they died? Would they be doing this in the 1980s, the 1990s, into the next century?

Brown introduced Troy to Walter and Ted—two men separated by a couple of stones in weight, a couple of years in age—roughly the same age as Brown and Troy—and a small round table bearing a crumpled copy of the *Manchester Guardian* and two half-finished half pints of bitter. They shook hands and said hello, and revealed a wider gap. The stout one, Walter, was clearly a Lancastrian, and the skinny one, Ted, just as clearly a Yorkshireman. Quite a melting pot, the British Legion, thought Troy.

'What'll you have?' the thin man said.

Brown asked for a half of the local brew—a Mansfield ale—and Troy followed on the Driberg principle that the first crack in the ice was usually to be achieved by drinking what the working man drank.

Troy looked around. It was a dull place. Inevitably, it was a dull place. But no duller than any London club he'd ever been in. Faintly hideous with varnished woodwork, it was neither more nor less pleasant than the Garrick with all its varnished portraits dulled with age—and no one had asked if he was wearing a tie. The new Queen had pride of place with a wall to herself, a public photograph in red robes. The war had its small memorials in the decorative plates hanging askew on the wall, to the local regiment—the Sherwood Foresters—and to the 1st Polish Parachute regiment. The illusion that the war had been England's war was a thin one, and only idiots ever believed it was. England had been too full of Czechs and Poles—and Yanks—for it to have been otherwise. In the background he could see a row of full-sized billiard tables, and the bar-room gossip was punctuated by the constant click of the balls. The gossip. He strained to hear, strained to make sense of a difficult local accent, and found, much to his amazement, that old soldiers talked about the weather and football and rugby league and what they'd seen on the 'telly' last night. No one mentioned the war.

He felt Brown's elbow nudge him, and turned to see him lighting up his pipe. The look on the stout one's face told him he'd just asked a question that Troy had not heard.

'I was just saying. Would you be Rod Troy's brother?'

'Yes, I am.'

'He's been up a few times and given us a talk. Came up for George in '50 and '51.'

There was a slight pause, possibly for Troy to fill, but he did not so the stout one added, 'Decent bloke,' by way of a coda.

At his best, Rod was a passionate believer in and campaigner for Love and Justice and Democracy. A man who hated lies. Troy could admire that, even if it was usually he who flicked up all three for him. At his worst, Rod was 'a decent bloke'. Troy hated the decent bloke.

The thin one returned, balancing a tray of drinks and the first rush of shag cloud billowed forth from Brown.

'The Chief Inspector's here about Arnold Cockerell,' he said through the smoke.

The two men looked at each other. Troy thought they both smiled. He was dreading the existence of another local double act and hoped to God they'd something sensible to say.

Walter spoke first. 'So it's not him down at Portsmouth? Must say I never thought much of the idea of Arnold as Bulldog Drummond.'

Troy put the obvious question. 'You knew him, then?'

'Moved here about the same time I did. I met him when I got out of the Army at the end of '45. Of course, he was with us then.'

'With us?' said Troy.

'Party member,' Ted put in across the top of his glass.

'We saw a lot of him,' Walter continued. 'He was very active on George's behalf.'

Troy looked at Brown, smacking loudly at the end of his pipe.

'By 1950 I was Satan, of course.'

'No,' said Ted. 'He was still with you in '50—he left us between then and the '51 election.'

'Very nearly lost my seat,' said Brown with a politician's self-absorption.

'I saw him change,' Walter said. 'Something quite drastic. It was like the road to Damascus. It was as though his own success couldn't coexist with his old ideas.'

Troy knew from trying to have rational conversations with Rod that the politically committed cannot grasp the notion that people simply and easily change their minds. It remained, however, that what the man was offering him was what he most needed, an educated guess at the motivations of Commander Cockerell.

'About the time of the Festival of Britain?' he asked.

The two men looked at each other again. Without the smiles, puzzled this time.

'Now you mention it,' Walter said, 'it was. Peculiar that.'

'The Damascus road of modern furniture,' said Troy, paraphrasing Janet Cockerell.

'No, no.' Walter mused, ignoring his beer. 'It was more than that. I know what you mean. Shop full of Scandinavian tat at high prices. It was more than finding his niche in the business, more than making a bob or two for the first time in his life. It was as though someone had picked him up and shook him.'

'That's fancy,' said Ted. 'Have you been at the Babycham? If you ask me, it's bloody simple. It's the British story, isn't it? Great Britain This Is Your Life—give a man a few quid more and he starts looking after self-interest. Give a man a leg up in life and he bites the hand that feeds him. It's what dogs us as a party and a country—we breed Tories. You'll see. We get back in next year or the year after, we improve the lot of the workers—do what we're committed to do—and the next election after that the buggers'll vote us out because they're making a bit too much money to trust it to Labour. That's what happened to Cockerell. He made a bob or two. And from then on he was determined to hang onto it.'

'Write that down,' Brown said. 'Gaitskell can use it next May Day.'

They all laughed at this. Troy managed a gentle smile, hoping he looked wry rather than humourless.

'I know his wife quite well,' Walter said. 'In fact she still pays her subs. Doesn't come to meetings or dos, but she's a member. She said, a few years ago now, must have been '52 or '53, when he became Treasurer of the local Tories, she said he talks such utter rubbish, she said, I can't believe he believes it. And then she said, "I don't know what got into him. He's like a schoolboy, smirking to himself, sitting there with his finger up his bum."'

Troy could imagine Janet Cockerell saying that. He could imagine the hell that was surely the home life of Mr and Mrs Cockerell, narrated by a tedious, self-obsessed bore, punctuated by the balloon-pricking, contrivedly vulgar wit of his wife. And if that wasn't bad enough, she voted Labour. God, how that must have annoyed him.

§46

'Dead?' she said.

'Heart.'

'So it's not connected? You don't suspect . . . ?'

She searched for a word or phrase. Her eyes looking down at the lawn, flicking up at the blank cartridge paper on the easel, and back to Troy.

'. . . Foul play. My God, I'm getting to use all the jargon, aren't I?'

She rolled 'foul play' around on her lips once more as though toying with the phrase.

Janet Cockerell had, he felt, been pretty straight with him. This was no time to allow another person's honesty to let him stumble into truth. The truth was of no use to her, the truth could do her no good.

'No,' he lied. 'I don't.'

§47

The interview room at Belper Police Station was designed to let paint intimidate. If the malefactor did not instantly feel the pangs of guilt on entering a room almost entirely denied natural light by the accumulated dirt on the windows, the brick walls, eggshelled over in dirty brown and dirtier cream, with a dividing border at shoulder height, would no doubt soon reduce him to gibbering confession along the lines of, 'It's a fair cop, guvnor. You got me bang to rights.' So reminiscent were they of the soothing shades of a good Victorian prison. It was at least sixty miles to Strangeways, but a short hop on the Brolac paint chart 'Snazzy Colours for Old Lags'.

Troy watched Godbehere riffle through a stack of papers, and waited.

Once, years ago, an old lag had accepted arrest by Troy with the words 'It's a fair cop,' and Troy could only ask, 'Are you taking the mickey?' There were moments when he loved the job.

Godbehere pushed a blank statement form across the table to him.

'You don't need me to put it into copperese, now do you, sir?'

Troy spoke fluent copperese and hated it. It went with black boots and silly helmets. He wrote an account of his finding the body of George Jessel in less than a hundred and fifty words, signed it and pushed it back.

'What have you got?' he asked.

'Three sets of prints. Quite clear. I'll run them by CRO and send you whatever emerges. I'll call you when the coast is clear.'

'And?'

'I couldn't do much else. Market day, you see. People everywhere. I talked to the obvious. The bloke outside the Kedleston selling newspapers. Always there, observant chap, but the only stranger he's seen is you. He knows all the travelling salesmen by name or by sight and they've all been regulars. Between you and me, I think he makes a bob or two fixing them up with tarts from time to time. It'd pay him to keep his eyes peeled. And I talked to the woman who runs the drapery right opposite the alley. Nothing. Nothing worth her remembering.'

'It needs a house to house, along the alley at least, and flyers. Posters up King Street. You know that, don't you?'

'I know. And I can't do it. If the boss knows I did what I did today he'll have my guts for banjo strings.'

Godbehere toyed with his ball-point pen, not quite looking Troy in the eye.

'You could make it official. Come in over his head, but we both know damn well what's going to be in the medical report, don't we, sir? Or you could take Mr Warriss into your confidence and tell him what you've got on the end of your handkerchief. But you're not going to do that, are you, sir?'

'No, I'm not.'

'You think he'll cock it up?'

'Maybe, but the problem is that he's already made up his mind. That's a bad start to any investigation. If I tell him what it is and it doesn't fit he'll just bury it in one of the vast vacancies of his brain.'

'Are you going to tell *me* what it is?'

'Gun oil. Lubricant for an automatic.'

Godbehere sighed and muttered, 'Oh shit. And you still want the house-to-house?'

'Yes.'

'And the flyers?'

'Yes.'

'OK. I understand, but if you want me do any more, you're going to have to talk to Inspector Warriss. And I think I should warn you that right now he's telling everyone in the station that we've got a rogue copper from the Yard trespassing on our turf—a right twat who can't tell murder from a heart attack.'

'Well,' said Troy. 'It looks as though I shall have to go on being a "right twat", doesn't it?'

§48

Warriss heard him out in silence. Troy asked for the house-to-house, and for flyers to be posted. Warriss nodded, and when Troy had finished said simply, 'Fine. When are you leaving?'

§49

He left on the next train. Half an hour sitting on a bench in front of the Swiss-style waiting room on the up platform, watching Oliver Hardy tend a flowerbed, bent over his charges, as far as his bulk would allow bending, clutching a trowel and tossing the weeds behind him onto the platform. He spoke not a word to Troy—Troy concluded he spoke to no one, but he thought it a great pleasure to watch a man delight quietly in his work—and ten minutes before the train was due, Hardy disappeared up the slope and came back down on his electro-trolley at the head of another caravan of burbling pigeons.

It was mid-afternoon. The train gathered speed slowly, out of the cutting and onto the flood plain of the Derwent, into a half-mile tunnel and out into the flatlands that in a mile or two were recognisable as the English Midlands. Khrushchev's words, as they often did, came back to him, more for their forcefulness than their poetry. There was little or no poetry in 'Bugger England', but 'Bugger England' it was that came back to him, and if this was, if this had been, his experience of Middle England, then bugger Middle England too.

§50

'Where ya bin?'

He could feel the weight of melancholy in each short syllable. He could not acknowledge it. He did not want to pick it up—to pick it up might be to make it his own, and he had no wish to do that.

'In the North of England.'

'Another murder, I guess?'

'Sort of.'

'Y'know—I never had you figured for the kind of guy who said "sort of".'

'It's vague. Possibly three murders.'

'Three?'

'One without a body.'

'OK. I'm followin'.'

'One without a face. Or a name.'

'Still with yas.'

'And one without a means.'

'Now you lost me.'

He wondered how he could explain. Drew a deep breath, and she cut him off.

'No—don't explain. Just tell me when you're comin' home.'

'I really don't know. It's going to keep me busy.'

'Should I come down to London?'

'Up.'

'Uh?'

'One always comes *up* to London and *down* to the country.'

'Jesus, Troy! You're beginning to sound like your sisters!'

He was. It was just the kind of nonsense they would utter.

'Are they giving you a hard time?'

'Not exactly. They say things like, "It's your house now, Larissa, you're the mistress of Mimram." Like we were re-enacting some plot by the fuckin' Brontë sisters. I'm the mistress of Hardcock Hall. And—they don't mean it.'

Troy knew damn well they didn't.

215

'They just use crap like that to wind me up. I should care who's fuckin' mistress of fuckin' Mimram. You know what's wrong? I got nothin' in common with 'em. 'Cept two languages. Has it ever seemed to you that those women are noddle-heads?'

'Of course. They are.'

'I mean. Here I am trying to educate myself, reading your old man's books and that, and they giggle and say things like, "Oh dear, Larissa's turning into a bluestocking." Like they never read a book in their goddam lives. Now what the fuck's a goddam bluestocking? I mean. I been wearing your trousers all week. I don't even own a pair of blue stockings!'

Tosca came to London, sad, unpredictable and unchanging. The job swallowed him whole; Troy had little time for her, but then she had so little time for him. Silent, nose buried in a book. Apologising for her silence. Then angry. Once he had explained the bluestocking remark, it rankled. Anger he could handle. Soak it up like a sponge. Unlike the sadness, it did not become his. He could see it but he did not share it.

Each night she crept into his bed, said, 'Don't touch'—and he didn't.

§51

Kolankiewicz could explode. You would be having, you thought, a perfectly reasonable conversation with the Polish Beast when suddenly—poof, yaroo, wallop—he was off into one of the rages that Troy ascribed to the occupational hazard of being Polish. There were half a dozen questions Troy would have loved to put to Kolankiewicz, but the risk was too great. Better by far to stick to the job in hand and ask him the nuclear questions later, when he was free to duck and cover.

He phoned down to Forensics. Kolankiewicz spent much of his time dashing between the new lab at the Yard and the old one at Hendon. It was possible he was in the building. A voice he did not know answered—one of a dozen young men that manned Kolankiewicz's department, much grown in size and importance in the last ten years.

'Is Mr Kolankiewicz about?' Troy asked.

'He's just scrubbing up after a job, sir. He'll be free in a few minutes. Shall I get him to call you?'

'No. I'll come to him.'

He found Kolankiewicz in his windowless, cheerless office in the basement, with a thermos full of milky tea, a row of jam doughnuts and his copy of the *News Chronicle*.

'Long time no smartyarse,' he said.

It was. They had not met since their evening with Khrushchev at the Bricklayer's Arms.

'You want doughnut?' he said through a mouth gushing red jam.

'No thanks. I just thought you might like to take a look at this.'

He put his Irish linen handkerchief on the open newspaper.

'What you want, I should examine your bogies? Troy, you getting to be bigger fucking pig than me.'

'Impossible,' said Troy. 'You are the most disgusting man alive.'

Kolankiewicz beamed at the compliment, genuinely flattered to hear the common wisdom of the entire Metropolitan Police Force and much of the constabularies of the home counties distilled into a single sentence.

'What I want,' said Troy, 'is your opinion on the brown stain at the corner.'

'Ah—brown stain! Troy, Troy, Troy. Brown stain—two of the most beautiful words in the English language. Why is it that a nation that has produced Shakespeare and Blake has no sonnet to the brown stain, no song, of experience, no song of innocence, that encompasses the mystery of the brown stain? We are old friends, brown stain and I.'

He picked up the handkerchief and sniffed loudly at the corner.

'Almost no odour,' he said. 'You had this a day or two?'

'Yes.'

'No matter, I can reactivate it. A dash of this, a soupçon of that and dear little brown stain will yield up its filth for all to sniff.'

'When?'

'Tomorrow.'

Kolankiewicz put the linen to his nose again and made revolting noises, worse than any schoolboy with a runny nose and bad adenoids.

'And you want it just between the two of us. Right, smartyarse?'

'How did you know?'

'I known you what now, twenty years? Look at your own habits, Troy. Everybody got habits. Onions picks his nose, Wildeve forever scratch arse—you close doors quietly, like you hope no one can hear you, whenever you expect secrecy. I see you close door when you come into room and I know we are in business for ourselves again and the Yard go flying fuck.'

Of course, he was right. The Yard did indeed go flying fuck.

§52

Troy went back to his own office and phoned one Angus Pakenham, his accountant of many years, a notorious one-legged RAF hero dry-drunk, and the husband of his recent mistress, Anna.

'Whaddyawant?' he barked at Troy.

'It's business, Angus.'

'I should bloody well hope so. Or did you think I lived on thin air?'

'Is there any chance we could meet up later? Perhaps a bit of a chat after work, at the end of the day?'

'Don't see why not. Meet me by the pump at six. And if you're late, y'bugger, I'll hobble off without you.'

The pump was their very occasional but habitual meeting place It stood, tall, black, elegant and, since the demise of the horse-drawn hansom cab, redundant, an ornament at the junction of Bedford Row and Jockey's Fields in Bloomsbury. Angus and his partners had the top two floors of a mews in Jockey's Fields, overlooking Gray's Inn. Angus had lost a leg leaping from the walls of Colditz Castle whilst trying to escape. He had spent the rest of the war as a POW, given a tin leg by the Germans, which they confiscated after every subsequent escape attempt. He had attempted to escape seventeen times. On his release the Roehampton Hospital had equipped him with a state-of the-art rubber and plastic leg and he had hated it and gone back to the hand-made tin leg the Germans had given him. He spent much of his life in pain—the missing leg, he said, hurt like hell—and much of his time escaping pain with a near-lethal mixture of pills and booze. He and Troy met by the pump because he could not stand to be waited on or watched as he negotiated the three flights of steps that led from his office to the street. He hobbled down them at his own painful pace, cursing all the way. By the time he got to the pump he was usually red-faced but relieved, and depending on the vicissitudes of the leg and his naturally bloody disposition, he was either the best company in the world or the worst.

Troy sat waiting for Angus. He was whistling as he came round the corner from Jockey's Fields—red-faced but whistling—a halo of scant ginger curls peeking out from under his bowler, his briefcase under one arm, the artificial leg in its pinstripe swinging out at an unnatural angle but at a cracking pace.

'Right, y'bugger. Lead on. What's it to be? The "Lot's Wife" or the "Whore of Babylon"?'

Troy had difficulty remembering what public house was what. Angus had privately renamed most of the pubs within hobbling distance of his office. They had perfectly ordinary names, like the Gryphon or the Three Tuns, but he had rechristened them to suit himself, and, the landlord of the 'Two Dogs at It' withstanding (Angus claimed to have found two of the creatures copulating on the pavement one day right outside the pub in question), no one seemed much to mind. It also had the added advantage that if his wife overheard him planning to meet a crony, she had little idea of where he was really headed.

'How about the "Frankenstein's Codpiece"?' said Troy without the faintest idea which one it was Angus had so dubbed.

'Right you are,' Angus replied and struck off north up Jockey's Fields, and Troy knew that they were heading for the Seven Bells in Theobald's Road.

Angus cut a swathe through the evening drinkers with cries of 'Mind the cripple!' Troy had known him wallop people with his walking stick on the days when the pain necessitated its presence, and when feeling particularly witty, he would elbow the drinking public aside with, 'Unclean, unclean, leper approaching.' He threw himself down in a chair and began to rub vigorously at the point on his thigh where stump and tin leg met.

'It's just about this time of day, when you've had the damn thing strapped on for nine or ten hours, that you get the most Godalmighty itch.'

He oohed and aahed at the relief, and then his eyes noticed the bulging briefcase Troy had placed on the chair between them.

'That's it, eh? The substance of your "bit of a chat"? Well, just looking at the outside I can tell you it's more than a bit and it'll cost you. However . . .'

He paused for a last deeply raking scratch at his stump, and let out a sigh of profound satisfaction.

'Ah me . . . However . . . before we get stuck in, there is one thing I've been meaning to ask you. Have you been fucking my wife?'

'No,' Troy lied.

'Good. I'm glad you have the decency to lie. 'Cos if you'd tried to brazen it out and tell me it meant nothing, I'd've taken off me tin leg and beaten the living shite out of you with it. In fact, for future reference, let me state it plainly. If I catch you sniffing around the old girl again, that's exactly what I'll do—in the street, and I don't care if it bends me leg and frightens the horses. Capiche?'

Troy nodded.

'Good. That's that out of the way. Now get the drinks in and tell me what you're after.'

'I thought you weren't drinking.'

'Look, Troy. Do you want me to thrash you silly or do you want to mind your own damn business and tell me exactly what's on your mind? A large malt. No water. No ice. Filthy American habit.'

Troy hoped it was not Angus's intention to get pissed. He needed him sober—God knows, he was the most difficult man alive sober, but he was unbearable drunk—and he wanted Anna's optimism to bear fruit. He knew that it was only Angus's month-long benders—when his business went to pot and he was about as priapic as a caterpillar—that had brought the two of them together, to cross the shaky line that had joined and separated them as lovers-not-lovers since they were in their twenties. Besides, right now he couldn't handle Anna back again. He cheated. Set a small malt in front of Angus and half an inch of ginger ale in the bottom of a glass for himself in the hope Angus would think he was on scotch too.

Angus held his glass up to the light. Before Troy could stop him he was yelling across the room to the landlord.

'Herbert! You mingy old bugger! You call this a double? You want your eyes testing!'

Herbert strolled over, a short fat bloke with hair like autumn corn stubble and the puffy face of an ex-boxer.

'What did you say?'

'I said,' Angus hauled himself to his feet, towering over the landlord at more than six foot two. 'I said, you're a mingy bugger. And you need to get your optics fixed. On the wall or in your face.'

A stubby finger struck him on the sternum and Troy watched as the little bloke firmly pushed him back into his seat.

'Mingy? Now you listen to me, 'ero. Mr bleedin' medals, Mr I-flew-a-bleedin'-'Urricane, Mr Battle of bloody Britain. We take a lot of shit from you. Every landlord between 'ere and the river takes a lot of shit from you. And we put up with it. You did your bit, you earned yer gongs, we all admire yer, Gawd knows some of the dafter ones even like yer. You're our bit of 'istory. Colditz on legs, and one of 'em tin. You're the only customer we got with a genuine 'ollow leg. But mingy? Short measure? Don't push yer luck, Angus. I was Hoxton and Shoreditch Under 21 Middleweight Champion. I went five rounds with Mickey McGuire when I was a lad. I'll wallop yer into rice pudding!'

Angus had not flinched. His expression had not changed.

'Nicely spoken, Herbert. Would you care to join the Chief Inspector and myself in a libation?'

'Very kind of you, Angus, but I never 'as shared a tipple with the Old Bill and I doesn't mean to start now.'

He nodded gently in Troy's direction.

'No offence meant.'

'None taken,' said Troy, knowing it was what pub manners—that arcane men's code—demanded of him.

It seemed wise to open the briefcase and let paper be a professional temptation. Troy would never understand it, but accountants could feel as strongly about their work as he did about his.

Angus sipped at his scotch and said, 'What's the beef, old boy?'

Troy gave him the potted version of the case of Commander Cockerell, moving as quickly as he could to the prospect of financial irregularities and the hypothesis of the wife.

'Well,' Angus said after a while. 'Who doesn't live beyond their means? The story of our times, eh? I know you're rolling in the stuff, but I'm stony most of the time.'

'But they weren't, at least not on paper they weren't.'

'Business doing well?'

'Too well.'

'Figures don't add up?'

'They do but . . . I'm suspicious. Look at it this way. If you were working a fiddle, who would you need on your side?'

'Book-keeper.'

'Cockerell looked after the books personally.'

'Accountant.'

'That too.'

'He'd still have to be damn clever with figures to get it past the auditor. Mind you, plenty of buggers are or we'd have no need of a Fraud Squad.'

'Which brings me to the case of George Jessel.'

'Who he?'

'Cockerell's auditor—crony—and a recent occupant of the mortuary. He died at a very convenient moment.'

'Murder?'

'I can't prove it, but I think so.'

'You think this bloke collaborated with the first bloke to do what? Cover up losses, fiddles, hide debts? What?'

'I don't know, that's why I need you. There's something not quite kosher about all of this. I just don't know what.'

Angus riffled the fat sheaf of papers. 'As I was saying, this will cost you.'

'Fine. Bill me.'

'And I'll need a letter of authorisation from you.'

'I have one ready.'

Troy reached into his inside pocket and handed Angus an envelope and the keys to Cockerell's shop.

'It's all there. A copy of the notes I took at the time. Bank statements, tax returns, the lot. And if you have to go up there, the wife's address, the auditor's address. Shop keys. Call the wife, she's bright and she's determined to nail her husband for something. And if you can, keep out of the way of the plod, and if you can't there's a young sergeant name of Godbehere who seems trustworthy. The local Inspector isn't, but then he was a crony of Cockerell's too.'

There was, Troy knew, quite a mind behind the bluster. Often in that rapid, expanding and seemingly interminable time between D-Day and the German surrender, Anna had described the RAF charmer who had swept her off her feet and into a do-it-now-we-may-be-dead-tomorrow marriage. He had been a looker, which he wasn't now, but above all she seemed to have been snared by his way with words and ideas. What she had called his 'egghead blarney'. It was increasingly rare to see the combative mask slip from Angus's booze reddened, pissed-out features, but something he had just said had engaged with the inner man, the mind, long enough for him to forget the outer man, the anger.

'Crops up a lot doesn't it, "cronies"? Has it occurred to you that it almost constitutes a principle of social action? A doctrine—"cronyism"? A frilly functioning set of *bon mots*. By their cronies shall ye know them, cronies in high places, one for all and all for crony, a crony in need is crony in deed. Bears a bit of thinking, y'know.'

He held up his glass and nodded at the bar.

'Be the death of this country, you know. Cronyism, clubbable Britain, the nods, the winks, the special handshakes, the blackballing. I used to think the war changed something. In fact I used to think it changed everything. I even thought six years of Socialism had changed something. But they didn't. We're still the same old place we were before the war.'

Herbert set another glass of whisky in front of Angus, without a word. A full double this time. Angus drank half of it and picked up his theme.

'And we'll rot on it. What was it Feste or some other clown says in Shakespeare—"Thou art like the medlar, rotten before 'tis ripe." That's Britain—we'll rot on the bone, long before we're dead or democratic. Cronyism has a lot to answer for. I decided in the end the war changed just one thing.'

'What was that?'

'It chopped off me fuckin' leg.'

Troy said nothing. If not at the root of the matter, they were certainly at the stump.

'And now there's only one thing to do. Get pissed and wait for the end of the fuckin' world. Hiroshima, Nagasaki, Bikini Atoll, and bloody Windscale. Pass the single malt, and don't let the kiddies drink the milk. The green, green grass of England is no longer green, it glistens in its thousand hues like a Strontium rainbow. We gather in the purple rain, lambs to the atomic slaughter. The centre never held. Things that fell apart have been badly stuck back together by a jealous child armed with a tube of polystyrene glue. What rough beast slouches two-headed and triple-bollocked, broad of bicep and limp of dick, towards the smouldering remains of Bethlehem to be illegally aborted?'

He surfaced a fraction, poking a feeler out for a reaction.

'I don't suppose you fancy a piss-up do you, Freddie? A pub crawl. Give a few landlords a bit more shit. I've a slate with every pub from here to the Embankment, as old Herbert so rightly says. Once more round the Great British Raree Show? There's a bloke in the Tit and Biscuit who takes out his glass eye and drops it in his pint—or yours if you're not careful. And this chap in the Pig and Bedpost has a steel plate in his head. Got shot up in a Spit—knew 'im in 1940 as a matter of fact—and the quacks stuck this steel plate in his bonce. So he's fitted a magnet to one of those snowstorm jobbies—y' know one of those glass balls that you shake up and snowflakes fall on a wooden hut in Switzerland or some such place. Won't take it off—even wears it under his hat. Every time the bugger so much as nods his head you get a blizzard up the Alps. And there's a bloke in the Lucifer's Arms who can fart the National Anthem—'

'And there's a bloke in this pub who's been known to whip off his tin leg and wield it like the jawbone of an ass. Angus, I haven't got the time!'

More than that, Troy had no wish to be drawn into Angus's world. It seemed to him hellish beyond measure to be made to share that awful malvision. A night out with Angus would be like treading lightly across a swamp in the vain illusion that you would not be sucked in. Lately he had come to think that survival in middle age demanded not simply the growing up that all men put off in prolonged adolescence, but also the avoidance of ways of seeing, ways of being, of miscalculated actions even, that—and he had no better phrase for it—sucked you in. Angus on the rocks was to be politely avoided, Johnny Fermanagh on the rocks needed the armour-plated heart.

'And nor have you,' he added.

Angus flicked a corner of the paper pile with his thumbnail, rippling it like a dealer shuffling a deck of cards.

'Tomorrow,' he said. 'I'll get stuck in tomorrow.'

He paused. Stared into the distance.

'Or the day after.'

Then he hoisted his glass aloft, yelled, 'Herbert, old boy.' And Troy left him to it.

§53

Special Branch was a hotbed of mangled Secret Service gossip. If the Secret State were an organism, MI5 and 6 were the two cerebella, the Branch was its arms and legs. Armwork—twisting and breaking—and legwork—kicking and breaking—were its function within Britain. Troy could ask the Branch for nothing. The time of day would be too much. They had nothing but contempt for him. He doubted whether his short spell under Inspector Cobb's wing had done anything to improve his standing with them. He asked Jack to put his ear to the ground.

'They'll talk to you,' he said. 'Just find out what you can about Daniel Keeffe. Something in Six. Don't know what.'

There were two D. Keeffes in the directory. Keeffe, D. J. P., in Drayton Gardens SW10, and Keeffe, D. S., in Notting Hill W2. Troy took them in alphabetical order. Keeffe, D. J. P. rang and rang without picking up. He dialled Keeffe, D. S. It picked up on the fifth ring and a woman's voice said 'Yes', bluntly and quietly as though he had woken her from sleep.

'Mrs Keeffe?'

'Who wants to know?'

'My name's Troy. I'm a detective chief inspector with Scotland Yard—'

She hung up. He had almost certainly found the right Keeffe. Ten minutes later Jack came into his office, helped himself to a cup from Clark's machine and pulled up a chair and confirmed the suspicion.

'There is gossip,' he said, 'about this chap Keeffe. I sat with a few of the heavies in the canteen at lunchtime. It would appear that a particularly nasty piece of Special work called Gorman, ugly bugger, ex-Military Police, a sergeant, was boasting a few weeks ago that he'd roasted Keeffe in his own flat. Given him the third degree and turned the place over. My source quoted Gorman as saying, "We turned over this nasty little kike."'

'Jesus Christ,' said Troy. 'Looking for what?'

'Not looking for anything. Just, as the saying goes, roasting.'

'Punishment?'

'I can't think what else to call it. When Five and Six send the Branch in to sort out their own it can only be threat or punishment. I doubt they learn anything directly. They have their own chaps for that, after all.

I think they sent Gorman just to make a mess, and God knows they can make a mess, can't they? Gorman took two constables and really turned him over. According the chap who was telling me, Keeffe had a collection of porcelain, Meissen, Limoges, that sort of thing. They smashed the lot. And as there was no mention of an arrest or even the prospect of one, I conclude that that this was the Branch operating in their purest form—bullying for the sake of it.'

'I think I just talked to his wife. She hung up once I'd given her my rank.'

'I don't blame her. Now, are you going to tell me who he is?'

'I think he's the man who sent Commander Cockerell out to spy on the *Ordzhonikidze*. He's certainly the man the FO sent to explain it all to Cockerell's wife once the Government decided to come clean.'

Jack looked blankly at him for a moment or two.

'Clean? Not the word I would have chosen.'

'Quite.'

Jack resumed the blank stare. Troy began to wonder if he had left half his lunch smeared across his chin.

'You're not going after Five and Six again are you?'

'Again?'

'You know bloody well what I mean.'

'No. I'm not. I just want to know.'

'Know what?'

'What happened to Cockerell.'

'You mean, who killed him?'

'I just want to be sure it doesn't fall within our brief.'

'And if it doesn't, we'll leave well alone?'

Troy said nothing.

'Freddie?'

'Of course,' said Troy.

'You know, somehow I don't believe you.'

Troy worked his way through the paperwork on his desk and cleared the afternoon. By three he was walking from Notting Hill Gate Underground station towards Kensington Gardens. He turned left into Linden Gardens, a looping cul-de-sac, a mixture of mansion flats and double-fronted family homes. He stood on the pavement opposite number 202, wondering what opening tactic would stop him getting an earful of the resentment that the Branch deserved. The door of the house opened, and a short woman emerged, wrapped in a belted mackintosh, headscarf and dark glasses. It was a warmish late-summer day. The inappropriate clothes looked to Troy like a crude form of disguise. Audrey Hepburn or Diana Dors trying to shop unrecognised in Regent Street, but making quite sure everyone would say, 'There's a film star in disguise.' She walked off in the direction of the Bayswater Road and stopped by a parked Morris Minor.

'Mrs Keeffe!' Troy called out to her, and she stopped fiddling with her keys, turned and pulled her glasses down to the tip of her nose, peering, at him over the top.

'It was you who called me?'

'Yes. Mrs Keeffe—I'm not Special Branch.'

'And I'm not Mrs Keeffe.'

'I'm sorry, I don't understand.'

'I'm Deborah Keeffe. Daniel was my brother.'

'Was?'

She took the glasses off entirely, folded them and put them in her coat pocket. Her eyes were red and the lids were swollen. She looked as though she had not slept for two or three days.

'No,' she said. 'You can't be Branch or you'd know. My brother took an overdose five days ago. He's dead, Mr—I'm sorry I've forgotten your name.'

'Troy.'

'I thought I'd seen you before. Or I'd've walked on when you called my name. I've seen you at the House. You're Rod Troy's brother, aren't you?'

'Yes.'

'I'm the Assistant House Librarian, Science and Engineering. I don't suppose you'd've noticed me. The members don't, so why should the visitors? I suppose you went through the telephone directory looking for Keeffes, didn't you? I don't know what your interest is in Daniel, but he lived in Drayton Gardens. As I said, if you were Branch you'd know that.'

'I'm with the Murder Squad, Miss Keeffe.'

'Who's been murdered?'

Increasingly Troy had no answer to this simple question. He gave the answer he was accustomed to give, even though it ran against the grain of what he now believed.

'Commander Cockerell.'

'Well, well, well, the chickens come home to roost at last.'

She pulled her dark glasses out again and slipped them on.

'The last few days I've been over to Drayton Gardens. Clearing up, clearing out, you know. I was on my way there just now, but I suppose that's the last place we can talk. Why don't we forget the car and take the underground? I've always found it a rather private place outside the rush hour. I doubt anyone will hear what we have to say.'

They walked back the way he had come from Notting Hill Gate and boarded a Circle line, on the clockwise run, the long way round to Chelsea, north through Bayswater, east via Baker Street.

Miss Keeffe said nothing until they were seated. She pocketed the sunglasses once more, pulled off her headscarf. Black curly hair fell free, and she brushed it clear of her face. Troy put her at about thirty. Short and Jewish, broad at the cheekbones, her eyes as dark as his, her skin pale, almost white by contrast, except where sleeplessness and grief had left it red and raw. It was a familiar face. England had received many immigrants in the first forty years of the century. She was, he guessed, Latvian or Lithuanian, a descendant of refugees from countries that no longer existed. Someone not unlike him. She knew this, too.

'You're Russians aren't you, you and your brother? Sir Alex Troy's boys.'

'From Tula,' he said, as he always did.

'My mother was from Vilnius. Her parents brought her over in 1899. Russian speakers, Jews, outsiders twice over. Trying to beat the pogrom. They got on a ship bound for Ellis Island. It put in at Tilbury. They disembarked, looked around for the Statue of Liberty, decided it was lost in the fog, registered, and lived here for the best part of a week under the illusion it was New York. My father was from Cork. He had no illusions. He had no adherence to the faith either. An odd marriage, but it worked. Half-Catholic, half-Jewish, guaranteed for neurosis, wouldn't you say?'

Troy saw the gap.

'Was your brother neurotic?'

'Yes. And that's why he killed himself. In the end. A more stable man might have ridden out the embarrassment, a more secure man might have seen it as less than life-threatening. Only a fool would ever have dismissed it as trivial. He didn't have to kill himself. It was always in him to do so, however.'

'I take it your brother had run Cockerell during the war?'

'Yes. He was in the Navy. Made commander. One notch higher than Cockerell. Ever since then there's been the usual rubbish about the reserve list and a job in the Foreign Office, and his rank became a sort of courtesy, concealing whatever rank he really held.'

'And he was blamed for what Cockerell did?'

'Blamed, interrogated, punished and humiliated. They posted him to Reykjavik at the end of June. Can you imagine the humiliation? Good war record. Bright young thing of the department, leading light in Soviet watching, spoken the language since childhood, still under forty—and they post him to a non-place, to a non-job. All he'd do for the rest of his tour would be to count fishing boats and spy on the amount of cod and halibut they landed. It was worse than sacking him. I always disliked Daniel's commitment to his job. In wartime it seemed fine. In peace it didn't. Don't ask me why. Maybe in war everything was bending to the common cause. The fabric of the old British prejudices stretching out of shape, holes appearing like fishnet stockings, holes through which men like Daniel passed. Outsiders became insiders. He thought it was permanent. Bloody fool. He lied to himself and he lied to me. He wanted to be accepted.

'The night before he left he came round to see me, already half cut. He finished off a bottle of gin in my sitting room and blubbered on about his job. I urged him to quit. He couldn't do that, he told me. Once they had you, you were theirs for ever. It would all blow over. He'd done nothing. Sooner or later they'd see that. Then he told me. Told me how Cockerell came to see him after more than ten years. Daniel had been in charge of him, his "case officer" or whatever the spooks call it, during the war. He'd retired him, because he was so obviously past it. Cockerell told him he wanted one last job before he finally hung up his flippers. Told Daniel he could tackle the *Ordzhonikidze,* described some crazy scheme he'd thought up for examining the hull of the ship. Why would we want to do that? Daniel asked him. And Cockerell rambled on about Russian secrets, and how it was a golden opportunity. Daniel said no. Told him he couldn't possibly get authorisation for such a harebrained scheme. But he felt sorry for the old fool. He took him for a drink at his club. But even that was showing off. Boasting that he had a club to take him to.

'And then the bubble burst. The rumours about Cockerell started. The papers got hold of it. Entry records were checked. They all had to produce their diaries, and there it was, just as the PM was trying to deny everything, Daniel's diary showed an appointment with Cockerell. The log on the door showed Lieutenant Commander Cockerell admitted to see Commander Keeffe in March. Too many spooks saw Daniel with Cockerell in his club, drinking like old comrades. And nobody believed a word of Daniel's version. That he put Cockerell on a train back to darkest Derbyshire with a couple of stiff drinks inside him and told him to forget about Khrushchev and enjoy his retirement.

'He spent two days with someone he called the "Soft Man"—he looked five years older by the time he emerged. Then the Branch called. Smashed everything that mattered to him. And the final humiliation. Three weeks before Daniel shipped out for Reykjavik the PM decided to own up and Daniel was sent up to Derbyshire to debrief the widow. And I think debrief is Newspeak for "shut her up". I don't know what he said to her. He hardly spoke except when he was drunk. Mind you, that was every day by then. He sailed for Reykjavik drunk, he phoned me up drunk. And he died drunk, swimming in gin and barbiturates.

'I was at work when they told me. I have an office just off the reading room. Chap called Woodbridge, Tim Woodbridge, called in. Parliamentary Secretary at the Foreign Office, MP for Upshire or Downshire. No one I knew. Most of my work is with the Opposition. Government doesn't much need the briefs we can prepare, they have the civil service at their beck and call. So, Woodbridge introduced himself, told me he had some bad news for me, started his how-sorry-we-all-are waffle. I cut him short and told him if Daniel was dead he should just spit it out. Had to be Daniel. My parents are long gone, and we were neither of us married. There was just me and him. And besides, it was in his nature to do the silly thing. Anyway, Woodbridge let me have a little cry, and when it looked as though I'd put on the stiff upper lip he came to the real purpose of his visit. Anything among Daniel's possessions relating to the job must be returned to the spooks, and I'm still bound by the Official Secrets Act. I must tell no one anything, and if I cooperate my prospects at the House are assured. Meaning if I don't, they'll finish me. All said in the nicest possible way, you understand and not a word of reference to what he really meant—just "recent events in which your brother may have been involved". Didn't mention spies or frogmen or Khrushchev. And all the time the bastard called me "my dear". I can take all the time

I want off work, all they ask is for assurances of my discretion. I felt like he was pretending all the time. Pretending I was one of them, pretending I wasn't a woman, pretending I mattered in some way, pretending I was part of "the club", pretending I played by the same rules, for God's sake pretending I wasn't Jewish!'

'Then why are you telling me this?'

'Because I'm not part of the club. Because faith, age and gender exclude me from it. Because I won't play by their rules. I like my job. I've worked hard to get there. Scholarship to Girton when I was seventeen, a Master's from the LSE by the time I was twenty-one. Commons Librarian at twenty-six. But they can't bribe me with it. They can't use it to hit me over the head. I don't know what I'd've done. I've almost cleaned out Daniel's flat and I haven't found a damn thing that would point a finger at anyone. But I know what I know. And if you hadn't come along I'd've found someone. Some bloody Ivanhoe would come along and rescue Rebecca. I hope to God he would. I'd've told somebody. God knows, I might even have told your brother, I've written the odd brief for him. At least he knows my name.'

'Don't.'

'Eh?'

'Don't tell him anything.'

She shrugged. 'If you like. I'm not sure what appealing within Westminster will achieve anyway.'

She paused. Troy could almost hear the action of memory.

'Tell me, do you remember that piece in *The Economist* last year, at the time the House debated Burgess and Maclean?'

'What piece?'

'I think the chap's name was Fairlie. He said something like the "Establishment closing ranks" to protect them? Does that ring a bell?'

It didn't. Troy had dim memories of poor old Harold Philby denying all the innuendo in the press conference at his flat, facing the likes of Alan Whicker, and doing his best to defend himself against the power of rumour.

'Vaguely.'

'It stirred up a debate in itself. One of those cultural rows that happen from time to time as a country and a culture redefines itself. That's what we're doing now. Redefining ourself. Doing it rather badly, as a matter of fact. And just because we don't have a Fourth of July, or salute the flag, and we have no notion of un-British in the sense of un-American, and no one stands up in the cinema for the national anthem any more, it doesn't mean we don't have a sense of identity, a sense of ourself. Fairlie put his finger on it. The idea of an Establishment—an inner layer of Britain that always looks after its own. Not a class or a hierarchy, and much harder to define than that. Layer's about the best I can do. It's about belonging. I don't belong. My brother did not belong, and he died of wanting to belong. He could not live with the accusation of betrayal. But he never grasped that without belonging there can be no betrayal. Do you see what I mean?'

Troy saw very clearly what she meant. For a moment it was like debating with his father. It was his kind of argument. It was his kind of structure. But she had got the important point the wrong way round.

'Of course,' he said. 'But the point of Burgess and Maclean is that belonging makes betrayal impossible. If you belong you cannot betray. Establishment, however you define it, is not country, is not *patria*. Betray and the country will disown you or prosecute you. This Establishment, this layer as you call it, never will. It is in that scheme of things perfectly possible to betray, to belong and not to accept that you have betrayed. It's perfectly possible that Burgess has kept up his subscription to whatever gentleman's club he was in on the offchance of his ever needing it again.'

He thought of Patum Pepperium, the Gentleman's Relish, and of the gentleman in Moscow, outrageous to the last, still thinking of himself as belonging to everything he had sold up the Swannee, still wanting betrayal with relish, holding a press conference to justify his betrayal still wearing his Old Etonian tie.

'Which,' Miss Keeffe replied, 'ought to be a paradox. But it isn't, is it?'

She put her hands up, the fingertips touching, the palms apart, the ribs and buttresses of a symbolic, make-believe cathedral.

'The Establishment closes ranks to protect and in so doing contains, that is includes and excludes. Even if you're living in Moscow on a KGB pension, you're still included. But God help the buggers caught in the gate when the ranks slam shut.'

She brought her palms together, the soft clap of flesh on flesh.

'Splat. That's what happened to Daniel Keeffe. Splat.'

It seemed to Troy that they understood one another perfectly. Rarely had he had a conversation with someone who so closely shared his own prejudices. But to what end?

'What do you want me to do?' he asked.

She looked surprised. Looked back at him with a puzzled expression on her face.

'Want? Why should I want anything from you? You came to me. Mr Troy. You do what you have to do. I haven't solved your murder for you. Nor have I added to the rollcall of the dead. My brother was a victim, as I'm sure you will agree, the perfect scapegoat, but he wasn't murdered and it will do no good for me to pretend that he died by any other than his own hand.'

Looking back on the whole sorry mess he always stuck at this moment, came back to it time and again, that this was the one person who had been lucid through the pain and anger, that this was the one person in the entire affair who had wanted nothing of him.

'Then let me put it another way. What are you going to do?'

'I'm going to finish clearing out Drayton Gardens. Then I'm going to go back to work. If, as a result of what I've told you, Woodbridge or any one of the Gentlemen accuse me, I shall not deny it. Nor shall I resign. They'll have to fire me. I've jumped through the English hoops all my life, so did my brother, we made ourselves in the required image, but they can't make me a liar, Mr Troy.'

But, of course, this was where they differed. He had long since, since childhood, since the coming of language, accepted the inevitability of lying. It was almost a way of life.

Troy looked out at the station sign, the line through a circle that marked every stop on the London Underground. He'd noticed nothing since Miss Keeffe had begun to speak, they could have been anywhere for all he knew, from Notting Hill to Charing Cross, but now she had so obviously finished. They were pulling out of Moorgate. One more stop and they'd be at Liverpool Street. He said goodbye and got out at the next stop. Found himself in front of the platform bar he and Khrushchev had propped up. Now it was shuttered and barred, or he'd have bought half a pint and thought a while. Instead, he looked down the tunnel, breathed deeply, searching to see if he too could smell despair, wondering what despair should smell like and why it should have a smell at all. He could not—only bacon frying.

§54

Warriss delighted in the call.

'Myocardial infarction. Or would you like that in words of one syllable, sir?'

'No,' said Troy. 'Just stick a copy of the report in the post. And tell me if there are any details I should know now.'

'No marks of any kind. No bruises, no cuts. Nothing. Your questions and your flyers were a waste of my time—yielded Sweet Fanny Adams. There is no evidence to suggest that Jessel died of anything other than a heart attack brought on by years of booze and figs and a history of angina. Dr Jewel is prepared to sign the certificate as "natural causes". Unless, of course, you know different?'

It was a taunt. The man was laughing at him. Troy hung up on him. Ten minutes later the telephone rang again.

'Mr Troy? Ray Godbehere here.'

'I've just had your Inspector kicking sand in my face.'

'I know, sir. That's why it's safe for me to call you. He's gone off to lunch laughing like a hyena.'

'I'm still the biggest twat in Belper, am I?'

'I wouldn't say that, sir. I've checked the three sets of prints I got off the desktop. One is the Inspector's. I know that 'cos we file all our own to cut down on the cock-ups. Clumsy of him to mess up a scene of crime, but then he doesn't think it is a scene of crime, does he, sir? The second set is left hand only. A prominent scar running the width of the index finger. You don't have a scar on your left index finger by any chance do you, sir?'

Damn. He must have leant on the desk at some point, though he had no recollection of doing so.

'Yes. I'm sorry to say that's me. And the third?'

'Also left hand only. Fingertips at various points and full palm right on the edge. As though someone had put most of his body weight on the left hand. No match anywhere. I didn't print Brenda or the cleaning lady—it's a man's hand, a big man's. I printed the late Mr Jessel. No matches. And nothing in CRO. At one point your print overlaps one of the unknown's, so it looks as though you were right. Between the cleaner and yourself, someone was in there.'

'Leaning on his left hand to wave a gun in George Jessel's face with his right. He racked back the slide, leant over and spilt a drop of oil on Jessel's side of the desk.'

'And Jessel died on him. Is that what you're saying, sir?'

'I think so. I think someone was trying to scare him and got lucky.'

'Lucky?'

'I doubt they would or could have shot him and walked away. The heart attack was very convenient.'

'Do you have anyone in mind?'

'Have you got a print for Cockerell?'

'No, sir. And I don't know how to get one. According to the papers he was washed up without hands.'

'Try the door of his car.'

'You mean go up there and ask Mrs Cockerell?'

'Yes. You can do that, can't you?'

'Yes, I can. But let me put it this way, sir. I did the last few days' legwork. I put out the flyers for the Inspector. I did the knocking on doors. No one saw anyone. That's the truth, but I'll tell you now the one person anyone hereabouts would remember seeing is Arnold Cockerell. He's the one man who couldn't walk into the town unnoticed, kill his accountant and get on the next bus to Shottle.'

Troy presumed the closing phrase was some local metaphor for the vanishing trick. Of course he had a point. It just didn't fit the pattern Troy was seeing. More and more he was coming round to Janet Cockerell's point of view. The man had vanished. And the delight in vanishing was to surface from time to time.

'I'm sorry. You're probably right. Let's leave Mrs Cockerell alone for the time being. How much does Warriss know?'

'No more than he did the last time the two of you met.'

'Thank you. I'm grateful.'

'Mind, if he does find out—'

'I know—I'll get you shot.'

'More than that, sir, you'd best find me another job.'

Troy took the hint. God knows, Godbehere seemed brighter than half the dozy buggers he'd worked with at the Yard. Perhaps too bright. Of course, Troy didn't think Cockerell had pointed a gun at George Jessel and scared the living daylights out of him, but it would have been so very neat if he had, and whilst he didn't really think this, the part of his mind that tacked intuitively, sailing close to the deceptive winds of imagination, would not quite surrender the notion that he *might* have done so.

§55

He needed the solidity of fact. He needed Kolankiewicz and Kolankiewicz was a day late with his promise. He pulled the post-mortem report on Cockerell off his desk and went to beard the Polish Beast in his lair.

'I bin busy. The dead keep crazy hours.'

He got up and closed the door behind Troy.

'You're forgetting your privacy,' he said to no reaction. 'But I have what you wanted.'

He pulled open the top drawer of his desk and put the remains of Troy's handkerchief in front of him.

'You cut up one of my best Irish linen handkerchiefs!'

'I cut off one corner. Don't be so damn fussy! Do you want to know or don't you? I got plenty of other coppers I can play with.'

'OK. Let's hear it.'

'It is, as I'm sure you surmised, gun oil. Or, in so far as any substance is qualified adjectivally by use, oil which is gun oil if you use it to oil a gun.'

This was Kolankiewicz in fully professional mode. The command of language that evaded him in the fractured colloquial was put to a precise scientific use that obfuscated beautifully.

'Can I have that in English?'

'It is what I would use on an automatic, if I had one. It is what many men do use, but it also has other uses. I used the same oil to loosen up the lawnmower last weekend. But unless you are about to tell me you're investigating a man run over by a lawnmower in Hampstead Garden Suburb—in which case I plead provocation and say I have always hated the man next door and killed the bastard in a fit of horticultural

236

madness—let us presume a gun. Low viscosity oil, high graphite content. Won't stick. Does not attract dirt, won't jam the slide, but it's fluid. It will run and you would need to oil the gun more regularly than you would with an oil of higher viscosity. You will get drips, you'll mess up your suit. Sooner or later.'

'And?'

'And what?'

'And speculate.'

'No common villain, no wide boy, would know such a detail. They'd put three-in-one on a gun just as they would on a bicycle, if they knew enough to oil it or clean it in the first place. A man who looks after his weapon in this way knows guns. An ex-serviceman—'

'We're a nation of ex-servicemen.'

'Most of whom never saw an automatic pistol in their life. There's a world of difference between the mechanics of a bolt-action Lee Enfield rifle and a Colt or a Browning hand gun. I mean an officer, or a professional, someone who takes no chances on a gun jamming at the wrong moment.'

'All this from a drop of oil?'

'You've never come to me with a grain of sand. I wait for the day you do.'

'You'll ruin your suit. Sooner or later.' Troy remembered the shirt he had never got clean after Portsmouth. Ruined by a few drops of oil. A heart-shaped stain. It was moment of odd recognition, seeing the point at which he had come in.

'Can you get down to Portsmouth in the morning?'

'Probably. Why?'

'The locals have a body on ice. Arnold Cockerell.'

'The spy?'

'Yes. Get him on the slab again. I want a second opinion.'

'You want me to upset a colleague? Tread on the toes of a fellow sawbones?'

'You know the local man?'

'Of course not. But does that make him any the less a colleague?'

Troy put the post-mortem report in front of Kolankiewicz.

'You read it. I need more than this.'

Kolankiewicz pushed it back at him. 'Have you read it?'

Troy pushed it back at Kolankiewicz. 'Of course I've read it.'

He had found it in his out-tray. That meant he'd read it. Of course he'd read it. But he had not read it all, and it did not occur to him that he hadn't. He had, after all, such a vivid picture of the corpse in his mind's eye.

Kolankiewicz was looking oddly at him. Was that concern he saw in the piggy eyes?

'You know me, Troy. The avuncular is not my *modus operandi*. But, I ask you, do you really want to stick your proboscis into Five and Six? Once more with the cats and foxes? How many hospitals I fished you out of? How many stitches I put in you these twenty years? You my best customer. I should keep a slab ready for you.'

It was the voice of Jiminy Cricket chirping in his ear. And it made not a damn of difference. The fox and the cat already sang to him. He danced down the cobbled alley with their song of seduction ringing in his head. Hi diddle di dee.

'I'm already in it,' he said flatly.

'Then I reserve my right to be Polish smartyarse and say, "I told you so" at some future date.'

'Fine,' said Troy. 'You've been saying that as long as I've known you. You'll no doubt have it chipped on my headstone. I'll see you at the mortuary mid-afternoon.'

§56

The weather was odd. The drenched August now promised almost an Indian Summer. The desk-bound idiot on the south door of the Yard had his theory, but Troy did not listen. He took off his jacket, wiped down the windscreen of the Bentley, saw the sun and the fleeting clouds reflected in it and decided it could not be a more beautiful day to drive down to the coast. The sky was Wedgwood, the clouds danced across it like blown candy floss and the sun was a checkercab yellow. He would tune the car wireless to the Third Programme and enjoy a couple of hours' freedom and sanity before he faced Kolankiewicz and a corpse, belligerence and death, for the umpteenth time in his career. He was trying to find the wavelength when Wildeve appeared through the gateway from the Embankment, jacket across his shoulder, sleeves rolled up, yawning widely.

'You off somewhere?'

'Portsmouth. A post mortem.'

'Cockerell? Keeffe?'

'Cockerell.'

'Mind if I tag along?'

'I thought you were in court all this week.'

'Our Mr Bayliss just changed his plea to Guilty.'

He grinned like a schoolboy in the sheer pleasure of victory.

'OK. Get in.'

Troy drove the Bentley out onto the Embankment and across Westminster Bridge, just as Big Ben struck the chimes of noon. Jack settled back in the passenger seat and closed his eyes.

'Are you going to tell me what you're up to?' he said.

'No,' said Troy. 'I'm not.'

'Fine. I'm knackered. Wake me up when we get there.'

Troy put the wireless on low, found the opening moments of a lunchtime concert. A Haydn symphony. He'd have fun guessing which.

§57

Kolankiewicz pointed at Wildeve.

'Why you bring him?'

Troy thought about it.

'For the ride.'

'Some ride. He faints. He throws up. Ach, ach!'

'This will be fairly clean, won't it? Hardly be bodily fluids left after five months.'

'Clean? Troy, you seen this fucker? He's a complete mess. They could not have done a better job if they'd deliberately set out to make him unrecognisable.'

'That's my point.'

'Eh?'

'It's too good to be true. It's all just a bit too neat.'

'Neat? I tell you, smartyarse, when Wildeve sees this one he turn green!'

He led off into the surgery. A modern room, all Formica and washable surfaces, strip lighting and plastic trim. As up to date, in its way, as Cockerell's living room. The unknown, numbered corpse tagged 'Cockerell?' lay on the stainless steel 'slab', a low sink more than six feet long with a spider web of radiating runnels to drain off blood and things worse, far worse. Whiter than white, he struck Troy as bearing only a passing resemblance to anything that might once have lived. He was neater than last time. A look of sterility rather than death. A wax impression of the parts of a man joined up with black thread. And it smelt of nothing. The room had the faint chemical trace of formaldehyde that was inescapable in a post-mortem surgery, but the smell of death and decay, the open gut, spilt shit and drying blood smell that so often surrounded death, was missing. Months on ice had reduced it almost to the clinical, the inanimate to the never-human. The body had been cleaned and, unlike the last time he saw it, did not look as though it had been washed up only hours before with seaweed stuck between the toes. The head and face were a black hole set in a rim of white bone. The absence of hands made him seem dwarf-like, a doll of a man. And there was a raised seam down the chest and abdomen like the rough stitching that held sacking together—it reminded Troy of the sackcloth body bag in which Edmond Dantés was dumped from the Château d'If, and in his mind's eye he could see the hand that held the knife emerging to slit the stitches, to burst into freedom and second birth, and a new life as the Count of Monte Cristo. An apt image, he thought, for the devious Commander Cockerell. Was he even now swanning around as the Count of Jasmine Dene, ducking his creditors and cheating his wife?

On top of a low cupboard to the side stood half a dozen glass jars, the pickled remains of the corpse's vital organs: stomach, duodenum, colon, liver *et alia*. Pickled, they had lost the fresh, roseate colour, the sheen of near-vitality, the rubescent light of lites—lost to a dun brown. All the same, Jack turned green.

'Out!' Kolankiewicz barked.

'No,' Jack protested feebly. 'I want to know.'

'You puke, I fuckin' kill you!'

'I won't puke. I'll just sit here. Quietly.'

He took a canvas and steel tube chair off a stack and sat by the wall, head tilted back, his eyes closed, his pallor unearthly.

Kolankiewicz slipped the loop of his rubber apron over his head, rolled up his sleeves and scrubbed up.

'He'll be fine,' Troy lied, thinking of all the times he had waited while Jack discreetly threw up in bushes at the scenes of murders.

'You better be right, smartyarse. Now tell me what you looking for.'

'I'm not looking for anything.'

'Give over.'

'Honestly, I just need to know.'

'Know? That's what puking Willy said. What you mean "know"?'

Kolankiewicz was right. Jack had not said 'see' he had said 'know'. He had definitely said 'know'. The choice of word struck Troy as odd. As odd as him showing up exactly when he did.

'I mean precisely what it says. Who is this bloke? I need to know.'

Kolankiewicz snapped on his rubber gloves and worked his fingers down to the tips.

'You mean you got no new evidence?'

'No, I haven't.'

'You going to screw my reputation, you know. Here I am down from the high and mighty Yard, redoing a job by the local bones without a shred of a reason. A little evidence would not have come amiss. All I have to go on is your suspicion that this isn't Cockerell, am I right?'

'No. I didn't say that. I don't know who it is.'

It was a fudge and Troy knew he had not got away with it. Kolankiewicz eyeballed him, raised the bush of grey hair that passed for an eyebrow.

'But you're pretty damn certain it isn't?'

'No.'

'Troy, you full of shit, as ever. OK. OK.'

They stood facing each other across the near-luminous white mass of the body. Kolankiewicz tapped the microphone suspended a foot above his head. Troy had not seen such a device before. The Yard, in the forefront of the science of detection, still had stenographers perched on stools with their shorthand notebooks. He looked around. There behind a glass panel in the wall was a young man equipped with one of the new

Grundig magnetic tape recorders. He gave Kolankiewicz a thumbs up and returned to looking at his dials and switches.

'Why don't we just take everything the first report has and check it item by item?' Troy said.

'Fine,' said Kolankiewicz. 'Who's on first?'

'We take the head first.'

'No, this is where you say, "I don't know." Then I say, I don't know's on second. Who's on first.'

'What?"

'No, Watt's on third. Who's on first.'

'Eh?'

'Forget it. Sometimes you so damn English I can hardly believe you real.'

Troy turned the first page of the post-mortem report. Kolankiewicz forsook Abbott and Costello and plunged a rubber finger into the skull.

'As I recall, cause of death was given as a blow to the head, shattering top of spine, killing brain stem. No water in lungs. Ergo he was dead before he hit the water.'

'Yes,' said Troy.

'However, very little of back of head left. Does our man describe the impact wound?'

'No. Just gives the blow to the head as probable cause. Remarks on the shattering of the skull. Possibly by propeller blades.'

'He's right. Sliced like a boiled egg. But below the cut is compression of skull and tissue I would not personally ascribe to the same action that sliced the skull. Upward motion sliced his head, entered via the face, hence no face, exit rear of skull, but the compression here is down. Hit from the back. What does our man say?'

'Nothing.'

'OK. It's easy to miss. Most of the actual wound is missing. And it could be that it *was* caused by the action of a propeller. It is in the nature of things that they swirl you around, clobber you over and over again. It's only my opinion. But if the blow that killed him was from the propeller you might deduce that he was alive when it hit him. But we know he wasn't. So what killed him? A prior blow? Ergo we look for evidence of a prior blow.'

'Sounds logical to me.'

'I could not make this stand up in court, but—'

'I hate sentences beginning that way.'

'But—I think he was hit once from behind with a round object.'

'Round? What happened to our old friend "blunt"?'

'He's at first base. No—I say round. I mean round. Like he been sapped. Good and hard. But as I say, with so much of the wound missing and with such violent action to the skull as a whole I'd have difficulty swearing to it. Now ze nick! Ze fangres, ze bilbow, ze nick! As our old pal Shakespeare put it.'

From Abbott and Costello to *Henry V* in a few short moves whilst poring over a corpse. Troy had to admire Kolankiewicz's sang-froid. He had wisecracked his way through a thousand autopsies.

'His wife mentioned a mole.'

Kolankiewicz turned the head around. The sliced side faced Troy and reminded him of nothing so much as an open oyster.

'There's no mole here. We lost a bit of the right-hand side of the neck, but there's no mole on what's left. Dig into my bag. Pass me the magnifying glass.'

Troy handed him a huge round glass, the kind Sherlock Holmes was often to be seen with on the lurid covers of paperback books, and watched his piggy eye blow up to a brown moon.

'Again, right on edge of remaining tissue, shiny patch.'

'Shiny?'

'Like recent scar tissue. Tiny. Maybe a thirty-second of an inch long.'

'What does it mean?'

'You going to hate this too. I can't swear to this either, being so close to an injury that tore off half his head and bits of his neck, but it looks like plastic surgery to me. If your man had a mole, it is conceivable he had it removed. Vain sort of bugger was he?'

'Yes.'

'Then let us press on.'

They worked down the corpse from the neck to the feet. Kolankiewicz reopened the chest cavity, and gazed through a glass darkly at the organs in the pickling jars. Every so often Troy would read out a section of the report and Kolankiewicz would say 'Correct', and every so often Troy would hear Jack sigh softly in the corner. 'Correct' became irritating. By the time they reached the toes, via hands, knees and sexual organs, tempers were frayed.

'There must be something.'

'What you mean, must be something? What you fuckin' want I stick on pieces like he was a puppet? Fingers where he got no fingers. Face where he got no face? What you think this is, Punch and Judy? Muffin the Mule?'

'All I meant was—'

'I know what you meant. What I don't know is what you want. You want it to be Cockerell or not? I don't know what you want, I don't know why you get me down here, but don't ask me to invent evidence where there is none. The guy done a good fuckin' job. If I say he got it right, he got it right.'

'He missed things.'

'No—he refused to speculate on two points that are scarcely big enough to measure. You pissed off with him, you pissed off with me because you want us to label the corpse, you want it tagged as Cockerell or not-Cockerell. I can't do that. Don't ask.'

'Speculation is the business we're in. Can we get on?'

Kolankiewicz leaned in close. Horseradish and roast beef on his breath. They faced each other across the corpse.

'Get on? Troy. We reached the feet. Beyond the feet he don't exist! How many men you met exist past their feet? The feet are where we touch the planet, beyond the feet is only Mother Earth.'

'All I'm saying is—'

Kolankiewicz blazed into anger, snatched the report from Troy's hand and shook it in his face.

'What you want me to say, cocksucker? I no longer know what you want me to say. That it is Cockerell or it isn't Cockerell? Fuckit Troy, I don't know what you want me to do. You jigger me every which way arsehole to elbow. I tread all over toes of local man for you. I make enemies faster than Hitler at a Jewish wedding. I tell you the man did a good job!'

He gave up shaking the report and began to leaf through it, turning the pages till he found what he wanted, stabbing at it with his stubby, rubber-gloved finger.

'I tell you Troy, this is all the evidence you going to get. The man is good. We quibbling over insubstantial matter. Every damn thing is here. Every last damn detail, the cuts to the hand and feet, the contents of the lungs, the dreadful condition of the liver, right down to the contents of the man's stomach and intestines. Dammit Troy, he even lists what the bastard had for his last meal.'

244

He threw his head back, rolled his eyes, and waved his hands in the air in mock horror.

'Ach! Ach! This is disgusting. Christ almighty, what kind of a man eats fish and eggs and rice mixed up altogether for his breakfast?'

Troy seized Kolankiewicz by the straps of his apron and bodily lifted him to eye level, suspended him over the corpse, all but nose to nose, speaking softly, scarcely more than a whisper in the wake of Kolankiewicz's racket.

'A certain kind of Englishman, that's who. It's a delicacy of the Raj. It's called kedgeree. And I saw Cockerell demolish a plateful for breakfast and then start on the toast and marmalade.'

Kolankiewicz smiled sheepishly, as much as he could, suspended by his braces, feet dangling, he shrugged—palms upwards in surrender to the logic on offer.

'Kedgeree, schmedgeree . . .'

'Yes?'

'Then it's him,' Kolankiewicz said quietly.

Troy put him down. Heard the click as his heels hit the floor.

'Yes,' he said, 'it's him.'

He turned round to jack.

'It's him,' he said softly.

Jack sat very still, the colour only just returning to his cheeks.

'Can we go now?' he asked.

§58

Kolankiewicz seemed not to bear the grudge. Out in the car park, dignity and hat restored, he stuffed his *News Chronicle* into his pocket and assumed a job-well-done affability. It was a moment Troy had been waiting for, and if he blew up at him now it would have little immediate consequence.

'I've been meaning to talk to you,' Troy said. 'You know, about that night in Stepney with Khrushchev.'

'No, no,' Kolankiewicz said quickly. 'There is no need. I quite under-stand your motives. Indeed, I did at the time. It requires no explanation. Since neither you nor I have the courage or the morality that would enable us to put a bullet through the man's head, a little education was perhaps the best thing you could have done for him, for you, for the world. I just hope you had a long spoon.'

He grinned wickedly at Troy over the last phrase.

'No,' said Troy, treading carefully. 'That isn't really what I meant. I wanted to ask what you and he talked about.'

'Poland, of course! He told me he could envisage a day when the Russian soldier need not stand one inch beyond the Russian frontier, that he could foresee a time when Poland would be free to call its own elections, elect its own government. And he could see this because he had no doubts that they would elect a Communist government. It was the inevitability of history's purpose.'

'Aha. And what did you say?'

'Oh—I called the bastard a liar to his face.'

In his mind's eye Troy saw Khrushchev rising red-faced from his seat at exactly the moment Eric the landlord had appeared with his handbell to cry, 'Aven't you lot got homes to go to?' It seemed to him now that both he and Kolankiewicz had been saved by the bell. The surprise was how quickly Khrushchev had recovered from what must undoubtedly be the worst abuse anyone had heaped upon him since the death of Stalin. Between Stepney and Claridge's he had slipped smoothly from the surly to the affable to the downright chatty.

'Shall we go?'

It was Jack, pulling Troy back from reverie.

'Yes. Of course.'

Troy turned back to Kolankiewicz.

'Do you need a lift up to London?'

'No,' he replied, tugging at the brim of his Homburg. 'For favours like this to buggers like you, I demand the bribe of a First-Class railway ticket, with which the fat bloke in your office has furnished me. While you boys struggle down the crowded roads, I shall eat a British Railways high tea, with sticky cakes and a little help from my hip flask, and finish the crossword puzzle in this morning's paper. In which there is no small measure of justice. So long, flatfoots.'

'Charming,' Wildeve said.

§59

Wildeve drove. Pleased as punch to be behind the wheel of the Bentley. He was a far better driver than Troy. Troy sat well back in the passenger seat, half-mesmerised by the rhythmic flashing of the sunlight through the trees, working it all out. They had reached Petersfield before he felt he had the pieces of the puzzle in place. Even then, they made no picture he could recognise.

'If that is Cockerell—' he began.

'What? What the hell do you mean "if"? You've just told Kolankiewicz it's definitely Cockerell!'

'Of course it's Cockerell, but—'

Troy got no further. Wildeve swung the car off the road, still doing over fifty, and brought it screeching to a stop on the forecourt of a roadside café.

'I! But! Dammit, Freddie, why are you even thinking about this? It is Cockerell. That's all there is to it and for God's sake let that be an end to it.'

'But—' Troy struggled pathetically.

Wildeve snatched the keys from the ignition, slammed the car door behind him and strode off across the forecourt into the café. Troy had little choice but to follow. To sit and wait in the car was so like the action of a sulking adolescent that he would have followed Jack through the gates of hell.

He found him at a Formica-topped, greasy table inside the wooden hut, two cups of murky-looking tea in front of him. The whole place reeked of cigarettes and bacon and egg. Burly lorry drivers in blue overalls and bobble hats turned to look at two toffs in dark suits, silk ties and polished shoes. As Troy sat down, self-consciously, accepting the silent invitation, Jack pushed the caked bottles of ketchup and brown sauce away from the centre, clearing the ground for what Troy knew damn well was bound to be confrontation.

'Spit it out, Jack,' he said, and sipped at the mess of tea.

'I don't understand you. I just don't understand you. Isn't it obvious what's going on?'

'Of course it is. It's a spook affair through and through. We knew that from the start.'

'Good. At least we see eye to eye on that. But it's because it's a spook affair that we get out now. All Cockerell's wife asked was to know one way or the other that that corpse was him. The Government had already said it was, but no one could blame her for clinging to one last shred of hope that her wandering hubby might still be alive somewhere.'

'There's more to it than that.'

'There's an infinite amount more to it than that! But it's none of our business.'

'Jack, aren't you the slightest bit curious? Someone sapped him and dumped him in the water. If he hadn't got caught up in a ship's propeller we'd have known it was him the day he was washed up. But it was a mess. Given that it was a mess, why were the local plod so anxious that it should be Cockerell? First they rip a page out of the register at the Henry, as though they want to conceal Cockerell, then they practically bully the poor woman into saying it's her husband when she cannot say for sure that it is. Doesn't that strike you as a mite odd?'

'You don't get it do you, Freddie? Let me spell it out for you. What did Onions say to us in 1944? He told us that he'd roast our balls over a slow fire if he ever caught us meddling in a spook affair again!'

Troy sipped at his tea. Jack's anger had not subsided enough to let him so much as touch his cup.

'To be precise, Jack, what Stan actually said was that if anything like that ever came up again he wanted to know at the outset. He didn't say we couldn't do our job.'

'And you're going to tell him, are you?'

Of course Troy wasn't going to tell Onions. Wildeve had him cornered now. Lying would be pointless.

'Not yet anyway.'

'Not yet, or when it suits you?'

'Much the same thing really.'

'So you're going after this on your own, knowing bloody well that the next step has got to be investigating some damn KGB spook or other, without telling Stan.'

'I hadn't thought what the next move was, but if you put it like that—'

'There's no other way to put it. The man is dead. Washed up in his frogman's clobber not two miles from the very berth in which even Her Majesty's Government has admitted he was spying on the Russian ship.

Who else do you think you're going to investigate? How far do you think you'll get?'

Troy shrugged. Wildeve was thinking so much quicker than he was himself. But then Wildeve was burdened by only half the knowledge Troy had.

'I'll tell you what the next move is. We drop it. You report back to the widow, give her the bad news, express your condolences and get back to honest murders. If you don't—'

Troy opened his mouth, about to speak. Wildeve's hand shot up, flatly and squarely in his face, like the point-duty copper halting the mighty roar of London's traffic.

'Shut up! If you don't do this, if I hear that you are pursuing the matter of the death of Commander Cockerell, in whatever direction, from whatever source, so help me, Freddie, I'll shop you. I'll shop you and I'll tell Stan everything. Do you understand me?'

Troy understood very well.

They drove back to London in silence. He could not, after all, think in what direction he could or should pursue the matter, nor, for the life of him, could he think from what source such a fresh impulse or initiative might come. It really didn't matter that Jack had taken such a hard line. In identifying Cockerell he had hit the buffers. The only Cockerell that could matter was the one who wasn't washed up on the Hampshire coast, the errant husband whom Troy had thought of as romping somewhere with a mistress, the errant husband whom his wife had thought was fleeing his creditors, and since the man on the slab *was* Commander Cockerell, none of the others existed. For the first time in days he could not hear the fox and the cat. Their song was silent and their feet were stilled.

§60

When he got home it was early evening. The September nights not autumnal, but no longer summer either in that you could not take their duration for granted. Tosca was sitting in the living room in her Chanel two-piece, the same suit she had been wearing when he found her in Amsterdam. Her going away suit, as he had come to think of it.

She blew a bubble of gum, and burst it neatly with her front teeth.

'Good,' she said. 'You're just in time to take me out to dinner.'

He had made no plans, had not even been sure whether he would find her in—of late she had wandered around the town very much on her own and at whim. Troy concluded she was revisiting old haunts, old memories, rediscovering London.

'OK,' he agreed. 'What's it to be? Posh or Soho?'

'Soho.'

'Gennaro's, the Hussar, or do you want music?'

'Dunno.'

They settled on Wheeler's in Old Compton Street. Troy had never much liked the place, or its emphasis on English cooking, but she professed never to have eaten there, nor ever to have eaten oysters, for which Wheeler's was famous. He doubted that the notorious, mythical effect of oysters could do much to lift his mood.

He watched her pulling faces and wondering whether the salt texture of oysters was an acquired taste or the emperor's new clothes, and he told her of his trip to Portsmouth. How he hated giving up on a case.

'Murder ain't what it used to be,' said Tosca.

'You'll have to explain that.'

'It was in one of your books I been reading—*Shooting an Elephant* by that Orwell guy. An essay called "Decline of the English Murder". How before the war—there we go, that phrase again—before the *goddam* war murders were like a family affair. But these days you get killing for kicks, and what that adds up to is the job of the cop is getting harder. Blamed the Americans, as I recall.'

The idea put Troy in mind of Neville Heath, a multiple killer of the first year of peace, who had 'played' murder as though it were a game between himself and the police.

'He's right,' said Troy. 'Not about the Americans, but about the way things have changed. Time was if you found a shallow grave and a woman's body, you looked for a fugitive husband or lover. Now, I don't know where to look. And I haven't a clue who I'm looking for. As you so succinctly put it, "Murder ain't what it used to be."'

Emerging from Wheeler's Troy instinctively turned right, towards the Charing Cross Road.

'No,' said Tosca. 'The long way.'

So they set off westward, further into Soho.

A buzz was coming from the 2i's coffee bar as they passed. A basic but raucous amplified guitar and drum kit bash to a horde of kids in sloppy Joe sweaters, amongst whom Troy recognised his nephew Alex.

Tosca paused, Troy did not.

'Isn't this the racket you've been playing?' she asked.

'No,' he replied. 'It's the boiled-milk version.'

She ran to catch up with him. They turned down Wardour Street towards Shaftesbury Avenue. She was looking around, scrutinising everything and everyone they passed. They crossed the avenue by the bombed-out shell of Queen's Theatre—bombed, Troy recalled, during a performance of *Rebecca*—and a sudden spurt of traffic stranded them on the concrete island in the middle, a stonesthrow from Piccadilly Circus. The thought that had been visibly nagging at her all evening surfaced.

'I don't recognise this country.'

'I do. It's the one we used to have. After the war ended we took the ticket back to the pawn shop and redeemed it. Dusty, musty and motheaten, but essentially intact.'

'What—like England was a jalopy up on blocks an' all you had to do was put the wheels back on, fill 'er up, grease a few nipples and hit the starter?'

'Pretty much. That's how my mother's car spent the war. It's pretty much how the institutions of the nation spent it too.'

'Y'know, I never saw England till '42. It dazzled me for a while, London under siege had such a feel to it, like we had something huge in common, something that united us, but it didn't take too long to work out that this wasn't the way it had always been. There was this WAC Lieutenant from Arlington I used to work with, classy a broad as you could ever hope to meet—Second Lieutenant Zadora Pulaski, daughter of a Republican Senator, who'd thought it was a good idea to finish his little girl's education with a spell in England. She was here from '35 to '37, and she used to say to me, "Hon, you'd never believe this place. You think they're uptight now, shoulda seen 'em before the war. A cat could not look at a king." Used to enunciate that last line like she was sucking a chili.

'I concluded that the black out was the best symbol for England at war. Under cover of darkness all the old rules and restraints were quietly ignored. Like meeting a plum-voice woman on a train who shares her lunchbox with you, or picking up some guy in the street who's not afraid to fuck you. And then the lights went back on. Shock, horror! Everybody dusts off their manners and hikes up their pants. So, what is England now? A place where they'd see you starve before they shared a goddam crumb with you, and where the men are too scared of women to admit they might even like them, let alone want to fuck 'em.'

The irony of this last remark was not something that registered with her. Troy almost winced at the jab of it, but Tosca rattled on as though it had no resonance at all.

'And it comes down to this, to a single question, what did the war change?'

'I have a friend, an ex-RAF flyer, who takes the line that it changed nothing. Absolutely nothing. Not a damn thing.'

'He's right.'

'Wrecking our cities, destroying our balance of payments, knocking our foreign exchange to pieces, cleaning out our gold reserves, sinking the Empire, and putting us permanently in hock to the almighty dollar don't count, eh?'

'Not in this equation they don't. Look at Germany, for God's sake. They lost the goddam war. By 1947 they were exporting Volkswagens. You know what Germany has that you guys don't? The Marshall Plan? They're born engineers? All they had to do was sweep away the rubble and start again? All those phoney-baloney arguments you get in the English papers? Nuts. It's far simpler. Nobody mentions the war.'

'With good reason,' Troy said to a deaf ear.

'The Brits? Fuckit Troy. They never shut up about the war. They relive it every minute of the goddam day. I mean, is there a movie house in London that isn't showing some goddam war movie?'

She had a point. The war had unimaginable importance to the English. 'Their Finest Hour' was also their ball and chain. Something in them yearned still for the simple truths of glory. Only a few years ago, there had been national rejoicing on an absurd scale when HMS *Amethyst* had run the gauntlet of Chinese guns and broken out of the Yangtse blockade, with the loss of the ship's cat to enenw fire. The moggie had been awarded a 'VC for Cats' and buried with military honours. Troy had never been quite sure whether this was touching or bonkers.

'I used to like London. I liked the unofficial freedoms of war. But times change, the world moves on. England hasn't. It's moved backwards, and it's done that by enshrining the war. It's become a touchstone. They remember all that was bad about it and go on celebrating it. And the good stuff, the way the barriers came down, the way you class-conscious bastards pulled together . . . all that's forgotten. You used to know you were all in the same boat, now you don't even think you're on the same river. It's a miserable, damp little tea-swilling nation. And I don't like it any more. England—stinking of old tobacco, wet gabardine and men who never dry clean those awful suits, and have hairy nostrils. Never put your head in an Englishman's lap. You'll gag on a miasma of stale piss and rancid nostalgia.

'There's one thing that's wrong with England and wrong in a big, big way. Apart from the fact that they never stop talking about it, it's as if the war never happened!'

There was a long pause. For the first time Troy became aware of the precariousness of their position, the traffic shooting by on either side at its busiest as the theatres emptied all around them. Marooned on a traffic island a hundred yards from the heart of an empire we no longer wanted.

'And how does that make you feel?'

'Like an American. Don't laugh, but after all I been through I kinda get the feeling I might just be an American after all.'

'Do you know what that makes me?'

'Nope.'

'A GI bride. Great title for a film. *I Was a Male GI Bride.*'

'*You* were a GI bride? Dammit Troy, if they did but know it this whole fuckin' island was a GI bride!'

Across Shaftesbury Avenue, down the short end of Wardour Street and into Coventry Street.

As they crossed Leicester Square, Tosca caught sight of the huge illuminated billboard outside the Odeon. Troy had been hoping she wouldn't. Kenneth More, Muriel Pavlow and Anton Diffring in *Reach For the Sky.* The tale of Douglas Bader, a flying ace with even fewer legs than Angus Pakenham.

'Oh Jesus, Troy. Will you look at that. Isn't that just what I've been saying. Another goddam war movie. I mean . . . I mean, that's where I saw *Gone With the Wind.* Five times in 1943.'

The brown eyes looked into his.

'And twice more in '44.'

It occurred to Troy to say that *Gone With the Wind* was just another goddam war movie, but her sadness at the sight of yet another bunch of stalwart Brits pitched against the sinister menace of Mr Diffring, a one-man repertory of jackbooted, steely jawed Fascists, was so obviously real. She pressed her forehead to his chest and he realised that she was sobbing gently, that she wept for Rhett and Scarlett and for herself too.

He bent his head to whisper in her ear.

'Da da daa daaa. Da da daa daaa.'

Her head came up, eyes smiling through the tears.

Troy slipped his arms into position, still humming the tune and plied her unwilling feet to motion.

'Come on,' he said. 'It's a waltz. You know. One, two, three, one two, three. Da da daa daaa.'

'But it's silly. We can't—'

'Yes we can. We're already doing it.'

He waltzed her down the square towards Irving Street, da da dadaaing in her ear till she giggled, and the tears stopped and her smile burnt him to the heart. She danced—they danced—more smoothly than he could ever have imagined. He danced so rarely. A married woman as a lover, of late, had meant that courtship was a hole-and-corner affair. He and Anna had never danced, had scarcely allowed themselves to be seen in public. The sound of Tara's theme swelled and he saw over Tosca's shoulder a bunch of drunks taking up the song, surprisingly in tune, and they waltzed to an improvised brewery choir, and her giggle became hysterics and she could dance no more for laughing.

They stopped. She reached her arms around his neck and hugged him and froze in motion as a round of applause broke the night air. Troy looked around, a little embarrassed to find they had an appreciative audience, a dozen Londoners for whom *Gone With the Wind* was also worth a dozen war films, the real memory of the way we were more precious by far than the celluloid one.

He took her hand and they ran for the Charing Cross Road, down the alley between the theatres and home.

She tumbled into his bed. For the first time they had not gone to their separate beds, only to have her crawl into his at some ungodly hour on terms of truce. Troy put out the light and reached for her. Already she had turned her back on him. He put out a hand to her backside. It was the arse of yore. She had regained all the weight she had lost in Moscow. It was the same round arse his fingertips and palms knew. In what ganglion of his body was this remembered? What neurone stored the imprint of an arse? It surely had little to do with that remote and unreliable organ the brain?

He pressed on, fingers sliding to the crack of her buttocks and further, his erection pushing against her, and down deeper, between her legs. And he began to think that she would not stop him. Then her hand took his, placed it back on his own thigh. The same hand reached for his cock and pumped him gently and quickly into a wet rush in the small of her back.

He heard the intake of breath that presaged speech. Trapped in the puddle between pleasure and the certain knowledge that in her way she had seen him off yet again, he craved the sweetness and nothingness of sweet nothings. Whatever she said next, please God let it be the inconsequentiality of meaningless affection.

'Y'know,' she said, and turned to bury her head in his chest, voice muffled by his body. 'I don't want to live in this town any more. Would you mind much if I went back to Mimram? Made another go of it?'

§61

Tosca lay face down in the sheets with her head in his ribcage, and one hand flat across his belly. Troy could not tell if she had fallen asleep at this odd angle or if she was holding it as a neutral position. The demilitarised zone, the 38th Parallel of the bed.

The phone rang. More accurately it clattered and buzzed gently, as he had long ago removed the bells to stop it sounding like a fire engine tearing through his bedroom.

A muffled voice rose from beneath him.

'Don't answer it.'

He reached for the receiver. Tosca stuck a finger in his belly button and pressed.

'Don't answer it.'

'I have to. This time of night, it has to be work.'

'It's turned midnight. I'm comfortable. I'm almost happy. One foot on the yeller brick road. Let Jack go diddle.'

'I can't.'

He picked up the phone. Button A clattered in his ear.

'You took yer time, y' bugger!'

'Angus?'

'No, it's the Archbishop of fucking Canterbury calling to tell you masturbation is a sin so knock it off and get out of bed.'

'Are you drunk?'

'Pissed as a fart.'

An echoing hoot of steam filled up the background. A mournful metal beast somewhere over the shoulder.

'Where are you?'

'St Pancras. Just got back from Derbyshire. Bloody train took four hours. Good job there was a bar full of miniatures. I drank British Railways dry. They had to restock at Kettering just for me. I'm coming straight over to you.'

He had forgotten Angus. He had put him so completely out of mind.

'No, no, Angus. There's no need. I was wrong. Cockerell really is dead. He really was spying on that ship.'

'No you're not.'

'Eh?'

'You're not wrong. I'll be over as soon as I can get a cab.'

He rang off.

Tosca rolled over. Bumped him with her backside, and bumped him again and again till he had to get out or fall out.

'I won't be long.'

'Don't matter now.'

'I'll get rid of him, and come back to bed.'

'Don't matter, so don't bother.'

He pulled on his dressing gown and went down to the kitchen and the kettle. He'd have to pour a few cups of coffee down Angus, thank him, tell him he'd had a wasted journey and pack him off home to Anna.

Ten minutes later he thought he heard a voice in the alley. Some idiot singing.

'Hey, hey, Uncle Fud.'

Or some such.

'Hey, hey, Uncle Fud.'

The voice stopped at his door and bellowed, 'Troy!'

Troy opened the door. Angus stood in the alley, looking as though he had been driven through a hedge in a wheelbarrow, stained from collar to crotch, tie askew, half his fly-buttons undone, and swaying gently, like a poplar in a summer wind.

'Hey, hey, Uncle Fud. It's a treat to beat your meat in the Mississippi mud.'

'Come inside and shut up.'

Angus fell into an armchair, his fingers still clutching the handle of his briefcase. His mouth fell open and his eyes closed. It was tempting. Troy could leave him there till morning. Instead, he nudged him and stuck a cup of black coffee in his hands.

'Are you trying to sober me up? Spoilsport.'

'Yes. And then you should go home to your wife.'

'Not till you've heard what I have to say.'

Angus stood up, flung off his jacket, rubbed his face with his hands and made blubbery noises, and then knocked back scalding coffee in a single gulp.

'If I sit down I'll be in the land of Nod in seconds. Got to keep moving. Got to keep moving.'

He put too much weight on the tin leg and Troy saw him wince sharply. He paused by the piano, rested his backside on the lid.

'The gist of it is, you were right. He's a crook. There's a most gigantic fiddle going on.'

'I told you, Angus. He's dead.'

'Doesn't matter a damn. You sent me up there because you smelt a rat. And I'll tell you now the bugger's the size of a small dog. A Jack Russell or possibly one of those snappy, ugly little creatures Her Majesty so obviously adores.'

Troy sat down, hoping Angus might follow suit, but he lurched about the room, tin leg flailing, bumping into the furniture, stretching and trying to drag himself one step nearer coherence and sobriety. He put his hands to his face again, gave a huge, muffled cry of 'Worraworraworra' and got stuck into the accountant's tale.

'Cockerell *was* a crook. Jessel was in it with him. They were pushing around an awful lot of money. I've been over the books for the last seven years. I've read all his tax returns. I've been to all those dreadful shops. I've talked to his bank manager. And I had, as you shall hear, a bloody good go at his building society. Troy, there was a small fortune being pushed through the books. Those shops can't turn over so much as fifteen per cent of what he's declaring. As for his foreign trade, he'd need a staff of a half a dozen or more just to handle the number of deals, the buying here, the selling there, he claims to have done. The truth is, he's using his business and his accounts to launder money.'

'Launder?'

'Wash. Money comes in dirty, that is illegal, goes out the other end clean, that is legit.'

'Why has no one caught him?'

'Ah, that's the beauty of it. How do most fiddlers get caught? They live too high, declare too little, conceal too much and our old pals at the Inland Revenue get them. Most fraudsters fall foul of the income tax chappies long before the Fraud Squad would ever spot them. Cockerell paid tax on everything that ever passed through the business. His books are a work of colossal fiction, but his tax returns are scrupulously honest. After all, what do the Inland Revenue look for? They look for people declaring too little from their work or their business, they haven't the time to bother with people who might be declaring too much. Why should they? They profit by Cockerell's honest payments on his dishonest earnings. Can't last. Take my word for it. Organised crime in the States has raised money laundering to an art—remember how the Feds nabbed Capone, not for murder or bootlegging but for tax evasion. Sooner or later the Inland Revenue is going to face the same problems as the IRS. But in the mean time your Commander Cockerell has hit upon a simple fiddle and it works.'

'It sounds crude to me, almost stupid.'

'Crude it may be, but it's beautiful. It's not foolproof, but it's ingenious. You get a bent auditor to keep Companies House happy, and you pay the full whack on all your fiddles. It's simple, Freddie, but it's not stupid. He could have got away with it for years to come. But—but—he was getting careless. Did the old girl show you his car?'

'Yes.'

'How much do you think a car like that costs? Now, I know you drive a Bentley, y'bugger, but don't think small of the Jag. Go on, how much?'

'Six or seven hundred?'

'More like a thousand. And he owned a Rover as well. And he paid cash. The best part of two years' salary for an average bloke. In cash.'

'How do you know?'

'Went down to the garage in Derby where he bought 'em. Unlike a lot of people, the proprietor was only too willing to chat about Commander Cockerell. One of his best customers. New cars every year. Top of the range. Walnut and leather interiors, built-in wireless, the works. And the last two years he paid cash. Now—that I would call stupid. He'd been neat, and honest with all his fake figures to the point where no one looked twice. God knows, maybe he wanted the bravura high of blowing cash. But it was stupid, because if I hadn't known that I might have just given the bugger the benefit of the doubt; I might just have assumed that trade on this scale could be carried by one hardworking bod and a couple of shop assistants. But I say now that it is my professional, if pissed, opinion that most of Cockerell's foreign deals are phoney, that much of what he pays out in England has nothing to do with the business, with goods delivered or services rendered, and they're kickbacks of some sort, and that if he brought cash into England from abroad to blow on posh cars, he was probably also doing it on a bigger scale and that too disappeared down various routes. Moreover, I'd say there have to be other bank accounts abroad that we and the Inland Revenue don't know about. I don't know the why of this fiddle but I do know the what. It's amateurish, and it's simple, but it works—and it's big. It starts in 1951, when he sets up his Swedish enterprise; it grows slowly over '52 and '53 and by '54 he's turning over a small fortune. Anyone looking at the figures with a sceptical eye who also knew his circumstances would have wondered why he didn't live better than he did. The wife said they lived, as she put it, "high on the hog"—with what he was earning I'd bath in Glenfiddich. I'd have me socks handmade in Jermyn Street. I'd have me tin leg gold plated. Sometime in 1951 something happened to turn this bugger's life around. He was doing fair to middling. No better than that. Somebody brought him an irresistible deal. And the money has spun around and around ever since.'

Angus was throwing too much at Troy too fast. He tried for a handle with which to grasp it.

'How can people cart money around like that? It's smuggling isn't it? Currency smuggling?'

'Wrong way, old boy. The state the pound's in, our lot are concerned about money leaving the country. Export sterling and they'll do you. And they spend so much of their time looking for people trying to smuggle sterling out, that I don't think it would occur to them, given our exchange problems, that anyone would try and smuggle it in. Of course he could have got bad luck, they could have opened him up looking for a few fag lighters or a bottle of scent and found him with ten grand in cash, but the gods smiled on him. I'd call it a reasonable risk.'

'The banks—why wasn't his bank manager suspicious?'

'Why do you think he banked in Great Malvern? So the bloke had no idea of the true scale of the business in Derbyshire. A local man would have put two and two together. Besides which he's a dim fucker. I know, I spent an hour on the phone to him.'

Angus sat down, the leg had stood all it could, but the eyes were bright, and there was an edge born of mathematical delight in his voice. He took a wadge of papers from his briefcase and waved them at Troy.

'Bank statements. Building society papers. A mortgage. The building bricks of life as we know it. The carbon, the amine, the deoxyribonucleic acid of our social being.'

'Yes.'

'In your notes you said the father-in-law bought the house for the Cockerells. Why the mortgage? I rang the dimwit in Great Malvern and he confirmed, once I'd convinced him of my authority to act, that one of the standing orders on Cockerell's bank statements was a monthly mortgage repayment. But—it was only taken out in 1952—the house, you will recall, was inherited in '43—and it was paid off in December last year. As far as I can tell, with all the loot Cockerell had floating around, the only purpose it could serve was the tax break. Mr Fiddle doing things by the book yet again. So, I rang the Ancient Order of Derbyshire Foresters and before they stonewalled me I did manage to get out of some poor woman in the chain of command that the mortgage was not on that bungalow in Belper. Freddie, the bugger had a second home somewhere. Some sort of bolt hole, I should think.'

'Where?'

'I just told you. I don't know. Some officious git, quite possibly the Ancient Forester himself, came on the line and told me to mind my own business. But if you ask me a bolt hole is the prime requirement of a vanishing trick.'

'He's dead, Angus.'

'You sure?'

'Yes. I held a second post mortem and in the end I identified him myself.'

'Then who's in the bolt hole?'

'I wish I knew.'

§62

He rolled Angus into a cab and tiptoed quietly upstairs. Tosca was curled up in the middle of his bed. He had half expected to find that she had sloped off to her own. He slid in beside her, listened to the regularity of her breathing. He kissed a shoulder blade and the rhythm stayed the same. He wrapped an arm around her and put his fingers to her left nipple. She took the hand away, held it to her lips and kissed it, and dropped it back on his side of the bed.

§63

In the morning Troy rode the underground to King's Cross with her. He could not recall that they had ever ridden the underground together. A flash of memory brought her voice to him from the war, telling him she would rather die in the open air than shelter underground, 'It stinks, y'know that, it really stinks.'

'Don't see me off. I can't stand waving and kissing. I seen *Brief Encounter* too many times.'

So they stood the among the shacks and sheds that made a shanty town of the station forecourt, in front of the left luggage office.

'You'll be home at the weekend?'

'Yes.'

'And Rod and your sisters?'

'They take the place for granted. Rod needs it, to be honest, for his work. But it's my house, I can tell them all to go to hell.'

'There's no need. I'll handle it. I just never had family before. It was always just my mom and me.'

Troy was shocked. He had never given a moment's thought to the possibility that she too might have family.

'Where is your mother?'

'I wish I knew. She's still young, y'know. Maybe sixty-three or sixty-four.'

He watched the tears form in the corner of each eye and a torrent begin to cross her cheeks.

'She must think I'm dead. I mean. They'll have told her I'm dead, won't they?'

'I'm afraid so. I reported you dead to the US Army myself.'

He paused. It seemed inevitable, impossible not to utter.

'*I* thought you were dead.'

And once uttered it seemed like an accusation.

An engine howled long and deep in the glass canopy inside—an iron beast in pain. She kissed his cheek and ran. It seemed to Troy that there might be no end to running.

§64

The Ancient Forester was ancient indeed. A wavering voice. An immovable man.

'You say you're a detective from Scotland Yard. How am I to know you're a detective from Scotland Yard?'

'Because I say so' was unlikely to convince. Nor, Troy thought, was a line about obstructing an officer in the course of his duty.

'It's perfectly simple,' he said. 'You call me back. You do know Scotland Yard's telephone number, don't you?'

'But,' said the Ancient, 'I would then have to pay for the call.'

'I'll send you a postal order,' said Troy.

It usually worked. He waited five minutes and five minutes became quarter of an hour. He had begun to think he had found the one person in Britain who did not know the number Whitehall 1212, and his hand was outstretched to pick up the telephone and dial the old fool again, when it rang.

'Is that Chief Inspector Foy of Scotland Yard?'

'Troy. The name is Troy.'

'Oh, I was just speaking with a Chief Inspector Foy.'

'That was me.'

Silence. Troy mentally calculated how long it might take him to get up to Chesterfield and rattle the address out of him.

'Cockerell, you say?'

'Yes.'

'We do appear to have had dealings with Mr Cockerell.'

'Yes.'

'But no longer.'

'What you had was a mortgage, taken out by him in the September of 1952, or thereabouts, which was paid off in December of 1955.'

Troy heard the sound of the Ancient shuffling papers. The laboured breathing of a man in the onset of emphysema.

'I believe that is correct.'

'What I need to know is where the property on which Cockerell had the mortgage is.'

Again, the slow, almost interminable shuffling of papers. Inhalation and exhalation that seemed to be wrung out of him by a mangle. The two short, disparate syllables.

'Bri–ton.'

Bri–ton? Bri–ton? Good God, the old fool was saying Brighton. Troy's heart leapt. The thrill of the chase, the heady pursuit of the agile criminal, the painstaking diligence of a good detective.

'Yes,' he said, 'but where in Brighton.'

'I beg your pardon?'

'Where in Brighton?!?'

Troy bit his bottom lip. The desire to interrupt was unlikely to be productive. He held his breath and waited.

'Number 2 ...

'Yeeees.'

'Number 2, Chatsworth Place, Cavendish Hill, Bri–ton.'

The mute voice in the head cheered and sang. For safety's sake Troy read the address back to him, with the Ancient saying 'yes' at every pause. At the last pause Troy had a 'goodbye-thank-you-don't-call-us-we'll-call-you' on his lips when the old man pulled out the rabbit from the hat.

'Property of Mrs M. Kerr.'

'What?'

'It says here ... Kerr. M. (Mrs).'

'You mean Cockerell didn't own the house?'

Another endless pause as the Ancient gathered elusive breath.

'Apparently not.'

'But he paid the mortgage?'

'Regularly. And to completion.'

'Isn't that a bit queer?'

'A little unusual, perhaps. But as long as the deeds are placed with us, as indeed they were—we still have them—all is proper.'

Very little about the case of Commander Cockerell was proper. It was a word Troy would never apply to anything Cockerell did.

'Who is Kerr. M. (Mrs)?'

'I could not tell you. Without, that is, examining the deeds themselves. I merely read you the reference as our records show it. Now, about that postal order ...'

§65

Troy had never worked in Brighton. His vision of the place was coloured more by Graham Greene and Richard Attenborough than it was by experience. The train down was crowded with holiday makers. He stood in the corridor all the way—the rattle of the bogies over the rails became monotonous, every jolt at the fishplates in the track assumed the words 'Kolley Kibb-er Kolley Kibb-er' in his mind as though the train were talking to him. They were not words he much wished to hear. He began to regret that the occasional aversion to the motor car led him to presume relief and pleasure in travelling by train.

Cavendish Hill took some finding. Largely because he had the map upside down. Only when he realised that the English Channel could not really be on the north did he turn around in Kemptown and head off to where Brighton blends smoothly into Hove.

The Hill rose steeply from the seafront about a quarter of a mile west of the West Pier. And a quarter of a mile or so up the hill, Chatsworth Place ran off from it, parallel to the coast. He had, he realised, been expecting a mews or some such. The address implied tucked away—which it was—it also implied that it would be less grand than Cavendish Hill—which it wasn't. It was a narrower house, but taller by far, and as he approached number 2, he could see clearly that it had been combined with number 3—there were no houses on the other side of the street—into a sprawling, double-fronted house with a commanding view across the town to the sea. Commander Cockerell had done very well for himself—if indeed it was for himself.

He stretched out a hand to the doorbell when he saw that the front door was an inch or so ajar. Suspicion fought a scrummage with plain nosiness—they called it a draw and he pushed on the door and entered. It was almost silent; the rumble of water running down the pipes echoed around the house, but little else other than the creak of his own footsteps broke the silence. Suspicion pulled ahead on points.

He turned right, and found himself in a dazzlingly modern kitchen that had the mark of Cockerell all over it. No more the clutter of little wooden tables, of higgledy-piggledy shelves askew on old iron brackets, of tin mesh larders to keep away the summer flies. This was seamless, as seamless as Brighton joining Hove, seamless in ivory-coloured plastic, dotted here and there with little splashes of blue and red. It looked to Troy like a dilute version of Mediterranean pottery. Best of all the gas stove and the fridge slotted in almost as though the places had been built around them. Where was the gap down which to lose a wooden spoon or half your dinner? This was Cockerell's world, the world of Mrs 1960, and Miss World's Fair. Who could guess, but that were he to open one of the many fitted cupboards—yes, 'fitted', that was the word—a double bed or a folding bath might unfurl before his eyes. At the very least it would be a fully functioning rotisserie, complete with skewered chicken, rotating as it opened to the beholder.

He set foot on the stairs. The first creak was enough to freeze him to the spot, but when the house offered no response he pressed quickly on and into the drawing room on the first floor. He knew as soon as he saw the room that someone else was involved. He had puzzled over the matter ever since Angus had told him that Cockerell had a second house. It could hardly be just to live alone in, away from a bad marriage. Logically, it would be a love nest. A little somewhere he could meet a mistress. But it was hard to imagine the man with a mistress, and this was not a little somewhere, it was a big somewhere, and here in this wide, airy room, with the sea laid out before floor-to-ceiling windows like a private panorama, was the evidence of the other woman. This room was Cockerell-ish, but his absurd proselytisation of the new was compromised, subtly leavened by someone else's taste. The heavy glass table on turned wrought-iron legs might well be him, but the close-packed wall of two hundred years of seascapes, in every medium from charcoal, through gouache and water-colour to heavily discoloured and darkened oils, was not. This must be the woman's work. As his first home had shown, Cockerell's taste ran to nothing better than Trechikoff's *Green Woman*. This living wall was breathtakingly beautiful, startlingly original—Troy would never have dreamt that one could pack paintings together so closely and not lose all they represented—and in it he saw the meaning of the mistress. Jasmine Dene was a war zone, divided into his and hers with a line through it like Korea or Jerusalem. Two minds, two sets of values met in this room and worked together. Yes—Cockerell definitely had a mistress.

He moved quietly up a floor. Bedrooms. Front and back, and all, it seemed, unused. Enough space to have four or five house guests at the weekend. The staircase narrowed; he was climbing to the top floor, there could only be attics above it. At the bend it narrowed further, as it carried on high under the eaves, and formed a small landing with a pair of slender double doors facing him. They offered the same invitation to nosiness as the front door had done. An inch ajar, asking to be pushed.

He pushed. He was back in the land of Cockerell, a feminised Cockerell, where everything was spanking new but deeply luxurious. The spareness of the Scandinavian look pushed through spareness to emerge the other side in a Hollywood style of smothering comfort.

He could hear nothing. The sound of running water had stopped. Two doors led off the bedroom, presumably to a bathroom and a dressing room, and the front wall of the room was made up of huge sliding glass doors, which opened onto a narrow terrace. He tiptoed pointlessly across a shag-pile carpet—pit boots would have made no noise on it—to the open door to the terrace. A gentle evening breeze had caught the curtain and was wafting it to and fro. He looked at the view. The beginnings of evening redness in the west gleaming like rubies in the sea. He looked at the bed. A happy man could lie abed and watch the sun rise or set in the Channel. A happier man could make love with a sea breeze caressing his nether regions. Then he noticed the photographs. Half a dozen in a column next to the door frame. Good bloody grief. Cockerell had surely developed these himself, perhaps he even had a darkroom in the cellar? No self-respecting chemist would fail to call the Vice Squad if he found these in the back of a Brownie 127.

A woman, back to the camera, was bending low, legs straight, face hidden from view—so that the length of the 10 C 8 print was made up of an inverted V of her legs with a full, well-lit view of her sexual parts. The one below showed the same woman—at least he assumed it was the same woman—leaning, back, crab-style, over a Bentwood chair, the face hidden again, but the view now as explicit from the front—a tiny spotlight trained on her seam to light up her halo of blondish pubic hair with an unnatural gleam. He fully meant to look at the rest. Out of sheer nerves he glanced furtively over his shoulder before doing so, like a man caught ogling *Health & Efficiency* in a newsagent's.

A woman of twenty-five or so stood in the bathroom door in a haze of steam and talc. All she wore was a towel, and that was wrapped around her head. At the best of times Troy did not much rate guns as fashion accessories, but when the gun was pointed at your chest it did at least offset nudity rather well by making it somewhat less than fascinating. Slowly he put his hands up and strained for a smile.

'You've been reading too much Raymond Chandler,' he said.

'Eh?'

'When in doubt . . . ?'

'Get on with it!'

'When in doubt have a man come through the door with a gun in his hand.'

'If you think I'm a man,' she said, 'you need glasses. Now—who are you?'

'I'm a policeman.'

'Aha?'

'I can prove it.'

Gently he lowered his left hand to his jacket front.

'I have a warrant card. I'm going to take it out very slowly.'

He held it up, lodged between his index and biggest fingers like a cigarette.

'Chuck it over here.'

He threw the card at her feet. It landed soundlessly on the carpet, and one of his own calling cards, with his rank and his Goodwin's Court address, spilled out from the fold. She knelt, kept the gun aimed at his chest, and quickly picked them up. Then she put the gun on the sideboard, tossed the warrant card back at him, whipped the towel off her head to wrap herself in, and as a last gesture tucked his calling card into the top of the towel, a sophisticated parody of a whore tucking a ten-bob note into her cleavage.

'Is this where you tell me it wasn't loaded anyway?' he said.

She flung herself in an armchair and reached for a cigarette box on the side table.

'Oh it's loaded all right. Look, there's a bottle of brandy in the bedside cabinet. Why don't you pour us both a drink. I'm sure we need it.'

She lit up her cigarette, a ridiculous king-size with a filter tip and a couple of gold bands, with a huge, clumsy, green stone table lighter. He did as he was told, wondering what next.

'What kept you?' she asked so bluntly the question threw him.

'I . . . er . . . I don't quite follow.'

He edged back towards her, feeling his feet sink almost to the ankle in the bedside carpet, handed her a glass and sat, daringly it seemed to him, on the edge of the bed.

'He's been dead the best part of five months. You took your time.'

'I've only just been able to confirm that Commander Cockerell is dead.'

'Oh? Really? I knew he was dead forty-eight hours after he failed to show up.'

'I suppose I've been rather in the dark.'

'What is it you want to know?'

'I don't know,' he said. 'What do you know?'

'Me? I know everything. Isn't that why you came?'

'Yes,' he said. 'I suppose it is.'

§66

Troy waited while she dressed. She—Kerr M. (Mrs). He had no idea who she was beyond the near-statistical tag of a building society record. Mary? Marilyn? And was there a Mr Kerr? He could guess who that might be. He sipped at the brandy. A good vintage, he was certain, but they all tasted a bit like soap to him.

The woman emerged in a simple dress for evening. Simple and brazen, the scarlet version of the little black dress in searing red. Sleeveless, cut very low at the back, and just preserving modesty at the front. Her hair was piled high on her head and she was twiddling with the fingertips of both hands to put an earring in place. It was a gesture to put him immediately in mind of Tosca with her squeamishness about body piercing, standing bolting her jewellery into place, of tiny gems or milky pearls on silver threads.

'I don't know your name,' he said.

'I can't say I recall your asking. But it's Madeleine, Madeleine Kerr.'

Her hands moved to the other ear, the same fine gesture with the same delicate engineering, to hang a gold leaf from the lobe.

'You're a Fred? Don't meet many Freds. Mind if I call you Troy?'

'Most people do.'

'Oh, and Arnold, Commander Cockerell. He's Ronald Kerr down here. Ronnie to you and me.'

Troy looked a little puzzled. He felt the name should make sense to him. The look on her face told him it ought to be self-explanatory.

'You don't get it, do you?'

'No, I'm afraid I don't.'

'Ronald is an anagram of Arnold. And Kerr is from Cock—*Kerr*—Ell. Geddit?'

It was so easy, he almost blushed at his own stupidity.

'And before you ask, whatever Ronnie was he wasn't a bigamist. The Mr and Mrs is all pretend. And a bloody sight more fun for being so. Now shall we go?'

'Where?' he asked lamely.

'To dinner. If you're going to play the copper and ask me a thousand questions, the least you can do is buy me dinner. After all, I've eaten alone for the last five months.'

'There is one thing before we go out,' he said.

'Yes.'

'The gun.'

'Yes.'

'I think you'd better give it to me.'

'Ronnie gave it to me. For protection, he said.'

'You won't need it with me. And I can't let you walk around with a gun in your handbag.'

'How do you know it's in my handbag?'

'Trust me. I'm a detective.'

She opened the bag, took out the gun and gave it to him. Then she tossed the bag onto the bed as though its only purpose had been to conceal and carry the gun.

Troy felt its weight. Feathers had more substance. It was a tiny, golden .22 automatic. What Chandler would have called a lady's gun. Pretty much like the one Tosca had had, the one he had dumped in the Irish Sea.

She led the way downstairs, out into Chatsworth Place and down Cavendish Hill. As they rounded the first corner she slipped her arm into his.

'We'll go to the Wellesley Hotel. There's a rooftop restaurant with a smashing view. It was called La Manche when it opened, but everybody called it The Munch, which sounded a bit common, so they changed it to the Clair de Lune. Much better name. Specially on a night like this.'

She looked up at the rapidly darkening, utterly cloudless sky.

'Plenty of Lune and pretty Clair wouldn't you say?'

He gave the shining sixpenny moon a passing glance and looked at her. A fraction taller than him, even in flat heels. She had looked beautiful before she had made up her face. Now, the beauty was layered in some imprecise way, as though she had assumed a gloss of sophistication. It worked, largely, but he remained somehow unconvinced. There was an inescapable element of the girl dressed as the woman, of the girl-*in*-the-woman, and it had begun the minute she had lit up her first cigarette, and she had pursued it through make-up and clinched it through clothes. The arm through his seemed like instant friendship. He had known the woman less than forty minutes. He had seen her naked, he had seen her posing for the camera—she surely was the woman in the photographs?—in positions he had never seen any woman assume, and now she strolled along arm in arm just as though they were old friends. Or new lovers. He detached his arm from hers. She was prattling on about the beauty of a full moon and seemed not to notice that he had done it. When she had finished, she simply closed the gap between them and slipped her arm in his once more.

The maître d' at the Wellesley greeted her like a lost sister. Madamed her to death. Showed the two of them to a table on the terrace. When the sound of his leather soles on the floorboards had died away, there was only the murmur of the room inside and the deeper, rhythmical murmur of the sea below them.

'I do hope,' Madeleine said, 'that you're not a meat and two veg followed by spotted dick man.'

'I've never been a spotted dick man in my life.'

'Good—then I'll order for us.'

She raised an arm. A waiter hurried over to her.

'We'll have the *lotte*, new potatoes, *mangetout*, green salad, followed by the *crème caramel*, and I think the '47 Château Lattre de Tassigny.'

'Nothing to start, Madame Kerr?'

'No, just bring the claret straight away.'

Troy admired her panache. He was paying, but she was calling the shots and meant to prove it to him.

'Red wine with fish?' he asked.

'Do you really believe all that tosh? Don't you think it's all part and parcel of the dreadful English snobbery, the curse of class? Surely freedom means having what you want when you want it?'

271

It was a startling little speech. He had seen his father glug best claret from a tea cup, seen him drink Pouilly-Fuissé with roast beef, seen him eat cheese with jam, seen him eat Christmas dinner still in his dressing gown. Of course she was right. The old man had spent much of Troy's childhood proving the same point. 'How do you think the English came to control half the planet, my boy? You know. The red bits on the map that the buggers are so inordinately proud of? With an army? Until 1915 they had never had conscription, nor had they maintained a large standing army, nor do they to this day. With their navy? Well, it helps to rule the waves, but it does very little to keep order in the hills of northern India or in the deepest jungles of Burma and Malaya. No—Britannia rules with her civil service. It is an empire of bureaucrats, of assistant district commissioners, of pen pushers and rule-writers. And thus are the rulers ruled, for they end by making as many rules for themselves as they ever did for the rest of us. Hence, your Englishman, hidebound, class-bound, who, given the freedom to have what he wants, will merely ask what the rules permit him to have.'

'No,' he said. 'I don't suppose I do.'

The wine waiter appeared with two bottles of claret, and whipped out his corkscrew.

'No,' Troy said. 'We only ordered—'

Madeleine's hand waved him down.

'He knows me. He knows what I usually have, don't you, Jean-Paul?'

She smiled at the waiter. He smiled back politely, uncorked the second bottle and left them to it. She poured. Knocked back almost half her glass in a single mouthful and looked at Troy.

'Well,' she said.

'Well?' he said.

'What do you want to know?'

'Well—it's perfectly simple. What was Cockerell up to, and for whom?'

She set down her glass, just for emphasis.

'No. Not now. Not tonight. It's not a simple question, as well you know. Tomorrow we'll go up to London. You give me an hour or so to myself, then we can meet up and I'll answer all your questions. There's just one or two things I need to do first. Ask me anything else. Anything at all.'

Troy was flummoxed. He had felt sure that this entire rigmarole was leading somewhere. Now, he couldn't think of a question innocent enough.

'How did you meet him? Here, in Brighton?'

'No. Brighton had nothing to do with it—at least not then.'

She took a huge gulp of red wine and denied him the prompt.

OK. Think of another.

'You're not from here?'

He winced inwardly. It was a line from a bad chat-up routine.

'No. I'm from Deeplydullshire. My father, God rot 'im, is a village GP in Berkshire. I'd done my degree at Bristol—my father would have preferred it if I'd done a commercial diploma in shorthand and typing, joined the civil service and hooked a diplomat for a husband. But I didn't, I kicked the dust of Berkshire off my heels and settled in London. That's where I met Ronnie.'

She had finished her first glass—he had not even touched his—and reached for the bottle.

'I met him at the Embassy.'

Alarm bells rang in Troy's head.

'Embassy? Which embassy? The Russian embassy?'

'No—silly—the Embassy Club in Bond Street. It was four years ago. The week the King died. I'd been stood up. A chinless wonder from the Grenadier Guards—Billy or Bobby something—he was squiffy when he called round for me. Swigged whisky from his hip flask all the way there in the cab, disappeared into the loo ten minutes after we got there and I never saw him again. I was stuck at our table, no cigarettes, no money. Then this dapper little chap came up and asked me to dance. It was Ronnie. He moved so beautifully, such confidence, so light on his little feet. Nice looking too. I've always liked older men. I was twenty-five, he'd be about fifty. Just the right gap, wouldn't you say?'

Troy had no opinion. But, then, the question didn't seem to require an answer. He may have broken his wrist crank-starting the woman but she was rolling smoothly now.

'We sat out the next dance. He bought me a martini and I was desperate for a ciggy by then, and he took out two from his cigarette case, put them in his mouth, just like Humphrey Bogart. Lit up both and passed one to me. I thought that was so good mannered. So romantic.'

Troy was getting puzzled. Not only did he not believe this woman was pushing thirty, he did not see how one gesture could be commended as good mannered and romantic at the same time. Romantic, he thought, usually wasn't much bothered by any notion of manners. And the voice. Something was not quite right. It had a languid beauty to it, but something seemed to lurk beneath it—the hint of a lost accent?

'The next dance was slow and gentle, and I felt his hand slide down to my bottom. So I did what a good girl should. I pulled it back up twice and let him have his little victory the third time. And he said—looked me right in the eyes—he had such lovely pale blue eyes—and said, "You're not wearing any knickers, are you?" Of course—I wasn't.

'We spent the night together. I had this beautiful little flat just off the Kings Road in Chelsea—but I had also had two flatmates. So Ronnie took a room at the Imperial. Mr and Mrs Kerr. It was divine. He spoilt me rotten with little touches of luxury. I could ring room service and ask for anything I wanted.'

Troy was more puzzled. He had begun to realise that she spoke like an advertisement. It did not seem to be a vocabulary of real responses, more an acquired surface of phrasing. A veneer over whatever, if anything, she felt, over whatever, and it had to be something, she was. The Imperial was not a hotel he would have chosen as a way to impress a new lover. It might once have been luxurious, but the last time he visited anyone there it struck him as long past its best, shabby even. A man with the money Cockerell had, and he knew from the bank statements he was not skint even in 1952, could have afforded the Dorchester in Park Lane, or Claridge's in the heart of Mayfair, and would have had little need of the Imperial, tucked away in its corner behind the British Museum.

'After that I saw him every time he came to London.'

'How often was that?'

'About once a fortnight, I suppose. Then one day, a couple of months later, he rang me the second time in a week. Said he was back in London, and would I meet him at Victoria. I had to drop everything and dash.'

'Everything?'

'Eh?'

'You had a job?'

'Well—yes. Of course I had a job.'

'So, what did you do?'

'I worked for a scientist.'

'A scientist?'

She ostentatiously drained her glass of red wine and held out her hand for him to refill it. If it was meant to wrongfoot him it almost worked. Too long in the company of women like his sisters, who had long since surrendered the formality of waiting for the man—as Madeleine herself seemed to have done until now—left him wondering for a second what she meant by the gesture. He topped her up and returned to the point.

'What sort of a scientist?'

'A boffin. You know, hush-hush. I was his private, personal assistant.'

'Private and personal?'

'Look—do you want to hear about how I met Ronnie or don't you?'

Troy nodded. He had lost nothing. She would not answer. There was no answer.

'Anyway—you listening?—we went to Brighton. Bit of a surprise really. I'd been there once or twice before the war, when I was little. I'd always loved Brighton. I don't know how Ronnie picked up on that. To this day I can't remember ever telling him that. It's . . . it's . . . exotic. Isn't it?'

Was it? He had never thought of the word as applicable to anywhere in the British Isles. Exotic? It could hardly describe the natural. It was man in his setting that made for the exotic. He thought of the places he loved: the view from his own verandah, willows, pigs and bats, but that was not exotic; the chiselled beauty of Ben Bulben, the most magnificent mountain west of the Alps, but that wasn't exotic either. Exotic was, according to cliché, dark, dusky, heady with spices—cinnamon and sandalwood—redolent of a market in Tangiers, in a thousand shades of brown, where every wild splash of red and yellow told. It wasn't Brighton. Brighton was the red and yellow of saucy postcards and the brown of warm beer. It was a step up from Blackpool or Skegness, but it wasn't Biarntz or Monte Carlo. You might toy with the notion on a warm summer's evening as you passed the Prince Regent's Pavilion, but you'd never actually mistake the place for the Taj Mahal. What was the woman on about?

'We had lunch, and we walked on the beach. He told me all about himself. I knew some things, of course. You couldn't not know certain things about a man after eight weeks together. But that day he told me everything. And in the end he told me his wife wouldn't divorce him.'

'You knew he was married?'

She sighed in mockery.

'You can tell a man is married just by looking at him!'

Try me, he thought. Go on, guess. But he said nothing.

'I told him I didn't care. Then he said, let's take another stroll before the sun goes. But I knew as he said it there was something . . . something he wasn't telling me. As though I could sense a surprise. But I like surprises.'

She pointed out over the balcony towards the Channel, glittering in the light of a silvery moon, to the West Pier jutting out into the water.

'We were down there. Right at the end. It'd be late summer, I suppose. Late afternoon, early evening, but not quite dark. We were standing at the end. And Ronnie said to me, "Get your tits out. I want to see your tits." So I took off my jacket and I took off my blouse and stood there looking out at the sea. "Turn around," he said. "I want you to look at me." Well, I knew the pier wasn't deserted. We'd passed enough people on the way down. But I turned around, and there was a middle-aged couple with a dog sitting there. And I heard something from the woman like, "Well I never. Come on, George." And she dragged the poor old bloke off. He walked sideways like a crab all the way back just to be able to look at me. There was only one other person left. A really old woman in a plastic mac, putting away her knitting. "Lean back on the rail," said Ronnie. "Flaunt it. I want you to flaunt it." So I did. And the old woman came up to me and said, "Nice titties, dear. I used to have a pair just like those. Mind you'll catch your death of cold." Then she turned to Ronnie and said, "Lovely titties, don't you think, dear?" And shuffled off.'

This was not the same man. This could not be the same man. This was not Arnold Cockerell. Yet it was. Was this the magic of a change of name? A simple shuffling of words, but as powerful as a sea change? Cockerell into Kerr. Weasel into lounge lizard. Frustrated little man, drearily thumbing a dirty magazine, into a pervert of preposterous imagination. A man with style, an élan of sexual provocation.

Madeleine showed enough sensibility to pause in her story while the waiter set the fish in front of them, but it scarcely broke the stride of the tale.

'I slipped my blouse back on and he walked me up Cavendish Hill. A little surprise, he told me. Wasn't so little. It was 2 Chatsworth Place. "Is it yours?" I asked as he showed me round. "No," he said. "It's yours." And then he bowled me over again. Took me next door to number 3 and said, "This is yours, too. Spread your wings, my lovely." It was the way he said it. "Spread your wings, my lovely." So I did. I went back up to London. Told the girls I was leaving the flat. Gave in my notice at work and moved to Brighton. All that autunm the builders were in. Ronnie let me do anything I wanted. A wall here, a doorway there. And of course—I let him do anything he wanted.'

She ran her index finger around the rim of her glass and then sucked it slowly, pulling it back and forth, smiling as she did so, and looking at Troy with eyes full of mischief.

'Ronnie never forgot the night we met. He said he knew I was the woman for him the minute he found out I'd no knickers on. So—I went everywhere without underwear. Ronnie's tickled my fanny or finger-fucked me in half the restaurants in Brighton.'

He had never heard the word 'fingerfucked' before. Its meaning was explicit. Its existence perfectly logical. It was the kind of word which—if she knew it—his wife would use. But he had never dreamt of such a word, nor that he would hear the notion it represented so neatly summed up in a single word—it was a single word, wasn't it?—on the lips of a middle-class Englishwoman.

'Tell me,' he said. 'Did he ever . . .'

'Yeeeeeeees?'

'Did he . . . well . . . did he ever ask you to . . .'

'Wear a rubber suit?'

'Well, no . . . actually I was going to say . . . did he ever ask you if *he* could wear a rubber suit? His frogman suit, to be precise.'

'Oh—we both wear them. We had his and hers wetsuits. You know—with holes in all the right places.'

She glanced down, a quick, unbelievably coy tilt of the eyes groinward, then she bunched up her breasts into an alpine cleavage with her hands, picked up her fork and returned to her meal as though everything she had said and done in the last couple of minutes had not been wholly outrageous.

Yet again her glass was empty. They were into the second bottle. He did not wait for the prompt. He topped her up and resigned himself to the fact that she was going to get pissed as quickly as she could.

§67

The tide was high. The gentle breeze of evening was chilling with the coming of night. She slipped off her shoes and dropped them on the sand.

'Are you coming in?'

'A swim?' He sounded incredulous.

'A paddle, stupid. Or did you think I was going to strip off and dive in?'

'Wouldn't surprise me,' he said.

'Touché.'

Troy watched her walk to the edge of the sea and stand where it was hardly ankle deep, barely washing over her feet. He heard the shrill squeak of delight as the cold water touched her blood.

Just under the sea wall was a solitary deck chair, a lost lamb missed by the deck chair shepherd. He pulled it upright, sat in it, watching her wade farther out until the water crept up to the hem line of her dress. And beyond. By the time she was through, the dress would be sodden.

He felt, he realised, the beginning of a reluctant admiration for Cockerell. He had got what he wanted: the classic, but often impossible dream of a double life. And it worked. Or at least it had worked for the best part of four years. Janet Cockerell surely gave him something or he would have left her long ago, and he did not for one second believe the line Cockerell had spun Madeleine about 'my wife won't agree to a divorce'. Janet Cockerell had never mentioned the prospect. Indeed, part of his idea of Cockerell was that the man enjoyed the double life, and without the wife it would have been singular, enjoyable—he looked at Madeleine in the moonlight, practically up to her hips in the water, arms outstretched like a crucifix, singing a wordless song to herself, beautiful, bizarre and pissed—hugely enjoyable, but singular. He could imagine the delight it had given Cockerell to sit with his wife amid the straining verbal violence of marriage and recall the last time he had fingerfucked his mistress in public. The weasel's revenge. It was bloody nigh perfect. 'What you want, when you want it.' Heartbreak Hotel with room service.

Madeleine hopped from one foot to another, splashing madly and shouting something.

'Ow, ow ow ow!'

Troy left the chair and met her at the water's edge.

'Bloody fucking hell. What kind of a bastard—'

She leant heavily on his arm and bent back her left leg.

'What kind of a bastard leaves bits of glass on the beach?'

He sat her down, where the sand was drier, and looked at the soles of her feet.

'Not glass,' he said. 'Shell.'

'Hurts just the same.'

'It's in deep.'

'Then for God's sake pull it out.'

He could get no grip on the fragment. It would need tweezers. He locked his teeth onto the broken edge of the shell, pulled back and spat out a sliver of shell over half an inch long.

She sighed with relief. He still had hold of her foot. Before he could let go she said, 'More. Just a bit more.'

Troy said nothing.

She propped herself up, her arms straight out behind her, her hands flat on the sand.

'Just a bit more. Won't hurt, honest.'

He knew he was being called out. The schoolyard cry of 'cowardy custard'. He sucked on the wound, salt and sand mingled with the taste of blood, and she squirmed gently and threw back her arms and stretched. Now all he could taste was blood. He let go of her and was wondering what he was supposed to do next. She sat up, put her fingertips to his lips and read his mind, to the very syllable.

'The woman's dilemma throughout history. Do you swallow it, or spit it out?'

She kissed the back of her hand, pinched his lips together and he swallowed on the reflex.

She drew back, a satisfying smile on her face.

'There. Told you it wouldn't hurt.'

§68

'I've something to show you.'

She peeled off the dress. Scarlet above the waist, black where the water had drenched it. Troy was delighted to find that this was one of the occasions when she had seen fit to wear underwear. She padded barefoot across the room, leaving a faint trail of blood on the carpet.

She opened a door in the vast wardrobe. There, side by side on the rail, were two rubber suits. Exactly as she had said. His, complete with frogman flippers, and hers. Madeleine unhooked hers, and held it up to show to him. Two large holes in the chest showed where her breasts would protrude when she wore it. Troy kept his eyes up, and tried not look at the unsubtle alterations that had been carried out on the lower half of the costume. It struck him as being a mould for woman—with enough plaster of Paris you could make a plaster woman. Your own Venus de Milo for the garden. Look nice next to the pond with the goldfish. And it struck him as shudderingly repulsive.

'I could slip mine on,' Madeleine said. 'You wouldn't have to wear Ronnie's. Wouldn't fit you, anyway. But I could wear mine.'

'I couldn't,' he said.

'Be a devil.'

'I couldn't,' he said again, thrashing around for an excuse. Any excuse. 'You've had far too much to drink. It would be taking advantage of you.'

She giggled. The giggle became a laugh. The laugh became the raucous mockery he had asked for.

'You don't mean to say you've never made love to a woman who's pissed before?'

Troy never had. Lately he hadn't made love to any woman. Pissed or sober. She danced up his cheekbone with her lips, setded on his ear lobe and nipped it lightly with her teeth.

'I can't,' he said. 'Really I can't.'

She whispered in his ear. The heat of her breath tingled through half the veins in his body, coursing down to the loins to stir the bits he would rather leave unstirred.

'Has anyone ever told you you're a bit of a spoilsport?'
Most of the women in his life had told him that.
Cowardy custard.

§69

He woke up alone and chaste in one of the many spare bedrooms in Madeleine Kerr's mansion. He had slept badly, waking often, dreaming deeply. It was something about her eyes. He felt awful. Again, the sound of running water. It followed him all the way down to the ground floor and into the kitchen as he searched for breakfast. Breakfast was not a meal of any importance in the Kerr household, at least not to the woman—the image of Cockerell alias Kerr shovelling kedgeree was permanently imprinted on Troy's brain—and all he could find was a packet of Ryvita and a jar of 'instant' coffee. Instant coffee, as well as being a perfect example of an oxymoron and a good bet for revised editions of Fowler's *English Usage,* was a novelty of the new world, the post-war world, instantly accepted like the ball-point pen and the plastic mackintosh—and it tasted instantly awful. It floated down to the bottom of the cup, as light as dust, a powdery scent already wafting off it, and when dissolved in boiling water it yielded up a strong and artificial aroma. It tasted like the coffee creme in a box of sickly chocolates, the merest approximation of what coffee tasted like, achieved by blending caramel and scouring powder. It brought pictures to the mind's eye. Troy could see the ribbon on the chocolate box, the guide to the contents of each brown blob, to find a centre by its shape, cherry cup and nut cluster and the one nobody wanted—coffee creme. It was faintly gelatinous and clung to the cup and to the teeth with a viscous smear. He drank half a cup with a Ryvita and a dab of orange marmalade, and poured the rest of it down the sink. As he turned off the tap, he was suddenly conscious of the silence. The sound of water roaring through pipes had stopped. She must be out of the shower.

'Are you ready?'

Troy turned at the sound of her voice. Madeleine stood in the door-way, dressed and made up, taking a last look at her artistry in the mirror of her compact. She clicked it shut and looked him up and down. Shirt tails out and no shoes or socks. Far from ready.

'I tend to save lines like, "You look like shit in the mornings" for more intimate relationships. But you do look like shit in the morning, don't you? Get your skates on, Troy, we've got a train to catch.'

He did up his shoelaces in the cab on the way to the station. She had wrongfooted him, almost literally, and he was wondering at this new organisation woman she had presented him with, wondering at the hurry they were in and wondering why she seemed completely free of the hangover she so richly deserved. If he drank the best part of two bottles of claret, he paid for it for days.

The cab pulled in under the glass awning of Brighton station. He paid and they stood before the huge wooden destination board, checking the London trains.

'We've missed the Belle,' Madeleine said. 'If you'd been ready we could have had kippers and coffee and be halfway to London by now. Still, doesn't matter much, as long as we go First.'

First—Onions would have a fit if Troy bought First-Class railway tickets on Scotland Yard expenses. But First it was. The look on her face told him she was used to no less and would accept no less. Cockerell had spoilt her—but then so richly, so inventively had she spoilt and satiated him.

Troy did not much care for First-Class travel. You met nobody. While there were times when he would quite like to meet nobody, most of the time copper's nosiness prevailed. The British public as the great human reference work. You never knew who was going to start talking to you. Particularly in the years just after the war when petrol was still rationed, hardly anyone owned a car and some vestige of wartime *bonhomie* pre-vailed. He recalled a trip to Manchester, out of Euston, sitting opposite a potbellied man with an RAF moustache who had explained at length the precise length of his artificial intestine, and just how much of his guts he had left in a German field hospital when the Wellington he had been co-piloting had been shot down over the flat plains of Prussia. And on the return journey a seven-year-old boy, being taken to London for the day by his father, whose vision of the capital seemed to be made up entirely from precociously lurid reading. He was dying to see Whitechapel and

Jack the Ripper, could hardly wait for 221B Baker Street and Sherlock Holmes. Troy tried to make his day. 'I'm a detective,' he said. And the child thought he was having his leg pulled.

'Troy?'

He blinked. He'd been miles away.

'You were daydreaming? Didn't you hear me? I said I could murder a cup of coffee.'

He looked at her through furred vision. She was neat, beautiful in her tight, two-piece outfit—red again, she adored red, a statement of her role as the scarlet woman?—with a sleeveless, high-necked silk blouse in white. She slipped off the jacket, laid it on the seat next to her and took out her compact from her handbag. Her arms were slender and tanned and watchable. He watched with a childish fascination as she again, and quite unnecessarily, looked at her own reflection in the mirror, pursed her lips, touched an eyebrow, but did nothing to change her appearance.

'Well?' she said across the top of the compact, green eyes flashing at him.

'Where are we?'

'Just coming up to Three Bridges.'

'Surely there'll be a waiter round in a minute?'

He did not much feel like moving.

'Or not,' she said. 'Troy, be a darling and get me a coffee. I'm gasping.'

She flipped the compact shut again, blew him a mock kiss from shiny red lips, and slipped it into the pocket of her red jacket.

He walked a couple of jolting coaches to the dining car. The attendant said he'd be round in ten minutes. Troy grovelled and persuaded the man to let him carry a tray and two cups back with him. The train stopped as the man poured, and Troy saw the sign for Three Bridges outside the window. He picked up the tray and with all the precision of bad timing the train started up again and quickly gathered speed. He cursed Madeleine Kerr the rattling length of two carriages, and as he had his hand on the door of the third the train hit the brakes and threw him onto his back in the corridor and the coffee flooded all over his crumpled black suit.

He'd never been on a train before when someone pulled the emergency cord, but he had no doubts that that was what had happened. There was hubbub behind him, alarmed voices and a child crying, and silence in front of him. He stepped into the last carriage, turned in at the door of Madeleine's compartment. Her head lolled towards the window, bobbing on her left shoulder, as the train gently recoiled and uncoiled like an overtightened spring. He had seen broken necks before and had no doubt that she was dead. He put his fingers to the side of her neck. There was no pulse. Her eyes were closed, her hands were in her lap, and her handbag was gone. He was succumbing to the stillness of the moment, the lateral force of shock, the absurd trick of nature that had left her looking beautiful in death, when the train jolted sharply and the door at his side swung open. Now he knew.

He leapt to the track and landed badly. All his weight on his left ankle and the leg slid from under him in a searing burst of pain. He dragged himself upright and caught sight of a figure running down the track, back towards the station. Troy took a step and felt his left leg drag him back down. The man disappeared behind a concrete shed. Troy took another step and another, trying as best he could to run. The man darted out from behind the shed. Troy had only a fleeting vision of a blur in blue but knew as the sinking feeling hit his stomach that the dark blob at the end of an outstretched arm really was a gun being levelled at him. The gun flashed and blew him green and blew him red and blew him black—into a dreamless hell.

§70

How often had he lain like this? Waking up, roaring earthward from a timeless, wordless hell, trying to recognise the hospital from its paintwork, knowing he had been walloped again and waiting for the rush of consciousness that brought it all back to him and told him who, when and everything but where. A nurse told him that. A pretty young woman in a staff nurse's uniform, and almost before the words were out of her lips he recognised the distinctive belt buckle and the unique configuration of starched linen that passed for a cap.

'You're in the Charing Cross, Mr Troy.'

'So I see.'

'Do you remember me?'

Troy looked as closely as his horizontal position and swimming vision would permit.

'I was a first-year nurse at the Middlesex in '51 when you caught Edward Langdon-Davies.'

The rush of memory—the past more vivid than the present. Troy had caught Langdon-Davies that winter. Cuffed, nicked, sentenced, hanged. And Langdon-Davies had caught him across the shoulder with a poker and broken his collarbone. Jack had bundled him into a squad car and taken him to the nearest casualty department, the Middlesex. This young woman had watched as a doctor jerked his bones back into place with a sickening jolt of pain, and then she had tied his arm in a sling and told him to salute Caesar for a month.

'Getting to be a habit with you,' she said, smiling, not knowing how near the truth she came.

'How long have I been here?' he asked from the depths of the habit.

'Just overnight. You came to at the Mid-Sussex. The X-rays were fine, so they let your brother hire an ambulance to bring you back to London. You came to a few times, but I don't suppose you remember a thing about that, do you?'

She took his pulse and temperature and bustled out. Troy felt the right side of his head. A bandage, bulging over a large swab. No pain, and once he had sat up no double vision or nausea. Perhaps he had got away with murder yet again. The phrase rolled around in his mind. Langdon-Davies had not got away with murder. Troy had not thought he should hang. Langdon-Davies, like Cockerell, like Angus Pakenham, and so many people into whose lives he had blundered lately, had been an irrevocable casualty of war. A born soldier, an officer to his nicotined fingertips. In the post-war he had been lost. No trade or profession worth mentioning, except killing and deceiving. He was, Troy knew, half mad. A series of failed business ventures, in none of which had commando skills been much use, most of which had turned out to be the local equivalents of the Ground-Nut scheme, or a latterday version of chicken-farming—either was ripe in the national argot as a symbol of failure and folly—had sent him into confidence trickery (fraud and forgery, the ignoble art of the bum cheque); trading on rank (Major), and accent (RP), and at the end of the last such trick he had killed his wife. As he had told it to Troy, they had argued badly, she screaming at him, all the names under all the suns in all the galaxies it seemed, him trying to be as calm as possible, the code telling him one did not abuse the 'fairer' sex. He had turned his back on her thinking the row over, and she had hit him from behind, and in reflex, as he would have it till the day they took him out and hanged him, he had jabbed her in the throat with his elbow, without even looking, and on the turn he had forced her head back with his other hand and snapped her neck. All, he said, in the twinkling of an eye, a textbook despatch of assailant-from-behind, as learnt, if not upon the playing fields of Eton, then upon the square tarmac of Aldershot.

Murder never fails to attract attention. But the run Langdon-Davies had made, eluding the police for weeks, living by theft and burglary, so like the Invisible Man that doors were bolted and windows barred the length of Britain for fear of a 'murderer', had reached the level of a national obsession, all but displacing Dick Barton in the imagination of the people. He became the man the papers loved to hate, a murderer on the run, sighted as far afield as Dundee and Barnstaple, and at that on the same day. 'Murderer', a species, in the realm of myth and popular journalism, rather than a demented individual. Troy had not thought he should hang. He even, it had to be said, liked the man. But the law, not seeing his madness for what it was, had no other penalty. He hanged. Hanged for the crime of never being able to forget what he had learned in war. He had talked, oh how he had talked, a confession so long it was little short of a novel. What story would Arnold Cockerell tell if Troy could but get the dead to speak? But then Cockerell had spoken, the drear tale of the carpet salesman. It had told him next to nothing. It was the mere facet of a life. Turn it this way, that way, another facet, another tale, another meaning would become apparent.

'I want the lot,' said Jack simply.

Later in the day, fourish, fivish, his watch was missing and he could not be certain, Jack stood before him, grim and pale. He threw a police 10 C 8 photograph of Madeleine Kerr onto the bedspread.

'I want the lot, and if I get the impression that you're holding anything back, so help me, Freddie, I'll sink you.'

He turned around the upright chair, visitors for the use of, and sat stiffly upon it, arms folded, his hat perched on the edge of the bed like a small species of slothful animal. It was unlike Jack to wear a hat. It was symbolic, the assumption of power in the garb of those old know-nothings in bowler hats and black boots who had been the 'Yard' when they had first joined before the war—a breed of dullards, inhibited and motivated by the constant humiliations of class—to which Onions had proved a savage exception.

'Where shall I begin?'

'Assume I know her name—Madeleine Kerr—and assume I recognised the photos dotted round her house as Cockerell. Take it from there.'

Troy told him. Everything from Angus's phone call to his leaping onto the track in the middle of Sussex into the path of a bullet and the blur in blue.

Jack heard him in near silence. He took no notes, prided himself on his memory and asked few questions.

'What do you have?' Troy asked.

Jack stood up and stretched, strolled a few paces around the room, rested the palms of his hands on the windowsill, looked out at the dwindling afternoon sunlight.

'He snapped her neck like a twig. No sign of a struggle. She died instantly. We found her handbag in the woods. Turned out, scattered. Impossible to tell what he was looking for, or what might be missing. Her driving licence and a couple of letters told us who she was. Just as well. You were in no fit state to ask.'

Troy wondered about the look Jack shot at him. Reproach?

'Her house had been turned over.'

'Ransacked?'

'No. A pro. Not a thing out of place. But it had been done just the same. You know the feeling when that's been done. You've seen it yourself. And I still don't know what he was looking for.'

Nor did Troy. Jack sat on the cold radiator. Troy twisted his head to be able to see his face, felt the lump beneath the bandage as his head touched the frame of the bed. What must he look like?

'What were you doing?'

'Eh?'

'Why were you taking her to London? She had a return ticket in her coat pocket. That and a powder compact. Why were the two of you on that train?'

'I don't really know.'

Jack pushed himself off the radiator, took a few steps into the room and Troy heard the deep breath that presaged rage. He was being so awfully dim. Jack, lackadaisical Jack, darting around a room like a cat on a hot tin roof, unable to stay still for more than a minute. It was his way of keeping control. He was seethingly angry with Troy and Troy had been too slow to realise it. He prised himself higher in the sheets and pillows, as near as he could an attempt to face Jack and diffuse him.

'I meant,' he began lamely, 'that she didn't tell me why. Simply that there were things she would only tell me once we'd got to London.'

'Such as?'

'Cockerell—what he was up to.'

'You mean you had a night alone with her and you couldn't get it out of her?'

'Yes.'

'Freddie. Did you sleep with that woman?'

It seemed like a challenge to his nature, one the severest moments of mistrust in all the years they had known one another.

'No, Jack, I didn't.'

'A whole night to ask her questions and you end up with her leading you around by the—'

'Jack! I didn't fuck her!'

Jack grabbed the chair, pulled it closer to Troy, and leant in.

'Do you have even the faintest idea what you've done? This is no time to be telling me lies!'

'I'm not lying. And what I did was investigate a murder.'

'Freddie, until you went to Brighton, there was no murder.'

'Yes there was. Cockerell was murdered. Jessel was murdered.'

'I've seen the medical report on your desk. Jessel died of heart failure.'

'Heart failure aggravated by having a gun waved in his face!'

Jack sat back, almost reeled at the shock.

'What?'

'I found gun oil on his desk. A drop no bigger than a pin head, but unmistakably gun oil. Some bugger thought it a good idea to put the fear of God up Jessel by waving a gun in his face.'

'Why is none of this in writing?'

'Jack—for Christ's sake . . .'

288

'I repeat. Do you know what you've done?'

Troy did not answer.

'You've left me bugger all to go on. You've ripped the lid off a can of worms.'

'Bonser. We talk to Bonser. Somebody told him to go round to the King Henry that day. We talk to Bonser.'

'We?'

Troy said nothing. He knew what was coming.

'We. Freddie, there is no "we". You're off the case.'

'You told Onions?'

'Did you think I was bluffing?'

'What's the deal?'

'You're on sick leave. You stay away from the Yard. When the medics pass you as fit, your return is discretionary. If I think you're going to stick your nose into this, I can and will prolong your sick leave.'

'Jack,' he said softly. 'That's the most colossal fiddle.'

'Quite. But it might just keep you alive. It might just keep you away from the spooks. Onions wants you nowhere near the bastards.'

This was bad news. What idea did Jack have about the next move?

'Jack, you surely don't mean that you're going to tackle the spooks? That's the last thing we can do.'

Jack picked up his hat from the bed. If the gesture was meant to end the meeting it was wasted. Troy sat bolt upright.

'Jack! You're not listening to me!'

Indeed, Jack was heading for the door.

'You can't approach them. Don't you see?'

Jack had the door open, one half of his body already hidden by it.

'They'll kill it stone dead!'

Troy realised he was shouting with all the power left in his lungs. The force made his chest ache and his head momentarily was reeling. Jack closed the door and leant against it, his palms flat against the boards.

'They'll take it out of our hands. Then they'll do nothing.'

'Let's hear it,' Jack said.

'Has it occurred to you that we don't know which . . .' Troy fumbled for the word and failed . . . 'which . . . side killed Cockerell?'

'I don't follow.'

'I mean that I don't know who Cockerell was working for. He wasn't official. We can't investigate this and expect any help from Five and Six.

Now the PM has owned up they'll want it all buried as soon as possible. If that means leaving the murder of an innocent woman uninvestigated, then that's what they'll do.'

Jack knew he was right. Troy could see it in his eyes. He was yet again buggering Jack about with irrefutable and utterly unpalatable logic.

'So I'm stuck with a case that has no leads?'

'Work around it. Follow the scent, pretend for the time being that spooks aren't involved. Just as though it were an ordinary murder. See how close you can get. We can only go to Five and Six when we've the making of a case. If at all.'

'Ordinary murder? Do you know that no one on that train can positively identify the man who broke Madeleine Kerr's neck? I've enough details to describe a small army, but so contradictory that you could never resolve it into an individual. Tall, short fat, thin. The only clear description I have is of you. Half a dozen people are perfectly willing to go into court and identify you as the man who broke Madeleine Kerr's neck, but nobody can pick out the real killer. Nobody saw him pass through the station. Nobody at Brighton can single out anyone in particular as boarding that train. And you want me to work "around it"?'

'Yes. And keep her name and mine out of the papers.'

'Well,' Jack said, 'it's nice to know I can do one thing right.'

He heard the echo of the door slamming for what seemed like an age afterwards, the trail of Jack's anger lingering in the air, glancing off the walls. But Jack was not the worst. The worst was yet to come.

§71

The next day, the day of his discharge. He had stuffed his pyjamas into his briefcase and was struggling with the sleeves of his jacket. Dizziness caught him, he fell back against the side of the bed, one arm in, one arm out, the jacket stranded halfway down his back. A hand reached out to help him. He looked up. Anna Pakenham, dour, unsmiling, standing over him, her hands guiding his arms through the momentary maze of his sleeves.

'What are you doing here?'

'Trust me. I'm a mistress.'

She was insistent. She would drive him home. He protested weakly that it was less than a quarter of a mile, but feeling his head spin knew he would probably end up face down in the gutter in the Strand if left to his own devices.

In his sitting room she unwound the bandages and checked the wound.

'Neat,' she said. 'There'll be a scar, but the flap of skin's retaking. You won't have a bald stripe. It looks for all the world as though the bullet bounced off your thick head. I don't suppose you need me to tell you how lucky you've been.'

'Story of my life.'

'Luck can run out, Troy. Have you ever met a boxer who's gone punchy? Mickey McGuire's a patient of mine. British and Empire Light Heavyweight Champion before the war, at least for two bouts until he lost it. He's been bashed to buggery in his time—and now he'd be hard pressed to tell you what time it is or what day it is.'

'I get the message.'

'No you don't. You can hear me but it doesn't mean a damn thing to you. Now, to more important matters than whether you live or die. I want to know—have you dragged Angus into anything that will hurt him?'

'No,' he said, 'Angus is out of it.'

Anna clicked her doctor's bag closed, kissed him on the cheek, called him a bastard and opened the front door. He was halfway to the kitchen, intending to put the kettle on, when he heard her voice, and then his brother's voice in answer. They were standing on the doorstep mulling him over. He put the kettle on anyway. He doubted he could get through one of Rod's lectures without something to do with his hands.

When he returned, Rod had thrown his jacket on the sofa, and was standing red-faced, tugging his tie to half-mast and groping for the collar stud. Troy stuck the tray in front of him.

'Not to beat about the bush, Freddie—'

He grunted at the constriction of his throat, sighed as the stud popped free.

'Not to beat about the thingumajig—what are you up to?'

He breathed deeply, looking Troy in the eye.

'Well?'

'I'm doing my job, Rod. That's all there is to it.'

'You're lying!'

Troy swung at him, his clenched fist floating uselessly off Rod's arm as he sidestepped the blow, his own weight plummeting him towards the floor, sending the tea tray flying. Rod grabbed him round the torso and dropped him onto the sofa in an easy movement. He was a head taller than Troy and a couple of stones heavier, he took his weight effortlessly and then let him go.

'Don't be bloody stupid! You think I don't know when you're lying? You've been a world class liar since we were boys!'

Troy had winded himself. Rod leant low over him. For a fraction of a second Troy thought he meant to hit him, and as Rod bent over him, legs wide, head low, he got ready to kick him in the balls and have done. But Rod reached behind him to his jacket, half-buried under Troy. He pulled something from the pocket and stood up.

'Just doing your job, eh?' he said, and flung a small shiny object into Troy's lap. It was Madeleine Kerr's gun.

'Just doing your job? Freddie, you're bloody lucky Jack didn't find this. Bloody lucky the local plods going through your pockets found your warrant card first and stopped searching. I found this when the quacks summoned me to that Sussex hospital. Why are you carrying a gun? Why are you lying to me?'

'I refer the honourable member to my previous answer.'

Even as he said it, it sounded cheap and adolescent. Cocking a snook at big brother.

Rod straightened up, began to pick up the fragments of the tea set. He could not sustain anger long, even when it might well be in his own defence. The edge went out of his voice, a saddened, concerned, irritatingly humane baritone took over.

'I'll tell you what I think. I think you're chasing this one out of guilt. That load of twaddle about the old man. You're chasing spooks because somewhere inside you, you actually believe the old man was a spook, and this is your way of expiating the guilt.'

'Guilt?' Troy said, compounding anger with a sneer. 'I don't know guilt.'

'How can you expect me to believe that you investigating Arnold Cockerell is just a coincidence?'

'Jack told you?'

'Of course.'

'Did he also tell you I was the last person to see Cockerell alive?'

Rod stood with the teapot in one hand and its spout in the other.

'No. Were you?'

'Yes. Bad luck really. I just happened to be in the right hotel on the wrong night.'

'The last I heard, Cockerell's wife had been unable to identify the body.'

'She won't have to. I've done it.'

'It's him?'

'Yes.'

Rod threw the pieces back onto the tray, and flopped into an armchair.

'So. That's it.'

'It? You mean final? Of course it isn't final. What do you think, that you've finally nailed Eden's balls to the floor? You knew it was Cockerell long before the Government owned up! But this isn't the last nail. Rod, you knew, but Eden didn't. None of the buggers knew. Cockerell was a loner. Eden probably found out after you did. Your theory of the great conspiracy, as is so often the case, comes down to the great cock-up.'

'I don't deny that I knew Cockerell's name right from the start . . .'

'Even on that day we got pissed at the Commons?'

'Yes. Even then. But I still don't see how you can say Eden didn't know.'

'The war cry of discredited leaders throughout the ages. "Nobody told me." I don't know what happened, but I know that SIS were surprised by this. And I think Eden was horrified.'

Rod sat back. Stared at a space somewhere over Troy's head, then lowered his eyes to meet Troy's gaze.

'Doesn't excuse them, though. Does it?'

'No. Their job to know after all. But it does put the ball squarely in my court.'

'How so?'

'It's murder. Three murders to be precise. I don't know who killed Cockerell, but it's conceivable it was the same person who killed George Jessel and Madeleine Kerr. It's not final because it's still happening, because it's murder—and murder is my business.'

'Shit,' Rod said softly. 'Shit, shit, shit.'

'Cockerell was a crook. Of what kind, I don't know. But he was working a fiddle worth thousands through his business. He wasn't your sophisticated spy, he was a common or garden crook.'

'But he was also spying? Why else was he down there? I don't follow.'

And Troy did not much mean to lead. There were things he would tell Rod and things he would do his best to avoid telling him. It was all a matter of phrasing. It was time to change tack or be caught out.

'Tell me. What is a spy?' he said.

'Bit bloody philosophical, isn't it?'

'Indulge me. What is a spy in his ... nature?'

Rod thought about this. Locking his fingers together, stretching out his arms and listening to every joint in his hands crack.

'I know it's a cliché, but they're whores aren't they? At heart your spy is a whore.'

'And what is the nature of a whore? The prerogative, if you like.'

'Oh, I get it. You mean that old saw about the chap at the Tory Party conference, Baldwin or somebody very like Baldwin, who described the press as exercising power without responsibility, which "has been the prerogative of the whore throughout history, arf arf". Then Devonshire turns to Macmillan and says, "Damn, there goes the tarts' vote!"'

'That's the one. The whore has power without responsibility. The spy has responsibility without power.'

'Now you have lost me.'

'What is the spy's stock in trade? What is the commodity at the heart of his trade?'

'Information.'

'Knowledge.'

'If you like.'

'Portable property Dickens would have called it. Knowledge he can carry, trade or deliver, but on which he cannot act.'

'Meaning?'

'Knowledge is not power. Bacon was only half right. Knowledge is only power if you can act upon it.'

'And if you can't?'

'If you can't, then knowledge is a dead weight. The fate of the spy is to know in impotence.'

'The burden of knowledge, eh?'

'Something like that.'

'And how do you come to know this?'

An honest answer might have been to say 'because I married one', but Tosca was a red herring to the argument. It was not her nature he was driving at, but Rod's and his own.

'A few weeks ago you called me a spy.'

Rod opened his mouth. Troy knew that his unspeakable decency would lead him to apologise for any truth. He raised a hand to shut him up.

'Of course I was a spy. I can hardly pretend otherwise. But what are you?'

'You're going to tell me. I can't stop you. And I'm beginning to wish you hadn't smashed the teapot.'

'A spy is someone in possession of information to which he has no right and is powerless to use. You got a lucky tip over Cockerell, but you couldn't come out and name him.'

'He wasn't exactly my priority. The point wasn't Cockerell or who killed Cockerell. It was the breach of faith by the Government.'

'Quite. You went after the Tories over Cockerell without Cockerell being the issue. You scored a victory, but the storm you whipped up won't die down. It's murder. It always was.'

'It won't die down because you're raking it up.'

Troy ignored this.

'The same tactic applies to Suez. You know what the buggers are planning, thanks to the CIA. But you can't come clean and say it. The information strangles you. Knowledge without power. You can't stop Eden without revealing your source. I'll go further—you *won't* stop Eden. You won't stop him, because you want to see him fuck up and then your party can step in as the saviours.'

Rod sighed deeply. There would be no angry outburst. This was its cue and it wasn't even waiting in the wings.

'Freddie. Believe me, I'd give anything to stop this war happening. But I can't. Not me, not heaven, not hell. All I can do is harass the bastards from the sidelines, see to it that my own party comes through it untainted and in a position to pick up the pieces.'

Troy pushed himself to the edge of the sofa. Rod was leaning forward, elbows on knees, fingertips to chin. He met his brother almost nose to nose.

'But, doesn't it hurt to know?' he whispered.

'Not the word I'd have put to it yesterday or even five minutes ago, but yes, that's exactly what it does.'

Troy got up. Walked a giddy walk to the kitchen. Rooted out the spare pot. God knows, Rod had earned his cuppa. He heard him sighing repeatedly over the gentle hiss of the kettle. He knew he had hit him hard, more brutal than any physical blow he could have landed on him. He stuck a second tray in front of Rod and poured for the two of them. The soft, oriental waft of Earl Grey floating to the nostrils, the airy illusion that they were good, solid Englishmen, at teatime peace with history.

Rod smiled, said, 'Let's see if we can avoid smashing this one, shall we?'

They sipped in silence. Troy could read Rod like a book. The pattern of guilt inscribing itself deep in the soft yielding tissue of his good nature. He stared at the ceiling, sighed from time to time and seemed to be working his way to some kind of conclusion.

'You know, I can't even tell Gaitskell. I mean, that is, I haven't told Gaitskell. In fact, you're the only person I have told. It's like holding the grenade in your fist. I can taste the metal pin in my mouth. Teeth clamped, fist tight.'

He stumbled to a halt. Troy sensed revelation slouching.

'You remember Ike called me?'

'I doubt I shall ever forget.' Rod did not ask Troy what he meant by this.

'I told you he'd heard Eden's address to the nation. It wasn't quite what prompted the call. Truth is, he'd heard Hugh's reply as well. He called not because he thinks Eden's war barmy—goes without saying—but because he fears Hugh and the Labour Party may well back him. Ike calls me up from the nineteenth hole almost every damn Saturday. "Only phone in America that ain't bugged!"—and he doesn't laugh when he says it. Last weekend he was all but shouting at me. He's really worried that the country will fall in behind Eden.'

'He has a point,' said Troy.

Rod looked sharply at him but declined the bait. The struggle simply to get out what he had to say was taking all his strength.

'Last month the Prime Minister of Malta paid us a visit. Hugh and I had a private meeting with him. He told us that the Royal Navy was amassing an armada off Malta. And that there could be only one reason for this. And blow me, Hugh said, "I don't believe you"! What the hell does he think is going on out there? A regatta? I can't tell him. I don't know how to tell him.'

Rod slipped into staccato. Each phrase dragged up as though it were poetry, costing him the price of his soul at utterance. The pauses getting longer and more maddening with every attempt he made at precision.

'We're embarking on a national madness—The last fling of Empire —It'll damn us for a generation—We'll be international pariahs—It'll create the biggest run on the pound in years—Sterling will go through the floor—Our gold reserves will be wiped out—And I can't find a way to tell him—'

Troy thought the last pause would be infinite. He could hear Rod breathing, he could hear cabs honking in St Martin's Lane, he could hear a London pigeon burbling on his windowsill. He could hear the blood pulse in the cut on the side of his head.

Suddenly Rod rounded on the argument in a move swifter than a cracker-barrel loop.

'You know, I can't stop what's going to happen—but you can stop investigating Cockerell.'

'No I can't.'

'It's Jack's case now.'

'You've known me all your life. Do you really think that's going to stop me?'

'Let it go, Freddie. We're both in over our heads. That's what you've been to considerable pains to tell me.'

'I know, but don't you wonder where it's leading? Guilt or no guilt. Father or no father. Doesn't the spook chase make you wonder into what corners it will take us?'

Rod mulled this one over.

'Corners. Corners? Not the word I would have chosen. Depths, perhaps.'

He sipped at his tea and mulled a new word.

'Yes—depths. I don't much care about the corners. Where would rooms, cardboard boxes and Pythagoras be without them? Depths. It's the depths that bother me.'

He drained his cup. Set it back on its saucer with a penetrating plonk. He looked at his watch.

'I must dash. I should be in the House.'

Troy was puzzled. The House did not sit in September.

'Eh?'

'Didn't I tell you? We recalled Parliament while you were in the land of Nod. You know, the great experiment—democracy and all that?'

That was a family phrase, the et cetera of 'all that'—their father's pattern of speech. It had been his pleasure and duty to educate his children by anecdote and aphorism, usually whilst doing something else, writing or eating, so that one always had the impression that such knowledge as he imparted was being imparted with extreme lassitude, the asides of a relaxed, occupied mind. Troy, as the youngest and sickliest, so often at home, so often just 'around', was the most frequent recipient of 'all that'.

'History, my little Englander, can be divided into two categories. The actions of history are either a bad thing or a necessary thing. Take the Revolution, our Revolution. A necessary thing. Take the present state of Mother Russia—the jury of history is still out. It will become a necessary thing or it will become a bad thing. There is no such thing as a good thing. Take the American Revolution. A necessary thing. Take their President—Mr Hoover—a bad thing. Take their present state. A necessary thing? Democracy and all that? Perhaps, but not a good thing.'

A few years later a schoolmaster and a journalist had got together and written a very funny spoof history of England, a terrific schoolboy howler in which there were good kings and bad kings and good things and bad things. They had called the book *1066 and All That*. Troy had often wondered if they had, at some point, met the old man in garrulous mood, and simply got it wrong.

There was no easy dismissal of Rod's 'democracy and all that'—the phrase carried too much baggage and most of it was doubt.

§72

He had lied to Rod. Thinking about the encounter afterwards, they were lies of imprecision rather than complete untruth. It all depended on how Rod took his line about the common crook and the sophisticated spy. Troy had loaded all meaning he could onto the nouns, knowing these would lead Rod away from where meaning really lay, in the adjectives. He knew in his bones that Cockerell was a spy—he just wasn't a 'sophisticated' spy. Perhaps he was even an uncommon crook. The more he learnt of the man, the more uncommon he seemed to be beneath the common façade. But Troy had surely and deliberately sent Rod away thinking that he had said Cockerell was not a spy. The less Rod knew the better.

The less Tosca knew the better. He could not face the explanations, could not face her with his head wrapped up in its skimpy turban.

He called her.

'It's Saturday tomorrow. Y' comin' home?'

It was as well she said—he had had no idea what day it was.

'No,' he said. 'I'm afraid I'll have to work this weekend.'

'The next then?'

'Yes,' he lied. 'How . . . how are you . . . managing?'

He heard the word crash down like breaking crockery.

'Not bad. Wish you were here. Bet that surprises you, don't it? One of the women turned out to be a mensch.'

'Which one?'

'Lucinda.'

He was not surprised.

'And the Fat Guy says you're not to forget the pig is due to something or other.'

'Farrow.'

'Farrow?'

'The pig is pregnant.'

They lapsed into silence.

Then she said, 'Is that all we got to say to each other? The pig is pregnant? The goddam pig is pregnant!'

He had never felt much like a married man. Now he did not feel like one at all. She had been gone a week, more or less? He wasn't really sure. Dreamless hell was timeless hell. He began to wonder why he had any clarity of thought, what motive force enabled him to make sentences and utter speech. Dreamless hell was wordless hell. Mimram and Tosca seemed like images from another lifetime. He caught sight of himself in the mirror. Took off the bandage and threw it in the bin. He looked worse than she had the day he found her in Amsterdam.

Jack phoned. His voice flat and emotionless. A courtesy call.

299

'I've seen Bonser. He says he acted on his own initiative. Tore the pages out of Quigley's book because he thought it was expected of him. Admits he was wrong. Even handed over the pages.'

'He's lying,' said Troy.

Jack exploded.

'Of course he's fucking lying! You think I don't know he's lying!?!'

'Jack, I was only—'

But Jack had hung up on him.

He sat most of the evening playing, and playing again, Debussy's *Estampes*. They fitted the night and fitted the mood. Limp and liquid. It was raining once more. The earth boomed and shook with thunder like the rage of Zeus, the rain tore down in sheets and lightning ripped the sky with a sound like tearing canvas. When he got fed up with Debussy he switched to Bach, those infuriating 'pieces to be played in another room', the *Goldberg Variations*. There was only one word for the *Goldberg Variations*. Flash. He loved the change of gear from first to top, especially that between the first and second variations. And he felt he coped well with the fast bits. It was the slow bits that did for him. Clunking through like a man with ten thumbs when, really, he needed three hands. The problem lay in the staccato nature of the work. Sharp—yes, staccato—but fluid at the same time. Tap, tap bonk just wouldn't do.

But the tap tap tapping was coming not from the keyboard. As a peal of thunder rolled away into a complaining grumble he stopped and heard, once again, the distinct tap of a hand at his door. He took the small golden automatic off the top of the piano and flipped back the slide, heard the metallic thunk as the bullet entered the breach. He seriously doubted whether a gun so small could fire through an inch and a half of two-hundred-year-old oak, but as he reached for the handle with his right hand, his left held the gun against the door at chest height. He prised the door open. Through the two-inch gap he could see a bedraggled figure standing in the alley just below the bottom step. The rain was falling so hard it was bouncing back off the flagstones to give the impression that here was some unfortunate northern Aphrodite, rising from the foam, shrouded in the mist—and shivering to death. As a crack of lightning shredded the sky above him he could see her clearly. It was Madeleine Kerr, in a sodden T-shirt and sodden blue jeans.

'You must be freezing,' he said and threw the door wide.

She stepped across the threshold, wiping the water from her face, and he ran to the bathroom for a towel.

She stood dripping on the mat. He kicked the door to and handed her the towel.

'Do you know who I am?' she asked.

'Yes,' he said.

'You don't seem surprised.'

'I've been around twins all my life. It doesn't surprise me to know that one person can precisely resemble another. Besides, they never do, precisely.'

This woman had the same blonde hair, the same pale green eyes, but she was, in some way he could scarcely pin down, better-looking than her twin, a remarkably beautiful woman. Perhaps the wet waif was a powerfully deceptive image. The difference he saw, he realised, was in the absence of a sense of decadence. The too-knowing look.

She rubbed at her hair in a desultory way.

'Madeleine told you about me?'

'She never mentioned you.'

He knelt by the fire, turned on the gas and put a match to it. It popped into life. Pink and human and friendly.

'Sit here and get yourself dry. I'll make tea.'

His hands shook as he reached down the tea caddy, rattled the tin kettle against the tap as he filled it. But that was, he had always thought, the purpose of the English Tea Ceremony. It bought time for nervous hands and hollow minds.

When the tea was ready and his hands were steady, he carried the tray into the sitting room. The woman was crouched on the hearth-rug, wrapping herself in the huge bath towel and pulling off her clothes. Her jeans and T-shirt steamed on the back of a chair. She reached under the towel, eased her weight off her backside and dropped her knickers onto the chair. An awkward motion—for any woman faced with a total stranger. But she just smiled sweetly at him, without a trace of coyness. He set down the tray and sat on the edge of the fireside chair. She moved closer to the fire, sitting on her haunches, pulled the towel off herself in a momentary flash of hands and breasts and held it in front of her as a curtain, while she dried her face on its top edge. The towel rolled about her once more, she pulled the slide from the knot at the back of her head and eighteen inches of wet, blonde hair cascaded down her back.

'I'm her sister,' she said.

'I know.'

'Shirley. Shirley Foxx. With two exxes.'

'Troy,' he said. 'With one of each letter.'

She smiled. Reached for the tea cup.

'Madeleine's real name was Stella. She made up the Madeleine Kerr name. Two of her favourite actresses rolled into one. Madeleine Carroll and Deborah Kerr. She loved Deborah Kerr.'

She paused, sipped at the tea.

'I suppose it must have made it a bit awkward for the police, trying to trace someone and not knowing her proper name. But they found me. I went down to identify her.'

He could hear the northern vowels in her voice. That was the trace of accent, he realised, that he had heard in Madeleine Kerr's voice. Derbyshire. God, how the woman had lied to him.

She reached for her handbag. Dug around inside it and produced a small, ivory-coloured compact. The same one he had seen Madeleine Kerr use on the train from Brighton.

'When it was all over, that young copper from Scotland Yard, the good-looking one ...'

'Inspector Wildeve,' Troy said.

'Yes, him. He said I could take away Stella's effects—I think that's what he called them—her effects, and this was with them.'

She flipped open the compact. Looked into the mirror at herself and then up at Troy.

'When we were kids. Eleven or twelve. At the end of the war. We were each given one of these by an aunt. Rationing made them so precious. Even though our Mam said we were nowhere near old enough to be putting powder on our faces, and Dad hit the roof at the thought of his girls wearing make-up. So we kept them for years. Unused. They became our secret place. Because—you see—if you ...'

She pressed the side of the compact and the mirror shot forward on a spring. She turned the compact around for him to see. In the space behind the mirror was his card, the one Madeleine Kerr had taken. And beneath that, Sellotaped to the stainless steel, was a small flat key.

'It was our hiding place. We kept our secrets there. It was a place we put things for ourselves and for each other. That's how I knew. She put your card there for me to find. She put the key there for me to give to you.'

Troy pulled the key free from its sticky tape. An elaborate K was on one side, an equally elaborate M on the other, in something like a Kelmscott typeface, and under the K was a stamped number so small one would need a magnifying glass to read it. Jack had said the killer had taken her handbag, tipped it out in the woods and abandoned it. The compact he had seen Madeleine slip into her jacket pocket. It must have been there when the local plod searched the body. The killer could not have found it.

'Did you,' he said, 'did you show this to the Inspector, Mr Wildeve?'

She shook her head. Not the faintest shred of guilt or doubt.

'For your eyes only,' she said.

It seemed to Troy that she was placing an awful lot of trust in him on the basis of a single gesture. But, then, he was the youngest child of four, stranded at the far side of a large family like a poorly used preposition at the end of a sentence. He had no experience of the shared intimacies, the common ground of siblings. He doubted that Rod did either; they were middle-aged men now, striving for the semblance of trust they had not shared as children, teetering constantly on the edge of each other's misgivings and Troy's evasions—but his sisters in the privacy of their twin-dom had a common language, a private language that was gobbledegook to anyone else, a mutual trust, a great *contra mundum*—it should never have surprised him that they conspired at the manipulation of gullible husbands to conceal each other's adultery—perhaps the trust this young woman had in him was only the transference of the trust she had placed in her sister. Troy had better be careful. He knew he had led Madeleine Kerr to her death, knew full well that whoever killed her had only found her because he had led him there. It was one of the most stupid things he had ever done. He could not tell Jack, although Jack would doubt-less work it out for himself, and he must certainly never let this woman realise how misplaced her trust in him was.

'Do you know what the key's for?' she said.

'Yes. It's a safety deposit box key for a bank in Hanover Square.'

'What, like the District or the National Provincial?'

'Not quite—a private bank called Mullins Kelleher.'

She seemed impressed by the readiness with which he recited this.

'I suppose it's your job to know things like that?'

'No, just so happens I bank with them too.'

'I know it's important, but I don't know why.'

Troy did. It was without doubt the reason Madeleine had insisted on the trip to London before she talked any further to him. Whatever was in that box was, in some unknown way, vitally important as a precondition to whatever she had meant to tell him. He put it on the mantelpiece with all the force of casualness he could muster. The tiny rattle of metal on wood cut through his nonchalance like a whisper in St Paul's.

'Are you hungry?' he said. 'I'm a fair cook.'

'And I'm a fair eater.'

He went back to the kitchen. But the cupboard was bare. There was a large tin of Heinz beans on the shelf, the hard, stale end of a white loaf in the bread bin and a jar of sticky peanut butter in the fridge—Tosca's legacy. Ransacking the drawers he also found a Mars Bar of indeterminate age. He had not shopped in days, he had not eaten in days, merely grazed until he was down to the bachelor's bottom line, the last tin of beans on the shelf.

It was nursery food, served in the best possible light. Beans on toast with peanut butter, best china and family silver, with an accompaniment of every proprietary pickle known to man: Pan Yan, piccalilli, Major Grey's and Branston, crowned by the *pièce de résistance,* his sister's home-made green tomato chutney—followed by half a Mars Bar each and a choice of Lapsang or Darjeeling.

'Don't laugh,' he said.

And if he hadn't said that she probably would not have—good manners more powerful than her sense of the absurd. And when she had stopped, she ate heartily and said, 'I haven't shared a Mars Bar since sweet rationing ended.'

'You must have got used to sharing.'

'Twins, you mean? Of course, we shared everything. Until ...'

The sentence petered out. But it was obvious. The missing word was Cockerell.

'When did they meet?'

She took the cue. Pushed away her plate, screwed the Mars wrapper into a ball, shook her hair, inched a little nearer the fire and stared into it.

304

'Hard to say. I can't much remember a time when Arnold wasn't a town busybody. He seems to have been the big fish in the little pond from the time he got there, and I suppose that's ten years or more. My parents bought their three-piece suite from him. On the HP, Utility-made. That'd be 1947 or 1948. Stella and I were there when he delivered it. We'd be thirteen or fourteen I suppose. Even Arnold Cockerell wouldn't flirt with a fourteen-year-old. Not in front of our Dad, he wouldn't.'

'A hard man?'

'That would be putting it mildly. An Ulsterman. Presbyterian. None of the faith left, just the rigours. We were bright girls. We both of us got scholarships to the grammar school. If Dad had had his way we'd have left at fifteen and got jobs, brought in a wage and paid our way till some man took us off his hands. But Mam was different. Derbyshire through and through—old-fashioned Labour. Education was everything; the only way out was up. So we took eight O-Levels apiece, and passed them all. After that we went to commercial college in Nottingham—shorthand, typing, French and German. That's as far as the vision went.'

She looked from the fire to Troy. Seeking the reaction in his face.

'Not much, was it? How to be one notch better off than your own parents is a lot like knowing your station in life. It means you don't think you can *do* anything you want or *be* anyone you want, you can just . . . well . . . do a little bit better.'

Foxx put a hand to the back of her neck, twisted her head slightly and angled the last of the wet hair towards the fire. She reached for her handbag, pulled out a brush and began to brush her hair in long, measured strokes.

'Then he died. Knocked off his perch by a heart attack at forty-two. We'd not long left college. The summer of 1951. Sweet seventeen. Stella was working for Cockerell, I was at the Co-op office.'

The look on Troy's face must have told her something.

'That's not what she told you, is it? None of this is what she told you.'

'No,' he said. 'It's not. In fact it's quite a way from what she told me.'

'Daddy was a country vet in Devon? Or was it a parson in Shropshire?'

'GP in Berkshire, I think.'

'That's a new one. I've not heard that one before. Stella was quite a liar you know.'

'So I'm discovering.'

'I rather admire it. If the fiction is better than the life you're leading . . .'

'Please, go on.'

'Dad died. That knocked Mam for six. He was a complete bastard, but it seems that he was her life and without him it wasn't worth living. She became an instant invalid. Took to her bed. Then in the autunm of the next year Stella announced she was off. She told me the truth, that Cockerell was prepared to set her up in her own place—a love nest the *News of the World* would call it—she told everyone else she'd got another secretarial job in London. I wasn't surprised. She'd been letting Cockerell have his way almost from the first day. They used to do it on the carpet samples with the lights out after work. Or, if he was feeling bold, in the back room during the lunch hour.'

'Good God,' said Troy almost involuntarily. 'Did his wife know?'

'I doubt it. But, then I've never met Mrs Cockerell. I know her by sight. It'd be hard not to in a town that size. But I've never spoken to her, and Stella said she never went near the shop. If Mrs Cockerell suspected anything she could have buttonholed me in the street at least once a week for the last four years. Never did. Never a word or a look. I told Stella she was a fool, but she didn't listen. I told her she was dropping me in it, an invalid mother to look after and only one wage coming in. She wept and wailed and said she was sorry, but I don't think she really gave a damn. By October she'd moved to Brighton. I threw over the Co-Op and went to the mill. There was more money to be made on a loom than taking dictation, and we needed it by then.'

'Did you see her in Brighton?'

'No. We always met in London.'

'Did you know what she was up to?'

'Up to? No, I didn't know what she was up to. But that's a leading question, isn't it? And in answering a leading question I'm admitting I thought she was up to something, aren't I?'

She'd rounded on him as swift as a Queen's Counsel nailing his evidence in the box.

'Yes, you are rather.'

'Let me ask you a leading question.'

'Fire away.'

She took him eye to eye.

'Did my sister make a play for you?'

306

'What makes you think she'd do that?'

'Well. I know my sister. And you're her . . .' She hesitated, tangled a finger in a long strand of hair, '. . . her type. I don't think I can put it any better.'

'Type?'

'Well . . . you do sound a bit like Robert Donat. You know the bloke in *The Thirty-Nine Steps*. The one who spends the night handcuffed to Madeleine Carroll. And you're a dead ringer for James Mason. You know—*Odd Man Out, The Wicked Lady*. And she was completely nuts about him.'

'Odd,' said Troy. 'Odd for her to have a type and then to choose so completely against it. If you ask me, Cockerell was much more the Edward Everett Horton type.'

Foxx smiled, laughed softly, but would not follow the tangent he had marked for her.

'But she did make a play for you, didn't she?'

'Yes. She did.'

'And?'

'And nothing.'

'Really? You didn't fancy my sister?'

'Of course I fancied your sister. But she was drunk—plastered, in fact.'

'And you were on duty?'

'Glad you appreciate it.'

'But you're off duty now?'

He said nothing.

'And I am, believe me, completely sober.'

He said nothing.

Foxx wound both hands in her hair. Toyed with idea of a beehive. She seemed to have either no sense of certainty—the hair, in the course of half an hour, had been up, down, over the left shoulder, over the right, and at one point gripped between her nose and her top lip like a fake moustache—she played with it constantly—or she lacked self-consciousness in a way Troy could only envy.

She dropped her hair, she dropped her towel and locked her hands around the back of his neck. It seemed like a long time since he had last been kissed, let alone so passionately as this. She drew back, placed a finger at the corner of his mouth, traced out the line of his lips with the edge of her nail.

'Let's go upstairs,' she said. 'I could fuck you silly.'

307

§73

Dawn was the time of day he hated most. It had none of the slippin' slidin', heartwarming glow of dusk—the horizontal sigh. It glared and it seared and it exposed. As the usage of centuries had it so rightly, it broke. Among the wreckage he found himself lying next to a young, blonde woman of extraordinary beauty. Her forehead was level with his chest. She stirred as he slid from between the sheets, rolled over and did not wake, shedding the covers as she turned to show the curve of her spine, the rising roundness of her backside as the last of the sheet clung to her. He crept downstairs to the kitchen, the tiles cold beneath his feet, the smell of the storm still poised in the air. He found half a bottle of flat Tizer in the fridge, and stood with his back to the door, swigging from it.

He was, in all probability, beguiled—he was most certainly bothered and bewildered—God knows, he might even be bewitched. But he knew beyond a whisper of a doubt that before the day was out he would be ... wild again.

He sank to the floor, still clinging to the Tizer bottle. However cold the tiles beneath his feet, colder still beneath the buttocks and balls. He drained the bottle, watched it roll away to the dark place beneath the sink, and then he stretched out on his side, full length across the floor.

Grab the thought now. Or lose it.

He was forty-one years old.

He had just let himself be seduced by a woman half his age.

It felt wild.

Wilder still.

> Awop
> > bop
> > > alubop
> > > > alop
> > > > > bam
> > > > > > boom.

And wild again.

§74

In the morning, Troy drove her to the station—St Pancras once more. Up the ramp to stop the Bentley by the red brick arch that led under the gothic hotel into the soot-blackened glass engine shed.

With her hand on the door, one foot on the ground and an irate cabbie honking behind them, Foxx turned to him and said, 'You'll tell me. Won't you? You won't just let it slip, you'll tell me?'

'Whatever I find out, I'll share with you.'

Her muscles tensed, the merest pressure on the car door, and then relaxed. She looked back at him again.

'You're married, aren't you?'

'What makes you think that?'

'Most men are married. Either to a woman or to the job.'

'Which am I?'

'Both,' she said.

§75

Dickie Muffins was the quietest of the four. At once the most and the least imaginative of the schooldays quartet of Charlie, Gus, Troy and Dickie. A born bookworm, with none of the daring of Gus or Charlie, and none of the intense, obsessive introspection of Troy. He had always followed the line of least resistance. To university at eighteen, a year at Harvard, and to the family business at twenty-two.

The family business was one of London's oldest private banks, with but a single branch, so small you might easily miss it altogether or mistake it for a private house, in Hanover Square, a stonesthrow from Regent Street.

He did not, Troy knew, give a damn about the bank. Joining had simply fulfilled his obligations to family—the line of least resistance—and allowed him endless free hours to pursue his first love—military history—in which field over the last ten years he had produced a definitive account of the Iberian Campaign and a well-reviewed life of Marshal Ney—uninterrupted save for the rare visit from one of his all too well-heeled customers. It said something for the scam Cockerell was working if he could afford an account at Mullins Kelleher for his mistress, without which Madeleine could not have had the use of the deposit box.

Troy did not see enough of Dickie, but that was entirely his own fault.

'Freddie. What a surprise. What brings you here?'

Dickie rose from a pile of books, his hand extended.

'It's business, Dickie.'

'Bugger—do I have to play the bank manager? What's up? Your sisters squandered the family fortune?'

Troy took the police 10 C 8 of Madeleine Kerr from his briefcase and laid it on top of the open book on Dickie's desk.

'Oh shit,' said Dickie. 'Oh shit. She's dead, isn't she? I saw a lot like that when I was in the ARP during the war. Not a mark on them, but dead as door nails from the blast.'

Troy laid the flat Mullins Kelleher key on top of the photograph.

Dickie stared at the juxtaposition for a moment or two, then reached behind him and laid a four-day-old *Evening Standard* next to it.

'MURDER ON THE BRIGHTON LINE.'

'It's her, isn't it, Freddie? She was the unnamed woman found dead on the Brighton train. And you're the unnamed policeman injured in pursuit of the murderer, aren't you?'

''Fraid so. Dickie, I need to know what's in that safety deposit box. I take it the box is in Madeleine's name?'

'Indeed it is. Mrs Madeleine Kerr. Never did come across Mr Kerr. I take it you don't have a warrant?'

'Not at this stage.'

'Or any stage?'

Troy shrugged. 'I do have the consent of Madeleine's next of kin.'

'In writing?'

Troy shook his head.

'There is the matter of probate. Probate takes a damn sight longer than four days.'

'She's dead, Dickie, and I do have the key.'

'Bugger. Bugger. Bugger.'

'Old pals' act?'

Dickie bustled out from behind the desk and its small mountain of books, pulling on his black jacket, trying to look like a banker.

'I'll need to get the second key, come on.'

Troy followed him down two floors to the vaults, through a thick steel outer door and a mesh inner door to a room of a thousand tiny doors.

Halfway up the wall Dickie inserted his key and beckoned to Troy. They both turned their keys at the same time and the tiny door swung sideways to reveal the handle of a long, narrow steel drawer.

Troy flipped the lid. Inside was a single envelope addressed simply 'Shirley'.

He tore it open. A single sheet of foolscap. A single sheet of utter gobbledegook. A numerical soup. And Sellotaped to the bottom were five small keys much like the one he had just used to open the box.

'Anything wrong, Freddie?' Dickie said.

Troy folded the paper.

'I'm going to have to take it away.'

Dickie slid the drawer back in and closed the door.

'My God, you ask a lot.'

'Tell me,' Troy said. 'Did Madeleine have much money in her account?'

'Now, you're asking too much. I can't possibly tell you that.'

'How far does the writ of the old pals' act run?'

'Not that far. You'll get me shot. Speaking of old pals. Seen anything of Charlie lately?'

'No,' said Troy. 'No, I haven't.'

Troy had tried ringing Charlie not long after his return from Vienna. It was news then. News he felt he should share with his oldest friend. It wasn't news now and he didn't feel like sharing it with anyone. Winding up the staircase, Dickie asked all the 'what's new?' questions and Troy muttered inconsequentially about things being 'much the same'.

He was letting Dickie down, and he knew it.

§76

Troy parked the car by St James's Park underground and went into the station to use a call box. He dialled his own number at the Yard. If he got Jack, then he would just press button B, get his pennies back and try later. It was Clark who answered.

'Are you alone?'

'Yes, sir. Mr Wildeve's in court today; the Old Bailey.'

'Do you know anything about codes?'

'You mean coded messages, that sort of thing?'

'Yes.'

'Trained in it, sir. Army Intelligence cryptography course at Camberley in 1947. And odd refreshers while I was in Germany.'

And, thought Troy, twenty years of doing the crossword in *The Times*.

'OK. I'm coming in.'

Ten minutes later he put the document he had taken from Mullins Kelleher in front of Clark.

Clark looked at it for less than a minute, and said, 'Piece of cake. Simple substitution. Number for letter. All you need to know is how far down the alphabet they start. Nobody's dim enough to go A–1, B–2—at least no one over the age of twelve. All I need is a little time without interruptions.'

He cocked his head in the direction of Wildeve's desk.

'If you catch my drift.'

'Quite,' said Troy.

Then it struck him that Clark meant more by the remark.

'Why don't you go home and read a book, sir?'

Clark pulled open the top drawer of his, that is Troy's, desk.

'Borrow anything you like.'

Not a bad idea, thought Troy, took *Lolita* off the top of the pile and shoved it in the pocket of his jacket. He made a quick telephone call to Nikolai, said goodbye to Clark and drove over to Knightsbridge. The only way Jack would ever find out he had been in Scotland Yard was if one of the blokes in uniform on the door mentioned it. That was pretty unlikely, he thought, as none of them would know that he was meant to be off sick.

Nikolai was outside Imperial College, waiting for him. Thin and grey, and looking smaller than ever—hatless and coatless in the summer sun. The flaps of a capacious double-breasted jacket waving unbuttoned as if to emphasise the slightness of his build. Without the winter weight of his astrakhan coat, he seemed to Troy to be stripped of all bulk, to be well on the way to becoming a wizened old man.

'You haff unerring copper's instinct, my boy. My stomach rumbles and tells me I will not get through to lunchtime, then you ring and invite me to early lunch. Leave your preposterous motor car here, and let us walk the length of Exhibition Road while giving thanks to the memory of Prince Albert.'

He slipped on a pair of ancient sunglasses, their lenses as dull and un-reflective as blackboards, and walked off southerly down the road. Troy found himself wondering about his gait. Was this an old man's shuffle? Prince Albert's achievement got very little of the old man's attention. He asked for family gossip and, when it seemed that Troy had none, loaded him up with his own.

'What's got into your sister?' he asked.

'Which one?'

'Sasha.'

'Dunno. I can't remember when I last saw her.'

'She is up and down, up and down. Moody is an inadequate word to describe her. She swings from elation to misery.'

This, to Troy, about summed her up at any time, and he could not see what Nikolai was getting at.

'God knows. She's forty-six. Do you suppose . . . ?'

'Ach. Don't ask me. I'm a physicist. I know nothing of biology.'

They crossed the Cromwell Road, by the Victoria & Albert Museum. Nikolai pointed to the tiny traffic island, with its thick bottle-glass floor— a skylight to the dark, miserable tunnel that lay below.

'Do you remember,' he said, 'when you were a little boy? How we would come down the tunnel from the Underground station and climb the steps to emerge over there? You used to think it was a kind of magic to pop up out of nowhere into the middle of the traffic.'

It was one of those drifts of memory that were so characteristic of his grandfather and were getting more typical of Nikolai with age. Troy now realised where they were heading. To the Polish caff at the end of the road. It was handy. Nikolai spoke passable Polish and, a couple of hundred yards from his office, it provided a substitute for the Russian he could not hear, and a choice of dozens of sickly-sweet sticky cakes. Troy had eaten with him there many times, although he cared little for Polish food, and doubted whether the countless Polish exiles who frequented the place cared much for an old man who spoke their language with a marked Russian accent.

They slurped their way through a bloody borscht, then Nikolai aired his cracked Polish and ordered Pierogi. Dumplings. With salmon and sour cream. Fried dumplings—Пирожки. Pirozhki—the code word Khrushchev's man at the embassy had given him.

'Tell me,' Troy said. 'Why would anyone want to spy on the *Ordzhonikidze?*'

'Who, if I might ask, is anyone?'

'The British. And I use the word loosely.'

Nikolai bit into his pierogi, chomped and shrugged.

'No reason I can think of.'

'Could you be a bit more forthcoming? Or do I have to wait till you've eaten your way through the menu?'

'The British—or if I may be so bold as to call them "we"—we have no reason to spy on the *Ordzhonikidze* because we know all there is worth knowing about it, and have done since 1953. It is a *Sverdlov* class cruiser. The *Sverdlov* itself sailed from the Baltic to Odessa in that year. It anchored at Spithead as the Soviet gesture for the Coronation. We surveyed it again from Malta, and again last year when it paid a visit to Portsmouth. There is nothing we don't know. The *Ordzhonikidze* is identical. A typical ship of her class. There are at least a dozen like her. I could show you a deck plan if you so wished.'

'Did you know Khrushchev offered to sell her to the Royal Navy while we were in Greenwich?'

'A joke, perhaps?'

'Of course it was a joke, but his jokes were never just surface. He meant what he said about it being almost obsolete. And if it is, why would anyone spy on her?'

'I don't know. Khrushchev allowed a British naval officer to travel all the way from Baltisk with them—if I am to believe MI5 gossip, the Russians even boasted that they got him drunk on Khrushchev's birthday and let him roam at will. On the weekend they were here they even threw the ship open to tourists. They have no secrets. We know they have no secrets. They know we know they have no secrets.'

'But Cockerell did spy on the ship.'

'So I'm told. You are certain it was Cockerell, by the way?'

'I identified the body myself.'

Nikolai shrugged again.

'Did they show you his kit?'

'His kit?'

'His frogman's gear. It was, I am reliably informed, ten years out of date. The sort of thing that had not been issued to a naval frogman since the war. Very far from being the new equipment he was supposed to be testing. None of the modern gadgetry.'

'Such as?'

'Closed-circuit oxygen systems.'

'Meaning?'

'It's like the condenser on a steam engine. It leaves no trail of bubbles. A frogman is virtually undetectable. No one would be able to see him.'

'Somebody did. Or we wouldn't be having this conversation. No, they didn't show me anything. But it fits, doesn't it? The man himself is ten years too old for the job. Ten years out of condition. And stupid enough to attempt an underwater swim on a full stomach. It's all wrong. It's an Alice-in-Wonderland kind of espionage, isn't it? A Looking-Glass War.'

'Indeed it is. Are you on for cheesecake?'

Troy wondered at the old man's skinniness. He had never known a time when he did not eat enough for two. Perhaps that was the paradox of wasting away. Nikolai was much his father's junior, but even so he must be seventy-five or six. How long would he go on playing war games? Grateful though Troy was that he played them for the moment.

'Doesn't it look to you like a rogue operation? A bunch of amateurs, not the spooks?'

'Yes it does, but the newspapers and my sources tell me otherwise. It is held to be official. And besides, Her Majesty's Government has owned up to it.'

'That's the oddest thing. Why did they do it? Why not just deny it? Until the body was washed up, it was just another Russian rant. Even with the body, it was deniable.'

'There I disagree. Enough people in Fleet Street knew about it. They knew Cockerell was missing. It was easy to draw the right and wrong conclusion. Besides, if the body were not Cockerell, where is Cockerell?'

'Fleet Street could have been smothered with a D notice.'

'Yes, but then there is the matter of your brother. Rod almost single-handedly forced an admission out of the Government. In fact, Sir Norman Spofford—you know who I mean . . . ?'

'No.'

'We're sitting in his constituency right now. I see him from time to time. He's one of those backbench Tories, utterly opposed to Eden—Spofford told me that Rod had almost certainly been wholly responsible for getting Eden to spill the beans. And Rod is not subject to D notices. There was virtually no way to shut him up. To own up may well have been the best chance of getting him to shut up. To let rumour run, and denial merely feeds rumour, was probably the worst solution. Someone up there took a decision to end the matter by admission, and by admission to contain it—damage limitation as Newspeak has it. Personally I think that was the biggest lie of all. But it was plausible. Whereas the notion that Cockerell might have acted alone was not. Am I to take it that you have confirmation of this from someone, that Commander Cockerell was indeed a rogue?'

'Yes,' said Troy.

'Fine. Someone you can trust? No. Don't tell me. I don't want to know. We are in this too deep already. It is almost a family affair. Rod has been stirring mightily. It does, by the way, prompt me to say that if it gets out that you were the last man to see Cockerell alive, then someone might put two and two together, your part in the matter and Rod's, and make five.'

Nikolai worked his way through a hefty slice of cheesecake. Troy sipped Russian tea, thinking as he did every time he succumbed to tradition that he much preferred it with milk, and that whatever their other failings—and they were legion—the English were still the only tribe that knew how to make a good cup of tea.

'What,' Nikolai asked, puffing out a fine dust of icing sugar from his beard, plucking words out of the air that Troy had thought he had uttered and discarded, 'do you mean by "a Russian rant"?'

Troy thought about it. 'Do it!'

'I think,' he began slowly, 'I think Khrushchev wanted something to happen. I think the incident came gift-wrapped and it must be pissing him off no end that it's not turned out to be a clear propaganda victory.'

Nikolai beckoned to the waitress, and ordered another helping of cheesecake.

'Suddenly you are the master of understatement. It is, in the language of football, an own goal. Or to put it another way, the Prime Minister has shot himself in the foot so many times that the cook at Number 10 uses his shoes to strain the vegetables.'

Out in the street, retracing their steps, Nikolai put on the sunglasses again, squinted up at the sky, decided he did not need them and dropped them into the breast pocket of his jacket. He set off. Yes. The walk was definitely sliding slowly into a shuffle. Once more he rummaged among Troy's words.

'You say you half not seen Sasha in a while?'

Troy did not answer. In the keen ear of the mind he heard the surface break over a rising 'you know what your trouble is?' The old man walked on slightly ahead of him, throwing the words over his shoulder.

'Yet she is at Mimram most weekends. Is she not?'

He paused. Troy declined the bait.

'Ergo you half not been to Mimram. Ergo you half not seen your wife.'

Troy quickly drew level. He was damned if he'd talk to his back.

'If you're about to utter a catechism of cliché along the lines of "marry in haste, repent at leisure", or "mixed marriages never work", then don't. I don't want to hear it.'

Nikolai looked up at him, the beginning of a twinkle in his eye.

'Far from it, my boy. The regret was all mine. The first time I saw her I wished I were thirty years younger.'

§77

He lay on the bed and opened *Lolita*. He read the first sentence: 'Lolita, light of my life, fire of my loins,' and by the second do-re-mi recitation of Lo-lee-ta knew he was defeated. He took the copy of *Casino Royale*

317

off the bedside table—the one he had pinched from Cockerell's office —and decided to read it again. He was less disturbed this time by its author's lush, almost surreal prose than he was intrigued by the mind of its erstwhile reader, the late Commander Cockerell. Was this how he saw himself? Smooth, charming and vulnerable in a brutal, mannish sort of way? Troy looked at the cover. More than a little lurid, with an artist's impression of James Bond in black and white at the bottom. Cockerell, with his weaselly face, pencil-line moustache and air of self-regarding weediness, looked nothing like this ideal. If anything it resembled the actor Eric Portman, a rather old-fashioned English face, strong in the nose and jaw—much more like Rod than like Cockerell. Cockerell was much more a poor man's—if not an outright beggar's—Ronald Colman. And that was the generous view. The painfully truthful view invoked the name of Edward Everett Horton, in all his spindly bumbling, once more. God save us all from self-awareness, thought Troy.

He had to admit it was still a good read, and he made a mental note to pick up a few more Flemings the next time he was in the Charing Cross Road. The plot, the outcome of this one, made him think of the Marlowe line: '. . . but that was in another country and besides, the wench is dead.' Dead wenches were terribly useful to plots in novels, particularly if, like Fleming, you wanted to keep your hero unencumbered and tortured in the soul. God knows, Fleming gave Bond enough torture of the body as it was—Troy winced as he read the scene in which Bond is thrashed across the bollocks with a rattan carpet-beater. What kind of a mind thought these things up? What kind of a man did Arnold Cockerell think he was, in his own mind? Did that drab, duplicitous little life long to see itself tortured, grieving at the grave of a dead bitch for the rest of his days, whilst carelessly fucking all the others? Troy had, he realised too late, just formulated the plot of the cheap novelette of his own life for the last ten years or more. And it hurt like hell. God save us from self-awareness.

The phone rang and saved him from a reflection that was utterly futile.

'Hello, Troy? You there?'

Troy heard the familiar if rare tones of Tom Driberg. Driberg had not called him at home in years. The precedent did not augur well.

'Yes, Tom. I'm off sick, as a matter of fact.'

It was a losing tactic. Appealing to Driberg's sense of tactful consideration for the poorly was as likely to put him off as it was a charging rhino, for the same pachydermous reasons.

'I don't suppose you could come over?' Driberg went on as though Troy had not said what he had. 'Bit of a pickle.'

Driberg was a master of understatement. In all likelihood, a bit of a pickle meant police involvement somewhere.

'Who is it this time?'

'It's not what you think.'

'Is it you?' Troy asked with visions of outraged bobbies in public lavatories, enforcing the unenforceable.

'Honestly, Troy. It's something else entirely. Take my word. Buggery has no part of it.'

'Delighted to hear it. I suppose you'll tell me it can't wait, all the same.'

'Well . . .' Driberg stalled.

'Don't worry, Tom. I'll be round in an hour or so. I could do with the air.'

He rang off. Driberg could lie for Britain. Troy knew in his bones that he had fallen foul of the law and was, as before, appealing to Troy's rank in the force to cover up some queer indiscretion. If not his own, then some crony's. Rod would have a fit. Just before the last election Driberg had asked Troy whether he could put in a word with Rod—in the eventuality of Labour winning he thought it was high time he got a ministerial post. No, had been Troy's answer. He knew damn well what Rod thought of Driberg. Almost without pause Driberg had shifted the conversation round to one of his escapades—the time he had blown a guardsman on duty at Buckingham Palace, after dinner with George VI and Queen Elizabeth. A couple of beers later he once again tried to coax Troy into 'having a bit of chat with your brother'. There was, it seemed, no natural division in the man's mind to prevent him rolling the distastefully disparate into a single conversation. Not that Driberg lacked all discretion. Or else he would have been nicked long ago.

The flat Driberg had was not the same one he had had during the war. Troy was relieved at that. His mildly superstitious sense bristled at the memory of finding Neville Pym there all those years ago, with all the consequences that followed. Perhaps he was wrong after all. Perhaps

Driberg just wanted to natter. The Driberg who opened the door to him certainly seemed to be relaxed. He had a glass in his hand, and as he led Troy to the narrow window terrace, no more than a shelf above the street, he snatched a bottle of malt off the coffee table. Troy glanced down at the table. Driberg was an inveterate reader of poetry. A slender volume of Philip Larkin lay face down—*The Less Deceived*—its pages splayed in lieu of a bookmark. The flat was tiny, serving Dnberg as nothing more than a London base, but the walls were lined with bookshelves. The man read more than anyone else he knew, short of his Uncle Nikolai. Troy remembered Ian Fleming, with whom he had passed a long afternoon, and for a fleeting second felt the pointless pinprick of cultural guilt.

Out on the terrace there was just enough room for two upright chairs, but the impulse was right. It was an evening to take in the passing of day and watch London wend its way home and then work its way out into the street again. Summer in the city. Well worth it as a spectator sport; beat the goggle-box any night. A pleasing variation on Troy's verandah habit.

Driberg sloshed three fingers of whisky into a glass and handed it to Troy. It might just turn out to be a pleasant evening after all. When he didn't have a bee in his bonnet, Driberg could be the best of company. Pushed, even Rod would admit that Tom was a wag.

'I've been in Russia,' he said.

'I know,' said Troy.

'I got my interview with Khrushchev.'

'I noticed,' said Troy. 'Congratulations.'

'Hang on, there's more.'

Driberg paused. Swirled his scotch, and then, almost against the grain of character, weighed up his words.

'When it was over—or at least when I thought it was over—this other chap was summoned, and I found myself interviewed. Tables turned. If you see what I mean?'

Troy didn't.

'What other chap?'

'Serov. Victor Serov.'

Troy began to see all too clearly.

'Ivan Serov?'

'Dunno. Could be, I suppose. Victor. Ivan. That sort of name.'

'The head of the KGB?'

'That's the feller.'

Suddenly Troy could see for miles and very little of what followed caused him to raise a single hair of an eyebrow. It might just be a pleasant evening, but Troy could feel it begin to slip away from him. Serov, after all, was a nasty piece of work. He had been shown the diplomatic door in March or April, when Khrushchev had been stupid enough to send him on ahead, and he was surely the man who, Nikolai had predicted, would not live to collect his pension.

'Khrushchev sends for this chap,' Driberg went on. 'The interpreter stays put, and the next thing I know he's asking me to spy for them.'

This was not sufficient to break the stride of the conversation. The only thing that disturbed Troy was that only Driberg would ever dream of having a conversation like this on a balcony. Down in the street the citizens of London, Her Majesty's subjects, in whose name all this cloak and dagger nonsense was conducted, shuffled around between home and job, stopping-off points on the way to the grave. It reminded Troy of Eliot's office workers teeming across London Bridge—he had not known death had 'undone so many'. Oblivious to the culture of deceit in which they swam like fish in water, dreaming dreams of better days—or as his wife had so bluntly put it 'still harping on about the goddam war'. One day, thought Troy, they might even come to look back fondly on the bizarre equilibrium of the cold war—if it ever ended.

'And what did you say?'

'I was a bit flummoxed. You can imagine.'

'Of course.'

'I found myself thinking what their next move might be after I said no—the Lubyanka? A salt mine? The Dissident Ladies' Touring Orchestra of East Siberia? But then, when it came down to it I was more interested in what happened if I said yes. I mean, it's not as if I know any secrets. Five years in opposition—Gaitskell doesn't tell me a bloody thing. If he were PM I doubt he'd give me the time of day. So I said, "What exactly is it that you want me to do?" I was expecting Serov to answer. The interpreter was looking at him as he spoke, but it was Khrushchev who chipped in. "We want you," he said, "to spy on the Labourites." For a second or two I didn't know what he meant. Then I realised he meant the party. Us. The Labour Party! I tell you, Troy, could have knocked me down with a feather.'

Troy sipped at his whisky. *Déjà vu*.

'That night at the Commons,' he said, 'when George Brown got right up Khrushchev's nose. He got it into his head that Labour was some sort of anti-Soviet group. George makes a strong impression at the best of times, and this was one of the worst, as I'm sure you'll recall. Khrushchev thinks George is really representative of the party. And he thinks he might be some sort of disaffected Trotskyite. Which is about as far from the truth as you could get. That, plus Rod giving him that list of missing East European dissidents and what-have-you stuck in his mind. In fact, I'd say it irritated the hell out of him. I told him what the party was, but it was all to a deaf ear. He's asking you to spy on the Labour Party because he seriously thinks it's a threat. Possibly the only man in Europe who does, but . . . What did you do, tell him Gaitskell would soon have his finger on the button?'

'Not exactly,' Driberg paused. Let Troy sip a little more of the malt. 'I told him I'd do it.'

Nice, thought Troy. Get yourself out of that one, Tom. But, of course, the whole point in Troy's being there was that Driberg expected something of him. Surely, even in his wildest imaginings, he did not think Troy could get him out of this?

'Tell me, Tom. Did Nikita Sergeyevich offer you a tot of vodka by any chance?'

'Well, yes. Several, as a matter of fact.'

'Fine. Now, let me get this straight. After a few too many, one over the eight, your hollow leg brimming with the spirit, you tell the leader of the Soviet Union and his head of KGB that you'll spy on the Labour Party for them?'

Driberg drew in his breath, let it out slowly, as though what followed needs must be precision.

'Sort of,' he muttered.

'Sort of?'

'Well. Obviously I won't but . . .' The sentence vanished into the vagueness from which it came. A hand waved out into nowhere indicating a vast whatever.

'Let me put it this way, Tom. What on earth do you expect me to do?'

'Well,' Driberg perked up, almost smiled. 'You know the bugger. You've spent more time with Khrushchev than anyone else in England. You must be the envy of half the spooks in MI5. Can you trust him? is what I want to know.'

'I'd hate to *have* to trust him,' said Troy hoping the remark was not too obscure for what appeared to be a bad day for Driberg's intelligence. And at the back of his mind dreading the day he would ever have to place his trust in a man like Nikita Khrushchev.

'But if push comes to shove?'

'Tom, he's a politician!'

'Bad as that, eh?'

'Yes. And if you take my advice you'll tell the spooks before one of their moles tells them first.'

'Yeees,' said Driberg slowly, musing. 'I was going to have a natter with them a bit later on in the week. It was just . . . the money, you see.'

'Eh?'

'The money. They weren't expecting me to do it for nothing. Gave me five hundred pounds up front. Told me they had a network. Absolutely untraceable. They could pay money to me in Britain, and it would never be traced back to Russia. I've spent a few bob of it already. You know, souvenirs. That sort of thing.'

Troy did not believe a word of this. The idea of Driberg blowing hundreds of pounds on concentric wooden Russian dolls and odd boxes to keep fags in was pretty well preposterous. This was simply Driberg's way of stating that he was broke. It was in Driberg's nature always to feel broke, regardless of circumstances—and his circumstances were that he was out of the House, after stepping down at the 1955 election, and probably feeling very broke and very sorry for himself—but Troy knew damn well that literary London was awash with rumours that he had recently taken a large advance—one never heard rumours of small advances—from a publisher, the Viennese *émigré* George Weidenfeld, to write a biography of Burgess. He was just about the last person Troy would have trusted to write such a book, and he doubted whether George would get his money's worth, but he rather thought that this had bankrolled the trip to Russia. All Driberg was saying was that if at all possible he'd like to have his cake and eat it—to tell MI5 and somehow hang onto the loot.

'If they've got a network, why did they take the risk of giving you cash?'

'Network temporarily out of commission,' Serov said. Asked if I minded cash, much the same way one asks a chap if he minds a cheque when one knows damn well the bloody thing'll bounce. I wasn't crazy about carrying that much boodle through customs, but then they hardly look for currency coming in. Much more concerned about it going out. And they'd be back to business as usual in a few weeks, Serov reckoned. I didn't ask what he meant.'

Troy knew exactly what he meant. Angus had used precisely the same argument to him when Troy had queried the money-laundering operation in which Cockerell was so patently involved. Driberg was an unlikely source for the confirmation Troy had sought, but here it was. The piece of the puzzle that made it all make sense. This was what the man had been up to with all those phoney figures and floating thousands. It was logical. Soon enough, they'd replace him. A new courier would be found, and any minute now some of the world's worst carpet-patterns would be magically transformed into a healthy row of noughts in Driberg's bank account.

'I think you've no choice about this, Tom. Tell the spooks. Give them the money and let them take care of it. At the very least you'll get an anecdote for your memoirs out of it.'

'Oh really,' said Driberg rather too keenly. 'Do you think anyone will want to read them?'

§78

A dozen times in the weeks since he had been summoned to Portsmouth to look at the bloated mess that once had been Arnold Cockerell, it had crossed Troy's mind to call Charlie. Each time he had put it off. He had never, on any Scotland Yard case, asked a favour of Charlie. It would break the silent agreement they had made many years ago, at the end of the war, when the fiction of Charlie the Diplomat had first been launched; it would make of his work the last thing either wished it to be, an issue between them, that ran the constant risk that it might divide them.

It was almost dusk when he got back from Driberg's, a little the worse for the whisky, clutching *The Less Deceived,* which Driberg had thrust on him. He reached for the phone, not at all sure what he would say if Charlie answered.

There was haste, a tearing urgency even in the word 'hello'.

'It's Freddie.'

'Freddie,' Charlie slipped into charm mode, effortlessly. 'Long time no see, but sad to say it may yet be longer. I have a cab at the door.'

'I just wanted to—'

'And a plane waiting. Sorry. Blame Colonel Nasser. I'm flying to Akrotiri tonight. If it can wait I'll call you the minute I'm back. Honestly. Must dash!'

Troy said a snatched goodbye and hung up. He remembered what Charlie had read at Cambridge in the early thirties—Arabic. All British diplomats were Arabists. That, too, was part of the fiction. It somehow lifted them onto a plane of academic respectability. To read German or Russian might mean you really wanted to be a spy, to read Economics or Philosophy might mean you were too bright to be a spy, and as everyone who was too thick to read anything else read History, Arabic did nicely, tinged, as it was, with a little learning and a little empire, smacking of T.E. Lawrence and St John Philby. He could not believe for one second that Charlie had ever thought he'd be called upon to use it, but what other purpose could there be in sending him to Cyprus? Cyprus, after all, did not matter. Everyone who was anyone knew that sooner or later the British would give Cyprus to the Cypriots. Egypt—Egypt was another matter.

§79

Clark called on Troy the next morning. It was gone nine. Troy was being lazy. Still in his dressing gown. Still sipping coffee and flicking through the morning paper. He had read a page of Nabokov and felt better about it, and a page of Larkin and felt even better about that. He opened the door to see Clark standing in the eastern light, staring up at the warmth of sun edging in over Bedfordbury, much as Troy's pigs would do at any opportunity. He turned to Troy and smiled.

'Cracked it, sir,' he said simply.

Troy swung back the door and Clark bustled in. He took a sheaf of papers from his jacket pocket and quickly unfolded them at the dining table. Troy sat down, pushed a cup and the cafetière towards Clark. Clark ignored it. He was brimful of enthusiasm, the customary demeanour of misery, his habitual disguise—all good coppers needed one, Troy thought—temporarily suspended.

'I can't stop long. It was a piece of cake. The only thing that threw me was the knock-on. Every repetition would move on two, but every pattern of five, she'd move on three. I think she must have been a darts player. Still, it was vowels more often than not.'

'She?' Troy queried. He had not been at all certain whether it was the work of Cockerell or of Madeleine.

'It was written by a woman, sir. You'll see. An amateur too, but a good one. Someone who took a real delight in deception. The satisfaction of a good red herring.'

It took Troy back a little to realise how much Clark had been able to deduce of the character of Madeleine Kerr from a simple cryptogram. She had been a delightful liar, he thought. She had paid a terrible price for her lies. Was this the reason?

'Skip the technical stuff, you're talking to man who's never finished a crossword in his life.'

'Right you are, sir.'

Clark sat down opposite Troy, breathed deeply and began to read.

'Dear Sis—does that make sense to you, sir?'

'Yes—just read the lot, Eddie.'

Dear Sis, if you are reading this then the chances are that daft bugger Ronnie's gone and got us both killed. And there's nothing I can say here that'll hurt you more than I have already so I'll tell you the lot and let you make your own mind up.

I know you thought I was a prat for going off with him. And I know you thought Brighton was nothing much. But it got me out of Derbyshire, didn't it? It got me out of an office and a life of shorthand typing. It got me out of the prospect of marrying some dozy bugger off the mill floor, who might just make foreman if he worked his balls off for the rest of his life. It got me out of a semi on a fucking council estate. Sorry. I said I wouldn't hurt you anymore. Didn't mean that. Well, my love, it wasn't Brighton. There was more to that, just as there was to Ronnie. You could never see that side of him, could you? I told you he'd whisked me off my feet and you should have believed me. I knew the risk and I took it—and I don't mean the risk of another woman's husband. Sis—I've seen Paris. I've seen Amsterdam, I've seen West Berlin. I've played Chemin de Fer in Monte, I've skied in Zermatt, I've browned me tits on the beach at St Tropez, I've been pissed as a fart in Biarritz—and I've watched Ronnie run circles round MI5 and the Russians.

Now, I don't want you to be alarmed at this. There's a lot of loose ends to be picked up. If you want to do it, it'll set you up for life. If you don't, put this lot on the fire and walk away from it.

Ronnie and me smuggled money. The Russians gave it to us in cities all over Europe and Ronnie pushed it through the business. Where it went after that I don't know. Ronnie never told me and I didn't ask. We were careful. None of the people Ronnie dealt with ever saw me. I saw them, but they didn't see me. But like I said, if you're reading this we slipped up somewhere, didn't we? There's money in five banks. At the Banque du Commerce Coloniale in Paris, and the National Bank of South Africa in Zurich, at Gebrüder Hesse also in Zurich, at The Merchant Orient in Amsterdam and at the Monégasque Premiere in Monte Carlo. Somewhere in the region of forty or fifty thousand quid, I think. It's all legit—Ronnie's cut. He swindled nobody. We deserved every last penny of it.

There's also a list of everyone I ever saw or everyone Ronnie ever told me about in the game. This is dangerous stuff, but it might protect you if you know. On the other hand, it might just get you killed. But—like I said—you can walk away from it if you want.

See you in heaven, my lovely.

Clark paused breathily. When he picked up again his voice had dropped almost to a whisper.

'It's signed "Stella", and then there's a list of numbers matching the keys you gave me to the banks.'

Troy felt the weight of silence. Clark's professional satisfaction had not blinded him to the inherent sadness in the letter. A dead woman who referred to the conspiracies of complex, devious organisations as a game. A romantic fool who'd paid with her life for what amounted to no more than a series of dirty weekends with a man twice her age in the fashionable watering holes of Europe—a deadly holiday in a class not her own—a deadly 'game' of which she could scarcely have grasped the purpose. Troy was stunned. He was not surprised. Since the day Angus had told him Cockerell was running a racket, what else could it have been? What else, after what Driberg had told him, could it be? How it must have appealed to the vanity of the man, to be so deliciously out of his depth in the gaming rooms of Monte Carlo, with a woman as beautiful as Madeleine Kerr on his arm. To be seen with her, simply to be seen with her—and all the time kidding themselves it was their secret, the fond illusion that they saw without being seen. What did she mean by 'Ronnie ran circles' round the spooks? What did she mean? When it came down to brass tacks the war had done for Arnold Cockerell as surely as it had done for those it killed quickly and those it killed slowly in the years that followed. He had died of not recovering, of not wanting to recover from that brief taste of adventure, that exhilarating rush of adrenaline. But Troy doubted that he had run circles around anyone—the spooks had him. They loved romantic fools. They were better than cannon fodder.

'Sir?'

Clark was looking quizzically at him, beckoning him back to the moment.

'I can't stay long,' he said again.

'Of course. How did you manage to get away?' Troy asked.

'Mr Wildeve's in Hammersmith, sir. Body under the floorboards. Terrible niff. The neighbours called the Yard.'

'And Stan?'

'Mr Onions? Funny you should ask, sir. Nobody's seen him since Saturday.'

'Not funny at all,' said Troy.

He went back to the kitchen and returned with the *Post*. He folded the paper open at page five—Overseas News.

'Read this,' he told Clark.

'What this? "British Soldier Murdered in Cyprus"?'

328

Clark's eyes flashed down the page; he read the whole piece in a matter of seconds.

'I don't get it, sir. Who is Flight Sergeant Kenneth Clover?'

'He was Onions' son-in-law. "Our Valerie's" husband.'

'I see. Poor bugger. Tortured to death and dumped in a ditch with a placard round his neck. Nasty way to go.'

'Not the first. Not the last. There've been a dozen or more this year. EOKA mean to have us out. Flight Sergeant Clover was the poor sod in the middle.'

'Did you know 'im, sir?'

'Yes. I knew him. I knew Valerie too. Onions will be in Salford with his daughter.'

'Why has he told no one?'

'He'll have told anyone who matters, the Commissioner, his secretary—he might even have told me if I'd been around—but he'd never let the reason be commonly known. This will make Stan mad as hell. Rage is one of the few ways he knows to register feeling. He'd be embarrassed to think his family and its troubles were being talked about.'

'Troubles don't come much bigger than this,' Clark said softly.

'Quite,' said Troy. 'But he'll handle it alone. I was a sergeant when his wife died. I've seen him this way before.'

Clark got up. Looked without loss at his cold cup of coffee.

'I'd best be off. I think Mr Wildeve may be in Hammersmith a while. I'll be able to call you a bit more often. I must say, sir. I thought I'd left my days of discretion behind me in Berlin. I've told more lies since I came to work for you than I have since I flogged black market stockings.'

Troy showed Clark to the door and stepped into the sunlight of the yard. Warm sun on his face, cold flagstones under his bare feet.

'I trust it's not an imposition?'

Clark blinked up at the sun, one hand to his forehead, shielding his eyes.

'Lord no, sir. I was born to play Leporello. And what's life without a bit on the side?'

Troy watched him amble off towards St Martin's Lane. He understood exactly what Clark meant. It summed up the fat, little rogue he had met in Berlin in the bleak years very well—but it was also the philosophy that had got Cockerell and Kerr killed. He wondered if he should tell him about Tosca. He never had. Simply let it be known that he had married quietly. On the Continent. An old flame. Clark had said a swift 'congratu-lations', and that was that. But he knew. In his bones Troy knew he knew.

Back in the house Troy could hear the telephone ring. He kicked the door to behind him, picked up the receiver. All his instincts told him it would be Onions. It was.

'You'll have heard by now,' he said without preamble.

'Yes, Stan. It was in the morning paper. Terrible news. I'm so sorry.'

He heard Onions sigh deeply, heard the laboured effort of self-restraint. The pause skirted infinity.

'D'ye think you could come up? She's askin' for you.'

'When?'

'Funeral's the day after tomorrow. I don't suppose you could get here today?'

'I don't think I could,' Troy answered, thinking on his toes. 'But to-morrow's fine. I could be there in good time tomorrow.'

He jotted down the address Onions gave him—a back street in the red brick wilderness of Salford's Lower Broughton. He was deeply sorry for Stan. The relationship with Ken had been nothing special, in fact it had often seemed to Troy that the two men had nothing in common but the link that was Valerie, but Valerie was emotional enough for the three of them, and to be left alone to handle her at a time like this . . . all that duty demanded of Onions would not be enough.

He had from time to time wondered how much Stan knew. That Troy and Valerie had been an item in the last, tense summer before the war, he surely knew. It had been no secret, and they had both been single. It was the reason he sent for Troy now—another emotional buffer-zone to place between himself and the whirlwind that Valerie could whip up. Troy prayed to God that Onions did not know that they had also briefly been an item once more in the spring of 1951, while Ken was in Korea. He doubted that Onions would sanction adultery, but more than that his attitude towards young Jackie Clover, his only grandchild, was protective in the extreme. Onions refrained from open judgement on Troy's morals—once, a few years ago, he had asked if he ever thought he would marry—Troy had uttered a decisive, if erroneous no—and any speculation on the sex life of a single, well-heeled man approaching forty had been left unspoken.

He shaved, dressed, felt through his hair to the ridge of torn skin and dried blood left on his scalp by the bullet, and rummaged around in the

330

small drawer set beneath the mirror on the hallstand. House keys, car keys and at the bottom, gathering dust onto its thin film of protective grease, a pair of gun-metal grey lock-picks. He took out his handkerchief, wiped them clean, slipped them into the pocket of his jacket, and caught sight of himself in the mirror. He felt at the scabrous ridge once more. It had ceased to hurt days ago, but he knew damn well that even if Wildeve had not imposed idleness upon him the medics would have, and if Kolankiewicz knew that he was about to cheat medicine once more—'fuck with the head,' as he would undoubtedly put it—he would call him smartyarse, call him crazy and explode with Polish anger.

He collected the Bentley. Drove down to Brighton. Picked the lock on the door of Madeleine Kerr's house. Stole four of her best outfits. Shoes to match. A suitcase to hold them. And was back in London by four in the afternoon. By six o'clock the next morning he was in the Bentley once more, driving north up a deserted Marylebone Lane, out of the Smoke, out of Cobbett's Wen, out in the direction of Watford and the Black Country and the Potteries and Manchester and the far-flung North. What the South, in all its imperial snobbery, still called the Provinces. England, Troy had learnt long ago, had few greater insults than to call you provincial. It implied you still wore woad.

§80

Clearly they were savages. It was a little after noon. He had just found St Clement Street, Lower Broughton, and was parked outside number 25. Before he had even pulled the key from the ignition a grubby face had pressed itself up against the window on the driver's side—nostrils flattened against the glass. Another head popped in at the open window on the passenger side.

'What kind of car is this Mister is it a Cadillac or a Packard or a Ferrari it's a big un in't it I've gorra dinky of a Caddy an a Packard an a Ferrari.'

The sentence had no pauses. An acute grammarian could not have driven in a comma with a sledgehammer.

Troy looked at the child—nine or ten at the most—full of curiosity, devoid of all knowledge.

'It's a Bentley,' Troy told him, trying very hard not to feel foolish.

'Bentley?'

'Yes.'

'Is it posh is it?'

'If you like.'

'D'thee mek dinkies of it?'

Troy waved the other child off the glass and opened the door. Over the top of the car the voluble child was just visible, craning upward, marginally short of climbing on the bodywork. A third savage had appeared from nowhere and was undertaking a personal test of the springs in the left-hand wing mirror with the flat of his hand. Behind him the vast bulk of Onions had appeared in the open doorway of number 25. A blonde, beautiful, sad-eyed girl of ten or so peeped round him at hip level.

'Probably,' Troy said to the boy.

Onions roared.

'Clear off. The lot of you!'

It had no effect. In the canteen at Scotland Yard grown men would leap to their feet and spill their pudding at such a sound from Onions. Indeed he had once seen Onions simply yell Constable Agnew's name only to see Agnew shoot bolt upright, recite his national service rank and number and click his heels together on the 'Sir!', deluded by the force of Onions' delivery into believing for a moment that he was back in the Army. They all looked at him, the newcomer even paused momentarily in his technical test of the mirror, but they also ignored him.

'I'll mind your car for a tanner,' said the first child.

'OK,' said Troy.

The boy held out a hand.

'C.O.D.,' Troy said.

'Yer what?'

'Cash on delivery. If the car's still here when I get back you get your sixpence.'

The boy shrugged his acceptance of the terms. Onions reached behind the house door, groping for his jacket. Jackie Clover stood on the step, the thin boundary between home and street, quite possibly the only one in the terrace that had not been freshly donkey-stoned, and scrutinised Troy. It was a disturbing gaze. Trying so hard to look as deep into Troy as she could. Surely she had no memory of him. It had been so long ago and she so small. She would not speak to him. Did not speak to Onions as he ruffled her hair and told her to tell her mother that they'd 'gone down the Grosvenor'. As they passed the Bentley Onions clipped the boy at the wing mirror round the ear without even looking at him.

§81

Onions ordered bread and cheese. A pint of mild each. Muttered that he had eaten nowt but his own cooking for three days. The barman slapped a doorstep of a slice in front of each of them. Silently Onions spooned a sticky brown pickle onto his plate, bent his back and shoulders into it and ate ravenously. It reminded Troy of the scene in *Great Expectations* when Magwitch, played by Finlay Currie, gorges himself out on the marshes with the food Pip has stolen for him. Was Valerie really that bad a cook? He'd never eaten a meal prepared by her; they'd always eaten out. He occasionally thought that this had been essential to the relationship. Even more than wanting to be fucked, Valerie wanted to be wined and dined. Life with Kenneth could not have been a box of delights. Even less so when he had returned home and whisked her from a backstreet in Shepherd's Bush to a backstreet in Salford.

Troy could stand the sound of stolid munching against the faint hum of lunchtime chatter no more.

'Had Kenneth been long in Cyprus?' he asked.

Onions unhunched from the food and looked across the table at him. There was relief in the stony eyes, their bright blue flattened to slate with grief and tiredness. He was glad Troy had broken the ice.

'Nobbut a fortnight. Went out there about the middle of the month. Bugger all notice. His entire squadron just told to pack and get on board a transport. Weren't even told where they were bound. Our Valerie found out where he was when she got a postcard. That was Friday. Telegramme came Saturday. Could be worse. Could have arrived before the damn card, I suppose.'

Troy could not eat. Would not have touched the beer in any case. He knew Onions well enough to know the explosion could not be far off.

'I mean. I ask yer. What in God's name was he doing there? What were British tommies doing in Cyprus?'

'Do you really want to know?'

'I wouldn't be askin' if I didn't, would I?' Onions snapped.

Troy knew that he could only let loose the wrath of Onions; he could not control or diminish it. He could only leach it and watch it flow down. It seemed to be what he should do.

'Cyprus has nothing to do with it,' he said. 'The nationalists have been bumping off the odd swaddie every so often, just like the Jews did in Israel under the mandate a few years back. That's just coincidence.'

'Ken died for a coincidence?'

'Yes. He wasn't there for any reason that matters to Cyprus, Cyprus is a floating island, the great Mediterranean aircraft carrier. A handy spot to launch the invasion of Egypt.'

'Jesus. Jesus,' Onions whispered.

Had he really not worked it out for himself? It was hardly more than six weeks since Nasser had seized the canal. Wasn't it obvious? Couldn't every sentient being in Britain see that we were heading into war?

'It's like . . . it's like Ken's death doesn't count.'

'Not to Eden it doesn't.'

'Eden?' Onions looked baffled by the word.

'He means to have Nasser. To humiliate him on the world stage.'

'He's mad.'

'Yes. Rod swears the man is certifiable.'

There was a pause. Troy felt the mood swing again. The softness of shock and incomprehension rising toward anger once more.

'He's the Prime Minister!'

'Yes.'

'I voted for the bastard.'

Troy should not have been shocked by this. The phenomenon of the working-class Tory was as English as morris dancing and the Last Night of the Proms. It was simply that he and Onions never talked politics, at least not domestic politics. He was, true to class, slightly in awe of it all, the party hardly mattered, he was unduly respectful of Rod whenever he came to the Yard. Yet the truth was clear. Stan had not voted for Eden, he had voted for Churchill through Eden, who in the eyes of men like Stan was no more or less than Churchill's shadow. That Churchill had to be booted from office almost gaga by his own party would be a mystery to Stan. Not worth the time it took to find it credible. Troy had seen this for himself. Waiting for Khrushchev at Number 10 he had bumped into Winston in a corridor, somewhat the worse for drink and by far the worse for age. Troy had no vanity that he would remember him. They had met a dozen times at his father's dinner table, but that had been during the wilderness years, the best part of twenty years ago, but he did expect that a man in full possession of his faculties might just remember where the bog was in a house he had occupied for the best part of ten years. He had shown him to the right door, and mimed zipping up his flies when the old man emerged agape with his shirt tail flapping like an elephant's ear.

'What the bloody hell are we doing in Cyprus? What in God's name have we got to do with the Gyppos? It's like the bloody Boer War all over again. What is this? The last bash at the wogs? I thought all that malarkey went out when I was a boy; I thought we'd just fought a war for a better world?'

Onions was shouting now. It was by far the longest political statement Troy had ever heard him make, wallowing in confusion and half-articulate sentiment though it was.

'No wonder the niggers are picking us off like flies. We've no business there. Let the niggers have bloody Cyprus, let 'em have the fucking desert!'

Out of the corner of his eye Troy could see the occasional turn of the head. Almost involuntary on the part of the odd lunchtime drinker. Not wanting to look. The entire street knew who Onions was. They must all know of his loss.

'What am I to tell our Valerie? That her husband was burned to a crisp with a bloody blow-lamp, had his teeth ripped out with pliers, just because we want one last go at the niggers before the Empire finally slips through our fingers? Is that it? Is that what I have to tell her?'

Silently the barman appeared at their table and set a large brandy next to Onions' elbow. Neither he nor Troy had touched their pints. Troy swapped his plate of bread and wedge for Onions' empty one. Stan downed the brandy in one, and started on his second plateful. He glanced up at Troy once or twice. There were tears in the corners of his eyes.

'Are you not hungry?' he said at last.

'I had something on the way. Stopped off just south of here at Dunham Park.'

Onions responded to the tactical shift. Accepted the burden of small talk.

'Know the place. Out Altrincham way. American base during the war, wasn't it?'

'From the look of it you'd think they left yesterday. Jerry cans all over the place, concrete bunkers, burnt-out jeeps. Mind you, a couple of centuries before that it was the delight of the landscape painters.'

'Sounds like a better reason for going.'

The silence fell like fine dust through sunlight. Onions ate. Fragments of pub talk began to filter through to Troy in meaningless snatches. He felt suddenly vacant in the teeth of Onions' unanswerable, so justifiable rage, and on the momentary *tabula rasa* of his mind the pieces of conversation scored an image so bizarre he turned around in his seat to see who was talking.

'Busby's Babes', the man was saying. It was the only decipherable phrase, and Troy saw in the mind's eye floating kaleidoscopes of pretty pre-war women dancing to formation camera-work and Irving Berlin tunes. Black-and-white glimpses of Dick Powell and Ruby Keeler. 'Remember My Forgotten Man'. The many death had left undone. Appropriate to the point of absurdity. Then the man holding forth jabbed the table top with his middle finger, drew a line in the sheen of beer-spill and said, 'Bobby Charlton's the man. He'll get us to the top this season,' and the image popped like a bubble blown from a pipe, as the reality pricked through. Football. He should have known. They were talking about football.

He turned back to Stan. He had all but demolished the second plateful.

'How is she?' Troy asked.

Stan did not look up.

'You'll see soon enough.'

'Taking it badly?' It was a lame remark. Stan looked up. Tears dried.

'Hysterical. You know Valerie. Any excuse.'

§82

They turned the corner from Great Clewes Street back into St Clement's. Troy's car stood out like a Sherman tank. The only car in the street. The donkey-stoned steps shone like false teeth—all except the Clovers', where Jackie sat exactly where Troy and Onions had left her. The boy with the model-car obsession was sitting on the bumper of the Bentley, a *Beano* in one hand, a slice of bread and dripping in the other. His lips moving softly as he read, oblivious to all around him. At the end house a young woman in a wrap-around overall and a headscarf stood in the doorway taking the sun and smoking a roll-up. Wisps of auburn hair peeped out from under the scarf. It was a stunningly beautiful face. Troy stared a moment too long and she puckered up, blew him a kiss and winked at him. It was the sort of thing Tosca would do, he thought.

'Where's your Mam?' Onions said to the girl.

'She said to tell you she's gone for a lie down, Grandad.'

Jackie paused, screwed up her face to look straight up at Onions.

'Will she be tekkin' me ter Lewises?' she asked.

'I shouldn't think so.'

'But she promised.'

'When was this?'

'Last week.'

'That was before ... before ...'

The child waited. Troy had little expectation that Onions would get to the end of the sentence.

'If Val's asleep,' he said, 'I've time to kill. No point in waking her. I'll take Jackie into Manchester, if you like.'

Jackie stood up, went through elaborate gestures of dusting herself off and smoothing down her skirt.

'Can I sit up front?'

Before Troy could grant her wish a small voice behind him said, 'Can I have me tanner now?'

§83

She let Troy buy her a pair of white ankle socks and an Alice band. They seemed to be all she wanted. The decision took most of the afternoon and necessitated a full, floor-by-floor tour of Manchester's largest department store, its cornucopia. For more than fifteen years there'd been next to nothing to buy. The modesty of her choice was entirely in keeping with the modesty of the times.

On the way home she peered out of the window less intently than she had done on the way into the city. As they crossed the Irwell Bridge she asked Troy who he was.

Onions served tea with bread and jam on the oilcloth-covered table in the back room. Valerie made no appearance. Onions took up a tray and brought it down an hour later untouched.

'Bugger,' he said under his breath.

Troy lied when asked if he would stay the night. Told Onions he had booked a room at the Midland. He could see little point in exhausting the pair of them with boredom if tomorrow he had to face Valerie, and do whatever it was that Onions felt himself ill-equipped to do.

§84

It ought to be raining, he thought. Pissing it down in knives and forks like it did that dismal November when they buried his father. Tearing across the sky in sheets as it had done at Debussy's funeral—a snippet he only knew because his mother had remarked on the weather and the similarity. He had never known that she had known the man. All those years practising the piano at her behest, and such was the woman's nature that she had never before bothered to tell him that she had known Debussy in her youth, that he had taught her the instrument when she was eight years old, that she had journeyed to France on a wet day in

1918 to see him buried in a godgiven storm, to the rival thunder of the German bombardment. A fact as buried as the corpse until the funeral of her husband prompted the randomness of memory in her, exactly as it was now doing in Troy. Perhaps funerals were Chinese boxes, always another within.

Streaming, dazzling sunshine seemed irreverent to the dead. Detrimental to the living. It showed the black of mourning in all its shabbiness. Every streak and speck and fleck turned the garb of mourning into a motley.

He had sat up front in the old black Rolls-Royce. Valerie sat between her father and daughter, crying silently throughout behind the veil. She had risen at noon that day, acknowledged Troy with the single use of his christian name, accepted a peck on the cheek from her daughter and said nothing to Onions' desultory attempt at chatter. She retreated to the bathroom with a cup of tea and emerged forty minutes later in her widow's weeds. They sat a long half-hour on the upright chairs in the front room, in the smell of lavender furniture polish and the stale air of disuse. When the hearse arrived bearing the body of Flight Sergeant Clover, Onions whispered, 'Are you ready?' and she had nodded.

Troy stood at the graveside with the detachment of a camera—'kodak-distant', as Philip Larkin so succinctly had it. Neighbours paid their respects and brought Valerie to the pitch of muttering. Onions stood holding Jackie's hand, and as the last of the mourners left, Valerie put out a hand to summon Troy. He gave her his arm to lean on. Jackie rode up front on the return journey, where she had wanted to be all along. Troy took her place.

There would be no funeral baked meats. No guests. No wake. Onions made plain tea once more. As he rattled around in the scullery, Troy heard a dull thumping through the ceiling from the room above. He slipped quietly up the stairs and found Valerie sitting on her bedroom floor with the contents of the fireside cupboard scattered around her. She tugged at the perished rubber of a World War II gas mask, watching it come apart in her hands.

'Will you look at this junk,' she said. 'He'd never let me throw a damn thing away.'

She threw the gas mask at the wall.

'Fuck 'im,' she said.

There were no tears now.

'Fuck 'im.'

Troy sat on the floor. A small folding-bellows camera, missing the eye-piece, lay on top of a photo album, where it had fallen from the cupboard. He took it off, set it gently down, and turned a page. There was Jackie in her mother's arms in 1946 in front of the house in Shepherd's Bush. Six weeks old. Then the same set-up, the same place and pose, except that a proud father, in uniform, now held his daughter.

'But you'd surely want to keep some things?' he said.

'Right now I could torch the lot. Starting with the bloody house.'

She slammed the album shut.

'I don't want to see it. He dragged me away from that to live in this hole. Did you know he asked for this posting? When he got back from Korea he took us away from everything I had, everything I knew. I was seven when Dad went to the Yard. I hardly remembered Lancashire. I was a west London girl down to my toes. I never wanted to move. Fuck 'im.'

'I didn't know.'

'He wanted to get me as far away from you as he could.'

'I didn't know he knew about me.'

'He didn't. He just knew there was somebody. My "fancy man", as he called him.'

Troy had no idea what he should or could say to this.

'Don't flatter yourself, Troy,' she said. 'You weren't the only one. And if you didn't know that then I'm surprised you call yourself a detective.'

It was almost a joke. A quick, grim smile flashed across her lips. Then the tears started to well in her eyes. She bowed her head and he could just hear her say, 'Jesus Christ, Troy. What am I going to do now?'

She stretched out her arms, draped them around his neck and sobbed into his shoulder.

'Fuck 'im,' she said between gasps. 'Fuck 'im. I hope he rots in hell.'

She sobbed an age away. Troy saw the light shift into late afternoon through the back window, looking out onto the privies and across the alley to the houses at the back. She had not moved in awhile. All he could feel was the slow, rhythmical rise and fall of her chest against him. He put out a hand to her hair. It seemed the right thing to do. It seemed that he had to do something. She stirred. Her face came up to his. Close in the dimness. She was only thirty-seven. Still very good-looking. Almost as blonde as her daughter, her father's piercing blue eyes set in a broad, pale face. She kissed him on the cheek. Pulled back. Looked at him expressionless. Kissed him on the lips and began to prise them apart with her tongue.

She could feel the lack of response in him. Lips like tentflaps.

'For Christ's sake, Troy.'

'I'm married,' he said simply.

'Hah? Married?'

'Yes,' he said, and it felt more like a lie than all the lies he'd told lately.

'I was married. What bloody difference did it make then? Troy, I don't want you to tell me I'm the love of your life. I'm not so green as I'm cabbage looking, but I know what's going to happen. Dad will ride to the rescue like a knight in shining armour. We'll lose the house. And good riddance. It's a RAF house, Married Quarters, NCOs for the use of—but Dad'll take me back to bloody Acton. I don't want Acton, Troy. I don't want to be a little girl in my father's house again. Fuck Acton, fuck my Dad. I just need a break, a chance, a chance to stand on me own two feet. Me and Jackie. Just put a roof over my head till I can do that. Acton'll kill me. He'll get me back and he'll never let me go. I'll be at 22 Veryneat Villas for the rest of my life. An eternity at Tablecloth Terrace. Do this for me, Troy. You don't have to say you love me. Just help me. I couldn't stand Acton. Help me, Troy.'

Troy said nothing.

§85

Onions had lit a poor excuse for a fire in the iron range of the back room. He sat in front of it smoking a Woodbine.

'I was beginning to wonder,' he said.

'She'll live.'

'In what state, though? There've been times when she was younger she'd work herself into such a tizzy I thought she'd go mad.'

'She's a grown-up now, Stan. She'll pull through quicker than you think. And I wouldn't expect her to wear her widow's weeds for long.'

341

'Eh?'

'She won't mourn for Ken any longer than she has to. In fact, I rather think somewhat less than protocol would demand. She's quite determined to get shot of the house, and Salford, and get back to London. She won't be erecting any shrine to Ken in this street or in her heart.'

'She'll be all right for money, though?'

'Of course. Ken was a regular. There'll be a full RAF pension. And he'll count as killed in action. Maybe a bit more money, and a medal. I called my brother last night. He's still the darling of the Marshals, for those two years he served as Air Minister under Attlee. He says Valerie will want for nothing. He'll see to that. There'll be money to put Jackie through school if you want it, and money to relocate back to London.'

'Relocate?' Onions said, querying the neologism.

'If I were you I'd dust off her old room in Acton and have the two of them back till she finds her feet.'

'Is that what she's asking for?'

Troy shrugged, letting the gesture say whatever Stan wanted it to.

'I'll have to stay here a while.'

'Of course. What do you want me to do?'

'You'll have to take charge at the Yard. I can't do without you any longer. The boy was right.' The boy was Wildeve. Thirty-six and he'd never be anything else to Onions. 'He came to me and insisted I lay you off. But you're more or less OK now, aren't you?'

It seemed to have slipped his mind that there were other, better reasons for Jack's request.

'I'm fine.'

'I'll put in for a week's compassionate leave. But I'll not do it till Monday. That'll buy you a few days to get a medical, get your life in order. You'll have to do some of my work, just for a bit. And you'll run the squad in your own right from now on—Tom won't be back. I heard on Friday. Doctors have given him a month. Friday was my day for bad news. Just get yourself back to the Yard and take over. You'll be confirmed as a superintendent as soon as Tom's papers are through. I'll handle things up here.'

Onions slipped into silence. An infinite sadness. The beginning of a tear once more starting to form in the corner of each eye. He puffed one last time on his Woodbine and threw the nud end into the range. Rarely had

342

Troy seen such a sense of defeat so manifest in Stan. For twenty years Stan had stood like a rock in his life. Rocks did not bleed stones did not weep.

All in all Troy could not believe his luck.

§86

Jackie was sitting on the doorstep again. At some point she must have slipped upstairs to see her mother. She had the disintegrating gas mask on her face, and had taken the precaution of wearing her Alice band on the outside. Its garish plastic colours and glass gems contrasted comically with the greys and browns of rubber and canvas. It seemed to Troy to sum up something about the country rather well, the fruitless way his generation had passed their legacy on to the next. She turned and looked through the cracked plexiglass at Troy. The car-boy was standing on the pavement.

'Go on. I'll give you sixpence fer it.'

Jackie turned back to him.

'Awright,' she said through the mask, sounding like an asthmatic frog.

Her hand came up and delicately removed the Alice band, and then tore off the mask.

'Tanner it is,' she concluded.

She put the small silver coin in the pocket of her dress, tucking it in below her handkerchief.

Troy was staring. She felt this. Looked up and said, 'I got a bob for me Dad's old camera.'

Troy said goodbye and walked round to the driver's side of his car. The boy circled the car, wings out, undercarriage running hard, the faint burblings of a propeller coming from inside the mask. He had got his history mightily wrong.

Troy wound down the window to let out the heat of the day. The boy touched down next to him.

'Why did you waste your money on that thing?' Troy asked him.

'Whatdeyer mean waste? It's good this is!'

'Good for what?'

343

'In case Jerries come again.'

'Don't be daft,' said Troy. 'That was years ago.'

'Could still 'appen,' the boy protested. 'Me Dad says it'll be Gyppos next.'

'Maybe. But they're not Germans, are they?'

'Me Dad says they're all foreigners.'

The irrefutable logic of xenophobia, in one so young. The infallible oracle that was 'me Dad'. Troy put the key in the ignition and decided to end the conversation. The boy felt otherwise.

'Me Dad says Gyppos killed Jackie's dad.'

Troy looked at the house. The door was closed. She had gone.

'That's not true,' he said softly to the boy. 'It was Cypriots. Not Egyptians. The Egyptians haven't killed anyone.'

'Me Dad says they chopped him up inch at a time, just like Japs did in the war!' said the boy with evident relish.

Troy smiled falsely and turned the key.

§87

It was a glorious drive. Over the Pennines with the western sun behind him. Through Whalley Bridge and down into the old spa town of Buxton. He stopped in the last of day at Monsal Head. He had never driven the route before and had long wanted to see the railway viaduct that had so offended Ruskin. The most beautiful valley in England, desecrated with a huge bridge and a high embankment simply that 'every fool in Buxton can be at Bakewell in half an hour, and every fool in Bakewell at Buxton'.

Troy stared at the bridge. High and narrow over the Wye. As elegant as a row of flamingos' legs. Ruskin was wrong. A hundred years on it looked as though God had put in an extra half-day's overtime on the first Sunday to see that this sat well with Mother Nature.

He had no wish to drive or to arrive in darkness. It seemed too compromising. He checked into the Peacock Inn at Rowsley. Dined late, breakfasted early, and by seven-thirty the next morning was approaching

Commander Cockerell's hometown from the north, along the crooked miles of the A6, snagged between the Derwent and the old Midland Railway line that snaked and burrowed its alpine way from Derby to Manchester.

He stopped by the cotton mill and asked for the Wirksworth Road. A man exercising a dog pointed up the hill with his walking stick. Across the river, off the Ashbourne road. North, poetically, by north-west.

He parked in front of number 44 and took the pink suitcase he had had since Brighton from the boot. There was no doorbell. He banged loudly with the horizontal knocker on the letter box.

She was not dressed. She stood in the doorway, in a terry-cloth dressing gown, her hair pinned into a bun high on her head.

She peered round Troy. Looked at the Bentley.

'Are you going to leave that there? It's wider than the house.'

'Why, do you think the neighbours will talk?'

'They'd better!' said Foxx.

§88

Troy watched as she dressed, hands flitting between a large mug of instant coffee and items of clothing. For a brief moment she stood naked, as she pulled on her knickers, then disappeared beneath American fly-button faded blue jeans, that he knew from his nephews were all the rage and hard as hell to get hold of, and a white T-shirt. As she flexed her arms in the air to ease the shirt down over her breasts, one hand hovered at the back of her head and pulled out the pin that held her hair. She shook it loose, sending it cascading halfway down her back. She opened the back door to a row of steep concrete steps leading down to a perilously perched garden, stood in the doorway's morning light and brushed out her hair.

'I suppose,' she said lackadaisically, 'that you're used to women with dressing rooms and dressing tables. Very working class to dress in the kitchen. But the reason everything takes place in the kitchen is that more often than not it's the only heated room in the house. Besides, I live alone.'

345

She looked down the garden, down to the valley, giving her a hair a last dozen strokes. Troy said nothing. Of course she was right, but then he'd relished every moment of it. When he was small his sisters, women devoid of self-consciousness and self-knowledge, had dressed and made up in front of him. It was curious, nostalgic even, hardly sexual but hardly devoid of sexuality.

'What's the suitcase for?'

It seemed as though she had only just noticed it, but he had walked in carrying it and she was not looking at it now—she had chosen her own moment.

'We're taking a trip.

'To the moon on gossamer wings?'

She closed the door on the view, lodged her hairbrush next to the stopped clock on the mantelpiece.

'No. To Paris. Possibly Monte Carlo.'

She sat on the arm of a battered Utility chair that stood in the corner between the door and the fireplace, and pulled on a pair of baseball boots, back bent, fingers moving almost quicker than the eye could see as she laced them up to the ankle. She stood up with a little bounce, up onto her toes like a boxer moving around the ring in the seconds before the gloves touched.

'I'm not dressed right for Monte Carlo,'

'What do you think is in the suitcase?'

'At a guess I'd say half a dozen of Stella's frocks. But they're not really me. Look, we don't have to leave right now, do we?'

'No,' he said. 'Not right now.'

'Then let's go out for a while. A walk. You are up to a walk, aren't you?'

She stepped lightly across the room to reach him. She stood eye to eye, shoulder to shoulder with him, put out her hands and pulled down his head. A gesture as gentle as Kolankiewicz's was bullying, but to the same purpose. She ran her fingers along the scar.

'It's healing well. If you're sure you're up to it, I'll show you around. There's a few things to be said before we pluck up sticks and disappear.'

All down the steep hill that led back into the town they walked thirty yards behind a group of chattering young women.

'Eight o'clock start at the mill,' Foxx said. 'I should be with them at this time on any other day.'

'Are you on compassionate leave?'

'What? Don't be daft. It's a cotton mill not the Royal Navy. I asked for every day's holiday due to me when that copper came up from Scotland Yard and told me Stella was dead. They gave me a fortnight like I'd asked them to chop off a leg. I've had more than a week now. And I still don't want to go back.'

She steered Troy off the road only a few feet before the Derwent Bridge and headed out along a riverside lane, high above the rushing white water.

'How long did you say you'd worked there?'

'I started there when I was eighteen. Later than most. I could have gone at fifteen or sixteen, I suppose. Wobbling around on heels, and me bra padded out, pretending I was Jane Russell, trying to look like a grown-up. I didn't. My mother always thought we were cut out for something better. Long after our Dad was dead she was still trying to better us. I did the same secretarial course as Stella. Typing and shorthand might be "better", but it didn't pay as well—and to tell the truth I was heartily fed up with being anybody's secretary. My boss was no better than Cockerell—worse, he thought he could stick his hand up your skirt and *not* set you up in a love nest. I went onto the mill floor. It was the obvious, the easy thing to do. Half the town works there, after all. And the half that doesn't is down the pit or on the railways. It took me less than a day to learn the job and within a week I could do it in my sleep. Or at least do it while I daydreamed. At the time I thought a job which used none of your mind was marginally better than one which used about a tenth—I thought of it as a kind of freedom. And it was good money compared to typing, brought in enough to run the house for me and Mam. Then Stella started sending money. I could have sent it back—I knew it was Cockerell's money—but I didn't. And I could have quit the mill, but I didn't. Mam thought Stella was doing another secretarial job in London. I suppose I was part of the cover. If I'd stopped working she'd have asked where the money was coming from. That we lived a damn sight better than we could on a mill girl's wages seemed to escape her notice. She wasn't all there towards the end anyway. But Mam died at Christmas. And I grew to hate the mill long ago. There comes a point when daydreams turn sour if you don't do something about them.'

The pace she had set up was almost winding Troy. They climbed steeply up the side of the valley away from the river, and onto a rough, ancient track that ran southward along the ridge of the Pennines.

347

'D'you know what makes a place like that tick?'

She pointed back at the mill chimney, the largest object on the skyline.

'Paypackets? Promotion? No—it's a running undercurrent of sexual innuendo. The men don't say "hello" on a Monday morning, they say, "Didst gerrowt?"'

'What?'

'Didst gerrowt? Did you get any? Meaning sex.'

'I see,' he said, unable to visualise the exchange in his mind.

'But then, nobody lays a hand on you.'

'All mouth and no trousers?' he queried.

'Yes. And you don't know how grateful a girl can be for that sometimes. I'm immune to the smutty remark. But then I was immune to the charms of Arnold Cockerell. If Stella had been too she might be alive now.'

Foxx hopped nimbly over a wooden gate. Troy followed gingerly, and found himself facing a colossal stone wall in the middle of nowhere—or, to be precise, since a herd of Scottish longhorns mooed lazily at them as they approached, in the middle of a field of grazing cattle.

Troy stared up at the wall. It was the best part of twenty-five feet high, solidly built of local granite, and pitted with small holes, out of a few of which sprouted ambitious sycamore saplings. It was a rifle range, clearly dated 1860 by an iron plate just below the parapet. A relic of the last time Troy's two nations had fought each other in earnest, in the Crimea. The futile, bloody stalemate of the 1850s. Several ancestors and kinsmen had died at Sevastopol. This wall halfway up the Pennines was the result, as the British Army sought to improve itself, realising at last that a good shire militia was worth a dozen charges by the Light Brigade. It was odd to think that old history should penetrate as far as it did. The date and the obvious purpose of the structure instantly brought to mind his grandfather's anecdotes of the brothers and cousins the old man had lost in battle. Whatever symbolic value the wall had for Foxx, she could hardly guess at its significance to Troy.

Foxx set foot upon the wall, working her toe into a hole probably made generations ago by a musket ball. She braced her arms against the almost vertical slope of the wall and climbed three or four feet off the ground.

'You don't have to stand and watch, you know,' she said, looking down at him under an arm. 'You'll put me off. How's your head?'

'Still aches a bit,' he said.

'I meant for heights. There's a ladder round the back. I'll meet you at the top.'

'You're going to climb all the way?'

'I wasn't intending to fly. I've been doing this since I was ten. As long as you don't distract me I'll be fine.'

Troy scrambled round to the beech grove at the back of the range and found a rusting iron ladder. It groaned under his weight, and he concluded he was the first person to set foot on it in many years. A few feet from the top, one rung snapped clean in two and sent his pulse racing, but he hauled himself onto the flat top, to find a view across the valley that stretched for miles.

A hand appeared on the parapet, followed by a foot, and in a moment Foxx had pulled herself over the edge. She lay a few seconds at his feet, breathing heavily, then she stood, dusted herself down and said a simple, 'Well?'

'Was that worth it?'

'Oh yes,' she gasped. 'Every time.'

She walked to the very end, gazed out across the valley, where the mill chimney still dominated everything in sight, breathed deeply and came back to him.

'You've news,' she said. 'You've news, or you wouldn't be here with your posh car and a packed case.'

Troy pulled the translated letter from his pocket.

'This was in your sister's safety deposit box. It was in code, but it was a simple code, and it's addressed to you.'

She sat on the edge, her legs dangling over the twenty-five-foot-drop, silently reading the letter. He saw her fold it once more. She paused, and was perfectly still for the best part of a minute, then she patted the stone next to her, indicating that he should sit. He did not look down.

She handed the letter back to him, pale and tense, but without a trace of tears.

'I think I knew all that. Not the money. And not the Russians. But I knew the rest. She was living pretty high on the hog.'

'Do you believe her?'

'Yes. And so do you. Or else you wouldn't have come here. I think it's time you told me why you came.'

349

'I want you to come to Paris and open the safety deposit box for me. Perhaps another after that if we don't find what we want. London was the old pals' act. I know the bank's director. It wouldn't work anywhere else. But if you cut your hair, change your make-up—"

'And put on one of those posh frocks you brought.'

'I brought suits. Two-piece jobs. Very discreet. If you do this you'll pass for your sister. In theory all you need to open a box is the key. Possession is everything. In practice no one's that green. They'll know their clients. This way we do what has to be done without arousing any suspicion.'

'Aha.'

'You'll do it?'

'We're not after the money?'

'It's incidental. I need to know what else there is. It's the only way we'll catch her killer.'

'She says the other stuff is dangerous.'

'She's right.'

'Then the money's not incidental. I don't see how forty thousand quid can be incidental to anyone. If there's a risk there's got to be some reward.'

'You'll do it?'

Again she did not answer. She stood up, turned to face the town, across the river.

'Look over there. Tell me what you see.'

He regarded the question with some suspicion, but took her hand as she pulled him to his feet, and looked out over the valley. What was he meant to be looking for? It might well be an entirely innocent question. There was, he saw for the first time, more than one mill chimney—perhaps the town had sprung up on cotton and stopped, frozen in time fifty years later—a host of church towers and spires—and street upon street of houses climbing the sides of a small valley at right angles to the Derwent Valley, in which, school geography told him, there was almost certainly a tributary stream. The houses looked to him like a precise illustration of a Grimms' tale. The lonely giant climbing his mountain with a sackful of custom-made houses for his model village, finds too late that there is a hole in his sack, and the houses tumble in their own order, which is no order, down the hillside. And there he leaves them, clinging scattered to the contours.

Nothing encroached on the river but the mill; the town stopped two hundred yards short in a well-defined flood plain. Up the hill towards them crept fields of every shape, the irregular rhomboids and trapezoids of the English quilt, dotted with sheep and oaks, ragged ribbons of hawthorn hedging, tangles of dog-rose gone to hip, the dried-blood red of ripening blackberries. Just below them an orderly row of hornbeam cut a line down to a cart track, and the track in turn led to a couple of farmhouses, carved in stone and seemingly half-buried in the landscape. It was a good time for hardwoods. Just past their peak, in the full glory of deep greens, that in a week or two would surely begin to brown with the onset of autumn.

He was, he realised, being forced to reappraise the place. The Orwellian sense he had had of narrow, cobbled streets and shabby northern houses gave way to this wider view. The town was like many northern towns, industry all but in a field. But it was unlike anything he had seen in Yorkshire. The town was smaller, neater, the countryside so much lusher, so verdant in its greens. It was, he admitted only to himself, a better-looking slice of the sad shires than his own home county.

'It's nice,' he said blandly.

'Nice?'

'All right—beautiful.'

'Fine. Then you can have it. You can keep it. You can stuff it. I don't want it!'

'What do you want?'

'I want,' she said slowly and carefully, enunciating like an elocution teacher, letting the words burst like bubbles on her lips, 'you to take me away from all this.'

Her arm swept out across the valley pointing to everything and nothing. Suddenly a pompous phrase from a penny dreadful seemed real and portentous and dangerous.

'OK,' he said.

'I mean it, Troy. We go home. Pack. I post the latchkey back to the council. We get in that absurd car of yours and we never come back.'

'OK,' he said again.

'Great.'

She grinned, widely, beautifully, turned on her heel and dropped to the ground. Instinctively Troy leaned out to grab her and almost fell over the edge. Instead he saw her drop into a crouch, roll over like a parachutist, and bounce up again onto her feet. The fall should have broken both legs—it seemed to Troy impossible. But there she was off down the track at a run. She turned, jogged backwards for a few steps and yelled up at him.

'I'll need an hour to pack. Don't get lost!'

§89

Foxx got more than her hour. Troy found a footpath leading back into the town, and trudged his way back up the stone streets to the opposite side of the valley, in search of Jasmine Dene.

Mrs Cockerell answered the door with a paintbrush between her teeth. She took it out.

'I always knew if I saw you again it would be bad news.'

She led off, back into the house, towards the rear, without another word. Troy followed. It had not occurred to him that he was the bearer of good or bad news. He had presumed that by now she simply wanted to know, one way or the other.

He thought she might be leading the way into the garden. Through the open french windows he could see an easel, set up for the southeast, and a large off-white card with a half-finished, almost abstract image upon it. But she turned into the kitchen, and he heard the pop of a gas ring going on. Tea and sympathy. But what sympathy he could bring he did not know. She stood with her back to the cooker. Paintbrush in one hand, battery-powered hob lighter in the other, hands crossed over her bosom. The housewife Nefertiti.

'It's him, isn't it?'

'Yes.'

'You're sure?'

'Yes.'

She put down the lighter. Wiped magenta paint off the brush onto her Joseph-coated apron and stuck the brush in a jam jar.

'Don't worry, Mr Troy. I'm not about to cry.'

He was pleased. He'd had enough of tears. And then she burst like a summer tempest.

§90

Troy chose a small hotel on the Left Bank, between the Boulevard St Germain and the Place de l'Odéon. The opposite tactic of his ventures to Amsterdam and Vienna. Concealment in the byways of a city. A hotel with none of the prominence—or elegance—of the Europe or the Sacher. If anyone wanted to find him, it would be like looking for a needle in a haystack. The room was tiny, but Foxx had no mark by which to measure it, and accepted everything without comment. She asked for money to shop. Essential to the deception, as they both knew, that she should look and sound like her sister. A haircut, some new clothes perhaps?

Troy was surprised at the sense of ritual Foxx brought to the task. She returned from the hairdresser's clutching another pink suitcase and a large green shopping bag, her hair wrapped in a headscarf, her figure hidden beneath the blunt lines of a sexless pea jacket and her customary T-shirt and blue jeans.

She unbuttoned the jacket and let it slip from her shoulders to the floor. Pulled the scarf off and shook her hair free. Eighteen inches of wild blonde mane had changed to a neat cut, about chin length, framing the face anew. Long, her hair had tended to flow backwards, away from the face; short, it fell forward, the razored tips almost curling under at the cheeks, hiding the face and with it half her expression.

She took one of her sister's suits from the wardrobe, stripped the wrapping off new underwear and lay them on the bed side by side, one by one, like paper cut-outs, dressing dolly—the bra, the knickers, the suspender belt and stockings—the double-breasted jacket, the matching burgundy skirt.

'Do you know what this is?' she asked Troy.

'No. I just picked the nearest in the wardrobe.'

'It's a Dior. What they called the H line unless I'm very much mistaken. The rage of Paris a couple of years ago. Costs a packet. If it hadn't been so random I'd almost have said you had taste.'

She peeled off the T-shirt, popped the steel buttons on her jeans, almost like shelling peas, and stepped out of them; put her thumbs into the elastic of her knickers, shoved them to the ankles and kicked them off. She stood naked, looking not at Troy, but at her own image in the looking-glass.

They were sisters. They were twins, but even now Troy could tell the one from the other. The tight muscularity of Foxx mentally juxtaposed with the naked Madeleine who had stepped from her bathroom to point a gun at him—which gun now sat among the fluff and old bus tickets in his jacket pocket. The Madeleine in his memory was paying the price of the high life, at twenty-two already slackening under the onslaught of food and fags and booze. Foxx rippled with muscle. Troy figured her biceps to be bigger than his own. Her legs were certainly longer—the thigh muscle standing out in a single ridge, the muscles of the calf over-lapping in taut tendons as she perched on her toes to turn her backside to the glass. The small breasts swung to face him, pectorals firmed, pink nipples tilting upward in best cliché of worst racy novel.

'Goodbye Shirley Foxx,' she said as she pulled on the pants. 'Call me Maddy, call me mad.'

Troy sprawled on the bed and watched the ensemble assembled. The bra clipped by that disjointing, impossible gesture with arms contorted behind the back, the stockings rolled up each thigh to the tune of infinity, hand over hand over hand, the skirt hooked up and zipped up, the reverse striptease of a total metamorphosis. Last of all a pair of new shoes emerged from a box, expensive shoes, good shoes, in red leather. She stepped into them, tugged at the cuffs of her jacket, stranded partway up the forearm.

'This suit's made to be worn with gloves, you know that don't you?'

'Never crossed my mind,' he said, still horizontal on the bed.

'Good job it crossed mine, then. Or I'd look a right twaddle.'

She opened the new suitcase, removed another, smaller, pink case from inside, and from that took out a pair of elbow-length white gloves, as though they were the prize waiting at the end of a game of pass the parcel.

'*C'est tout*,' she said.

'*Non*,' he replied. '*Ce n'est pas tout*.'

He took a black jewellery case from his coat pocket and flipped the lid. A single strand of pearls lay on a bed of velvet. She turned. He fastened the clasp at the back of her neck and spun her around to face him.

'There,' he said. 'Now it's complete.'

'They're hers?'

'I found them on her dressing table,' he said.

Foxx stared into the looking-glass again. And from the looking-glass to Troy.

'Are they real?'

'Probably.'

She fingered the strand of pearls, the traditional neckwear of the upper-crust Englishwoman. Part of the uniform.

'God. The things she did. Who would ever think she'd want to be a fake Englishwoman? Did you believe her?'

'Mostly. There was something that didn't quite ring true, but mostly I believed in this girl from a good home in the shires. I didn't quite believe in the sophisticate. It looked like a layer of lacquer. Perhaps the fake Englishwoman was what Cockerell wanted?'

'No. It was Stella. This was Stella's game. Arnold put up the money, and did what he did, but this part of it was Stella. It's got her written all over it.'

Foxx turned back to the looking-glass, scanning her own image.

'I'm not me any more, am I? I'm her.'

'Surfaces,' said Troy. 'Not even skin deep.'

'I wonder. I really do. Will I ever find me again?'

'There's one way to find out.'

'Aha.'

'You could take it all off again.'

'All?'

'Everything. Bit by bit.'

'Sort of a striptease?'

'If you like. But at the end of it there you'll be.'

He watched the process reverse itself. The static charge as her skirt slid over her hip to run the length of her stockinged legs and pool at her feet. The Dégas angle of the body, the balletic tilt, one leg absurdly longer than the other, as she unhooked stocking from suspender, locked the muscle in her thigh and peeled off the nylon. And the stretching of the torso, the stretching out and up of the ribcage, the flattening of her breasts as her arms went over her head once more and she flung off the bra, poised with her fingertips out to the ceiling, balanced on her tiptoes. She stood naked again. Troy didn't care if she never wore clothes again. Just to look at her burnt. Simply to touch drove him wild. She leant over him, wearing only the pearls. He thought he'd go mad. It had been years since he felt uncontrollable lust. He was accustomed to reasonable lust,

355

lust that allowed itself to be negotiated, the polite sex of the middle-aged, the wants that wait.

He put out a hand to one small breast, slid the other between her legs. She put her hand over his, held it poised on her mound, his palm cupped to it.

'Steady on,' she said. 'We've got all night.'

He could not but disagree. He had no sense of all. No sense of for ever. He'd known heaven like a tent . . . how did the line go? . . . 'to wrap its shining yards and disappear'.

In the morning when he awoke she was sleeping soundly, one leg across his. He moved it gently, and noticed for the first time the last irrefutable difference between Foxx and her sister—a small tattoo on the inside of the left ankle. A bird of some sort, a bird ascending with something in its mouth. A dove? It had to be a dove. A dove holding an olive branch. He had sucked the seashell from Madeleine's left foot. He liked to think he would have noticed a tattoo. When she was dressed, the next time she was dressed as her sister, the fake Englishwoman, as she herself had put it, he would think of the tattoo—so utterly un-English, un-middle-class—hidden beneath nylon stockings and good shoes.

§91

The Banque du Commerce Coloniale was all but indistinguishable from a private house, tall and narrow as a London terrace. Indeed, it stood in a street of largely private houses, into which the fashion houses were just beginning to intrude—the Avenue Montaigne, cleaving from the Champs Elysées at forty-five degrees, aiming straight for the river at the Pont de l'Alma. Like Mullins Kelleher, only a small brass plaque told you it was a bank. And if you weren't looking, you'd miss it.

From his seat on a bench, on the tiny triangle of muddied grass in the Place de l'Alma, Troy had a clear view to the bank, and an equally clear view of the Crazy Horse in the Avenue George V. He wondered about the proximity of the two. Did this say something, anything, about

Cockerell? Drawing out money from his bank, only to blow it at the conveniently close capital of tit and titillation? He could not concentrate on pretending to read the newspaper that was meant to be his disguise. Paris was a city of mnemonics—the republican habit of remembering every odd and sod in place names nudged the memory constantly. The English scarcely did this. Where in London was the Avenue Churchill or the Rue Ernie Bevin? Or, for that matter, George V Street? He was captivated by a world of small symbols and fleeting coincidences. Place de l'Alma: the French equivalent of a street he had walked in his beat days in the East End, and the name of yet another Crimean battle at which ancient Troys had perished; and Montaigne, Montaigne, what was it Montaigne had called lies? . . . the wretched vice? No . . . the accursed vice. Lying, Madeleine Kerr's accursed vice. He played pointlessly with the 'kerr cur' rhyme, and missed her exit. Before he knew it Foxx was at the bank door, shaking hands with someone and then standing, blinking into the sun, while the man hailed a taxi for her.

Troy caught a taxi as it came down the Avenue George V, pointed at the back of Foxx's cab as it crossed the bridge and said, '*Suivez.*'

The driver rolled his eyes upwards—boredom and exasperation as though all the English ever wanted was that you should waste time following another taxi. As they swung left on the opposite bank, onto the Quai d'Orsay, Troy could see Foxx's blonde head through the cab's rear window. His own driver was muttering and cursing, but they had her clearly in sight, and he turned his attention to what mattered. Was anyone else following? He looked behind him every few seconds, he peered into every car that drew level with them and watched the cab in front with one hand on Madeleine Kerr's little golden gun as they paused at traffic lights all the way along the Boulevard St Germain.

He was pretty sure they were not being followed. The cab turned off the Boulevard into the Rue de l'Odéon, with two cabs behind them, then off the Rue de l'Odéon and into Rue Racine, and then there were none. His cab and hers were the only cabs in the street. Foxx turned right, and Troy knew she would stop outside the hotel. He stopped his cab at the corner and walked the last fifty yards.

Five minutes hanging around in the lobby and no one else had entered. He went up to their room. It was empty. The smallest of the pink cases lay on the bed unopened. Her shoes lay on the carpet where she had kicked them off. He pushed at the bathroom door, stepped inside. Only the rush of air told him the blow was coming. He ducked and a Perrier bottle wielded like an Indian club smashed on the wall above his head.

'I thought you'd be here,' Foxx said, standing over him. 'You said you'd be here. I didn't know what had happened to you.'

Troy got to his feet. Knocked the shards of glass from his hair.

'I was watching you,' he said. 'If I'd told you, you'd have been looking out for me, whether you resisted the impulse or not, you'd've had one eye cocked for me.'

'Someone's following us?'

'No. I don't think anyone is. But this was the only way to be sure.'

'Who'd be following us?'

He took a towel, mopped the mineral water from his head and face as they moved back to the bedroom. It was not a subject he wanted to pursue.

'How did it go?'

He sat on the bed next to the pink case, shrugged off his jacket and rubbed at his hair with the towel.

'Fine. Just the one awkward moment. I addressed the manager in French; he replied, and told me my accent had improved, then he switched to English, and we stayed in English till we got out to the street. Me with "how now brown cow" running through my mind and trying to sound home counties. I think he and Stella had a routine—a bit flirty I should think—but I couldn't work it out, I could only fit in with what he did. But I don't think he suspected a thing.'

'And the box?' said Troy.

Foxx flipped the catches on the case. Huge bundles of white five pound notes, a brown envelope and several strips of gold coins in plastic covers.

'I took everything. I don't know how much there is in paper money, but each of those strips holds fifty sovereigns and there's six of them.'

Troy tore open the envelope. Five sheets of paper. Five double-spaced typed sheets of the five-block numerical code he had found in the London bank. He was not good with numbers. Hated numbers. It would take him all day to decode this using the instructions Clark had given him.

He looked at Foxx. Standing, arms folded, in her stockinged feet, the tight, red burgundy skirt, the crisp cotton blouse and the token string of pearls. She shook her newfound fringe from her eyes. Pale, green, looking back at him, trusting him and waiting on him. He had a day's work cut out for him, and all he wanted to do was fuck her. He held the heart of the mystery in his hands, gold and revelation, locked away in cellophane and cypher, and all he could think of was her on her back with her legs locked around his waist.

'You're soaked,' she said, in a matter of fact tone of voice. 'Your shirt's wet through. Here, let me.'

She pulled at the knot in his tie and began to pop the buttons on his shirt—a maternal, sexless gesture he could not take as maternal or sexless —and he knew he was lost. *She* was the heart of the mystery, locked away in cotton and nylon. Down there was the dove. All he had to do was strip off the wrapper.

§92

It was past noon before they surfaced. While Foxx bathed he set out the five sheets of foolscap on the small table in the window. By the time she emerged from the bathroom he had decoded the first sentence and ground to a halt on the second. It was going to take a lot longer than he had thought.

'What can I do?'

'Nothing. Why don't you see the sights? I'll meet you for dinner.'

'Where should I go?'

'There are plenty of places within walking distance. The Jardin du Luxembourg is only a quarter of a mile or so from here, and the river's even less the other way. Why don't you see the jardin, walk over to the Île de la Cité, do Notre Dame, and then if the sun's still out, sit in the little park at the opposite end of the island. It's a beautiful spot. Read a newspaper and watch the Seine barges go by. I'll meet you at Lapérouse about eight o'clock.'

"Where's that?'

Troy sketched the flattened U of the Seine on the back of the room service menu, drew in the elongated blobs for the two islands and marked the Quai des Grands Augustins with an X.

359

'There,' he said. 'See you at eight.'

But by eight he was no wiser. He had tried every variation on the crib Clark gave him, all twenty-six possible starting points. To no avail.

He found her in a dark corner of Lapérouse, buried in its deep black and gold, her burgundy suit blending into the near-subterranean setting like natural camouflage. A corner table, lit by a single sputtering candle. She held a half-empty glass of champagne in her hands, and was leaning back against the panelled wall with her eyes closed. They flickered open momentarily as he sat down.

'I'm dreaming,' she said. 'I've died and gone to heaven. I went up the Eiffel Tower. It was magical. You wouldn't believe the day I've had.'

He would and he did. He'd known Paris magic. His mother had taken him to Paris half a dozen times in the 1920s. They had heard recitals by Ravel and Stravinsky. They had eaten in this very restaurant. She had reminisced about her own Paris magic, her first visit when she was seventeen, when she had been introduced to Maupassant and Zola, and seen the Eiffel Tower half-built, and had considered it 'vulgar'.

'It seems a shame to go back so soon.'

Foxx opened her eyes fully, smiled at him.

'You're not,' said Troy.

'I'm not?'

'I can't crack the code. There's something wrong somewhere. I have to go back and set my sergeant to work on it. I'm due back at the Yard anyway, and I doubt I can stall them a day longer. You have to go on. I need to know what's in the next box. It might be different. It might be easier.'

'Go on where?'

'Another city. Monte Carlo, Zurich, Amsterdam. Take your pick.'

She held out her hand.

'Pencil,' she said simply, and Troy took one from his inside pocket.

She tore thin strips off the wine list, scribbled down the three cities, and arranged them like a game of three card monte. A quick shuffle and she asked him to 'pick a card'.

He had difficulty in believing her lack of volition, but picked.

'Zurich,' he said. 'It's Zurich.'

§93

Onions had a civilian secretary he referred to behind her back as 'the gorgon'. Her real name was Madge.

'You're late,' said Madge, standing in front of his desk, a huge sheaf of papers pressed to her bosom. 'I was told to expect you this morning. I called you four times.'

'Doctor,' Troy lied. 'Had to see my doctor.'

He had stayed with Foxx, wrapped up in Foxx till dawn, and travelled back in the wan light of early morning. He felt dreadful.

'But you're fine now?' Madge said without concern.

'Yes,' he said.

The sheaf of papers hit his desk with a thud.

'Good,' she said. 'Mr Wildeve's in Hammersmith. Mr Clark's trailing along behind him. The boss is in Manchester and Mr Henrey's dead. So somebody round here had better do a bit of work. Read and initial, except where it says sign, and you sign pp. Mr Onions.'

She strode to the open door. Troy stopped her with a hand on her arm.

'When?' he said.

'When what?'

The woman had the sensitivity of a reptile.

'When did Tom die?'

'Last night. I wasn't ringing you to check on your health.'

It was not that Madge had no regard for Tom. She had no regard for anyone but Onions.

'What word from Manchester?'

'The boss'll be there till Thursday he reckons.'

'I have to talk to him.'

'He says not to call. I don't know what you've done, Troy. But you seem to be a major bone of contention with "our Val". If I were you, I'd do as he says and let sleeping dogs lie for a while.'

He let her go. He felt a moment's pointless guilt. The fleeting surrender of intelligence to coincidence. An old colleague had breathed his last while he was in the arms, between the thighs, of a woman half his age. And then it passed. He and Tom had not been the best of friends, and he was a lousy copper.

Troy wondered if he could get through the next three days without a major case he could not delegate dropping onto his desk. His share of Onions' work was routine; he found himself initialling orders for paper clips and truncheons. He found his mind wandering. Could he work Clark's coffee machine? Could he conjure a cup from this Heath Robinson affair? And as he stared at the Thames, cup in hand, he found he could conjure the image of Foxx like a genie from a lamp.

In the morning Clark returned from a house-to-house search. Troy gave him the new papers. He looked at them like a master plumber confronted with a blocked lavatory and sucked air through his teeth.

'I'll need time,' he said.

In the afternoon Jack returned from Hammersmith. Troy sat while he brought him up to date on bodies rotting under floorboards in the terraces of Bedford Park, a case that at any other time would have had him gripped. And at the end of it, he could see guilt in Jack's eyes, much as it was so often writ in Rod's.

'You're fine now, aren't you, Freddie?' Jack said. 'I mean, that was a narrow scrape.'

Jack had had him suspended, shoved him into hole and corner.

'Yes,' said Troy. 'I'm fine.'

On Thursday morning Madge graced his office with her steely presence to tell him Onions would be a day late.

On the Friday there was no sign of Stan. And no sign of Clark either.

'I have to phone him,' Troy told Madge.

'Tough tittie,' she said. 'Val's had one of her fits with the poker. Smashed the china, smashed the mirrors, smashed the phone too. Boss calls me from a box now. You'll just have to wait.'

But he could not wait. He was out of his depth and he knew it. He had to tell someone. Stan was the best person. Stan was the logical, the legal conduit between the Yard and the intelligence services. He had unearthed a crime beyond the scope of his powers. Worse, he had no idea who the criminal was. He had worked out, and he was pretty certain Clark had too, that either side could have killed Cockerell, Jessel and Kerr.

And so, he made the call he had put off for weeks, and in the larger context had put off for twenty years.

'Charlie, I need to talk. It's business.'

'Yours or mine?' said Charlie.

'Both,' said Troy.

Charlie paused so long Troy had begun to think they had been cut off.

'Fine,' Charlie said at last, with no music in his voice. 'I'm up to my neck today, and come to that tomorrow morning too. But we could meet tomorrow afternoon. How about tea at the Café Royal? Fourish?'

They had crossed a line, one he had never wanted to cross. One he was sure Charlie had never wanted to cross either.

§94

Troy sat in Goodwin's Court in the encroaching dusk of Friday evening. He had left messages everywhere for Clark to call him—at the Police House and in every pub within walking distance of the Yard. He sat by the telephone in the darkness and silence, willing it to ring. And when it did his spell went awry—he had summoned Madge from her circle in hell.

'The boss is back in Acton. He says he'll be in in an hour.'

'I'll be there,' Troy said.

He put the phone down, and it rang again at once. He almost ignored it. They did it of their own accord half the time.

'Freddie?' said Johnny Fermanagh's voice. 'We have to talk. I must see you.'

'You've picked a lousy time,' said Troy.

'Please. S'important.'

Troy heard the sound of laughter in the background, the umistakable roar of pub jollity.

'Johnny, where are you?'

'Colony Room. Dean Street.'

'What happened to "on the wagon" and "the love of a good woman"?'

'Nothing happened. I stuck to it. I'm sober as a judge.'

'Then what are you doing in a place whose sole function is to allow Soho layabouts to get pissed at any time of the day or night, with no restriction from the licensing laws?'

'Freddie, I'm sober! It's just that after twenty years a drunk you've nowhere else to go. All you know are the old places. You try killing a wet Friday afternoon in Soho!'

'I don't believe you.'

'I'm on Britvic, and bloody awful it is too! Here, Muriel, you tell him. I'm sober aren't I?'

Troy heard a remote voice saying, 'More's the pity.'

'We have to talk. You put your finger on it. Woman. The love of a good woman.'

Troy looked at his watch. He knew he'd only wear holes in the lino waiting for Onions. Why not give Fermanagh a crack? It had the attraction of true banality compared to his present problem.

'All right. Back room of the Salisbury in fifteen minutes.'

He would head him off at the door. That way they could talk in the street, neither in the pub nor in his house. It would make it so much easier to stop when he'd heard enough.

It had come on to rain. A steady drizzle, putting a haze around the street lamps, and a come-hither glow onto the pub windows. Troy turned up the collar of his overcoat and stood in the doorway of the Salisbury. A couple of minutes later, he saw Johnny coming down St Martin's Court from the Charing Cross Road, in the uniform of their class—the black cashmere overcoat, the brown trilby and the red scarf, wrapped up against the drizzle, but smiling. He seemed genuinely happy to see Troy.

'Are we not going in?' he asked simply.

'No,' said Troy. 'Not if you're telling me the truth. It will be no hardship to stand on the pavement for ten minutes. It will test your willpower and your liver.'

'I've not had a drop since June, Freddie. Not since the last time we met.'

Troy was not wholly sure he believed him, but looking at him closely, peeking under the brim of the hat, his skin was tighter and healthier and for the first time in years his eyes were not bloodshot. They were his sister's eyes, a deep, beautiful bottle green.

'Then say your piece.'

This flummoxed him. He scraped a foot across the paving and could not look Troy in the eye.

'Johnny, just spit it out.'

'You know I said there was a problem with my . . . er . . . my good woman's marriage.'

'I thought that was the problem, that she was married?'

'Quite. I'm not putting things too well, am I? Well, it's simple really. She's willing to leave him for me.'

'So, she's told him?'

'No. But she's going to. This weekend.'

Troy wondered if Johnny was really as gullible as he sounded.

'How often have you heard that in a film or read it in a novel, Johnny?'

'No—Freddie, I know what you mean, but it's real this time. This time it's for real.'

'How do you know?'

'Because . . . because . . . because she has courage.'

Troy groaned aloud at the innocence of it all.

'Johnny, Johnny, Johnny. For God's sake.'

'Because . . . she's your sister!'

'Which sister?' Troy said involuntarily, and as soon as the words were out he knew how stupid a question it was. Which sister? It could only be Sasha. She had been having an affair with somebody for months. He'd seen Masha set up her alibi for adultery time after time. He'd seen the friction between Sasha and Hugh all but strike sparks at the family dinner when he had introduced them all to Tosca. Of course it was Sasha.

He knew then that there was no dismissing Johnny. He would have to give the poor sod all the attention he could muster.

'You picked a lousy time,' he said.

'I know. You told me.'

Troy fished into his coat pocket for his keys.

'I have to go to the Yard. Take my keys and let yourself in. I'll be back in an hour and a half or so. We can talk then.'

They rounded the corner into St Martin's Lane. Out of the shelter of the alley, the rain whipped up.

'You'll get soaked,' said Johnny. 'Take these.'

He took off his hat and placed it on Troy's head. He undid his scarf and wrapped it loosely around Troy's neck. A curious gesture, almost touching, almost fraternal.

Troy looked back at Johnny. The eyes apart, they were the same physical type. Small dark men with masses of black hair, flopping down onto the forehead. He had never really noticed before.

§95

He cooled his heels for an hour or more. Madge went home. Jack yawned his goodnight and went in search of the next single woman. There was no sign of Onions. There was no sign of Clark.

He set off back home in the drizzle and the unaccustomed hat. Irritated by the wasted time, trying as best he could to find the right mental gear in which to handle Johnny and the impending divorce and scandal that Sasha was about to unleash upon the family.

There was no light in the court. The street lamps of St Martin's Lane did not penetrate beyond the first three yards, and for some reason the lamp at the other end was out. He fumbled down the alley blind as he had done a thousand times, and on his own doorstep tripped over something solid. It pitched him forward, onto his hands with his knees across the obstacle. His palms braced his weight, face down on the paving stones, and came up wet. But rain did not smell like this, rain did not smell of anything, and nothing on earth had the unmistakable scent of blood. A mad phrase of Kolankiewicz's flashed through his mind: 'sweet shit, sweet shit,' that was how the beast had precisely caught the smell of spilt, congealing blood. And Troy was covered in it.

A light went on two floors up in the building at the back of him, reflected off the windows of his house and bathed the alley in a dim glow. The body at his feet was a man. A man wrapped like him in a blood-sodden black overcoat. Troy lifted the head.

'F ... F ... F ...' burbled from the lips.

He laid Johnny's head in his lap. Tore at the buttons of his overcoat and laid it over the man like blanket.

'Fr ... Fr ... Fr ...' Johnny said.

Troy wiped the blood from his face. Cleaned his lips and eyelids with a fingertip. And the lips opened once more.

Troy leant nearer, strained to hear, shifted his grip and found one hand sinking into the back of the crushed skull, a smattering of grey matter seeping between his fingers.

'Freddie,' Johnny said clearly.

His eyes opened once. As wide as they could go. Then closed. Troy heard the deep exhalation, felt the chest fall, and the life ooze out of him.

Troy sat an age. Time he could not measure. The light above him went out, and sometime later came on again. Into its pool a figure came. Troy looked and could not focus. Looked and could not speak. He heard someone call his name, then the same voice said, 'Oh my God,' then he heard the shrill blast of a police whistle.

'Freddie, Freddie,' said the voice close to him. 'Let go now. You can let go now. He's dead.'

A second figure joined them, running down the courtyard. They resolved into focus, leaning over him, prying his fingers from the body. One was Diana Brack, the other was Ruby the Whore. Ruby, Ruby, he'd not seen Ruby in years. She married a punter and went to live in Leamington.

'Ruby?' he said weakly.

'Oh bugger,' said the first voice. 'He's out of his fucking head. Get an ambulance. Call the Yard. Give them my name. Wildeve, Inspector Wildeve. Tell them I want Kolankiewicz a.s.a.p.'

And Troy saw Ruby run, skirts flying out behind, her, boots clattering.

By the time the short, fat, ugly one appeared they had prised his keys from the corpse's fingers and laid Troy out on the chaise longue in the sitting room. He was shivering uncontrollably, so they had stripped the eiderdown from his bed and draped it over him.

'Oh no,' the short, fat, ugly one was saying. 'Not again. How many times I tell you, smartyarse?'

'Just take a look,' said the young one. 'There's blood everywhere. I've no idea how much of it is his.'

Ugly probed his skull with short, hard fingers. Then unbuttoned his shirt and wiped away the blood with a towel.

'There's not a mark on him. It's all off the other bugger!'

'Then he's in shock.'

'Of course he's in shock. Wouldn't you be in fuckin' shock? No, you'd have tossed your lunch all over the evidence. Out of the way. Get out of the way!'

Ugly produced a hypodermic syringe, the fluid spurting from the needle. Troy's hand shot out and grabbed him by the wrist.

'No,' he said.

'No? Fine, Troy. Who am I?'

Troy thought about it. A short, fat, ugly man. He knew a short, fat, ugly man. He'd got his own short, fat, ugly man. Had one for years.

'Kolankiewicz. You're Kolankiewicz.'

The pair looked at each other like a double act of music hall comedians.

'And who am I?' said the young one.

Troy dragged up a word from the pit of consciousness.

'Jack?' he said.

'Maybe he's OK after all?'

'Bollocks,' said the ugly one. 'Troy, listen to me. What year is it?'

'1944.'

'That does it.'

The ugly one pulled his wrist free and aimed for a vein in Troy's arm.

'No,' said the young one. 'Half the dose. I'll need to talk to him in the morning.'

Troy never heard the ugly one answer. Pink washed him into scarlet and scarlet into burgundy and burgundy into black, black night.

§96

Johnny's blood turned the bathwater brown. Troy pulled the plug and watched it vanish into its spiral, hit the pipe at the end of the bath with his foot and waited while the geyser delivered its meagre four inches of clean.

Jack appeared with a large mug of black coffee, and sat on the bog seat while Troy drank it. It was the old scene—the court of the ablutions, only Jack was him and he was a bubbleless, death-scented, flat-chested substitute for Tosca.

'You know,' Jack said, 'I knew Johnny Fermanagh for the best part of thirty years. Since school, in fact. As older boys went, a decent chap even at the age of twelve. As an adult he was the most useless pillock alive, but he was also the most harmless. No one could have any reason to kill him. I conclude therefore that he was not the intended victim. You were. It was you they meant to kill.'

'Out in the lane,' Troy began, hardly louder than a whisper. 'Insisted on giving me his hat and scarf. Watched him walk off down the alley. Turned up his collar against the rain. Anyone watching who'd been a bit slow would have thought I was him and he was me. Even I thought he was me.'

'I've asked myself. Who would want to kill you? And the answer I come up with is . . . the same people who wanted to kill you last time. So, tell me what lead enabled you to pick up the case?'

'The sister. The one you found in Derbyshire. She found the key to a safety deposit box. Madeleine Kerr left a will, of sorts, blowing the whistle on what she and Cockerell were up to.'

Every time Troy looked over at Jack he nodded as if to say 'go on'. And in ten minutes he had the whole story in half-sentences and breathless mumbles.

'How much does Clark know?' he said at last.

'Everything. Well, almost everything. Don't get on the high horse. He's simply played the role you used to. What's a conspiracy without a conspirator?'

'Have you told Stan?'

'I've tried. I tried all week. He's not there to tell. But perhaps it's all for the best. You know what he's like where the spooks are concerned. He'll get formal, he'll get flustered and he'll get angry. Then God help us all. He won't handle it well. I'm going in through the back door.'

'Aha, 'Jack nodded. 'That friend of yours, Charlie?'

'Yes.'

'When?'

'Today. Late afternoon. About four. Unless I can get to him earlier.'

'I'll be home all evening. Call me. Whatever the outcome, call me. I think it's time we stopped fighting each other and fought the enemy.'

'Whoever he is,' said Troy.

'Quite,' said jack. 'And I've no more idea than you have.'

Troy lay back, the nape of his neck on the roll of the bath's rim, and closed his eyes. The water was almost stone cold, he was scarcely covered by a watery scum of blood and soap and the ghostly trace of Tosca's bath salts, but he didn't much care if he never moved again.

'The tearaway toffs,' he said softly.

'Eh?'

'That's what the Yard used to call us, before we garnered enough rank for them to pretend to more respect—the tearaway toffs.'

'Good Lord, so they did. I haven't heard that phrase in years. The tearaway toffs ride again, eh?'

§97

There was no reason to feel this way. No logical reason, that is. But when Troy saw Charlie sitting in the Café Royal at the same table at which he and Anna had ceremoniously dumped each other, his fingers tingled and his thumbs pricked.

'You look bloody awful,' said Charlie. 'Any particular reason?'

'Dozens, hundreds,' said Troy.

Charlie had clearly been there a while. He'd finished a plate of sandwiches and marked up the late runners for Sandown Park in the morning paper. He flagged a waiter and ordered the same again.

'Unless,' he said, 'you feel like something stronger. We could always adjourn to one of the watering-holes.'

'No,' said Troy. 'I'd only feel worse.'

'Then perhaps you'd better tell Uncle Charlie all about it, and I'll kiss it better.'

'Cockerell. It's all about Cockerell.'

There was only one thing Troy wanted to hear from Charlie. He stumbled into his preposterous tale, and within a couple of sentences Charlie said it.

'Dammit, Freddie. What are old friends for? Why didn't you come to me sooner?'

They both knew why.

Charlie reached into his jacket pocket, and finding he had no paper, opened the back of his chequebook and began to scribble. He filled the back of one cheque—those ludicrous, giant pages, the size of pre-war banknotes that Mullins Kelleher favoured—and began on another. Troy wondered if he'd end up filling the book, tearing off the stubs in summary of this mess of mayhem. And then it would make sense. He would only have to read the stubs to see meaning. Deposit—one mystery. Withdraw—one life.

As Troy told him a cloud appeared in the telling. It hovered at every stage. It was clung to every question Charlie asked. He suddenly felt that he had dreamt last night, that it had not happened. Washed and dressed, the smell of blood smothered in talcum powder, he felt suddenly stripped of its certainty, as though he had set foot upon a dream. He could feel Johnny's weight in his arms, he could see the mask he had made of his face as he wiped the blood from his eyes and lips, a blood-red nigger-minstrel mask. But he could not hear him, and he could not smell him, and the weight floated from him and the vision dissolved, and he began to think he had dreamt it and because he had dreamt it he could not talk about it. He could not tell Charlie.

'Where is it now?' Charlie said.

'Where's what?'

'This document you say you found in Paris.'

'Oh . . . my sergeant has it. He knows a bit about cryptography.'

'And where's he? At the Yard?'

'I don't know. I don't know where he is. He seems to have vanished.'

They had reached the point at which chronology dictated that he recount the previous night. He tried to see it all again. The moment when Johnny had placed the hat upon his head and they had symboli-cally exchanged identities. The sound of his last uttered word—Troy's own name. It was a dream. He had floated in pink somewhere. It never happened. And he knew he could not tell it.

And then he saw her. Picking her way between the tables and the afternoon shoppers of Regent Street, taking the tea they all held to be earned, heading for him, waving fussily, coming up behind Charlie. He rose from his chair. Charlie looked around to see who had joined them, and seeing a woman, rose too.

'This is unexpected,' Troy said.

'Aw ... I came up with your sisters. They wanted to hit town and blow some money. It was nice for a while but goddammit, all those women can talk about is shopping and fucking, fucking and shopping.'

Then she noticed Charlie. And Troy saw the tiny spark that passed between them.

'Charlie. My wife—Larissa Troy,' said Troy. 'Larissa. Charles Leigh-Hunt.'

Charlie beamed his famous smile at her, took her hand.

'At last,' she said. 'I heard a lot about you.'

'Nothing good, I hope?'

Troy watched. Even Tosca basked in the attention of a man like Charlie. He was not sure what it was, but he knew he didn't have it. This animal magic that could corrupt the common sense of women. Height helped, the elegance it gave, and the beautiful blue eyes spoke as loudly as his perfect smile, but these were only parts of the puzzle, and the sum was greater than the parts. She waved a hand, mock dismissively, almost seemed to blush at one of the corniest lines in the book.

'Naw—just lotsa stuff about all the things you and the gang used to get up to.'

'The gang?'

'Oh ... you know ... Huey, Duey and Luey.'

Charlie looked quizzically at Troy.

'Gus and Dickie,' he said.

'Baby. I gotta run. Or they'll come looking for me. You be home soon. Nice meetin' ya, Charlie.'

She pecked him on the cheek, waved cutely at Charlie and dashed for the door. A ten-second whirlwind.

They sat down.

'Well,' said Charlie.

'You were abroad,' said Troy.

'Was I?'

'I tried phoning you.'

'I suppose congratulations are in order.'

'If you like.'

'You know. I never really thought that we'd either of us marry. Funny really. No rhyme or reason to it. I just never thought we would.'

'Nor I.'

The pause that followed was one of the most awkward Troy could ever recall. Until Charlie said, 'Now—where were we?'

§98

Troy ran. All the way home. Out of the Café Royal, into the Quadrant and hell for leather towards Piccadilly Circus. He tripped crossing Leicester Square, tore the knee out of one trouser leg, pushed away the kindly hands that helped him to his feet and ran for the Charing Cross Road, St Martin's Court, across the Lane and breathless to his own door. He could still feel the imprint of Charlie's bear hug, the palms clapped to his shoulder blades, like demonic stigmata.

Tosca was home. The pipes banged and creaked with the telltale noises of a bath running. Troy threw off his jacket and ran upstairs. She was half undressed, down to her blouse and suspenders, padding around her bedroom in her stockinged feet, humming softly to herself

She draped her arms around his neck. The best of moods, smiling, jokey. The wise-cracking, wise-ass, all-American broad she could be when the mood took her. He slipped his arms about her waist out of nothing more than habit. A reflex in no way connected to what he was thinking.

'That was quick. Just as well. We're goin' out. On the town. It's time to rock'n'roll!'

She kissed him. A real smackerooney—a parody of a kiss—pulled herself back, arched her neck, put her weight on his arms and beamed at him. He felt the provocative stroking of one stockinged heel on the back of his calf. It was the peak of irony, that the best should surface in her at the worst moment.

'Well? Cat gotcha tongue?'

'Sit down,' Troy said.

'What?'

He pushed her to the edge of the bed and made her sit.

'Where have you seen Charlie before?'

'What?'

'Where have you seen Charlie before?'

'I never seen him before. You introduced us not half an hour ago.'

'No,' said Troy. 'No. I've known Charlie since we were boys. He tried, and he put on a damn good show, but he could not hide it. He recognised you. He knew you.'

'Baby, I never—'

He took her face in his hands. His fingers splayed across each cheek, and looked right into her eyes. It was better than shouting at her.

'Think!' he said. 'Think! Where have you seen him before?'

Tears started in the corner of each eye.

'He knew me?'

'Yes.'

'I didn't know him. I mean I thought I'd just met your oldest friend.'

'He is my oldest friend. But he's a spook.'

'You said, but high up—like diplomatic. I was a nobody. I had no reason to think he'd be anyone I'd ever dealt with.'

'Nor I. But I can read Charlie like a book sometimes. He's met you, and in the only guise that matters.'

'On the job?'

'Yes.'

'You don't think maybe in the war? I mean it's a goddam miracle I never bumped into your brother in the war. I met so many Brits.'

'If it had been in the war, don't you think he would have said?'

She sagged with the weight of his logic. He felt that if he let go of her now she would simply fall into a heap on the bed.

'Yeah. Of course. I'm clutching at straws. I know the type. He's not the klutz with women that you are. He's a fuckin' smoothie. A lounge lizard if ever I saw one. If there'd been any intro he could have used he'd 've flirted with me till his balls fell off. Damn, damn, damn!'

The tears flowed under his hands, and behind him he heard the sound of the bath running over, of water splashing onto wood. He let go of her and went to the bathroom to turn off the tap. When he returned she had buried her face in the pillow. He picked her up and wrapped her in his arms. She sobbed into his shoulder. He heard her strangled voice say, 'There's never going to be a way out is there? There's never going to be an end to running.'

She slept and he let her sleep.

When she awoke it was dark. He was sitting on a chair in the corner of her room. He saw her stir, watched her rub her hair and blink at him. For a moment it seemed that she did not recognise him, the hands left her hair and clapped onto her open mouth as she muffled a scream.

'Jeeezus. Jeezus. I remember! I remember! It's him!'

Troy crossed the room, pulled her hands away from her mouth, and held them.

'Just tell me.'

'November. Three years ago. 1953. I was on a live drop to Lisbon. Regular run. I'd been doing it since the spring. Same guy, same method, same exchange. He'd show up clutching a two-day-old copy of *The Times,* with the eyes of the Es filled in, and I'd hand him a parcel. They never told me what it was, but I knew it was money. I'd done half a dozen in a row. Then in November a different guy shows, clutching the paper marked up in the right way. So I gave him the money. Didn't take fifteen seconds—we neither of us asked any questions—and he didn't try to flirt with me. But it was Charlie. Only time it ever happened. In December the regular guy was back and I never saw Charlie again. The regular guy showed up every other time. Lisbon, Paris, Zurich. Regular as clockwork, till they pulled me off it.'

Troy went downstairs and came back clutching his briefcase. He tipped it out on the bed and held up a photograph of Cockerell he'd cut from a newspaper.

'Is this him?'

'Sure. That's the guy. Ronnie Kerr. But how did you—?'

'His real name's Arnold Cockerell.'

'The frogman? The guy you've been investigating? I don't get it.'

'You should. It's simple. You were the service end of a grubby little operation.'

'I was?'

'Where did you think the money went? What did you think it was for?'

'I didn't think. You lose the habit. You just do it and hope to get by. Y'know. Maybe it's not as bad as it seems. Nobody knows. I mean, nobody else. Nobody that could tell. Charlie won't tell, will he? I mean he can't. If he blows the whistle on me he blows it on himself. It's a Mexican stand-off. So we're safe. Nobody really knows. I mean, who else has ever seen me?'

Troy could not tell her pleading from her desire to reassure him, and hence herself. He picked up the police 10 C 8 of the dead Madeleine Kerr.

'Did you know her?'

'Nah. Never met her.'

'She was Ronnie Kerr's wife. Or at least she pretended to be. Twenty-two years old. Thought it was all a lark. She was murdered. Less than two weeks ago. You remember the case I was on in Derbyshire? That was Ronnie Kerr's accountant. That leaves you—you're the last person in England who knows Charlie was running a racket for the Russians. Everyone else has been killed.'

'Oh shit. Oh shit. Oh shit.'

The phone had rung persistently over his words. He picked it up, meaning to hang up and silence it.

'Mr Troy?' The operator's voice.

'Yes.'

'Reverse charge call from Leicester. A Mr Clark. Will you accept the charge?'

Tosca was right. No one but Charlie had ever seen her in her old guise. No one except Clark.

'It's me, sir.'

'Eddie. Where are you?'

'I'm on Leicester station, sir. I've forty minutes between connections. I'm waiting for the slow train from Nottingham, but I thought I'd better tell you as soon as I could. I'm on my way back from Derbyshire. I've cracked the code.'

'The code?'

'Madeleine Kerr's last letter, sir. I was getting nowhere with it. Couldn't get past the first sentence. Then it dawned on me. She hadn't written it. Cockerell wrote it. So. I had to look for the key.'

'Key?' Troy said feeling like an ill-informed parrot.

'Yes, sir. Codes like this need a text. An acrostic grid that both writer and reader know to use. At its neatest you have two code pads, one-time pads they're called, five letters in a block, and you tear off the page every time you use it, so it's never the same code twice. At its most complex you have a machine with lots of rotating cogs that makes Babbage's engine look as simple as an alarm clock, and a few thousand assorted boffins and WRENS in wooden huts in Bletchley Park to work the damn thing. I didn't think Commander Cockerell quite that sophisticated, so I knew I was looking for a printed text. The letter opens in the old alphabet code—Dear Sis. That's a pun in my opinion sir. SIS. Get it?'

'Just tell me, Eddie.'

'Then it says 49AA. However I worked the code I always ended up with gibberish from those four letters. I thought I must be working it wrong. But then it was obvious, there was a new code for everything that followed and this was the key, they weren't actually in code themselves. What we in the police force call a clue, sir. I began to realise that Madeleine Kerr had written only the first two lines, something to steer her sister to the real code that Cockerell was using. And it had to be something Cockerell had access to every day. So I took his shop keys out of your desk and went up there yesterday afternoon. I missed it. It was out in the open and I missed it. I spent all last night and half this morning turning out his desk drawers. Then I saw it, sticking out of one of those pigeon holes above his desk. The Automobile Association Handbook for 1949. At the back of the book they give you the distances between the major towns of the country. A simple A–Z graph on two axes. The perfect reusable code. Unless you know what it's based on, you'd never crack it! So A is for Aberdeen, and the first use of the letter A is the distance between Aberdeen and Aberystwyth—which is 427 miles, therefore the code is 427. The second use would be based on the distance between Aberdeen and Barnstaple, which is 573 miles, hence 573. And as there are fifty-seven possible codes for the letter A, you can write a page or more before you have to repeat any one code. Occasionally you'll get overlaps—for example the distance from London to Brighton is the same as from London to Cambridge so you could in theory have 53 standing for both B and C, but as London is at the bottom of every column you'd be on at least your thirtieth use of the letter by then, so . . . And the tricky bit is there's no major British city beginning with the letter J, so the second I, which is Ipswich, becomes J. You'll never guess how he managed Z.'

'For Christ's sake, Eddie. Just tell me!'

'Ashby de la *Zouche*. Not bad, eh?'

Clark clearly was not getting the message. Troy turned around in search of Tosca, but she had gone downstairs.

'You cracked it. Well done. Now just tell me what it says.'

But he knew what it would say. Knew it at its worst.

'Cockerell was a double agent, sir. I doubt he had the brains to work out exactly what that meant, but the people running him did. They were using him as a courier to channel information out of Britain and money in. They bounced him all over Europe—Paris, Milan, Lisbon. You name it. He was recruited by a man called Charles Leigh-Hunt in the summer of 1951 on a trip to London, ostensibly to visit the Festival of Britain. Says Leigh-Hunt's MI6, and that he'd known him in the war, but I have no real confidence in Mr Cockerell on matters like that. Could be a fake name, could be a line they spun him. But there's no doubt about who was his immediate control—would you believe our old friend Inspector Cobb?'

'Yes,' said Troy. 'I would.'

'Then there's a list of seven names of agents Cockerell claimed to have on his payroll. Earl, John—Smith, Alan—Harwood, Antony—'

'Don't recite the lot. Just give me what's important. The big fish, not the sprats.'

Clark paused, as though Troy had set him a dilemma.

'Well, sir. There's only one other big fish as you put it. The courier the Russians sent. He records every meeting, every date, every place, but then he says she always used a different name, so he doesn't bother to record them, as they'll all be phoney.'

Clark paused again. Troy could hear his own heart beat.

'But he does describe her.'

Again silence. Troy not wanting to break into it, for fear of what must follow.

'I will say, sir, it sounds familiar.'

'Does it?'

'About five foot tall, close-cropped hair, although the colour varies from blonde to ginger, built like Jane Russell, bit of a looker, and what Cockerell calls an "irritating American accent". But, sir, and here's the clincher, "always clutching a copy of *Huckleberry Finn*". Now, sir, who does that sound like to you?'

He wanted so much to be able to see her. He wanted to look into her eyes. He wanted to fling her "we're safe" back in her face in all its overconfident stupidity. Why had she chosen now to wander off? Now—when the lies she had constructed were about to come crashing down like crazy paving.

'Eddie, do you still live in the Police House?'

'I do, sir.'

'Don't go back there. Watch your back all the way home. Check into a hotel. Go to the Ritz, give them my name. There'll be a room for you. She'll meet you there.'

'I don't quite follow, sir.'

But he didn't ask who Troy meant by 'she'.

'There's been another murder. Someone Cobb mistook for me.'

'Bloody hell.'

Troy went downstairs to the sitting room. Tosca was sitting in one armchair. Foxx in the other. Like hell's bookends. Foxx was the new Foxx—the Dior suit, the good shoes—the matching pink luggage in a heap between the two chairs. Tosca was the old Tosca, wishing looks could kill.

'Well,' she said, 'looks like we caught you suckertush, doesn't it?'

She crossed her legs, let her foot swing, a metronome of her own impatience. Foxx looked at him. Baffled and not far short of angry.

'You gonna explain, or what?' said Tosca.

Troy seized her by the hand, dragged her into the kitchen and kicked the door shut. He didn't see the fist that came flying at him, and a direct hit to the jaw knocked him off-balance. He deflected the second blow, and the third went wild, colliding with a saucepan. She bruised her knuckles and yelled in pain.

Troy slipped in and slammed her back against the wall.

'You bastard,' she hissed. 'You complete fuckin' bastard. You couldn't wait for me could you? You couldn't fuckin' wait! I mean was that a lot to ask? Just to wait for me!'

He took her by the jaw, tilted her head and levelled her eyes on his. Her feet still kicked, but the hands stopped flailing.

'Shut up. Shut up and listen to me. Whatever's running through your mind, whatever it is you think I've done to you there's something more important.'

Tosca managed an 'Oh yeah?' through pursed lips.

'They killed a man last night.'

'They?'

'Them. The people you were dealing with.'

'Oh God.'

'Right here. On the doorstep.'

379

Her eyes widened. He felt her body slacken and knew the fight had gone out of her.

'They thought he was me.'

'Oh God. Oh Jesus. Oh God save us.'

He let go. She slithered to the floor, wrapped her arms about herself and he saw tears forming in her eyes.

He squatted down to her level.

'Who was he? This guy they thought was you?'

'An old friend. You might have heard me mention him. Johnny Fermanagh.'

'And this guy looked like you?'

'A bit. Well, a lot.'

She leant her head against his thigh and groaned.

'Whatdafuckaweegonnadooo?'

He stretched out a hand to her head and ruffled her hair, picked out the cobwebs she had gathered slithering down the wall.

'Exactly what I tell you.'

'I'm all ears.'

'You take Shirley. You check into the Ritz. You take three rooms.'

'Who's the third one for?'

'My sergeant. He'll get in touch with you in a couple of hours.'

'How will I know him?'

'He's an old friend—Edwin Clark.'

Her head shot up so fast he thought she'd crick her neck, and her eyes were the size of saucers.

'Edwin? Edwin? You mean fat little Eddie Clark from Berlin? Sweet little Swifty who did that nice line in women's underwear and black-market coffee? The guy who got me my black strapless Schiaparelli?'

'Yes.'

'And he's your sergeant?'

'Yes.'

'Jeezus! Jeezus, Troy. Why didn't you tell me about Clark? He knows me, he knows me! You could have told me, you could have fuckin' told me!'

'It doesn't matter. It would only have alarmed you. Besides, he's one of us now.'

'Us? Us? Troy, I don't even know the word!'

'Leave a message at the desk telling him which room you're in. Lie low and do nothing till you hear from me. Now—get your shoes and coat. You haven't time to pack.'

He opened the kitchen door, and she ran for the stairs. Foxx was standing by the fire, with her back to him. She turned and slapped another large brown envelope against his chest.

'When I said you were married, you told me you didn't live together any more.'

'We didn't, or I didn't think we did,' Troy said, not wholly sure what the truth was.

'But here she is, and here am I.'

'And you'll be together a little longer.'

'Are we in trouble?'

'Yes.'

'I was prepared for that. I don't think I was prepared for a wife.'

§99

Troy put the two women in a cab, and went back to the house. He took the little golden gun from his coat pocket, pushed off the safety and racked a bullet into the chamber. He put the gun on the table next to the telephone. The tools of the trade. One or other had to get him out of this.

Time was he and Charlie would discuss every aspect of their lives. Once, the best part of twenty years ago, Charlie had rung him and said 'I'm engaged. Talk me out of it.' Troy had. And he had never even learnt the unfortunate woman's name. But to call him, and square off, to call him and draw a line in the sand, to call him and be willing to go as far as blackmail—that he had never done, and he had no idea how to set about it. With any luck Charlie would call him. 'We're in a mess Freddie, let's get out of it.' Time was, Charlie could talk his way out of anything.

Half an hour had passed, and he had not reached for the phone. It rang first. He picked it up. If it was Charlie, so be it.

'Troy? It's me—Foxx. I'm at the Ritz. Something happened. We took the taxi to King's Cross. Larissa gave the driver new instructions after we'd set off. Not the Ritz. She said it was dumb to go straight to the Ritz. "Trust me," she said. "I'm a pro." She said she'd been followed before. She knew how to shake off a trail. We changed taxis at King's Cross. I flagged it down. She was behind me, paying the first taxi. She dropped her handbag, and when I turned round she'd vanished. The bag was still there, lying on the ground, but she'd gone, Troy. She'd just gone. I waited for more than ten minutes, but she'd vanished into thin air! Vanished, Troy. Just . . . vanished!'

§100

It had been years since he had last been in Edwardes Square. He had always thought it beautiful, in its sylvan way, but he had never found any reason to go there and enough of a reason not to. One thing had changed. There was now no Special Branch plod outside number 52. There was now no need for him to lurk in the shadows. He parked the Bentley outside Mrs Edge's door and yanked on the bell pull.

'You're late,' she said as she saw him framed in the doorway.

Troy looked at his watch. It was a quarter to eleven.

'I'm sorry,' he said. 'I'd no idea of the time.'

'I meant late in the lifetime of your favour, Mr Troy. Not the hour. However, I've been expecting you these ten years. Do come in.'

She pushed the door to and drew a heavy curtain across it, locking out the night.

'Almost autumn, you know. Mists and mellow fruitfulness, to say nothing of cold draughts and rising damp.'

He followed her down the hall and into an overheated sitting room at the back of the house.

'I retire at Christmas. If you had not come soon, you would never have been able to collect what you're owed.'

'I wasn't thinking in those terms.'

'Don't be coy. It doesn't suit you.'

She sat down in a high armchair next to a hissing gas fire. Troy had the vaguest memory of a yappy lapdog, but a fat tabby cat occupied pride of place on the hearthrug, opened one eye as Troy approached, and did not stir from its place in the artificial sun. A game of patience was set out before her on a low, green baize card table, the latest novel of Kingsley Amis spread open on the footstool. Time had not been kind to Muriel Edge. The lines around her myopic eyes had sunk into Audenesque canyons. The high chair was clearly intended to cater to the onset of arthritis and an inability to bend without pain. The disease had locked her fingers like claws, bent and angular, the knuckles swollen to the size of conkers. The very shape bespoke pain to Troy.

'I should have gone in the spring, at sixty. But when Dick White went off to run the other show, the new chap asked me to stay on. See the section through the handover, as it were. I was only too glad, retirement will bore me into an early grave. God knows, I can hardly while away the time writing a memoir, now can I?'

She waved Troy into the chair opposite with a crooked hand.

'Now, tell me what you want. I do hope it's something within my reach. I do so dislike to leave a debt unsettled.'

Troy had told her the truth. He had no sense of calling in a favour. But he would never have called on her had he not been able to bank on her sense that he had done her job for her all those years ago—tracking Jimmy Wayne where she could not, bringing him to book when her powers had reached their limit. He saw it as a connection, not a debt, but if that was how she saw it, it was but a small difference. He wanted a favour. Whether it was owed or not was of no matter if she granted it.

On a small oak table in the alcove of the chimney breast sat two telephones, at arm's length from her chair. A black one and a white one—the white had no dial. The standard equipment of a senior officer of MI5. Muriel Edge was a section head. The white phone would lead directly to MI5's own switchboard. She would have only to lift it to find a duty officer waiting to address her by name. The favour Troy had to ask would be almost effortless for her.

'Do you know Norman Cobb?'

'Yes. I know Inspector Cobb. He did one or two jobs for me. But not lately. He is . . . ah . . . too heavy-handed. I can't have that. There are better officers in the Branch, though God knows, subtlety is not their middle name.'

'Some time today he will have requested use of a safe house. I need to know where it is.'

'Is that all?'

'Yes.'

She shrugged as though he had accepted a shilling for a quid and reached for the white phone.

'Yes. I need to speak to Norman Cobb of Special Branch. He's in a safe house of ours. I don't know which one. No, don't put me through, just call me on the other line when you know.'

She turned back to Troy.

'He'll be a few minutes. Why don't you pour us both a drink. You're as white as a sheet, you know. I think we could both use a brandy.'

Troy followed where the bent finger pointed, to the sideboard and its array of spirit bottles. He returned, set the glass next to her deck of cards, and sipped at his own. It still tasted like soap, but she was right—it was just what he needed.

'I've been following your career. From time to time, that is. You do have your ups and downs, don't you?'

It should not have puzzled Troy—though it did—but she had not yet asked why he wanted Cobb in his MI5 safe house. And, it seemed, she would not.

'You were the talk of the town a while back.'

'Was I?'

'Oh yes. I felt proud to have known you. When you told Ted Wintrincham you wouldn't spy on Bulganin, but you would spy on Khrushchev.'

She was chuckling softly now—not at him, but, it would seem, with him.

'You heard that? I wasn't aware it was common knowledge.'

'It's not. It's what you call uncommon knowledge. Ted's quite a wag. Told the story with all the pauses, mimicked that overblown public-school accent of yours and then laughed fit to bust. He told anyone who'd listen. Thought it was the funniest thing he'd ever heard.'

'I'm afraid I didn't manage to see the joke,' said Troy.

'Nor should you. That's when they got you. You should never have agreed to any part of their plan. You should have got to your feet and told them to do their own dirty work. You should have walked out of the door with not so much as a glance over your shoulder for fear of the salt pillar. It was madness. It was vanity in its crudest form. You were flattered they wanted you. You were flattered by the chance to meet Khrushchev. You fell for hobnobbing, for rubbing shoulders with the great and the monstrous—but that's when they got you. You've been theirs ever since. And once they get you, you're theirs for ever. You, you of all people, ought to have known better. I find it hard to believe that you didn't know this. Once they get you, you're theirs for ever!'

Her voice had risen in a steady crescendo to this final reiteration. 'Once they get you, you're theirs for ever'—these were the last words of Daniel Keeffe.

'I'm taking steps to be un-got,' he said.

'Oh? You are? Inspector Cobb, I take it?'

The black phone rang. She picked it up, said 'yes', and put it back almost at once.

'Narrow Street,' she said, 'Cobb is at number 11a Narrow Street, in Limehouse.'

§ 101

Narrow Sreet was the dream of a perfervid imagination. A fragment of Dickens, a figment of Edgar Wallace or Arthur Machen. The sort of mist-shrouded Limehouse riverside alley where dead dogs would be found floating in green puddles, where the younger sons of peers, silk-hatted and black-caped, would stagger stoned from the opium dens of London's Chinatown, where Dorian Gray would walk the night for ever young, for ever evil, where scarlet whores in scarlet dresses would flounce their skirts beneath the gaslamps and solicit with a cry of ''Allo ducks', where every other man was a cutpurse who would slit your 'froat from ear to ear' and dump your body in the Thames to float downriver.

Troy had walked Narrow Sreet as a beat bobby. He rather liked the place.

It was almost one in the morning. He stood with Jack in the drizzling rain, looking up at number 11a from the opposite side of the street. He had got Jack out of bed, and he had picked Troy up at the Yard in his plain black police Wolseley 4/44, so much more discreet than a Bentley. He had called Leman Street police station and asked for the Divisional Detective Inspector of J Division, and caught him only minutes before he signed off for the night.

'Paddy—it's Troy. Do you still want a chance to even the score with Norman Cobb?'

'Lead me to him,' Milligan had said.

'He's on your patch. Narrow Street.'

'Bingo,' said Mulligan.

And he had called George Bonham.

'George, can you still get into your uniform?'

'O' course,' Bonham had said. 'What's up?'

Troy could see Bonham now, lumbering down the street from Limehouse Cut. His boots clattering on the cobblestones, splashing through the puddles, his shadow thrown before him, immense in the moonlight, his pointy hat towering above them, the best part of seven feet off the ground.

Milligan stepped out of the shadows under 11a, and crossed the street, soft shoes treading soundlessly.

'He's here all right. There's a squad car under a tarpaulin down the alley next to the house. They've blacked it out pretty well, but there's definitely lights on the first and second floors.'

'You know George Bonham, don't you, Paddy?'

'Of course. We were at Leman Street together for a while, weren't we, Mr Bonham?'

Troy turned his attention on Bonham. He was the one who would most need the explanation and be least capable of grasping it.

'George, we're all of us off duty. Do you see what I mean?'

'I'm not,' said Bonham. 'I'm retired.'

'Same difference,' Troy said.

Bonham looked puzzled, scratched one ear beneath the pointy hat. 'We're all coppers, though?'

'Yes—we're all coppers, but this is not a police operation. We're ...'

Troy racked his brains for a euphemism that would explain and not alarm.

'We're freelance tonight.'

'Oh, I gettcha. Sort of a posse like?'

The idea had not occurred to Troy, but that was exactly what they were, and the word suited very well.

'Yes. A posse. We're a posse.'

'And who are we chasin'?'

'Norman Cobb.'

'What, that bastard from the Branch?'

No one, it seemed, had a good word for Inspector Cobb.

'All you have to do is get them to open the door. That's why we need a uniform. Cobb will have a constable with him at the very least. He'll be the one to open up. Make an enquiry. Ask him about the car. Don't be fobbed off with a flash of warrant card. Take out your notebook, ask him for the registration number and the log book. I'll go in the back. And I'll create the disturbance we need to let Jack and Paddy steam in. You just sit on that constable.'

'Freddie—what's in there?'

'It's an MI5 safe house, George.'

'I see,' he said, but plainly didn't. 'MI5—aren't they our blokes then?'

'Usually,' said Troy. 'But . . .'

'But,' Milligan cut in, 'when they use a safe house on your patch and don't have the courtesy to tell the local nick they're doing it, they're not playing by the rules, are they? So there's no reason we should either.'

'We rescuing someone, George. If we do it right no one will say a thing about it afterwards. It will be as though it never happened. Your pension's safe, and who knows, the rest of us might live to collect ours.'

'Say no more,' Bonham said. And Troy hoped he meant it.

Troy and Jack slipped between Cobb's car and the corrugated steel fence that ran down to the river.

'Are you sure you're up to this?' Jack asked.

'Yes.'

'I could go, you know.'

Troy pointed to the top-floor window at the back, where the building jutted out over the river.

'It's tiny,' he said. 'I'm the smallest. It's best if I do it. Give me ten minutes to get in, then set George to rattle the door. Keep out of sight. Give them a clear view of him. If they think he's a passing beat bobby being dutifully nosy, so much the better. When I've found her, I'll kick up a racket. If needs be enough of a disturbance to make a forced entry perfectly legal . . .'

'I think we should stop using that word. George might need the reassurance. As far as I'm concerned it's irrelevant. Cobb's got it coming.'

'Whatever . . . just come in fighting.'

Jack cupped his hands to make a foothold and eased Troy over the fence.

'Tearaway toffs!' he whispered in the same tone in which one told actors to 'break a leg'.

'Jesus Christ,' said Troy, and dropped clumsily down the other side.

The rain made everything slippery. Troy grabbed hold of the soil stack and began to wonder if ten minutes would be enough. The stack, an eight-inch diameter iron pipe, was old, stout, and solidly bolted to the wall. At the first floor it swung through forty-five degrees and crossed from the side of the building to the back, sticking out precariously over the mudflats of the Thames. Troy felt like a human fly clinging to the pipe as it rounded the corner, but it took his weight, realigned to the vertical and seemed to lead privy by privy to the top of the building, and the open window on the top floor—the only one that was not barred or bricked up. At the third floor he lost his footing and found himself spinning into space, seventy feet above the river, the rain spitting in his face, clinging to an overflow pipe and staring at the looming cranes of Canada Wharf.

The odd thing was the trembling of the knee. He eased himself quietly through the top-floor window into a long-abandoned lavatory, and slid down onto the bog seat. Ancient distemper flaked at every touch and covered his clothes with its fine, pale ash. But the knee, the same knee he had scabbed dashing across Leicester Square, the leg that lost its grip on the pipe, jerked with a life of its own. He held it down with both hands and willed it to respond. Any minute now Bonham would thump his giant's fist against the door and set the house to rattle to its roots.

The top floor was abandoned. Rain and moonlight poured in through missing slates in the roof. Troy took the gun from his pocket and went down to the fourth. The floor was empty. Down to the third. Gently turning the doorhandles one by one. And in the second room he found her, just as Bonham began to pound the door.

Tosca lay on a bare mattress by the far wall. She was not bound or gagged; she was out cold. Troy knelt down, placed the gun on the seat of a bentwood chair, and turned her face to him. She had taken a beating.

Her face was a blue patchwork of bruises, her right eye was closed by swelling not by sleep, and one of her front teeth was chipped. But the knuckles of her right hand were skinned and bloody. She had put up one hell of a fight.

He put his mouth to her ear and spoke as loudly as he dared.

'Tosca. Tosca.'

She stirred, groaned, mumbled and beneath the mumble he heard too late the tread of feet upon the boards behind him. He turned sharply. All he could see were legs, then an arm swung down at him—his own gun, held by the barrel, the butt aimed at his face. He rolled backwards, kicked out with both legs and connected loudly with Cobb's shins. Cobb went down. Troy flung himself on top of him and got both his hands around the hand that held the gun. He found himself looking straight into Cobb's face. A bloody bruise beneath one eye bore witness to the struggle he had had taking Tosca. But Troy was scarcely bigger than she. Almost smiling at the task, Cobb simply rolled Troy off him and reversed their positions. Troy still clung to his gun hand. Cobb twisted the wrist. The barrel still pointed off to nowhere, but slowly he was turning it on Troy.

Troy put his thumbs over Cobb's trigger finger and squeezed. The shot rang out and a shower of plaster cascaded down on both of them. Cobb reared up, his left hand thumping Troy in the face, but off-balance and without the strength or skill of his right. Then Troy heard feet on the stairs and a truncheon thwacked Cobb across the shoulders, and he felt his weight roll off him, and the rush of air returning to his lungs, and saw Milligan whacking Cobb into a corner.

Jack helped him to his feet. Milligan had knocked Cobb senseless, and now scooped Tosca in his arms as though she weighed no more than a leaf and vanished through the door.

'You OK?' Jack said.

'Yes. He danm near had me, but I'm OK.'

The knee that trembled suddenly refused to bear his weight. Jack caught him, and the bullet Cobb was aiming shot between them, drawing a bloody line on the outside of Troy's right thigh. Cobb was sprawled full length on the other side of the room, blinking as though unable to focus, clutching the little golden gun at arm's length. In two strides Jack was across the room. One foot on Cobb's wrist, and the other delivered a cracking kick to the jaw. Cobb's head shot sideways and his grip on the gun relaxed. This time he really was out. Troy lurched across the room, all his weight on his left leg, but Jack caught him in both arms.

'Leave him, Freddie! He's not worth it. Leave him!'

And he bundled him out of the door and down the stairs.

Of course Cobb was not worth it. But it was not Cobb Troy had gone after. It was the gun.

Out in the street Bonham held a young constable, no more than twenty-five or six, pinned to the pavement with a size fourteen boot across his throat and a truncheon aimed at his balls.

Troy stopped on the threshold, clinging to Jack's arm, blood coursing down his leg and filling up his shoe.

'You,' he said. 'Warrant card!'

The man fumbled in his pocket. Troy looked at the card. He was a regular Special Branch constable. Troy had no way of knowing whether he was a stooge of Cobb's or someone who honestly thought he was doing his duty.

'Do you know who I am?'

The man nodded.

'Then take some advice. If you want a career as a copper, forget this ever happened. Go back to the Yard and ask to be transferred out of the Branch. And keep well away from Cobb until you get it. If you don't, I wouldn't give tuppence for your chances. Do you understand?'

He nodded again. Bonham showed no inclination to lift his foot. Jack tugged at his sleeve and gestured upwards with the flat of his hand. Bonham let go, and the young constable sucked in air with a painful wheeze.

Milligan had lain Tosca on the back seat of the car. She had not come round. Now, he lifted Troy into the front seat as Jack started the engine.

'Hospital,' Milligan said to no one in particular.

Troy put a hand on Jack's arm to stop him, and reached down to the floor of the car, acutely conscious that the wetness he could feel beneath his fingers was as likely to be blood as rain. His fingers grasped the hard, round object he sought.

Troy handed the potato to Bonham. He took it in his huge paw and regarded it quizzically. Then it dawned on him. A disarming smile of uncertainty, swept by good manners into a display of gratitude.

'Ta, very much. It'll bake nicely with a couple o' parsnips and the Sunday joint.'

'No, George. It's not a present. I want you to shove it up the exhaust pipe of Cobb's car. If he's any notion of following when he comes round, it'll buy us a few hours till he gets his hands on another.'

Bonham looked at the potato, once more an object of mystery where he thought he had perceived a simple household vegetable.

'Up the exhaust? Wherever do you learn such things?'

'At an English school, George. It was either that or learn how to blow smoke rings.'

Troy thanked Milligan, Jack put the car in gear and roared off towards the Highway and Cable Street.

'Hospital,' he said echoing Milligan.

'No,' said Troy. 'The Ritz.'

'The Ritz? What the bloody hell's at the Ritz?'

'Clark and the sister.'

Jack nodded towards the back seat and the horizontal Tosca.

'What about sleeping beauty?'

'Take her to Mimram. I'll join you as soon as I can.'

'Can you drive like that?'

The gash didn't hurt. There was a lot of blood, but the wound was a nick in the flesh; it was too shallow to have hit an artery and most certainly had not hit a bone. Sooner or later the blood would stop.

'Yes,' Troy said optimistically.

'We could be at the London Hospital in less than two minutes.'

'A hospital—with a gunshot wound. Jack, they'd have to call the police.'

'We are the police.'

'I'd hate to have to defend tonight's actions with those four words.'

§102

'You can't go in there looking like that.'

Jack was right. His jacket was peppered with flaky green paint, he looked like a Martian with a bad case of dandruff. The knee was out of one trouser leg, the other slashed at the thigh and crisp with the browning mat of his own blood. His shoe squelched when he walked.

'Why don't you take my mac?'

Jack was a six-footer. The mac covered a multitude of sins and reached almost to Troy's ankles.

Jack's hand swept the hair from his eyes.

'You still look absolutely bloody awful,' he said.

'Thanks, Jack.'

The night porter at the Ritz knew Troy by sight, and took evident pride in his own sense of discretion. He glanced once at Troy's shoes, and gave him Clark's room number.

Troy heard Clark's voice answer through the locked door.

'If you're Chief Inspector Troy, what was my nickname in Berlin in 1948?'

'I'll tell you what it is now—it's Fat-rogue-asking-for-a-demotion-and-a-posting-back-to-bloody-Birmingham!'

'Right first time,' Clark said and slid back the chain on the door.

Troy threw himself into a chair and felt his muscles uncoil for the first time in hours and the breath seep out of him in a trailing sigh.

Clark was in his shirt-sleeves and braces. Last night's papers strewn across the floor, a pocket chess set and two empty pale ale bottles laid out on a coffee table beneath a single lamp. He was playing against himself. Troy would never understand minds like Clark's if he lived to be a hundred, and he felt as though he'd be lucky to make forty-two.

'Foxx?' he said.

'Next door. I've got the key to the connecting door.'

'Are you in the picture?'

'Pretty much. Our American friend?'

'Safe and fairly sound. Jack's driving her to Hertfordshire now.'

Troy mustered the last of his energy and peeled off Jack's mac and his jacket.

'Call room service. We want a typewriter, a stack of foolscap and a half a dozen sheets of carbon paper. How long will it take to type out your version of Cockerell's cypher?'

'Half an hour or so. I was clerk of store stores for a while back in Berlin. I learnt to touch type,' said Clark, and then added a telling, 'among other things.'

He picked up the phone, and placed the order.

'And a pair of trousers,' he said looking at Troy.

Troy whispered a 'what?' at him, and he put his hand over the mouthpiece.

'Well, if they can find us a typewriter at two o'clock in the morning, a pair of trousers should be no problem. What size?'

'Twenty-nine by thirty-one leg. Do you think they could throw in a pair of socks too?'

'And a triple helping of roast beef sandwiches,' Clark concluded, and hung up.

'Ten minutes or so, sir.'

'Fine. Three copies. I have to go next door.'

§103

Foxx was not sleeping. She was sitting up in bed, wearing a fashionable shortie nightdress. He heaved his leg to the edge of the bed.

'You look like something the cat dragged in.'

'I know. People keep telling me.'

'Did you find her?'

'Yes.'

'You'd better take those trousers off.'

He could not do it. He could unbutton his own flies, but he could not bend as far as his ankles, and with the weight of dried blood the trousers would not bend either. Foxx pulled off his shoes, tugged at the trousers, and he sat on the edge of her bed in sodden socks and shirt-tails staring down at a leg black with gore, and a flap of loose flesh gaping on the thigh.

'Bloody 'eck,' she said. 'That needs stitching.'

'It will have to do. I can't go to a hospital.'

Foxx went to the bathroom and came back with all the towels and a flannel soaked in hot water. She bathed the wound and worked down the leg, wringing out the flannel in the basin four or five times and mopping him dry with the towels. The towels were filthy now, and there was still a mess of blood on him, but the flesh was visible again, and the wound clean.

'How did it happen?'

'Someone took a shot at me.'

'The same someone who killed Stella?'

Troy said nothing.

'Troy!'

'Yes.'

'Did you get him?'

'I don't know. It isn't over yet.'

Foxx rummaged around in her handbag and came up with a pack of needles and a reel of synthetic thread.

'This won't be totally sterile, but at least it won't fester. Brace yourself.'

Troy saw the needle go in and re-emerge between his torn leg and her bobbing head.

'It doesn't hurt. Why doesn't it hurt?'

'I don't know why, Troy. Perhaps because you love me truly, and true love can know no pain. But—I haven't believed that since I was twelve. So, God knows. It should hurt. You deserve it.'

She moved slowly. It seemed to Troy that she knew little of medicine, but enough of dressmaking, and sewed him with a perfect seamstress's hemstitch. Her head moved up and down with her hands, the tips of her hair brushing his leg. The charge ran through him, up his spine to raise the hairs on his head, the delicious tightening of the scalp—but the flesh was willing and the spirit weak as a guttering candle.

'What now?' she said. 'What is to become of me?'

'How much money do you have?'

'Thirty-eight thousand six hundred and forty-five pounds in cash. And seven hundred in sovereigns. I've no idea what they're worth. And two boxes to go. We haven't looked in Amsterdam or Monte Carlo. But it's still a lot more than Stella said it would be.'

'Take it.'

'I already have. Did you think I was daft? I opened an account in Zurich in my own name.'

'Take it. Go to Brighton. They won't follow. You're free. The house is in her name, and it's yours now. Get yourself a solicitor and apply for probate on your sister's estate. Once it's through you can do anything you want.'

'Anything?'

'Anything. You have the money.'

'Is that what it comes down to? Money?'

'Tell me. Have you ever read the Count of Monte Cristo?'

'Years ago. 'When I was a nipper.'

'Do you remember the Abbé Faria? The old man who tunnels through the Château d'If to find Dantès? He's the most knowledgeable, the most educated man Dantès ever meets. He attempts to pass on his wisdom to Dantès, but in the end the only legacy that matters is the fortune, the boundless fortune walled up in a cave on a Mediterranean island. Wisdom was as nothing compared to money. I used to think my father was Faria and Dantès rolled into one. He bought us all freedom, bought his entire family choice in the tide of history, but I'm still not sure whether it was his genius or his money.'

She bent low to snap the thread between her teeth, and said, 'And what about you?'

'I appear to have . . . obligations.'

'Obligations you didn't know you had?'

'Sort of.'

She raised her head, pulled the broken thread from her teeth and wafted the word at him like a last-blown kiss.

'Liar.'

§ 104

It was almost dawn by the time Troy reached home, the sun breaking the skyline off to his right, occasionally visible in the rear view mirror as he steered the Bentley round the last snaking lanes between the main road and Mimram, following the course of the river.

Jack was right. He had his work cut out driving with the muscles of his right leg torn. It hurt like hell every time he put his foot down on the accelerator. Once out of central London, and into fewer stops and gear changes, he abandoned the clutch, used his left foot on the brake and accelerator and changed gear on the sound of the engine.

Jack stood leaning in the porch, wrapped up against the early morning cold in Rod's dirty-white riding mac, a double-barrelled shotgun dangling at his hip, one finger through the trigger-guard. He looked for all the world like Jesse James.

'I found it in the umbrella stand. It's just for show. I couldn't find my shells.'

'I shouldn't think it's been fired in years,' said Troy, thinking of the gun Jack had made him leave in Narrow Street. 'Have you had any sleep?'

'No. I popped a couple of bennies about an hour ago. When I crash, heaven will fall with me, but that won't be for several hours yet. I'll . . . er . . . ride shotgun while you sleep if you like.'

He swung the gun round by his finger and it slipped effortlessly into place in the crook of his arm, almost as though he'd practised the move. No, thought Troy, it wasn't Jesse James. It was John Wayne playing the Ringo Kid in *Stagecoach*.

Troy was yawning. It was too good an offer to refuse.

'We'll have to clear the decks. It's Sunday. There'll be an absolute horde arriving for lunch unless we stop them. Call Rod and the women, tell them "no go". The cook'll be here about ten, and there's a chap comes in to mow the grass sometime before noon. And so on, and so forth. Just tell anyone who shows up to come back tomorrow.'

Jack woke him at eleven. Sat on the bog seat once more, while Troy watched the bathwater turn bloody brown yet again, and examined the neat line of black hemstitch that closed the fleshy flap in his thigh. He could see the speed in Jack's eyes, his pupils enlarged to bottomless black wells.

'I talked to them all over breakfast,' Jack said. 'Except Sasha. I got Hugh instead. He said they weren't planning on coming anyway, and seemed to take it as an impertinence that I should be calling. There was a silent "fuck off" between every sentence, so I fucked off.'

Troy wondered if Sasha knew yet. Or was she breaking the news that she was leaving Hugh for a lover already dead? He had found it hard to believe that Sasha would ever leave Hugh—it was too easy to cheat on him, and go on cheating on him—but Johnny's death had left him with a superstitious respect for Johnny's belief in her.

He looked in on Tosca. Sleeping soundly. He pulled back the sheet. Her face was a mess, but her body was unmarked. Then he and Jack took their coffee upright on the porch, Jack still absurdly toting the shotgun, his eyes so wide Troy knew he was popping pills like jelly beans, and watched the Indian Summer toss down a last, sunny, breezy afternoon. Troy felt clean for the first time in days. The starch in his shirtfront was an inexplicable source of pleasure. Clean, but lame. The same umbrella stand that had yielded a shotgun now delivered up a walking stick, unused since his father's death more than ten years ago.

It was turned four o'clock when next Troy pushed open the door to Tosca's bedroom. She was up, bathed and dressed. She was wearing his clothes again. The grey gardening trousers, the worn Tattersall shirt. She was just finishing her make-up. It seemed to Troy that they had carved an arc in time, an arc that had become a circle. Tosca was bruised and bloody as when he found her in Amsterdam. She put down the jar of flesh-tint, turned to look at him, the bruised eyelid like a stuck venetian blind, and as she did, pulled a glove over her right hand to hide her battered knuckles, and the circle was complete. Before he could speak he heard Jack bounding up the stairs to the half-landing.

'There's a car at the end of the drive, in the lay-by on the other side of the road.'

They stood on the porch again. Jack handed the binoculars to Troy. Troy saw Charlie get out of his car, saw Cobb in the passenger seat, saw Charlie saying something to Cobb and setting off up the drive.

'He's coming.'

Jack looked at Troy. Not so stoned he didn't know what was coming next.

'I have to do this alone.'

'I know.'

'Just me and Charlie.'

'You don't owe him that, you know.'

'No, I owe it to you. Whatever happens now, it's best you don't know.'

'I'll be at the the Blue Boar in the village.'

Jack stopped his car halfway down the drive, wound down the window. He and Charlie exchanged half a dozen words and Charlie walked on. He looked pale, tired, but still inescapably handsome. A lock of blond hair waving in the breeze, hands sunk deep in the trouser pockets of an olive-coloured summer suit. A mannequin elegance Troy could not aspire to this side of rebirth or plastic surgery.

'Another fine mess, eh Freddie?' he said standing in the drive, observing a sense of threshold.

'It must be fourish. You're just in time for tea.'

'Good-oh.'

Troy limped down the long corridor into the kitchen. Lit the gas under the kettle for another round of the English tea ceremony, and found he could not reach the shelf with the tea caddy—his leg would not stretch. Charlie handed it down, shoved his hands back into his pockets and mooched up and down the kitchen floor, head down, leather soles tapping softly on the tiles, like a schoolboy in search of a stone to kick.

'Where did they nab you?' said Troy. 'Cambridge? Along with Burgess and Maclean?'

Charlie ceased his shuffling, looked up through a wayward curl. Then his hand swept it from his eyes.

'If you like. It's not strictly true, but Cambridge is a good enough symbol. Maclean and a few others came over in that sort of way—but if you know for a fact they nabbed Burgess, you know more than I do. To this day I'm not certain that Guy's one of us.'

'So you're the infamous Third Man?'

'Good God no. I'm not even the fourth or fifth man. Philby's the third man. He'd be most put out if he thought I was laying claim to the title.'

Troy was setting tea cups on the tray. The rattle of crockery felt like thunder in the head. He hoped he did nothing by way of hesitation that might give away his reaction. It was only a year or so since Philby had broadcast his innocence at a press conference, only a year since Macmillan had exonerated him in the House. Charlie would not be telling him this if he thought there was any way he would blab. One way or another, Charlie meant to shut him up. And Troy had no idea how far he would go.

The kettle blew, Charlie leant his backside against the dresser, Troy filled the pot.

'You carry,' he said, reaching for his walking stick. 'I haven't two hands, I'm afraid.'

Troy limped across the lawn to where a small wicker table and two chairs were set out in the fleeting sunshine, and Charlie followed with the tea tray. The same wind that had whipped the overnight rain from the grass now blew clouds slowly across the western sky—large clouds, lenticular clouds, tabby clouds, rippled like plump brindle cats rolling lazily head over heels in heaven.

Charlie set down the tray. Troy sat down on a wicker chair, and propped his stick against the arm. Something hard dug into his backside. He stuck his left hand behind his back, moved it, winced sharply, pressed his hand to his hip and stretched his back muscles.

'Sorry about the leg, Freddie,' Charlie said. 'Does it hurt much?'

'No. But it will. I still get gyp off the wound to the kidney and that's more than ten years ago.'

Charlie had come through the war, and every subsequent skirmish not deemed worthy of the title, unscathed. He sat opposite Troy, tucked back the knee of his perfect trousers, crossed his perfect legs, and touched together the tips of perfect fingers. He spoke calmly, an affection in his voice that was bound to provoke.

'Freddie, we have to find a way out of this, you do see that? Don't you?'

'No. I see nothing. I hear nothing. I've listened to you all my life. All my life I've been the brave to your chief. Now, you're going to shut up and listen to me.'

'Freddie—'

'Shut up! We're into endgame, Charlie. Can't you see that? This is no time to be spinning me blarney. I'm going to tell you what's what and you're going to listen.'

'What, like the last page in an Agatha Christie? Poirot Sums Up.'

It seemed so sweetly pleasant, not the sneer which it surely was.

'If you like.'

'Fine. But if you're going to go all the way back to Cambridge we'll be here for a week.'

'I don't give a blue fuck about Cambridge. 17 April. That's where it starts, when those two poor buggers from the Branch wrapped their car round a tree on the Portsmouth Road.'

'I'm all ears.'

His fingers stayed paused in their gothic position, the fingertip church, deceptively serene, while the pale blue eyes locked tightly onto Troy's.

'When the Branch roped me in, they did the last thing you had expected and certainly the last thing you wanted. If there was one copper in London you wanted nowhere near Portsmouth, it was me. Not because of the proximity of me and Khrushchev—as my brother so rightly put it, guarding Khrushchev was a red herring—you wanted me nowhere near Arnold Cockerell. Bit of bad luck really that I was ever roped in. But your luck got worse. You tried to talk me out of it, and we ran into Johnny Fermanagh. Johnny always costs me a good night's sleep, blasts me into sleeplessness. So I caught the late train to Portsmouth, and tough luck again, I found myself sharing a breakfast table with Cockerell, an hour or two before you sent him out to his death under the naive illusion that he was spying on the Russian ship. Am I right so far, Charlie?'

'Of course. So far, so good.'

'Then a few days later the balloon went up and Detective Inspector Bonser dashed round to the King Henry and covered the trail. That puzzled me. Bonser is not an impulsive man. I don't think he's got the imagination to work up initiative. Now, I haven't had the time to pull Cobb's service record, but what's the betting that if I do I'll find that Cobb was in the Special Branch in Liverpool before he got the Yard posting? And that in Liverpool he worked with a sergeant named Bonser? When Bonser heard about the frogman spy, he called his old friend Norman Cobb—if he did, there'll be a record of the call in the duty log—and without you to turn to Cobb panicked and told Bonser to bury the evidence. So, Bonser ripped out the page from the register at the King Henry, a page that also had my name on it. Then, Cobb caught up with you. You told him he'd been a fool, that above all else you wanted the body identified as Cockerell. Because if it isn't Cockerell, where's the scandal?

'Now, unless I'm mistaken you were out of the country in June and July—I know, Gus Fforde said you'd passed through Vienna on your way somewhere, and I tried ringing you myself, just to tell you I'd married and to introduce you to Tosca—but Cobb wasn't, was he? Cobb was at the Yard handling this fiasco on his own. So, the body finally washed up in July, Bonser called Cobb again, and received new, contrary orders—forget covering up, it's got to be Cockerell, Cobb said, at any price. God knows what Bonser told Cobb, but if you'd been around I doubt you would have paid the price of his next move. When no one in Portsmouth could identify the body as Cockerell, Bonser consulted the torn page, talked to Quigley and then he called me. Bonser's a good copper, follows orders to the letter. He got me down to Portsmouth, asked me to look at the body, asked me to meet the grieving widow. And once again the worst thing that could happen to you happened—I investigate the death of Arnold Cockerell. More than that, I investigate the life of Arnold Cockerell.

'It took me till yesterday to work out that it was Cobb following me around. Stupid of me, damn near got me killed. It wouldn't have been hard for him to keep track of my movements at the Yard, he'd only have to put his ear to the ground to know I was going down to Derbyshire to see Cockerell's wife. I found Jessel, and before I could get anything out of him Cobb killed him. I don't think he meant to, but he overdid the bully boy routine and scared the poor bugger to death. I've got fingerprints from Jessel's desk. One of the prints will surely match Cobb's.

'Then . . . then I fucked up. Cobb had no idea Madeleine Kerr existed. No idea that Cockerell had a mistress. I led him straight to her, and he killed her. No accident this time. He snapped her neck, pulled the cord, jumped from the train, and if he'd been a better shot he'd have killed me too.

'I found myself on enforced sick leave and in the detective's doghouse. But that meant I wasn't at the Yard, and with Onions' wrath hanging over me it meant that I was a damn sight more secretive about what I was doing. Cobb lost me. He didn't pick up the next lead, he didn't follow me to Paris because he didn't know I'd gone. In fact you none of you knew a damn thing about it till yesterday, when my wife blundered into the Café Royal and blew both our covers.

'But we were all on borrowed time. If you'd been around when I first brought her home with me, it would all have come apart in our hands weeks ago.

'So, I found Arnold Cockerell's insurance policy—the document Cobb suspected he'd left behind, and for which he killed Madeleine Kerr. And now I not only know what happened—I know why.'

Charlie's reactions had been minimal. A slight twitch in the muscles of the cheek—a little like the King's nervous tick during the abdication speech—a tilt of the head forward so his lips touched the tips of his extended fingers.

'I'm still listening,' he said, scarcely more than a whisper across his fingertips.

'Now we will go back a while, not as far as the thirties, and not to Cambridge, but to, let's say, 1951, to London. You and Cobb are setting up a new network for the Russians. I presume you knew both Cobb and Cockerell from the war?'

Charlie straightened up, smiled, almost happy to be able to make a contribution.

'Of course,' he said. 'They were SOE. Very much our operational arm in those days. I knew Cobb fairly well. He'd no politics to speak of, but he always needed money, and I knew he'd do almost anything to get it. They don't make the best agents, but then you've always some degree of power over them, because they're so damn greedy. A greedy man is a weak man. I met Cockerell a couple of times at best, but I didn't know him. Norman was the one who knew Cockerell.'

'And when the Russians told you they needed a money-laundering service and a courier, Cobb suggested Cockerell?'

'Of course, I'd forgotten all about the chap. He hardly stuck in the memory, did he? Cobb knew he was in business, and it seemed like just the cover we needed.'

'1951,' Troy went on. 'Cockerell told his wife he was going to visit the Festival of Britain. At the same time Cobb arranged a meeting for the three of you. And I've wondered, what lie did you tell him, Charlie, what yarn did you spin him?'

'None at all. Told him the truth. It was a Russian operation. Not my fault if he couldn't grasp the reality. And he did go to the Festival. We met him in the Dome of Discovery, as a matter of fact.'

'You recruited Cockerell to bring in and distribute money to your network. You created a plausible cover, you told him to set up a foreign business, to inflate it to heaven, and he brought in Jessel to keep everything looking kosher. Jessel worked out the trick of paying tax on the money, effectively legitimised it—but nobody told Jessel the truth. Jessel just thought it was a fiddle. And if there's one thing the age of austerity did for us, it made us a nation of fiddlers. Sid James is our national archetype. Jessel saw very little wrong with this. God knows, until I showed up he probably thought of himself as honest. It was just one more piece of spivvery—the economic *modus operandi* of the ration book society.

'Strangest of all—you told Cockerell to turn respectable. He improved his cover, left the Labour Party, joined the Tories and the Rotary Club—he became a pillar of the local Establishment, the middle man of Middle England, and all the time you were pushing thousands of pounds through his Contemporary tat business to a network of Soviet agents working to overthrow everything Cockerell now appeared to stand for. A nice sense of irony, I'll give you that.

'For the best part of five years it ran like clockwork. Then something got into Cockerell. I've had a high old time trying to figure out what, but at some point he came to you and said he wanted a real mission, he wanted one more crack in the field, didn't he, Charlie?'

'It was almost insane,' Charlie said. 'He came to me and said he had to swim again. It was something he had to do for himself. He said, "I must have a mission"—you're quite right, his exact words—he suggested some crack at Bulganin and Khrushchev, not me. I said "Arnold, we're on their side." And he didn't seem to grasp it. It was as though a button had been pressed in his brain and he was back in the war. Swimming into Brest, a recce out to the beaches of Normandy, or whatever. I couldn't get through to him what we were doing. He seemed to have grasped so little of it. He seemed to think that in some way it was all circular, that in doing this for me he was party to some double- or triple-agent scheme whereby it would all turn out to be for Britain in the end. And you're wrong about his cover—I never told him to go Establishment. He did all that off his own bat. Worse still, I think he genuinely believed it all. He was the man he pretended to be. Pretty much the fate of all of us when you come to think about it. You invent yourself.

'As you will imagine, by March he was a liability. I told the Russians about his crackpot scheme and asked what to do with him, and they said, "Fine, send him out to the *Ordzhonikidze*." Could've knocked me down with a feather. I was staggered. But I did it. I didn't know they were going to kill the poor sod.'

'But they didn't tell you why they wanted him sent out, did they?'

'Not till I'd done it, no.'

'It was a black joke. One of Khrushchev's finest. Cockerell was sent out to spy, by the Russians on the Russians, and they in turn used him to create a scandal that rocked the British Government. It really spits in your eye, doesn't it? You thought you'd finally got Cockerell off your hands and they toss him back at you like a sprat. Can't you see the contempt they had for you in pulling a stunt like that?

'But, it didn't go smoothly. On the Monday night I heard Khrushchev say, "Do it." I'd no idea what he meant. I didn't know who he was talking to, but sure enough the next morning the Captain of the *Ordzhonikidze* complained to the Foreign Office about a frogman spy. That Monday night, while Khrushchev and I were out pub-crawling, they dumped the late Commander Cockerell overboard. That was "Do it"—"dump the body now!" But in the morning there's no body. It had vanished, when it should have been floating belly up in Portsmouth Harbour like a dead mackerel. God, Krushchev must have been furious. He'd been saving Cockerell to create a diplomatic crisis when he felt like having one, and he felt really bloody after the row with the Labour Party, so he told the Russian captain to "do it"—but nobody allowed for the currents and Cockerell's body got washed along the coast for five miles and as many months, and it became a scandal without proof. Only my brother raising hell in the Commons and Eden's stupidity ever allowed Khrushchev so much as a whiff of victory. He got his scandal, but all too late and too little for his purposes. What he wanted was all hell to break loose while he was still here. Two birds with one stone—the public embarrassment of the Government and the disposal of a useless former agent. Khrushchev probably thought Cockerell was more useful dead than he'd ever been alive.

'When the body finally washed up, it'd been chewed beyond recognition by fish and propellers and God knows what. It was still important that it should be Cockerell, but by the time I gave you the positive identification you wanted, the proof of the pudding as it were, none of it really mattered much. Yesterday's rice pudding. Eden had opted for damage limitation, owned up to something he didn't do, and it was all old hat. And besides, the perfect scapegoat had been found. Both sides needed a victim, both sides needed someone else to blame, and once he'd been nailed the matter could be safely buried by everyone concerned. Scandal, retribution, sacrifice and finally justice. Tell me, how did you manage to pin it on Daniel Keeffe?'

'Oh, that was easy. I told Cockerell to report to his wartime controller. Keeffe. I knew Keeffe would dismiss his plan as rubbish, but by then it would be too late. His visit would be a matter of record. It didn't matter what Keeffe said, no one in Five and Six would believe him.'

'So Keeffe died for your sins. The perfect scapegoat.'

'If you like.'

'And now your chickens come home to roost.'

'I don't quite follow you.'

'When you pulled Cockerell off the money run, the Russians had no further use for their courier—Tosca. They pulled her from their end of the operation, knocked her about, and she fled for her life—to find me, and eventually, inevitably, she would find you. Doesn't it strike you as a mite ironic, that you set in train the sequence of events that would undo you when you sent Cockerell to his death?'

'Irony's wasted on me, Freddie. I'm not open to it. Underline it, put it in red. Do what you will. It won't affect me. I'm a believer.'

'And I'm not. And first and foremost I don't believe you.'

'I'm sure you don't, but now we've had the what and the why and the irony, if you've reached the end of your little speech perhaps we can get down to brass tacks and do business. Ten out of ten for detection, but Tosca, after all, is why we're here. There's got to be a way out for both of us. We can still horse trade, but we can't leave things as they are.'

'No.'

'What do you mean—"no"?'

'No. No deals. Not while you're still lying to me.'

'Freddie, I'm not lying.'

'You said you'd no idea the Russians would kill Cockerell. Maybe you're trying to spare me, I don't know, but Cockerell was dead when the Russians got him. Cobb killed him.'

'Why would he do that?'

'Because you told him to. Because Cockerell knew too much for you ever to let the Russians take him alive. They told you to send him out to them, but they didn't say dead or alive, so Cobb sapped the poor fool across the back of the head, and dumped him in the water in full frogman's gear for the Russians to find. They sent a couple of frogmen out from one of the escort ships as they steamed up the Solent. Whatever they were expecting, Cobb gave them a body—and he only just made it back to Portsmouth in time. He was sweating like a pig and he was frazzled. I was there. I saw him. He was on edge, and I put it down to his temperament. He was someone who got high on power, but it was more than that—he'd just killed a man, and the adrenaline was still ripping through his veins like a shot of heroin.'

'Speculation, Freddie. That's all.'

'No—fact. If Cockerell was alive until the Tuesday when the Russian captain put in his complaint, there'd have been no evidence of his last meal in Portsmouth still in his stomach—he died within an hour of finishing his blasted kedgeree. For all I know the Russians stuck him in the fridge for six days, but he was dead when they got him. And he was dead because you couldn't take the risk of him telling them the truth about your network. I've read Cockerell's insurance policy, Charlie. His last will and testament. He only wrote it because he didn't trust you. He knew it couldn't stop him being killed; it could only make life hell for you and Cobb afterwards. He names seven agents on your payroll. Some bloke in GCHQ, an old don at Cambridge to spot likely undergraduates, a couple of minor civil servants at the War Office, whom you appear to be blackmailing, two MPs and a dotty lord. Now, how many have you told the Russians you've got? Twelve? Twenty? Because you're pushing more money through Cockerell's books than you could ever spend on that threadbare list of would-be traitors. And where does the rest of the money go?'

Troy paused, but Charlie volunteered nothing.

'Do you remember when you last borrowed money from me? I do. It was the summer of 1951. You paid me back the same year—in cash, and you never asked for money again. You and Cobb are skimming like a pair of cheap croupiers. You pocket the money that the Russians think is going to your list of phoney agents.'

'It wasn't my idea, Freddie. Give me some credit. I believe in what I'm doing. It was Cobb. And I didn't tell Cobb to kill Cockerell. He acted on his own.'

'I don't believe you. "They're so damn greedy. A greedy man is a weak man."'

'Eh?'

'That's what you said ten minutes ago. You were describing Cobb, but I think it sums you up rather well too. You've always been profligate, Charlie. That's the next thing to being greedy.'

'Freddie. I did not kill Cockerell. Cobb killed him off his own bat. Just like he killed Jessel and Madeleine Kerr.'

'Was it his idea to kill Johnny Fermanagh and snatch Tosca too?'

'What?'

'Was it his idea to beat Johnny Fermanagh to death and snatch Tosca?'

It seemed to Troy that this must be the make or break question. There they were, each on the edge of their seats, shouting in each other's faces.

But, it should somehow make a difference to the inevitable end of their friendship if Charlie would answer 'yes'.

The question seemed to halt Charlie in his anger. He looked baffled and his mouth opened soundlessly. Troy never got an answer. Cobb lumbered round the corner from the front of the house, as Troy always knew he would, aiming for them in huge strides, an errant sunbeam breaking the clouds to pick him out like limelight, big feet thudding down like shire hooves, all that grim determination screwed up into an ugly scowl.

Charlie got to his feet.

'No, Norman. No!'

But Cobb was not listening.

'I've had enough of this bloody farce.'

Cobb reached into his jacket with his right hand, to grasp the Browning sleeping snugly in its leather holster in the armpit of his generously tailored suit. A double-breasted suit may flatter the bigger man, may smooth out the bulge of a concealed weapon, but it adds precious fractions of a second to the action Cobb attempted. Before his hand could clear his lapel once more Troy had shot him five times through the heart.

He had not been wholly sure he could do it.

The Mauser had nestled under the cushion of his chair most of the afternoon, and he had slipped it into his waistband as he sat down. He had taken it off its wooden pegs that morning, felt its weight and wondered. There was ammunition, years old but sound, in the bottom drawer of the old man's desk. Troy had loaded the gun and found it heavier, longer than any gun he had ever wielded. Worse, his father had been right-handed, and Troy was left-handed, and whilst this mattered not a damn with ninety-nine guns in a hundred, the Mauser, as his wife had so vividly demonstrated, was designed as a cavalry weapon to be cocked by a roll on the thigh as the arm came upwards from a saddle holster. Hence there were models with the hammer on the left, for right-handed people, and, rarely, models with the hammer on the right for left-handed people. He could not draw the gun in any conventional way. He had settled on sticking it in his waistband, in the small of his back with the butt facing to the left. With a little practice he could draw the gun left-handed, cock it almost on the hip as he pulled it up and under and shoot with it held sideways, hammer uppermost, sights to the right—and he found he could do it quickly. But, he had wondered, how quickly would he have to do it?

Every rook in every tree squawked skyward. Cobb fell like an oak struck by lightning—he did not crumple or cry out, but keeled over backwards, with a crash that shook the ground. His hand flew clear of his jacket, the arm extended at right angles to his torso, still clutching the Browning.

Troy had not anticipated the effects of recoil. He had squeezed the trigger and half the magazine had discharged, and the force of it had knocked him off his feet and onto his knees. He put his weight on his right hand. Cobb was still. Stretched out cruciform. He looked to Charlie and found that he, too, was on his knees only a yard away, his face buried in his hands, and a sodden whisper of 'Jesus, Jesus' seeking through the mask he had made for himself.

Troy levelled the gun on him, saw an eye open and peep between the fingers like a child pretending to be invisible.

Cobb rattled as his last breath escaped his throat. Troy kept his eyes on Charlie, whipped the gun sideways, shot Cobb once through the forehead, and put the gun back on Charlie.

'Look at me, Charlie,' Troy said.

Charlie took his hands from his face, still whispering 'Jesus, Jesus' to himself like a fragment of half-remembered prayer, the magic word to undo all he had seen. His cheeks were glazed with tears.

'Look at me, Charlie.'

Charlie looked up at Troy, then glanced at Cobb as though confirming the worst, then looked back at Troy, still propped up on his right arm, still aiming the gun at him.

'In case you're wondering,' Troy said breathily, 'it's an 1896 Mauser Conehammer semi-automatic machine pistol. It holds ten. I rather think I just put six into the late Cobb. Whatever you're carrying, take it out and throw it on the lawn.'

'Carrying?' Charlie's voice was shrilly incredulous. 'You mean you think I have a gun? Why on earth would I have a gun?'

'Of course—you had Cobb. You don't need a gun. But I'm not going to take that risk. Stand up and take off your jacket.'

Charlie did as he was told. Got shakily to his feet. Held the jacket out and shook it.

'Please believe me, Freddie. I didn't know Cobb was going to do that. Really I didn't. I told him to stay in the car. The last thing I said to him was, "Stay in the car."'

'Turn around, drop the jacket, roll up your trouser legs.'

When Charlie stood with his back to him, calves bared like a ludicrous freemason, looking wry-necked over one shoulder, Troy eased himself off the grass and back into the chair, let the gun hang loosely at his side, and waved Charlie down into his chair with his free hand. The move cost him dearly, knocked the breath from his lungs, and he and Charlie faced each other in a crackling, electric silence until Troy found the energy to speak once more.

'Charlie, this is the deal. And it's the only one you're getting. I've put everything I've just told you on paper, and it's on its way to lawyers in three different cities, in three different countries, together with copies of Cockerell's last letter. You'd be well advised to keep me alive, Charlie. If I die they have instructions to send everything to MI5. But you're safe—your shabby little network is safe—as long as I never hear from you again. If I, or my wife, or any member of my family is ever troubled by either side—it doesn't matter which—I'll shop you to both. I want to be left alone. And if I'm not, then we'll find out the hard way just how convincing the proof is.'

'The British are gullible, Freddie. Look what mugs Philby made of them. And do you really think you can get anything to the Russians without me knowing?'

'I've already done it.'

'Eh?'

'Check the duty log from the watch on the Russian Embassy. You'll find a man answering my description dropped a letter in their box about 4 a.m. this morning.'

'You're being naive. The KGB will—'

'Пирожки,' said Troy, softly pouting over the first syllable.

'What?'

'Пирожки.'

For the first time Troy felt that he had really got through to Charlie—with a single word in a language he did not speak.

'Oh God. Oh my God. Khrushchev gave you an embassy code, didn't he?'

'There has to be an end to running. I dropped him a line. Told him where she was, that she will say nothing of what little she knows to anyone and how grateful we would both be to be left in peace. You could say I

409

gave you a head start. But you'd better pray the First Secretary grants my wish. If he sends the dogs, we've both had it.'

'You're mad, Freddie. He might do just that.'

'And then again he might not. And if he doesn't, the status quo pertains. You and me with a common cause once more—*contra mundum* as you used to say when we were kids.'

The silence fell on them again. Troy thought he had said it all. He'd had most of the day to rehearse it, but he'd never been able to work out how it should end. There were no famous last words on the tip of his tongue.

'I'll miss you, Charlie.'

Charlie's eyes flashed. The finality of what Troy had said seemed to sting him.

'That's it, eh? Just like that?'

'We've nothing more to say to one another.'

'You've said an awful lot, Freddie, but you haven't asked me why.'

'I'm not interested in why. I never much cared for ideologies.'

'It's got bugger all to do with ideologies. Isn't it obvious why?'

Troy said nothing.

'Hasn't it been obvious since we were kids at school? Didn't you swear oaths to kill every last one of the bastards every time they beat us black and blue? Didn't you ask a dozen times a day what all that hidebound ritual had to do with you and me? Didn't it send you screaming into the world hating God and King and Country? And every last damn thing they stood for? Don't you still look around and ask what all this has to do with you or me? Don't you still ask yourself how you can ever belong to all this?'

Charlie's arm swept out inclusively—the house, the garden, the pig pens, the willows and the river, so English in their deepgreenness and their mild eccentricity, so Russian in the human choices they represented and the extremes they struggled silently and secretly to reconcile and if not reconcile contain. The irony of this was lost on Charlie—they were simply symbols close to hand—but hardly on Troy, and Troy knew that he did belong to this, as much as it to him, and knew that he could not explain this to Charlie.

'We don't belong, you and I, Freddie. We never did. It was you and me *contra mundum* for so long.'

His voice dropped to a whisper, the darkness of the confessional.

'And if you don't belong, you can't betray.'

It seemed to Troy like the distillation of all that Deborah Keeffe had said to him—her intelligent, heartfelt argument boiled down to a ruthless conclusion, to a licence to kill.

'We all said things like that. It didn't mean a thing,' he said, knowing full well that it did.

'Oh no—I meant it. I meant I was out to get them. I was fit to kill.'

'And who did we kill in the end, Charlie? A weaselly, clapped-out ex-frogman, a pissed-out chartered accountant, a gullible, innocent girl—'

'And Cobb, Freddie. We killed Cobb.'

'That doesn't change anything, Charlie. Cobb's not my responsibility.'

Charlie looked at Cobb's body. The chest drenched in grume. The forehead pierced by a clean, bloodless black hole. He looked back at Troy. Whatever it was he was about to say, Troy had heard enough.

'You can go now, Charlie. We've said all we're ever going to say.'

Charlie stared at Troy, but did not move.

'I mean it, Charlie. Go now.'

Charlie got to his feet. His lips parted. No words came out. He turned on his heel and began to stride briskly away.

'Charlie,' Troy called after him. 'You're forgetting Cobb.'

Charlie stopped.

'What? You can't seriously expect me to drag his carcass after me?'

'Yes I can. Think of yourself as Hamlet with Polonius. Lug the guts behind the arras.'

Charlie came back a few paces, drew level with Cobb's body.

'What the hell do you expect me to do with him?'

'I don't know, Charlie. I don't care. But you'll think of something. You always do.'

Charlie seized Cobb by the collar of his jacket and tugged. The body moved a couple of feet, the heels of his shoes scoring parallel furrows in the turf. The look on Charlie's face was expectant, as though Troy must inevitably see the impossibility of his disposing of Cobb's corpse, but Troy just stared back at him and said nothing. He watched Charlie all the way to the gate. It took fifteen minutes of tugging, resting and sweating to get there—Troy watching all the time. And when Charlie's car had roared off he sat and watched a green and yellow dragonfly dance in eccentric circles across the lawn, watched the first tinge of dusk reddle the sky, heard the tuneless rattle of a wren singing—sat until he felt the chill of evening raise his skin, sat until the last swallow had caught the last fly on the wing, and the first bats had glided into the weft of evening.

He was still clutching the gun, his fingers wrapped around the butt as if it had grown out of his arm. He reached for his stick. The leg hurt more than ever. He leant on the stick and limped into the house.

In the semi-darkness he could make out Tosca sitting halfway up the stairs, pale of face, knees under her chin, arms clasped to her shins, the white-gloved hand wrapped around the other, staring at him.

He flipped the magazine from the Mauser and emptied the clip.

'You can live with that?' she said softly as the bullets fell into his hand like peas shelled from the pod.

'We're not going to talk about it.'

'Jeezus, Troy. That was murder.'

'We're not going to talk about it . . . because if we do then we'll have to ask how many lives you've been responsible for in your time.'

'Troy, I told you a thousand times. I was just a spy. I dealt in information. I never killed anybody!'

'Do you really believe that?'

She stamped her feet all the way upstairs. He heard the door of her bedroom close.

Troy hobbled into the kitchen. The light was on. The kettle sang on the gas ring. The Fat Man sat at the kitchen table eating a roast beef sandwich.

'How long have you been here?' said Troy.

'Long enough,' said the Fat Man. 'Like I said, yer Old Spot's due to farrow tomorrow, so I thought I'd best look in on 'er today.'

Troy sat down opposite him. Put the gun on the table.

'Ah,' he said. 'Of course. The pig. I'd forgotten about the pig.'

'Anything I can do to help, old cock?'

'Can you get rid of this?' Troy said with his hand still on the Mauser. 'I should think so.'

'Permanently?'

'Consider it done, old cock.'

Troy slid the gun across the table, like a pint of beer sent skidding along a bar, and the Fat Man slipped it into his belt and pulled his ragged pullover down over it.

'Now,' he said, 'do you fancy a cup o' rosy lea?'

§105

For three days they ate their meals in silence—a precise illustration of cartoons by Osbert Lancaster, they sat at opposite ends of the dining table in an atmosphere that would straighten a corkscrew. Between meals they found occupation at far corners of house or garden and at bedtime retired, Maxim and Mrs de Winter, to their separate rooms.

On the evening of the fourth day Troy motored up to London and spent a night at Goodwin's Court. The next morning he went into the Yard, still in pain, still leaning heavily on a walking stick. Onions sat by the gas fire in his office waiting, puffing gently on a Woodbine. It was a familiar scene. Troy had arrived at his office dozens of times over the years to find Onions there, in just that pose—hunched over gas fire and ashtray regardless of the time of year, regardless of whether the fire was lit or not.

He drew deeply on the stub of his cigarette and looked up as Troy sat down opposite him.

'I been hearing rumours,' Onions said.

'Of course,' said Troy simply.

'Rumours the like of which I've never heard about a copper at the Yard and never did expect to hear.'

'I know.'

'It's got to be taken care of. I've got to take care of it. You do see that, don't you, Freddie?'

Troy slipped a long white envelope from his jacket pocket and handed it to Onions. Onions turned it over in his hand. It was unsealed and was addressed to 'Ass't Commissioner Onions' in Troy's overelaborate, near-cyrillic hand. Onions stuffed it in his jacket pocket unread.

'How long do you think you've got? How long do you think you've got before they come for her? One side or the other.'

'It's taken care of. I've taken care of it.'

Пирожки.

Onions lit a fresh cigarette from the dying glow of the first.

'I never thought it would end like this,' he said.

Troy drove home, pushing the Bentley for all it was worth along the Great North Road. Rounding the bend that took him clear of the beech trees at the top of the drive he could see the house in the first light of autumn. The sun was low on the skyline, cutting sharply through the trees, dappling the house with shadows of hawthorn's stripped boles. He wound down the window—the air had that unmistakable autumnal smell, the sharp, clean smell of ploughed earth displacing the dusty tang of harvest. The Indian Summer was over. In a single night the seasons had changed, and October had been claimed. The porch door was ajar and filling up with golden leaves rustling gently in the breeze. The house was empty.

He called out as though hearing his own voice in a dream, as though returning to a house he had seen only in a dream, lived in only in some other life—but no one answered.

Up in Tosca's room a note was propped against the mirror—a stiff foolscap sheet of crested Mimram House paper.

§106

Troy was left with the problem of how to close four cases. The death of Arnold Cockerell could be left exactly as it had been in April. The death of George Jessel exactly as it had been in September. The deaths of Madeleine Kerr and Johnny Fermanagh needed some conclusion—for the record if for nothing else the Yard had to state a reason for looking no further. Then a circular memorandum appeared on his desk informing him of the disappearance of Cobb on MoD business. Wintrincham drew no conclusions in public. If he knew what Onions knew, he kept it to himself. It was obvious what Charlie had told the Branch. God alone knew what they had told Cobb's family—if he had one. It had not occurred to Troy to ask before. Troy then issued a description of a man, that fitted Norman Cobb precisely, as wanted in connection with the murders of Kerr and Fermanagh, and placed it in front of Jack. Jack accepted it without a murmur and quietly let the cases drop.

§107

Autumn brought the world to the brink of madness. A surge of bellicosity that looked like the willed fulfilment of some collective death wish. Russian tanks rolled around Poland as Poland offered the promise of a political spring in autumn—Khrushchev flew into Warsaw and flew home again with the promise nipped in the bud. Kolankiewicz phoned Troy and said flatly, without the faintest trace of humour or histrionics, 'I told you so. You have supped with the devil.'

November brought the meeting of the stones. The world went wild again. Over the brink of madness and into the abyss. Britain and France invaded Egypt. Russia invaded Hungary. Bulganin casually threatened to blast London and Paris.

Stones met.

Troy read the papers every day, saw the newsreels in the Eros Cinema at Piccadilly Circus—British paratroopers floating down over Suez like great white jellyfish; an armada of French and British ships steaming south—his natural cynicism taking no pleasure in being proved right. The victorious allies of the last war spanned the world, bestrode it like squabbling colossi.

Stones met.

He stood awkwardly in Onions' sitting room, clutching a brown ale, with a bewildered, angry Onions, a silent, resentful Valerie-in-her-moated-grange, while Jackie sat at the table drawing endless concentric circles in fifty different colours on a large sheet of paper, and watched the nine-inch television set the new generations had imposed on Onions—watched Gaitskell address the nation, a rousing, faultlessly moral speech, damning Her Majesty's Government for their 'criminal folly', and across his face was written the pain of a man who knew himself deceived. The Prime Minister must resign, he said, it was the only way to 'save the honour of our country', and in that ringing phrase he felt the hand of Rod. It took him back to Janet Cockerell, and the matter of her husband's honour. She had had no time for honour, so male a notion. It was guilt that mattered.

Stones met.

He stood with the raggle-taggle British dissidents in Trafalgar Square. Duffle-coated optimists flying in the face of their country at its most banal, as it burst with British patriotism, 'their finest hour' rendered down to 'an ignoble loneliness'. Heard Nye Bevan, the finest political orator in the land, argue for 'law not war'. Rod should have been there. On the platform, side by side. It was a Rod moment, but he was nowhere to be seen.

Stones met.

Ike tore up the 'special relationship'. Lit a bonfire in the White House. New wars consumed by old flames. The British forces ground to a halt in the sands of Egypt, no 'right wheel at Ismailia', no 'next stop Cairo', no hope, no glory—starved of economic fuel and political will. Vanity, folly and fire. New war. Old flames.

And Troy went in search of Angus. He found him in the third pub he tried—the 'Two Dogs at It'. The landlord had dug out a framed photograph of Churchill and a pair of Union Jacks on little wooden sticks, stuck Winston over the bar and crossed the flags above him. Troy entered at an opportune moment—Angus was yelling, 'What the hell is that supposed to mean? Battle of Britain part two? What do you silly sods think the last ten years have been? The commercial break? And where did you get 'em? The national dressing-up box?'

It came rapidly, instantly to blows. Troy dragged Angus out still hurling insults at simple-minded men who saw themselves as simple patriots and were baffled to simple violence by his abuse of them. He felled three of them before Troy could even bundle him to the door. '*Dulce et decorum est,*' he was yelling. '*Pro* bunch of arselickers *mori!*'

Troy watched the anger in them subside as quickly as it had flared up, the sad shake of heads—'and him a war hero too'. The two of them fell out onto the pavement, Angus's tin leg skidded from under him in the gutter, his briefcase flew through the door and landed at his feet—his bowler hat followed, Troy reached up and caught it neatly at full stretch, heading for the boundary and a probable six.

'Right y'buggers.' Angus got to his feet, but he wasn't facing the 'Two Dogs at It', he was looking to the muted orange glow leaking out into the November night from the 'Lucifer's Arms' on the other side of the street.

'Right y'buggers,' he said again, and pursed his lips—a burbling raspberry sound—and it dawned on Troy that this was the noise small boys made when playing aeroplanes. Angus's arms levelled at the horizontal.

'Chocks away,' he said. 'Takkatakkatakkatakkatakkatakkatakka.' And shot through the doors of the 'Lucifer's Arms' and into another dogfight.

Troy waited. Stared at the dented crown of the bowler. Looked at his watch. Five minutes passed with no sign of anything more than the usual pub hubbub. He pushed open a door. A man at the bar was farting out the rhythm of the national anthem, 'God Save the Queen' played without melody upon the human sphincter, and no one paid a blind bit of notice. Angus was seated at one of the small, round pedestal tables, two enormous scotches before him, his face buried in his hands. All Troy could see of him was the balding pate and the ginger halo spiralling out into the ether. He sat down next to him. Angus took his face from his hands and looked up at Troy—a flurry of burst veins; a relief map of Arizona, criss-crossed with dry river beds; a rough sketch of the moon pitted with open pores the size of craters; Passchendaele the day after.

'You can tell a man what boozes by the company he chooses,' he said.

Troy knew the doggerel. His father used to recite it. God knows where he learnt it . . . 'And the pig got up and slowly walked away.'

Angus knocked back his scotch. Troy almost beat him to it. Their glasses returned empty to the table top at the same moment.

'Quite,' said Angus. 'Same again?'

Stones met.

When Troy was eight or nine yet another seemingly interminable childhood illness had floored him, his head swam, his eyes refused to focus. He could not read. As ever he recuperated, bound in blankets, on long summer evenings on the south verandah. His father came home each day and read aloud to him from *The Golden Bough*. An old Aztec ritual had Troy chilled to the bone. He could never forget the sickening horror he had felt on first hearing the tale of the meeting of the stones—so phrased that the life that was crushed to pulp as the stones met did not even figure in the title. He was reminded once more of Nikolai's lament for the apparatchiks—the little people he had called them, only to have Rod and Troy dismiss him with a sneer. But—the world between the stones was the world of little people—who could be crushed without care if they spoke a language that sounded like an accident with a Scrabble box, or were so unfortunate to have skins of dusky hue. The world between the stones was full of gooks and niggers.

From Cyprus arrived a plain card in a plain envelope, saying simply, 'Forgive me'. Troy never replied. The stones met. He felt again the sickness of horror. The stones met. He had supped with the devil.

§108

Christmas rose up at speed. The sisters descended upon him, complaining and hooting about the petrol rationing—the sense of deprivation was undeniably nostalgic, so British, so very British—and whipped the local tradesman up in a flurry of pheasant and venison and turkey and decked the house in holly. On Christmas Eve all the Troys gathered at Mimram, as they had done for thirty or more years. He stood on the porch with Rod, coatless and shivering as Rod, last to arrive, knocked the first flakes of snow from his hat and said softly, 'I've lost the Foreign job. Gaitskell's batted me sideways into Home. I suppose I'm paying the price of being right.'

'No,' said Troy. 'I rather think it's just the price of knowing.'

Rod tilted his head gently towards the house and the burr and hum of the women revving into Christmas.

'I could do without all this right now. But I suppose I have to get through it.'

'We,' said Troy. '*We* have to get through it.'

Troy ducked questions on the whereabouts of Tosca. Pretended it was all jolly, skived off charades and lost twice a day to his uncle at chess. On Boxing Day a deceptive calm lay across the house and the white landscape. The elder children usurped the servants' hall to watch the television without which they could, it seemed, no longer live. The younger gathered around the Christmas tree in the red room, assembling the vast train set Nikolai had given to Masha's boys. In the drawing room Nikolai disappeared behind a newspaper many days old. Only when Troy, playing host, asked him if he wanted another glass of something did he realise the old man had nodded off. Hugh drank glass after glass of something scotch and rapidly got roaring drunk. The row that had been simmering for so long between him and his wife boiled over amidst the tinsel and the sherry. They stood either side of the fireplace shouting at each other, until Hugh raised an arm at Sasha and Rod broke a truce of many months and blocked Hugh's arm with his own and told him he'd had too much to drink and should sit down.

Hugh looked across Rod at his wife.

'I'll swing for you, you selfish bitch,' he screamed in best B-feature cliché.

'Hugh, you haven't got the nerve. You're all mouth and no trousers!' Sasha yelled back.

'Oh haven't I?' he replied, struggling against Rod's restraining arms. 'I'll do for you just like I did for your fancy man!'

Rod let go sharply and thrust Hugh backwards into an armchair. Sasha had a hand across her mouth and seemed to Troy to be screaming silently.

'What?' Rod said softly. 'What did you say?'

'I said,' Hugh hissed, 'that I'll do for her like I did for that snivelling ponce Johnny Fermanagh.'

Rod looked at Troy. Desperation in his eyes.

'I didn't hear what he said,' Troy said. 'He's drunk, and he's rambling. I didn't hear him. And nor did any of you.'

He looked around the room, making sure they all acknowledged what he had said. Then he went upstairs to Tosca's room. Lay on the bed and wept silently for Johnny Fermanagh. It seemed to him now that his life would be for ever tangled up in Bracks, that neither Johnny nor his sister would ever be out of his mind or out of his dreams. He had lost Tosca, he had lost Charlie and he had lost Johnny with too little realisation that the man meant anything to him. So he wept for himself. Never in his life had he felt this alone. He slept. He did not know how long. When he awoke he switched on the light on the dressing table. There, propped against the mirror, was the note Tosca had left. He had never moved it. It stood where she had placed it weeks before.

On the vast white emptiness of foolscap her words read simply, 'We cannot live like this.'

'Who has not committed treason to something or someone more important than a country?'

GRAHAM GREENE
(from his introduction to Philby's '*My Silent War*' 1968)

Historical Note

This is a novel. Not fact—not even faction—but fiction. Here and there I've bent history a bit, usually because it did not suit the exigencies of the plot I wanted.

First, in putting invented figures into an historical context, real people are displaced. Most obviously Commander Cockerell displaces the real Frogman Spy Commander Lionel Crabb. The plot of Crabb's mission was (still is?) too drawn out for my purposes. The body was not found until 1957, and has never been positively identified as Crabb. I didn't want to be bound by the facts of the matter, even though they were the starting point for the idea that became this book. Rod Troy, my fictional Shadow Foreign Secretary, displaces the real one, Alf Robens—sorry, Alf, but if anyone forty years on remembers you were ever Shadow Foreign Secretary I'd be amazed.

Second, I've stolen time from Khrushchev's meeting with the NEC (National Executive Committee) of the Labour Party. He ranted, and he stormed out, but nearer 11 p.m. than the 9.30 p.m. I give. I had other uses for the time. What George Brown, the only one of these historical players I ever met, said on that occasion is taken from his own account. What Khrushchev said has never been made public—the press were not present—but exists in fragments in the memoirs of the Labour bigwigs.

Suez. The revelation I put into the mouth of Rod Troy, at the end of August/early September, on the Anglo-French conspiracy to invade, is—again for purposes of plot—deliberately out of synch, though hardly against the spirit of the times. The French, the British and the Israelis did not actually sign an agreement until 24 October. The British copy was given to Eden and has never been seen since. To say he burnt it is not provable, but not fanciful either. The text of the Israeli copy appeared in English in the memoirs of General Dayan (Weidenfeld & Nicolson, 1976), the original surfaced in the archive of David Ben-Gurion and was made public some ten years ago. The notion that the CIA got a look at the Israeli copy is fanciful, but I doubt impossible. That said, what the US knew about Suez before and during owed more to the U2 plane than to spies on the ground. It's stated by several historians of Suez that the CIA made much use of the U2 over Egypt and Israel at this time, and also that the CIA monitoring station at Rome NY probably broke the codes used by the British, the French or the Israelis or any combination thereof, and quite possibly all three. If anything in my exercise of invention might be deemed fanciful, it's the idea that what the CIA knew was dutifully passed on to Ike.

As to Tom Driberg being asked to spy for the KGB, the published source for this is obviously Chapman Pincher's *Their Trade is Treachery.* In the introduction to his excellent life of Driberg, Francis Wheen is dismissive of Pincher's allegations. Instinctively, I share his scepticism. However, about two years after Driberg's death, and, if memory serves, two or three before Pincher's book, rumours were flying fast and wild about Tom spying for one side or the other or both. I asked Peter Cook, so often, in his capacity as proprietor of *Private Eye,* Tom's employer, if he thought Tom had been a spy.

'Yes,' he said, in a voice not unlike E. L. Wisty. 'And a very bad one. He'd tell anyone who'd listen. The first time I met him he came up to me in a lavatory, stood at the next urinal, cock in hand, and said, "I'm a spy for the KGB y'know."'

I cannot hold up this anecdote as proof or anything resembling proof—after all, the constant danger in asking Peter any question was that he would use the answer to take the piss—only as seductive, just about plausible, and dovetailing very neatly into the story I wanted to tell. The Tom Driberg to whom I ascribe a fictional encounter with my hero is not the vile beast of Pincher's books, but the engaging couldn't-give-a-piss artist of Peter Cook's memory.

Read on for a preview of

A LITTLE
WHITE DEATH

The next
INSPECTOR TROY
novel by

JOHN LAWTON

§ 1

When the snow lay round about. Deep. And crisp. And even. England stopped.

First the roads, from the fledgling six-lane autobahns, known as 'motorways' – a word used as evocatively as 'international' or 'continental' – to the winding, high-hedged lanes of Hertfordshire, disappeared under drifting snow. Then, the telephone lines, heavy with the weight of ice, snapped. Then the electricity supply began to flicker – now you see it now you don't. And lastly, huffing and puffing behind iron snow ploughs as old as the century and more, the railways ground to a halt at frozen points and blocked tunnels.

It was the worst winter in living memory, and when and where did memory not live? It squatted where you did not expect it. And where you did. Not-so-old codgers would compare the winter of 1963, favourably or not, to that of 1947. Old codgers, ancient codgers, codgers with no calendar right even to be living at all, would trounce opinion with a masterly, "T'ain't nothin' compared to 1895."

Rod Troy, Home Affairs spokesman in Her Majesty's Loyal Opposition, a Labour MP since the landslide of 1945, had reason to be grateful to his father, the late Alexei Troy. When refitting the stately Hertfordshire pile he had bought in 1910, as a final refuge after five years a wandering exile from Imperial Russia, he had installed electricity and the telephone – the first in the village – and omitted to remove the gas lamps. Gas was a hard one to stop. It wouldn't freeze and it had no wires to snap. So it was that, in the middle of a blanketed white January Rod found himself cut off in Mimram House, marooned in snow, stranded in a post-Christmas limboland, bereft of wife and children, hunched over a traditional English pastime, by the romantic glow of gaslight, facing a short, dark, irritating alien he ruefully acknowledged as his younger brother Frederick.

'How can you?' he yelled. 'How can anyone cheat at Monopoly?'

'That's what it's for,' Troy replied. 'If you can't cheat, I can't see the point in playing.'

'Grow up, Freddie. For God's sake grow up. That's just the sort of attitude you had as a child.'

'It's a childish game, Rod.'

'It's about rules and trust and codes of conduct. All games are!'

Rod should have known better. Such argument had never cut mustard with Troy when they were children and in middle age it was inviting the pragmatic scorn he seemed to store up in spades.

'No it's not, it's about which bugger can be the first to stick a hotel on Park Lane.'

Rod swept the board to the floor. 'Sod you then!' And walked out.

Troy passed an hour in his study, staring at the unchanging landscape, the monotony of white. He put John Coltrane's 'Giant Steps' on the gramophone, but was not at all sure that he was not kidding himself that he had a taste for the music, and he was damn sure it didn't go with England in January. Did Delius write no *Winterreise*? Had Elgar left no *Seasons*?

It occurred to him that he should go and look for Rod before Rod found him. He would only want to apologise and Troy could not bear his apologies. It seemed wise to head him off at the pass. They might, after all, have to spend days cooped up like this, and while the house was big enough to lose a small army within, they would inevitably end up together and if Monopoly brought them to grief, God help them when Troy started to cheat at pontoon.

The cellar door stood open, a gust of icy air wafting up from below stairs.

Troy called out his brother's name and waited.

'Down here in the wine cellar!'

Troy moved cautiously down the stairs, the light dimly orange in the distance as Rod waved his torch beam around.

'I think I've made a bit of a find.'

Troy could not see him, only the dancing end of the torch. Then the beam shot inwards, and Rod's face appeared, pumpkin-headed, in the light.

'Hold this a mo'. I'll get the gas lit.'

A rasp of match, a burst of flame, and Rod reached upwards and lit the gas jet. In the flickering hiss of gaslight Troy found himself framed by vast dusty racks of wine, countless bottles in long rows stretching away under the house. Rod stood facing him, absurdly wrapped up against the cold in the eiderdown off his bed, belted around his chest and waist, looking like the rubber man in the tyre adverts. He appeared to be clutching a solitary bottle of wine.

'What have you found?' Troy asked.

Rod wiped the label with his sleeve.

'The paper's a bit perished, but it says 1928 and I'd lay odds of ten to one it's Veuve Clicquot.'

'Does champagne keep that long?'

'Haven't the foggiest. But there's only one way to find out.'

He unhooked two glasses from the side of a wooden rack, where they had sat untouched since before the war and wiped the dust from them.

The champagne burst into the glass in a healthy stream of bubbles. Troy swigged some of his and pronounced it 'OK'. Rod sipped his gently and said, 'OK? It's bloody marvellous.'

Then the pause, the reflective stare into the glass. The thought so visibly running through his mind and across his features that Troy grew impatient and wished he would speak.

'Whenever I pull the cork on one of these . . .'

Troy knew what was coming. He could see the curve of Rod's illogic arcing between them like static.

'Or whenever I watch you . . .'

He sipped and stared into his glass a little more.

'I think of the old man. Every time. Never fails. No matter what is on my mind or whatever shit you are giving me, as you are so wont to do – and age does not diminish it – it gives me pause. I think of our father.'

'Sort of like unholy sacrament. An atheist communion?'

'Don't piss on it, Freddie. I'm serious.'

'So am I. Has it ever occurred to you that's why he left us this lot, so that we should think of him from time to time?'

'I didn't say from time to time, I said every time. And who else would he have left it to? And I wonder, what else did he leave us of himself? If this is blood of his blood, where is flesh of his flesh?'

Troy was not sure he could follow this.

'Come again?'

'Who the hell was he? Was he the same man he was to you that he was to me?'

'Doubt it,' said Troy.

'I mean . . . I'm his first born, you're his last, the child of his dotage—'

'Hardly dotage. He wasn't that old.'

'There, there's my point. How old was he? Did you ever know? When was he born? Did he ever tell you? Or where?'

'Must've done. Moscow, Tula, I don't know. And if he didn't, his dad lived with us for fifteen years. *He* must have mentioned it. God knows he rambled on enough.'

'Quite. He rambled. His stories never went anywhere. But the old man was a master of precision. He told us everything – at least it seemed like everything – yet when I come to look back on it there are gaps you could drive a tram through.'

Again the pause, long enough for Troy to refill both their glasses. Troy could see his brother's point even if he could see neither the gap nor the tram. Personally he was sure such minor details as the date and place of his father's birth were simply and temporarily lost in his memory; it was not that he didn't know, it was not that he had not been told. But at the heart of the matter, the man was an enigma.

'You're right, of course,' Rod resumed his musing. 'He wasn't the same man to both of us. I got sent away to school before you were so much as a toddler. You hung around the house almost till adolescence—'

'I was at home because I was a sickly child, Rod, they weren't doing me any favour.'

'Nonetheless you were there. He talked endlessly to you. You were his favourite.'

'Rod, this is bollocks. I was the youngest, that's all.'

'Youngest. Hand-reared. Privy to his wisdom.'

'Recipient of all his gags and anecdotes, if that's what you mean?

Child corrupted by his view of history and politics, if that counts for anything.'

'Corrupted?'

'OK. That's a bit steep. Let us say I was nurtured into an unfortunate precociousness by prolonged exposure to his didactic asides. He taught me the Theory of Surplus Value when I was seven. Had me on the Second Law of Thermodynamics before I was ten.'

'Bugger me! More booze, I think. I cannot listen to sentences like that and stay sober.'

Rod stuck out his glass again. It seemed a daft thing to be doing, sitting on beer crates in a dark cellar, scarcely above freezing, getting pissed on vintage champagne and pretending not to mind the cold. Rod might not be feeling it, but Troy had on nothing thicker than his Aran sweater. Still, if this was how Rod wanted to spend the last hour of daylight, Troy would humour him.

'Think of it,' Rod went on. 'I mean, think of him. Of what he did for us. I always felt secure in the world as he made it for us. I can't help but wonder if my kids can ever feel what that means. Wonder if they'll ever feel the same security. The world he built around us.'

'Troy Nation,' said Troy softly.

'Eh?'

'That's how I used to think of it. So often I ended up housebound, one damned ailment or another. The house was the world for a time. I used to think of it as Troy Nation. A country entire unto itself.'

Rod looked up at the ceiling. Troy knew what he was thinking. In the mind's eye, he was looking through the ceiling. Stripping away the layers in time and putting them back on in an order of his own choosing. This house, these five storeys of junk-packed, book-lined, history-ridden rooms, looming above them like the edifice of memory, a world of its own through which the old man moved mysteriously even now. The house ought to be haunted. It was made to be haunted. Yet they conjured him in words not spirit; he haunted not the structure of their house, but the structure of their minds. Most of the time Troy could take him or leave him. He had long ago got used to being Alex Troy's boy. At forty-seven, Commander of CID, Scotland Yard, half a dozen commendations and an ex-wife to his name, he was still 'Alex Troy's boy'. Doubt caused him little conscience, but such conscience all but made a coward of Rod. Doubting the old man would nag and nag at him, and he could not dismiss it. If there was one gift Troy would have given his brother, it was to free him from such doubt. He had, he knew, probably sown the seed himself.

Away over their heads Troy could hear a bell ringing. It seemed an impossible noise. Logic ruled it out as being simply the doorbell. In households such as this someone else usually answered the door and told the caller whether or not you were at 'ome, regardless of whether you were. And no one had fought their way up the drive from the village in days. Clearly Rod was not going to answer, half-pissed, wrapped up too cosily in his eiderdown, the Michelin man, still sipping the last of the Veuve Clicquot.

'You'd better go and see,' he said, smiling faintly. 'It's probably Titus Oates or Captain Scott.'

It was Driffield the postman. The surliest bastard alive, as far as Troy was concerned. Or – to be precise on the matter of titles – the surliest sub-postmaster, a man in whose eyes Troy was still twelve and simply his father's son, requiring no more in the way of courtesy than a clip 'round the ear 'ole from time to time. He was attired much after the fashion of Rod: at least two overcoats had been added to a layer or more of pullovers and onion rings of collars and scarves obscured most of his face. All the same, Troy could see from the eyes that it was him, and from the expression in them he was, as ever, not best pleased to have trudged up the hill. To do so in several feet of snow had merely refined what was fundamental in his nature. No doubt he missed the days, long gone, when Troy's father would send a donkey and cart to the village to collect the mail.

'I don't know why I does this for you buggers, but I does,' he said. 'Tel'grammes it is, you hev got tel'grammes, the blarsted pair o' ye. Why ye gaht to hev tel'grammes on a day like this, Gahd knows.'

It was, it seemed, deeply inconsiderate of the Troys to be in receipt of tel'grammes of which they knew nothing.

A mittened hand shoved two envelopes at Troy, and then returned to sink into its pocket once more as its owner set off back down the drive, ploughing the trench in the snow he had cut on the way up.

'Aren't you going to wait for the reply?' Troy yelled after him. More often than not the man would tell you what was in a telegramme before you could open it, would stand on the step and recite it to you before you could so much as break the seal, but now nothing, it seemed, would keep him a moment longer.

'Phone it through,' he said over his shoulder. 'There's two blokes from the GPO up a pole in the lane. Ye'll hev phones again in half an hour or so they reckon.'

Rod appeared behind Troy. Troy handed him the small brown envelope and tore open the one with his own name on it. The telegramme meant nothing to him.

```
hugh turn for worst stop fear he may
not last stop suggest come soonest stop
bill stop
```

Troy read it again, wondering if the author's economy with language and cost had left him to guess at a vital aspect of its meaning.

Rod snatched it from his hand. Stuck another in front of him.

'Dozy sod's put them in the wrong envelopes. You've got mine and I've got yours.'

The new telegramme scarcely made more sense than the last. But at least it was written with scant regard for cost in fully grammatical sentences.

```
dear freddie stop long time no see stop
i wouldn't be writing to you out of
the blue if it weren't important stop
i don't think i have much time left
```

stop i'd like to see you one more time
before the end stop i'd like to think
that our friendship survives on that
level and that i can ask this of you
stop could you come to beirut? stop
now? stop i've reserved a room for you
at the st georges stop come as soon as
you can stop i've no idea how long i've
got stop charlie stop

It felt as though a ball and chain had tipped softly from the
envelope in some sleight-of-hand magician's trick and wrapped
itself around him. The old weight, the old friend, the old lie. Was
he dying? Could Charlie be dying? Why couldn't he just say so?
Troy had not seen Charlie since 1957. He had asked much the
same of him then. 'I've taken a job in the Middle East. See me
off. Just for old times' sake. It'll be the last time.' Now this was
the last time. The last time for what? Could Charlie be dying?

'Gaitskell's dying.'

Rod's voice cut through his reverie. Troy looked up from the
telegramme to see Rod suddenly sober, casting off the Michelin
outfit.

'I have to get up to London. God knows how, but I have to.'

Gaitskell was the 'Hugh' of the telegramme Rod had just read.
Leader of the Opposition and, since it was received wisdom that
1963 would be an election year, the next Prime Minister. He and
Rod, of much the same age, class and education, fought like cat
and dog and were stubbornly loyal both to each other and to the
party. For Gaitskell to die now would be a political inconvenience
and a personal tragedy for Rod.

'The phones will be on soon,' Troy said. 'Driffield just told me.'

'Did he say how the roads were?'

'See for yourself,' said Troy, pointing out through the open door
at the snowbound drive and the three-foot-deep trench Driffield
had carved in it.

Around the corner at the end of the drive, where the curving
line of beech trees – resplendent green in summer, crisp brown
in winter – shielded the house from the road, a petrol-driven

that in the last ten years alone. Troy never knew why it was that the army amassed such surpluses and in such quantities – and perhaps mountains were climbed and wildernesses crossed just to diminish the stockpiles – but they did, and without them Sir Edmund Hillary might stand atop Everest in a string vest and half the working men in Britain would be left khakiless and wondering what to wear for the messy jobs or, in this case, how to wade through three-foot snowdrifts down to the pigpens lugging half a hundredweight of compressed dry pig fodder.

'When was you last down there?'

'Yesterday.'

The Fat Man regarded him sceptically.

'Honestly,' said Troy. 'I took her fresh water, a huge bundle of cabbage leaves and a bucket of last year's windfall apples I've been saving.'

'And?'

'And what?'

'And how was she?'

'Fine,' said Troy. 'Happy as a pig in . . .'

He could not quite think of the word. But it was straw. His Gloucester Old Spot sow, the third such he had bred in the last ten years, was happy as a pig in straw, if only because he and the Fat Man had had the foresight to build an insulating wall around her sty late last autumn with twenty-odd bales of straw. Whatever the Fat Man thought, and it was his usual banter to deride Troy's pigmanship, he had looked in on his pig and had thought her sty somewhat warmer than his own house.

The Fat Man hoisted his sack, slipped his feet into the leather loops of the snowshoes and set off for the pigpens under the oaks.

'I'll be back,' he said.

Troy did not doubt it. He had known him on and off the best part of twenty years, and, apart from an increase in his girth, he had changed very little. He was still the committed cockney, determinedly unpredictable, quite the most secretive man he had ever met, and utterly, totally reliable. He had minded Troy's pig, and pigs plural when she had farrowed, at no notice on countless occasions. It had occurred to Troy that perhaps he read minds, for, whilst one could never be at all sure when he would turn up, or from where, he did so exactly when one needed him. Not that Troy needed a pigsitter right now, that went without saying; what he needed the Fat Man had provided almost inadvertently. Transport. A vehicle that could get through snow and ice, something that could get him to London. Something with wheels that did not spin pointlessly on the spot as Troy's Bentley had done when he had tried her a couple of days ago.

He rushed upstairs and began to pack. From his bedroom window he caught sight of the Fat Man cresting a humpbacked ridge of snow like Ahab astride Moby Dick, the snowshoes stuck to his feet like giant leaves miraculously letting him walk on water.

He had no idea what to pack for Beirut and threw an assortment of clothes together. Across the other side of the house he heard the phone ring. The first time in days. Heard the urgent tones in Rod's voice without actually hearing any of his words. Clutching his suitcase, he almost knocked Rod down on the stairs. He was dressed for a journey. Overcoat, trilby, gloves. He was carrying his briefcase.

'I have to get up to London.'

It seemed to be a remark hovering between apology and explanation.

'I heard you the first time.'

'He has to take me, Freddie. Hugh's dying. Unless you can tell me it's a matter of life and death I'm getting in that sidecar and he's taking me as far as that piece of Heath Robinson machinery will get us.'

Troy did not know what 'it' was – a matter of life and death? A matter of life and lies? It was half-formed or less in his own mind. He would not have dreamt of discussing Charlie with Rod at this point. He said nothing. Just followed Rod down to the front door.

'Are you going to tell me?' Rod said, pulling on his wellies.

'There's nothing to tell. But I do need to get up to town.'

'Secrets, Freddie. Secrets. You're worse than the old man. You play every damn card so close to the chest. Well, I'm telling you now that if you can't tell me honestly that your business is more important than mine, I say sod you for your secrets. I'm commandeering the Fat Man and his motorbike and I'm going.'

Troy said nothing. The very word 'commandeering' made

him wince inwardly. This was Wing Commander Troy in fully operational mode. Playing by the Queensberry Rules. Rules that let him hijack the bike, but did not permit him to read a telegramme addressed to someone else.

'Quite,' said Rod. 'Silence.'

When the Fat Man trudged back to his bike Rod made his pitch, plain and simple. A fiver to get him, as he put it, 'to civilisation'. The Fat Man looked to Troy. Troy nodded almost imperceptibly and, as Rod made a racket clambering into the sidecar, leant over and whispered.

'Dump him at the nearest station and get back here. I may need you for a few days.'

The Fat Man tapped the side of his nose.

Rod looked ridiculous sitting in the sidecar. Knees tucked almost to his chin, hat rammed down to his ears, goggles over his eyes, briefcase pressed to his chest. He looked like an owl.

'There is one thing,' he said from his preposterous perch.

'Of course,' said Troy.

'What's the Second Law of Thermodynamics? Is it Einstein or one of those blokes?'

'It's Kelvin.'

'Never heard of him. What did he say?'

'Entropy. Everything expands into . . . nothing.'

'Don't quite follow . . .'

'Everything turns to shit in time.'

'And we need a "Theory" to tell us that?'

The Fat Man raised a giant's foot off the ground, slamming down on the kickstart, and brought four 250cc cylinders spitting and roaring into life. He was back in less than an hour.

JOHN LAWTON

THE INSPECTOR TROY SERIES

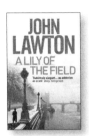

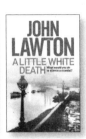

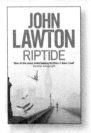

Grove Press UK

Also available as ebooks
www.atlantic-books.co.uk